THE

CATERPILLAR

GIRL

ADAM LONGDEN

A CIP catalogue record of this book is available from the British Library.

Published by Goldcrest Books International Ltd
www.goldcrestbooks.com
publish@goldcrestbooks.com

ISBN: 978-1-911505-06-8 (paperback)
ISBN: 978-1-911505-07-5(.mobi)
ISBN: 978-1-911505-08-2 (.epub)

This book is dedicated to my family and to music, without both of which I would never have had the inspiration to write it.

'But I tried, didn't I? God damn it, at least I did that.'

R.P. McMurphy, *One Flew Over the Cuckoo's Nest*

Author's Note

Whilst the majority of this novel is set in a real area with real places, some topography, geography, bus routes and journey times have purposely been altered to suit the story. I hope you can forgive me! All characters are entirely fictitious.

A.L.

PROLOGUE

I ce, like patterned lace, on the inside of window panes in a
darkened bedroom – a howling wind presses its face and
hands blackly against the glass, rattling it in its frames as if
trying to get in. A tall man with lank hair hanging in his eyes
stands hunched at the foot of a bed. He is manic, agitated,
sweating despite the cold.

In his hands he is juggling a slippery, bawling newborn
– mucus-covered and outraged at its sudden expulsion into
the world. He holds the infant at arm's length, repulsed and
horrified by it in equal measure. For a moment its life hangs
in the balance.

A little girl is shivering in the hallway outside, drawn by the
foreign sound from within. A doll with half of its hair tugged
out dangles from one of her fists. She pushes open the door
to survey the scene inside, but she is groggy and her vision is
blurry. Nothing makes sense.

Through the gloom she can make out the hidden shape
of her elder sister, seemingly asleep, beneath covers that have
developed dark patterns. Stranger still is the stooped and
spectral form of her father. What is *he* doing in here? He is
staring, oblivious to her presence, at what looks like a baby in
his hands; the source of the commotion that had woken her.

'Father?' she says.

He turns with a look of shock on his face that quickly changes to a scowl when he sees her. 'Get back to bed!' he barks. The girl runs, scurrying and frightened, back down the corridor, trying to make sense of what she's seen. In her slumberous state she stumbles on an uneven floorboard, stubbing her toe and crying out in pain. She climbs back into bed, clutching her foot and sobbing loudly, alone in the dark. No one comes – they never do.

During that bleak and momentous night, the temperature plummets further still and the wind abates. It leaves behind a curious white sediment in its wake – Jack Frost; Mother Nature's errant son. The house and everything surrounding it are covered with a sprinkling of fine, white powder. Nothing is spared. The fruit trees are all minted and furry, their branches looking so brittle they could turn to dust at the merest touch.

The next morning, the girl rises bleary-eyed and confused. Still clutching her doll, she heads to the only warm spot in the house; by the stove in the parlour. When she gets there, to her surprise, her place on the rug is taken by a usurper in the form of a basket. She rubs at her sleepy eyes as if she's seeing things, and then totters over to peer in.

Inside is a tiny, pink baby with blue eyes and black hair, caked in dried blood. So it wasn't a dream, she thinks, and her stomach does a little dance. Just then her father looms at the kitchen doorway. She cowers at the sight of him. He looks haggard, more so than usual, as if he hasn't slept for days. She turns her attention back to the baby and stares at it, captivated. 'I think he needs a wash,' she says.

As her father watches, the girl looks up to stare out of one of the parlour windows with its many panes of glass. Her gaze goes past the melting pools of water on the sill, through the circular holes where the ice is beginning to melt and drip, to the hoary frost outside. It is the first time she has noticed it; everything is twinkling under a weak, winter sun. She appears contemplative, as if considering something, then looks back to the baby in the crib, decided. 'I think we'll call him Jack,' she says, then stands up, dropping her doll, and hurries down the hallway to tell her sister.

CHAPTER 1

The Bus

The sun followed Jack home on the bus again, keeping pace with him as it raced past the scrolling East Midlands landscape. Over claustrophobic buildings and factories, the lonely embankments of the glistening River Trent, and then a railway track – turning its lines to glowing copper before they disappeared from view, giving way to rolling hills that eventually soothed his mind.

Jack breathed more easily and settled into his journey, sitting in his usual seat on the left-hand side near the back. He caught the same bus home every day after work and, it seemed, so did the rest of the people on it. He recognised pretty much all of them, with their quirks and routines, and, more to his disgust, their physical defects. He sometimes felt as if he was part of a travelling freak show or a human menagerie on wheels.

There was one man with a huge boil, like an egg on his forehead, who always sat on the same side as Jack, with his protuberance next to the window. Jack could see it in the reflection as the man sat down and, like clockwork, got his comb out and proceeded to comb his hair into place, trying to cover the boil.

There was a woman who had one fat leg and one thin, and

as she hobbled down the aisle Jack could never decide which was the normal one. Another regular passenger – a woman who must have been all of four feet tall – sported full facial hair. No matter how revolting it was to look at, Jack's eyes were always drawn to it in morbid fascination.

Then there was the old couple. The man was still tall, straight and proud, yet on his arm was his shrunken wife. Where once he had probably courted a beautiful young woman, now, like a cruel magic trick, he paraded a shrivelled, balding monkey – as wrinkled as a prune.

As for our boy Jack, well, he also had his own little imperfection: a black speck on his right eye – too tiny for anyone to notice, but always on the periphery of his vision. It came and went; sometimes insignificant, other times a black cursor – menacing and winking. He could never look directly at it as it moved with his eyeball, as if floating – the result of falling off a ladder propped high up in a Victoria plum tree when he was young. He'd taken a nasty blow to the head on the way down and been knocked unconscious upon landing. This was followed by days of severe concussion – the lasting consequence being this pesky, black dot which, as he'd grown up, had become almost psychosomatic in nature, being more pronounced at stressful moments.

On the bus home Jack stank of fried mince and onions from his laborious toil at the processed meat factory. He was always conscious of this and sat as far away from everyone else as he could, putting his rucksack on the seat next to him. He dreaded the day when she, the girl, would catch the same bus home. His heart hiccuped when he thought of her, and he tried to think of something else. Out of the window red-faced students were cycling home up the steep incline from the polytechnic. He let his mind wander.

Jack imagined the countryside was his beloved America –

the America of his dreams anyway; a place of rust-coloured mountains and pine trees, where eagles soared and pickup trucks hurtled down lanes with dust flying out behind them, like in *The Dukes of Hazzard*. Red and white gingham-check cloths lay on kitchen tables in whitewashed, clapboard houses, fronted by verandas, screen doors and porch swings. He pictured the Palomino horses, the ranches and saloon bars in the cowboy films starring his hero, John Wayne. He conjured up the magical, faraway-sounding places in the songs he'd grown up with – Rocky Mountains, Michigan, West Virginia, Tennessee and Colorado – all of which he'd studied, over and over again, on the well-worn map of America that he kept, folded up, hidden in his money tin along with his savings.

Talking of money, today was Friday – payday for Jack – and he patted his jeans pocket to feel the satisfying bump of folded notes. A simple arrangement: two pounds fifty an hour, a hundred pounds a week if he worked through his lunch breaks (he always did, so he didn't have to speak to anybody), cash of course; no tax, no National Insurance, no questions asked. Not bad money for a lad of his age; all courtesy of a dubious, long-standing favour his father had called in from the owner of the factory (an old acquaintance of his) thanks to some shady dealings with pigs back in the sixties, the true nature of which Jack still wasn't sure of.

It was a cold February day (the month that he had turned sixteen), earlier in 1989, that Jack had finally been allowed to make his first foray into the big wide world. Surprisingly, when the time had come he hadn't actually wanted to go. That morning he'd felt naturally scared, but excited too. As the bus had pulled up, however, and he'd seen all the people on it, a terror had gripped him like he'd never known. Fortunately, his elder sister had got on with him that first day and escorted him all the way to the factory.

He hadn't dared look at anyone on the bus and had just kept his head down, trying not to inhale the unfamiliar and odious stink of other people. When it was time to get off at the other end, he'd shuffled down the aisle on rubbery legs and thrown up on the pavement. He'd begged and pleaded with his sister not to make him do it. It was her father's wish, though, not hers, and she didn't dare disobey him: 'the boy needs to start paying his bloody way!'

His sister had cried when they'd reached the huge iron factory gates; it felt as if she was abandoning him outside a workhouse in a Charles Dickens novel – never to be seen or heard of again. Little did Jack know at the time that he was being delivered from the hands of one tyrant to another.

The owner, Mr Peasgood, hadn't known what to make of him at first; this taciturn boy (a nephew, did he say?) who'd turned up early. Neither had the rest of the workforce: they'd all presumed he was kind of simple – not quite 'all there' – so they'd avoided him. He wasn't, just petrified; but this reaction had suited Jack as it meant they left him alone to get on with his work – under the watchful, beady eye of Peasgood. Funnily enough, Jack had grown to enjoy the bus journeys: they'd become his favourite part of the day – away from his father, and staring out in wonder at the world.

Back to the present … and the downside to Fridays. Even though he'd been paid and had got the whole weekend away from the stinking factory, Jack wouldn't see *her* again until Monday; those all too brief moments before work had become the highlight of his day.

When Jack got off the bus, he immediately reached into his rucksack for a bottle of the home-brewed cider he'd been craving. He took a long, thirst-quenching swig. How delightful, you may think. How refreshing and well deserved after a long week at work. But how wrong you can be. This potent, pernicious brew, which had started out as a hobby of his father's – an innocent experiment in home brewing – had become the curse of his family's life. Jack had been practically weaned on it from birth. With no mother around, the only way to shut him up at night (in his father's befuddled brain) was to dip a dummy in the stuff, squeeze it until it filled with the amber liquid, then let it knock the little baby out.

The cider had been a constant ever since, and Jack had found himself increasingly dependent on it in his teenage years. It had been the ruin of his father: he'd become addicted after his wife had died, then raged and bawled his way through life, taking most of his anger out on his offspring.

The only person immune to its devilish, deceptive charms was Jack's sister, Anne, who, after seeing what it had done to her father, wouldn't touch the stuff. Ironically, she had borne the brunt of its effects. She had, like Jack, physically suffered at the hands of her father, mainly because she had the misfortune of being born a woman. She wasn't as quick as Jack – who from a very early age had learnt to run and hide like a fox. Worse than this, much worse, was that she had lost a sister and a mother, and this hurt more than any beatings her father could dish out. Yet she had sacrificed her life to serve him, and to bring up her little brother; no wonder sorrow sat upon this girl's head.

CHAPTER 2

Home

Jack waited till the bus was out of sight, then climbed over a gate as he began the familiar trek home. He swigged from his bottle, relishing the comfort it brought and enjoying the warmth of the evening sun.

His destination was a somewhat ramshackle white bungalow in need of a lick of paint. Despite being situated near a main road, the property was almost totally hidden by the impenetrable hedges that surrounded it. It was halfway up a long, steep hill, slap-bang on the border of Leicestershire (county of the fox) and Nottinghamshire (home to Robin Hood folklore) – in the heart of the countryside, yet in the middle of nowhere. To the north, it was protected by a huge row of mature poplar trees that bowed alarmingly when gusts of wind blew across the exposed fields. But these sentinels stood strong and firm, sheltering the house from the worst of the elements.

The bungalow was set in a large, rambling corner plot, once a nursery, with various different levels. Access was provided by a long, pot-holed lane that bordered a meadow, beyond which was a spinney. These, along with the wild garden and orchard, were Jack's playground.

The lane continued to another house, a farm more than half a mile away, where it ended. Jack never went up there; it was strictly forbidden. The boundary of his world in that direction was the cattle grid, about a hundred yards or so from his home. Sometimes he stood at the cattle grid and stared longingly at the farmhouse in the distance, wondering who lived there and what went on inside it.

Jack's father and his beloved wife, Carla – both teachers at the time and still full of the promise of what life had in store for them – had bought the run-down bungalow almost outright, a devil's bargain for losing both her parents in their fifties. This episode had permanently estranged her from her only sister (as wills so often do) – exacerbated by Carla's choice of husband. They had bought the property for a snip as no one really wanted it: the uneven land and thick clay soil had been major factors in its failure as a nursery. Most people thought they were mad taking it on, but Carla had been obsessed with the idea of self-sufficiency.

It was the early sixties when they first moved there, more than a decade before *The Good Life* came to British living rooms. Despite the programme being a sit-com, and a genuinely funny one at that, it made Jack's father cry drunkenly into his cider. He reminisced through rose-tinted glasses about those early years, forgetting all the bad stuff and romantically identifying with the couple – ignoring the fact they'd had two children themselves and it had all turned to hell. He wasn't the easy-going, good-natured Richard Briers either – far from it.

The land was Carla's thing; it was the bungalow that interested him more. He had grandiose ideas about renovating and extending it, but the furthest they got was the beginnings of a loft extension. Plans were drawn up, planning permission was granted and work began. Supporting beams for the floor were put in place via a hole knocked through the side of the house, and all the flooring was laid. Then Carla fell seriously ill. Work halted and the window was bricked up, but never painted over. Jack would stare up at the square of red bricks, high up on the wall, wondering what secrets lay hidden behind it.

To the front of the house was a lawn, the only one that was mown regularly, surrounded by a crumbling sandstone wall. Near the poplars there was more grass, but this was wild and overgrown, over a foot high and bordered by tree stumps. These once magnificent Victoria plum trees had been hacked down and now resembled stepping stones – another part of Jack's very own adventure playground.

Hardy wild primroses grew here, scarlet, magenta and yellow. No longer were there any cultivated flowers on the site, just what nature intended: nodding snowdrops in winter, daffodils at Easter, and clouds of speckled blue forget-me-nots in spring. When the glorious aubretia that tumbled over the sandstone wall came out, it was the signal to check on the apple blossom in the orchard. The abundance of this (or lack of it) was an early indication of the autumn fruit the trees would bear.

To the rear of the house was a driveway and Jack's father's workshop – a hulking place of mystery and deafening, lethal machinery – all paid for with his late wife's pension and a large part of her life insurance. When she died, he had to bring up two girls he'd never wanted in the first place and had never cared for. He'd been jealous of them from the moment he'd laid eyes on the first born, Charlotte, suckling at his wife's breast, and he felt as though he'd had to share her attention thereafter.

At the time of Carla's death he'd been out of work; the predictable conclusion to his ill-fated teaching career. Never had a man been less suited to the profession; he was quick tempered, short of patience and didn't like children. As with a lot of things in their early years, Carla had talked him into it. He'd already had two warnings for overstepping the mark, and was getting a reputation as a bit of a bully. He was eventually dismissed for 'excessive use of force' when the governors got tired of defending him to parents. It had been an unsavoury period and he'd tried, but failed, to appeal – bitterly losing faith in the education system in the process. 'How can you discipline children, Carla, without the use of proper force?'

He was left, in his early thirties, with no income, two mouths to feed, and dependent on the money left by his wife's passing. The small mortgage was paid off, but they still needed money to live. He wasn't a lazy man per se, and would work around the clock if something interested him, but he was prone to bouts of indolence, introversion and daydreaming. A carpentry business on the premises was the perfect answer. It had been his family's trade, and he was doing something he enjoyed, more of a hobby. Carla would have approved; that's what he told himself anyway. He could also keep a watchful eye on those troublesome girls.

Next to the workshop, up some stone steps, was a square yard used for chopping logs. It housed a huge caustic tank, raised up on breeze blocks and used to strip doors and furniture. Between the yard and the house was a timber junk shed with a corrugated roof. The shed was filled with all manner of unusual items, including an old lawnmower, a bike, various scythes, a cracked sink and, most bizarrely, some old gas masks – the purpose of which Jack could never figure out. The only logical explanation he could think of was that his father was of Nazi descent, which would explain a lot.

Jack had spent hours tinkering in the shed when he was little, pretending he was an inventor. One day, being an inquisitive child, he'd got hold of a box of matches, and had decided to see what happened if he dropped one into the petrol tank of the defunct lawnmower. He'd unscrewed the rusty lid, lit a match and dropped it in. A cylindrical tower of orange flame had shot up towards the roof of the shed, singeing off his eyebrows and fringe and nearly setting the shed on fire. He would never forget the smell that had stayed with him for days, even after his frazzled hair had been cut off and he'd had countless baths. Needless to say, he'd got a good hiding and had never played with matches again; he'd been afraid of fire ever since.

Further up the garden were the remains of two long greenhouses. The original idea had been to knock them down, flatten the area and build a tennis court – Lord knows there was enough room – but this was just another daydream that never materialised. It was now a wasteland littered with rubble, occupied by an incinerator. A path cut through the long grass up to it, negotiating a gaggle of gooseberry bushes and a large rhubarb patch. Beyond this were the top garden and the hallowed orchard, the abundant source of the family cider.

The top garden was divided by a row of apple trees and a few pear trees. Jack and his sister half-heartedly tried to mow part of this area, as it was home to their rusty old swing, which they both still enjoyed. It was secret and peaceful up there, a good place to get away from their father. Anne often rocked herself gently, with a sad, faraway look on her face, when there had been a fight. The other section was overgrown, bordered by dilapidated outbuildings, chicken runs and sheds.

Although all this area was run down and forgotten, in its heyday, whilst Carla was still alive and the girls were young, this had been the epicentre of the smallholding. Before Jack's time, it had been a hive of activity and organised chaos.

There had been chickens, guinea pigs, ducks, geese, two pigs and even a goat. The goat, incidentally, was the last animal to survive from this era, as if it was somehow destined for a higher purpose.

As it turned out, it was. The creature had been one of Carla's last acquisitions, when she didn't have long left to live; she'd never tried goat's milk before. Many years later, the stubborn, bad-tempered old thing still refused to die, as if it was waiting for something. It remained tethered on a long, frayed leash so it didn't escape, and wandered the orchard nomadically, stripping the fruit trees of their bark. Little Anne was the only one who paid it any attention; the goat seemed wise to her and reminded her of her mother. It had lasted for twelve months after Jack was born. There were times when without its milk he possibly would never have made it through that first year. It passed away during the harsh winter that followed, as if its job on earth was done.

Back in the old days, all these animals had kicked up an infernal racket and spent most of their time trying to escape. Jack's father had put up chicken wire to contain them all, and when this was trodden down by the animals or the children he had been driven into fits of fury. Looking back, though, these had been the good times; the girls had helped to pick the never-ending glut of fruit, feed the animals and collect the eggs from the birds.

In summer, the children had a stall by the roadside selling excess produce – plums, apples, pears and eggs. They sat at a table with an old-fashioned set of scales and a drawer for money, and for a few years did a steady trade. Once Carla died, and the girls grew up, this disappeared: all that remained was an old sign embedded in the thick undergrowth at the bottom of the lane: 'Victoria Plums for Sale – 50p a lb.' Any passing customers from the old days who pulled in on the off chance, and made their way up to the house, were barked at and sent away with a flea in their ear: eventually they got the message and stopped coming.

CHAPTER 3

A Storm

On reaching home, Jack took a deep breath before entering the back door. Anne was cooking dinner, and they briefly acknowledged each other with a resigned half-smile. Their father – who was always in the house or his workshop – could be heard snoring from the living room, no doubt sleeping off an afternoon drunk in front of a television quiz show. Jack went straight to his room and removed his savings tin from beneath a loose floorboard under the bed. He added his wages to the considerable wad of cash, carefully covered with his map of America. He replaced it, then had a quick bath and change of clothes; glad to wash away the smells of work.

By the time he returned to the kitchen, dinner was ready but his father was still asleep. They both knew better than to wake him. 'Go on, you have yours, I'll wait,' Anne said, putting his plate on the table.

'Are you sure?' asked Jack. Their father hated eating alone as much as he hated being woken up; he found it disrespectful. It was as though he had to hold court at the head of the table in front of an audience of loyal subjects.

After a nod from Anne, Jack tucked in – eager to get outside into the fresh air. Although he felt guilty leaving her to face the brunt of his father's foul mood, equally he didn't want to be around when he awoke. He wolfed down his dinner, thanked his sister, then paid a routine visit to the cellar to get some supplies.

He paused halfway down the cellar steps and, as his sister watched, braced himself before jumping to the bottom of them. He cleared the remaining stone steps easily, pretending they were the mouth of a crocodile. Anne shook her head, wishing he wouldn't do it. One of these days he was going to misjudge and smash his face into the wall; it was time he grew up. Jack filled two fresh bottles of cider, then tilted the keg, which felt fairly light. Although there was another full one, he decided against a third bottle. From experience, he and his poor sister knew what happened when the cider ran out in this household: it wasn't worth the risk.

Jack left the house, grateful that his father was still asleep, and headed off up the lane to one of his favourite evening haunts. These were the spinney, Bunny Wood, the stile or the brook. He chose the stile this evening, on the edge of Bunny Wood. Jack had always traversed the lane as other children negotiated a dangerous stretch of railway line; with his senses on high alert, listening out for the distant rumble of a vehicle – a farm truck, the weekly dustbin lorry or the postman. This feeling had diminished a little, only slightly, since he'd started going out to work.

He walked briskly with his rucksack clinking on his back, drinking in the sights and scents of late spring. They reminded him of when he was little, especially the nostalgic, redolent aroma of cut grass from the top lawn drifting over the hedge; his sister must have done the year's first mow earlier in the day.

He could smell the rapeseed in the fields and the cow parsley in the hedgerows that bordered the lane. There was the tick-tock of dandelions, and the glow of buttercups and daisies, warmed by the sun in the long grass of the meadow. Midges buzzed about, making his scalp itch. They annoyed him, but he loved them too, as they were evocative – all of these things were – of a simpler time. A time when things just happened, and days drifted along, without all these thoughts whirling round his head as they had lately. Now he seemed to be waiting for something to happen, or felt that he needed to force something to happen to create future memories.

Jack veered off the lane and walked across two fields to sit on his favourite stile, taking his time now that he was out of sight. The view was amazing at this time of year – a riot of pure yellow from the rape fields. This is where he felt most at home, with the whirr of nature all around him. Cracking open a bottle of cider, Jack took a long swig and surveyed his kingdom. The sun was a striking tangerine hole now, sitting low in a bruised sky. He tilted his bottle to it in salute. There was something in the air that he couldn't quite put his finger on. It was slightly darker than normal, and the crows in their nest at the top of the dead tree, usually squawking and squabbling, were subdued.

Jack's thoughts returned to the girl. He mused, glumly, that Monday seemed an eternity away. But come Monday, 'What then? You're only going to stare at her as usual.' The voice in his head always doubted him, always put him down. 'I'll tell you what!' he challenged it, holding aloft his cider, 'I'm going to speak to her!' And he made a resolution there and then that the next week he was going to pluck up the courage and do it.

The little black speck in his eye reared up, joining in like a tag-team, and mocking him: 'I'm still here, you know, and I know you; you haven't got the guts, you're a scaredy-cat!' Jack tried to ignore it, but sometimes that made it worse. This was the problem: he knew he had to remain calm, otherwise he would start acting like a total idiot in front of her, talking to himself and fighting off invisible black dots. But this was easier said than done, when just the thought of her sent him into a spin.

Time drifted. Lulled by a second bottle of cider, Jack didn't notice the last chink of the sun bid farewell, dropping behind the wood. He was startled by the squawk of the crows as they left their nest. They looked in a hurry. It was still humid and the air was heavy; too heavy, brooding with suspense.

First he felt it, and then he heard it – the unmistakable patter of raindrops, light at first, intermittent. He stuck his tongue out, trying to catch them. They grew more persistent, each one large and warm, tingling his tongue, refreshing him. It had been a while since it had rained. Jack grinned, threw back his head, and brayed with mule-like laughter as the drops got heavier. This needed to happen, he thought. It's a sign that everything is being washed clean, a new beginning. He felt revitalized, with a newfound zeal, sure of what he had to do come Monday: the sky had spoken! And he sprinted for home as the thunder rolled, lightning flashed, and the sky ripped open with a roar.

On reaching the lane his mood quickly changed, as despite the onslaught, he could just make out the creak of the swing behind the hedge. He could visualise his sister, her straight brown hair soaking wet, staring off into the distance. 'Bastard!' he hissed. He stopped and called out, but she didn't answer him – perhaps she didn't hear him through the rain and thunder.

Jack was getting drenched himself and so he left her to it; it wasn't the first time and it wouldn't be the last. The house was deadly silent when he entered the kitchen. There was no sign of his father, or of any fight, until he spotted some broken crockery, stained with gravy, in a dustpan by the bin. When he saw it, he burned with familiar, impotent rage. Rushing to his room, he took solace by counting his tin of money for the umpteenth time and looking at his map; his comfort blanket. He rocked backwards and forwards on his bed; cold, wet, and longing for maternal arms around him.

*****

Breakfast was the normal routine; his father sitting there, brooding and impatient, as Anne brought him a mug of tea to have whilst waiting for his food – one of three things: two slices of poached egg on toast, baked beans on toast, or tinned tomatoes and cheese on toast. He always sniffed his plate and either complained that it smelt, or grunted if it was OK. Next, he liberally sprinkled salt and ground black pepper onto his breakfast. He then cut the four corners off his toast and worked his way into the middle of each slice. When done, he grunted again, and Anne cleared away his plate and mug, replacing them with a cup of coffee. Then she did the washing up, whilst her father sat there watching.

Jack had watched the same thing morning after morning, year after year, and it depressed the hell out of him. It angered him that his father was incapable of doing anything for himself, or of even saying thank you, whilst his sister waited on him hand and foot. Jack ate his toast in silence, thinking that he would wash it down afterwards with his first cider of the day. Talking of which, his first job of the weekend was to make a fresh brew...

The cider recipe (if you could call it that) had developed considerably over the decades, and so had the method of making it. Ongoing trial and error had resulted in a very rudimentary product, brewed for alcohol rather than taste. It certainly wouldn't win any awards; in fact, most cider lovers would have turned their noses up at it and its insipid flavour, but its beauty was its simplicity. Making it was still a messy and

26

tedious job, requiring a strong nose at times and a good deal of kit, but through necessity they had found a way of brewing it almost all year round.

Come harvest time, all the precious apples (and pears) were picked and stored. During this frenetic period as many as possible were chopped up and frozen, which helped to pulverise the fruit. Once they'd run out of the stored apples for the cider, they went onto the frozen ones.

The process had been a gradual learning curve, with many mishaps along the way. Carla had originally insisted on using the wild yeasts on the fruit for fermentation – as true to nature as possible – but this could be inconsistent and took too long. Jack's father didn't have the patience, and after she had died he introduced bought yeast.

Again, this was a case of 'learn by your mistakes', as he soon found out that you couldn't store the cider in glass bottles; the first few batches exploded like grenades. As a result, they stored it in plastic kegs and only tapped it into bottles when needed. The yeast also took a while to master, and could be annoyingly temperamental. For example, in the autumn and winter the cider had to be made in the kitchen rather than the cellar, where it was warmer.

The right combination of sugar was critical too, as no two batches of fruit were the same; it was pretty much 'taste as you go'. The introduction of crab apples was another major breakthrough, giving that extra bit of sourness to the mix.

These days the whole family was perfectly capable of producing the same, consistent result – well, Jack and Anne anyway; their father just drank the stuff. He saw himself as the master brewer and they his underlings.

CHAPTER 4

The Girl

The weekend that had stretched out before Jack like a death sentence was over, having passed without any major incident; albeit at a snail's pace. It had been taken up with the usual work, chores and aching hours of boredom under his master's rule, and trying not to do anything to enrage him. Jack's only respite had been in the evenings, when his father was too drunk to pester him anymore, and he was left alone to wander and dream of the coming week.

When Jack awoke on Monday morning and remembered the task he had set himself – to pluck up the courage to talk to the girl – he wanted to crawl back under the covers. I'll do it tomorrow, he told himself; already talking himself out of it. He had never felt like this before, so … desperate. His head pounded and his stomach had cramps, half in agitation and half from the gut rot he had consumed the previous evening. The black spot danced in the corner of his vision, and by the time he left to walk to the bus stop he was a wreck. He'd already had one bottle of cider and was drinking a second, in a somewhat futile attempt to dull his jangling nerves.

The weekend's storm had washed away the clouds like soapsuds, leaving everything brighter and cleaner. It was a perfect, fresh, spring morning and the sun throbbed in a beautiful blue sky. All the birds were chattering as if gossiping about it, and normally Jack, too, would have been rejoicing. But today he just felt hot and flustered. How had this happened? Why was he putting himself through this? He recalled the day when he had first encountered this angel – who had somehow fluttered into his life and shaken him up.

*****

It was the Monday morning after the weekend when the clocks had changed – or were supposed to have changed. That weekend as a family they hadn't done anything, as usual, hadn't gone anywhere, and had barely watched telly. Living as they did in isolation, and with nothing to prompt her, Anne had simply forgotten to put the clocks forward. Jack's father was usually too drunk to remember anything like this – it wasn't as if he had to get up to go to work, so what was an hour here or there? As for Jack, he didn't even have a watch; he'd never needed one and relied on his sister to drag him out of bed in the morning. So they'd spent that whole Sunday an hour behind. Early on the Monday morning Anne had woken at her normal time and followed her normal routine: put the kettle on, rake the stove (or remake it if it had gone out), and then a cup of tea in front of *Good Morning Britain* – her little bit of time to herself before she woke the men up. It was then that she noticed, to her great alarm, the clock in the corner of the TV screen, and realised her mistake.

Up till now, Jack had always caught the seven o'clock bus to work. This was Anne's doing: on that first day she'd been worried that they wouldn't get there in time for nine o'clock. The buses only ran every hour, and it took at least fifty minutes to get to the edge of town. Jack, being a creature of habit, had caught the same bus ever since – even though he always arrived early. He had even started getting off at an earlier bus stop and walking that bit further, to take up more time. When he got to the factory, he began work a lot earlier than he had to – much to Peasgood's satisfaction, as he didn't have to pay him for it.

So, when Anne broke the news to Jack as she shook him awake, it sent him into a bit of a meltdown. He paced and muttered and cursed whilst he waited for the next bus, supping from his cider bottle. When it finally arrived and he got on, he couldn't look at the new driver. His normal seat was already taken, so he hurried to the back with downcast eyes. Thankfully, there was space to the right, and he sat there panicking about being late for work.

As the bus drove into the first village there was a gaggle of five or six people at the bus stop. Jack cursed again at how long this was going to take. At the back of the queue, something caught his eye – a vivid flash of colour – a girl with hair of the deepest auburn. It reminded him of looking through one of his red marbles at the sun. She disappeared from view as she waited to board the bus. Then there she was again, paying for her ticket and turning to walk down the aisle. Her hair bounced as she walked and hung about her face in curls. It took Jack's breath away. He was immediately bewitched, and his panic over being late for work melted away.

He had only seen her face briefly and she certainly hadn't noticed him, so he spent the remainder of the journey furtively glancing at her, entranced by the colour of her hair. As the bus neared the outskirts of town, it occurred to him that he would have to get off soon and walk past her. A fresh wave of panic washed over him. As he was running late, Jack decided to get off at the stop near the factory; he pressed the buzzer and stumbled down the aisle. His face was burning as he waited for the bus to slow. He disembarked without looking back, then waited for the bus to leave before running all the way to work.

All that day he couldn't get her out of his mind. He couldn't think about anything else. The next morning (much to his sister's bemusement), he caught the later bus to work again, and sure enough, the girl got on and sat in the same place. Jack had caught the same bus ever since.

He had slowly been building up a mental jigsaw of her face and fitting it back together later; those deep brown eyes, those cherry lips. He took delight in her every movement – the clothes she wore, the way she walked – there was something about it, something in the way her hips moved that was hypnotic and self-assured. Some days she rummaged in her bag for a book, or fished out a personal stereo and put headphones on. The distinct smell of her perfume reached him further down the bus, and when he walked past her he couldn't help but surreptitiously take a deep breath, hoping her scent would stay with him all day. It was like some sweets he'd had as a child...

*****

So here he was, hopping from one foot to the other as the bus pulled up – with no plan of how he was going to put into motion the crazy goal he'd set himself. In his drunken daydreams he'd swept her off her feet and delivered a winning kiss, John Wayne style. But now reality bit. He wasn't John Wayne; he was plain old Jack Hemsley – 'Mad Jack' if you like – paying for his bus ticket and fumbling the change as the black spot on his eye emerged.

The bus was busy as usual on a Monday morning, already half full. Great, he thought. But then an idea came to him: why didn't he just sit where *she* normally sat? Or would that look too obvious? What if she *did* sit next to him? Would he be able to handle that? What if he made a fool of himself? What about when he got off the bus? He'd have to clamber over her to get off!

All these thoughts flashed through his head in the seconds it took to reach her usual place. For better or for worse, the decision was taken out of his hands: for once, her seat was already taken. He exhaled heavily and continued to his normal spot, clutching his rucksack and feeling a mixture of relief and disappointment.

As the girl got on in the village and paid for her ticket, Jack watched to see where she would sit. He stared intently out of the window as she approached lest his face should betray the secret thoughts he'd been having about her. With a heady waft of musk and a jangle of bracelets, she plonked herself down just in front of him.

Jack gulped, but it was hard to swallow. He didn't dare breathe and was conscious of his every move. It took him several minutes to shift in his seat and face forward again. As the girl settled down, she reached back and flicked her hair loose from under the collar of her jacket, releasing another heavenly wave of scent in the process. To be so close that he could reach out and touch her hair – and the smell of it as it washed over him – made Jack feel drunk; it was ambrosial, intoxicating – like shampoo, blossom and … Parma Violets. That was it, Parma Violets!

Needless to say, he didn't speak to her; he sat there in a dreamlike stupor, content to be so near to her and awash on her fragrant sea. That was enough, he told himself; maybe it would always be enough. His goal temporarily went out of the window. He didn't speak to her the next day, nor the next day, nor the day after that – despite the fact that, to Jack's utter delight, she sat right in front of him every day.

As the weeks went by, the days got hotter. Jack had got over the initial shock of being so close to her, and his thoughts returned to wondering how on earth he was going to strike up a conversation with her. When he wasn't doing his father's endless list of jobs, he wandered restlessly in the fields, seeking solace in the bottle. It was eating him up inside; he had lost his appetite and wasn't sleeping well. It was as though he had a rare, ardent form of Stockholm Syndrome; his heart had been taken hostage, and he had fallen in love with its captor.

It was a Thursday morning on the bus. Jack was already feeling the familiar pressure of the approaching weekend and the disappointment of another week wasted. It was stiflingly hot as she walked down the aisle towards him. Her hair was up, bunched together in a large clip, and she was wearing a cotton top with thin straps, as opposed to the normal band T-shirts she wore. As she sat down in front of him, he stared longingly at the back of her neck. It was ivory coloured and slightly fuzzy like a peach; and her shoulders were freckled and pink from the sun.

In the reflection of the window, Jack watched as she removed a book from her bag and began to read. Then she appeared to change her mind, taking the card she always showed the bus driver, placing it in her book as a bookmark, and putting the book down next to her. She stood up to open one of the windows. As she did so, Jack's eyes were drawn to the graceful contours of her body; how her bracelets slipped down her slender arms as she reached up, and the way her jeans clung to her. A welcome breeze blew over his face as he drank it all in. Suddenly she turned her head and spoke. 'You don't mind, do you?'

Jack was startled; ashamed that he'd been caught looking at her. No words would come out. Did she just speak to him or had he imagined it? He looked up slowly and their eyes met for the first time. She gestured to the window and all he could do was blush and shake his head. It seemed to happen in slow motion, but was all over in seconds, and she sat down again. As she did so, her book fell on the floor and the card in it fell out. Before she reached down and picked it up, he saw the black letters 'NUS' and a photograph of her. He also had time to make out her first name; it was Daisy, which made him think of Daisy Duke.

Jack spent the rest of the day in tortured misery – cursing himself and his rotten shyness. The opportunity that he had been trying so hard to engineer for the last few weeks had presented itself, and he had blown it. He hadn't uttered a word; he was pathetic – what must she think of him now? He built up a brief trifle of a moment into the ultimate failure and humiliation, replaying it over and over again.

He could barely concentrate at work. Tears smarted his eyes as he pulled trays of sausage rolls out of the huge, steaming, convection ovens. He hated himself and he hated his life – and on the spur of the moment he took the back of his hand and pressed it against a red-hot oven tray. The pain was immediate, shocking and intense, but despite this, he left his hand there for maybe two or three seconds and it felt good; it took the other pain away. He had never done anything like that before, and he instantly regretted it. An angry red welt, white in the middle, rose up on the back of his hand. It stung like hell.

He made straight for the staff changing rooms and stuck the burn under a cold tap. As the icy water numbed the searing pain, he looked into the mirror at his tear-stained face. He threw the ridiculous paper hat he had to wear on the floor in disgust and looked again. From somewhere deep in the recesses of his fuzzy mind, a voice told him not to give up; calling on the last remaining dregs of resolve and spirit he had left. It urged him to try one last time to speak to the girl, Daisy; otherwise he would regret it for the rest of his life.

34

That evening, despite being in excruciating pain, Jack managed to get through dinner without his father or sister noticing the burn on his hand. As soon as he dared, he slunk down to the cellar to retrieve two bottles of cider, then retreated to his room like a wounded animal. He left it only once to go to the bathroom for the Savlon, their good friend over the years. He covered the back of his hand in the cooling ointment and it provided some welcome relief. It didn't take him long to finish the cider.

Jack sweated through a restless night of delirious sleep. He dreamt he was walking down a country lane where all the hills were bedecked with tartan – as if someone had laid a huge blanket over them. In the distance, he saw tall, thin, stick people walking towards him, and dead trees lining the road. Down the tartan hills came huge, rolling balls of matter. They looked like fluff, but were really thoughts and worries – and they knocked over the trees and stick people, snapping them like twigs. The balls swirled around him, making him spin in a confused, dark world that melted into liquid, until he was inside a huge teacup, being stirred by a giant spoon.

CHAPTER 5

A Birthday Dinner

The next morning, Friday, Jack was woken by the dull throb from the back of his hand. He examined the burn in morbid fascination, astounded at how a huge blister had swelled up overnight. He prodded it lightly and it was firm to the touch. It served as a reminder of his cowardice, and he vowed not to succumb to it again.

After bathing, which helped to clear his mind, Jack made his way into the kitchen. He expected a volley of abuse from his father over disappearing so suddenly the previous night, but he wasn't sitting bad-temperedly at the table. His sister was bustling about, placing breakfast items onto a large wooden tray. Jack's stomach rumbled at the sight of boiled eggs with their tops cut off, little wisps of steam unfurling from them. 'Mind out the way,' Anne tutted as she passed. It was then that he noticed the envelope on the tray. 'It's his birthday,' she sighed, as she headed off to their father's bedroom.

His birthday … oh no, Jack groaned; just another excuse to lord it over them. Jack had totally forgotten as usual. He resented it, and resented even more the effort his sister made, especially considering their birthdays went by without so much as a whimper. It was the same routine every year: breakfast in bed, drinking from lunchtime and his father's slap-up birthday dinner, for which he was usually plastered. Afterwards, he would descend into rare and morbid sentimentality over his long-departed wife. Jack covertly listened to his drunken ramblings in the hope of some information about his origin. So far this had proved fruitless; he'd heard the name 'Carla' bandied about over the years and something about cancer, but that was it. At least this year he would be out at work for most of the day.

His sister returned to the kitchen. 'Would you like a boiled egg? There's one left.'

'Yes please,' he mumbled, his thoughts already on the bus journey to work and Daisy; no longer just 'the girl'.

After preparing toasted soldiers to go with his egg, Anne brought it to him at the table. It was a relief not to have their father there for once. Jack could tell that Anne felt it too; she was humming to herself as she sat down. She never usually did this, and for once they had a chance to talk, albeit in hushed whispers. 'Now, Jack,' she said. 'I want you to do a favour for me today.' Jack was half-listening, more interested in dipping his toast into his egg. 'I want you to nip into town on your lunch break and get Father's chocolate gingers for me this year.'

Jack's ears pricked up at the mention of town. He had an irrational fear of it and everything it represented: people, traffic, buildings, noise. He'd never been into a shop in his life – he'd never been allowed – never mind gone into town properly; his work was on the outskirts, on an industrial estate. It would mean a huge change in his routine. 'Why me?' he asked.

'Because it'll save me the hassle of getting the bus in. You're in town anyway, and I've got enough to do with getting the meat from the butcher's and preparing dinner. Besides, I think it'll do you good, you know, starting to do a few bits like this; meeting people and having a bit more responsibility.'

Jack stared into the bottom of his empty eggshell; the day wasn't getting off to a very good start. The thought of what she was asking terrified him. The thought of *any* new situation did. Anne was well aware of this, and she half-considered backing down – she was too soft with him and always had been; she'd always felt so sorry for him. None of this was his fault, after all, but she had to tell herself to be firm. It was for his own good: he was no longer a child, and it was high time he became more independent, more worldly-wise. Otherwise someone was going to take advantage of him. 'Please, Jack, for me – it'll be a big favour. The buses run every fifteen minutes into town, so you'll have plenty of time. Just get off at Broadmarsh bus station, which is the last stop; you can't go wrong. Go through the doors into the shopping centre and the shop's immediately on your left – you can't miss it. You know which ones he likes, the dark chocolate ones.'

'I know which ones he likes!' Jack said. When was the last time *he* had ever got anything for his birthday? When was the last time his birthday had even been acknowledged? Never; that's when. He begrudged doing anything out of his way for his father at the best of times – and especially something that was going to ruin his day.

'Now you won't forget, will you, whatever you do – *don't forget!* Do you want me to write it down for you?'

'No, it's fine. I'll remember,' he replied, getting up from the table.

'Here, let me write it on your hand for you.' She fished a pen out of her apron pocket and reached for Jack's hand. It was then that she saw the huge, ugly blister. 'Jack!' she cried in distress. 'What have you done?'

'It's nothing,' he muttered, trying to pull his hand away.

'It's not nothing!' she said, and then more quietly, 'Here, let me look.'

Jack reluctantly let her examine the burn. She winced at the sight of it and sucked in her breath; it looked so painful. 'How did you do this?'

'It was just an accident at work; I was getting a hot tray out of the oven.'

She searched his face, not knowing whether to believe him. 'That needs wrapping up. You're not going to work with it like that.' And she stood up, knowing they had to work quickly. She applied more ointment to the back of his hand and wrapped it in a small bandage, tying it off neatly as she'd done many times before. The smell of Savlon always reminded him of Anne; that and the comforting smell of scorched rubber from a hot water bottle on a winter's night – soothing, nurse-like. 'Now, try and keep it out of sight tonight as well. We don't need any drama, not today!'

As if to emphasise the point, they heard their father bellowing for his coffee. 'Coming!' Anne hollered back. Jack thanked her; he was running late and needed to get some cider. 'Oh God! One more thing – I nearly forgot,' Anne said. 'Are you OK paying for them – the chocolates? I'm a bit short this week, and I've got to get the joint and that.' Jack looked at her. This was the final insult; it was bad enough having to *get* them for him, but paying for them as well? 'You'll get it back; it can come out of your board money,' she added.

Jack had to hand over forty pounds a week to his sister out of his wages; that was the whole reason for him going out to work. He couldn't really complain, though; save for the bus fare, the rest of it was his – and so far he hadn't spent a single penny. That's why it riled him so much. Not because of the inconvenience, or because he was running late, but more that he had to use his money. It was for one purpose and one purpose only – and that was to get as far away from this hell hole as he could.

It struck Jack as he waited for the bus that the morning's break from routine had been a welcome distraction. He'd only consumed one bottle of cider by the time the bus arrived; just enough for courage, but not so much that he wasn't clear-headed. He boarded the bus with a steely determination that today was the day he was finally going to speak to Daisy. He sat in his usual spot, and butterflies in his stomach began to flutter at the thought of seeing her. The black spot on his eye vied for attention as he stared out of the window. He refused to look at it or indulge it.

As the bus rounded the bend, he watched out expectantly for the familiar blaze of her conker-coloured hair, but didn't see it. He sat up straighter, drawing a few stares from his neighbours, who already considered him a bit peculiar. He craned his neck to see better, thinking perhaps she was at the front of the queue. But she wasn't. Jack was confused. Perhaps she was running late and would arrive at any second. He turned round, peering out of the rear window in hope. People were still paying; there was still time – but she didn't arrive. He was still looking out as the doors closed with a hiss and a whoosh, and the bus pulled away.

He wanted to cry out to the driver, to tell him to wait, but would never have dared. After one last look behind him, he shrank back into his seat in crestfallen resignation. This wasn't part of the plan; he felt cheated. Where was she? Why wasn't she on the bus? Was it his fault? What if he never saw her again? He looked about in blurry-eyed envy at all the other people – normal, contented people, going about their business. The thought of a day ahead of him at the factory compounded his misery. Such was Jack's anguish that he briefly considered getting off at the next stop and not going in. But this would mean killing time for the rest of the day. And when his father found out from the boss that he hadn't turned up he'd get a hiding. As his sister had said, 'We don't need any drama, not today'…

*****

Jack sauntered home after work with his head down. A dirty sun looked down on him in pity, painting a crooked black shadow on the ground as company. Today had been awful, beyond awful. The only thing that got him through the day had been taken away from him, so cruelly, that morning. What he'd give now to turn back time and relive those moments she had sat so close to him. He wouldn't have to speak to her; he'd been greedy, he knew that now. Just to see her again would be enough.

As he opened the back door to the kitchen, his mind still preoccupied, the smell of roasting meat hit him. His sister looked more flushed than usual, and also a bit more stressed. There was something different about the kitchen too; an incongruity that he couldn't put his finger on. Something had been changed, moved or added, and he surveyed the large room, searching for it. There it was; a flash of bright colour on the table – pretty blue and yellow flowers, intermingled with sprays of white ones – all carefully arranged in a dainty, mosaic-effect vase. This had belonged to Anne's mother, and was older than she was. It made the normally drab and stained pine table look very different.

Anne saw him looking at the flowers. 'Pretty, aren't they? I got them from the shop in East Leake; the joint cost less than I expected!' Jack looked at her, confused, without answering. She looked at him oddly in return. And then it dawned on him.

With a sinking feeling of dread, he realised he had forgotten all about his father's birthday … along with the chocolate gingers.

With all the commotion over his burn, and the subsequent bandaging of his hand, his sister had never written that reminder on it. And then not seeing Daisy had meant that all day long he'd been lost in his own little world of pain. He had clean forgotten … and now it was too late; it was gone six o'clock and all the shops were closed – and miles away.

As the colour drained from Jack's face, it took only a moment for the sickening realisation to hit his sister. She froze, and her voice trembled as she spoke. 'Oh, Jack … you haven't. Please tell me you haven't forgotten the chocolates?' His silence, and the way he lowered his head in shame, was enough of an answer. She put down the tray of roast potatoes she was holding before she dropped it, and leant heavily against the counter. 'Oh no. They didn't have any joints of beef at the butcher's either. He'd run out. I had to get pork.'

Despite the bombshell Jack had dropped, and her mounting trepidation, Anne managed to hold herself together whilst she finished preparing the rest of the dinner. She was a good cook; she'd had to be, learning over the years that the best way to placate her father, and to keep things running smoothly, was through his stomach. It was a form of defence, part of her weaponry and armour. She pulled out all the stops. There were crispy roast potatoes and mash, leeks in cheese sauce, roast parsnips, buttered carrots, apple sauce (made from their own Bramleys), stuffing, and a proper meat gravy made from the juices of the joint; all the things her father liked. The crackling on the pork was perfectly crisp and golden, confirmed by a satisfying crunch as she removed it with a knife before slicing the joint.

Jack could barely contain himself, full of guilt as he was at the trouble he knew he had caused. He didn't have the heart to leave the kitchen, and felt obliged to help his sister as much as he could by setting the table, trying not to get in the way. He had a feeble effort at mashing the potatoes, but struggled to do it with his left hand; his right hand felt too tight to grip with. Anne took over, worried that the mash would end up with lumps, whipping it up till it was creamy and fluffy. The last job was to ensure that the plates were nice and hot (cold plates being another of her father's bugbears). She put them in the oven to warm whilst placing a fresh bottle of cider on the table. The time had come, and despite her inner unease, she called her father through for dinner in the most light-hearted voice she could muster.

By the time their father had graced them with his presence, everything had been laid out. It was a fine spread. Jack and Anne sat at opposite sides of the table, eyeing each other nervously. Their father appeared, announcing his arrival with a charming belch. He was a large man and filled most of the kitchen doorway, his hair unkempt and abundantly grey at the sides. His face was bright red, indicating that he was already drunk, a fact confirmed when he lurched to the table and sat down heavily.

Jack forced himself to say 'Happy Birthday' in a timid voice, but hated doing it; it felt like chewing on grit. His father surveyed the table, and grunted at the vase of flowers. With a shaky hand, Anne began to serve roast potatoes onto his plate. Unable to put it off any longer, she said, 'They didn't have any joints of beef left at the butcher's, I'm afraid, so I had to get pork.'

He slammed his fists on the table, banging his cutlery against the wood and knocking his plate in the process. It made them both jump. 'No beef?' he bellowed, as spittle flew from his mouth. 'Roast pork on my birthday?'

'Well they didn't have any beef, so it was pork or lamb

'… and I know how much you love your roast pork. There's proper crackling and apple sauce – just how you like it.'

'Well, you should have ordered it in advance shouldn't you, you stupid girl!'

'I know, I'm sorry, Father.' But he cut her off and leant forward in his chair. Anne cowered and Jack squirmed in his seat.

'Or is that too much to ask?' There was silence as the rhetorical question hung in the air. 'WELL, IS IT?' he shouted, making them both jump again.

'No, I'm sorry. I should have thought.'

He grabbed hold of his cider bottle and raised it to his lips. Most of it missed and ended up down his shirt. He rocked back in his chair, eyeballing Jack, daring him to say anything. Jack tried not to meet his gaze. This was how he worked, how he exercised control; making people feel small and inferior.

When he'd stopped shouting, he began piling his plate with food in an ungrateful manner. Jack waited for him to finish before serving his own dinner. Forgetting what he was doing, he used his right hand, letting his bandage show. He instantly realised his mistake and tried to pull down his shirt sleeve, but it was too late. Out of the corner of his eye, he saw that his father had noticed; he didn't miss a trick.

To Jack's surprise, he didn't say anything, which was somehow worse; his father reached for the gravy boat instead, then stopped what he was doing and stuck a fat finger into it. 'Gravy's cold!' he barked, and shoved the gravy boat across the table at Anne. The gravy wasn't cold, but she had forgotten to warm the jug. She quickly got up and returned the gravy to a pan on the stove, placing the jug in the residual heat of the oven to warm.

Jack looked down at his meal: he wasn't the least bit hungry. His sister returned to the table with the now steaming gravy.

Their father helped himself liberally to it. Anne helped herself to a meagre serving and they both did their best, for decency's sake, to eat.

For a while the only sounds to be heard were the clink and scrape of cutlery and their father devouring his dinner. This temporarily abated his anger. It didn't take him long to clear his plate and then to pile seconds onto it. With his humour improving slightly he looked up, and for the first time became aware of the silence at the table. It was always quiet at dinner – something he was normally oblivious to – but this seemed suspiciously so … and it *was* his birthday. By way of breaking the silence, he said, 'What's the matter with you two? Cat got your tongues? Next you'll be telling me they didn't have any chocolate gingers either!'

He snorted and swigged from his bottle, waiting for a response. Nothing. The same expression on both their faces, the same plates of food barely touched. The penny dropped. His face began to turn an alarming shade of carmine. 'Where's-my-chocolates?' he growled, pausing between each word for emphasis and looking from one of them to the other. They both had their heads down. 'WHERE'S MY SODDING CHOCOLATES?' he erupted in Anne's face. She flinched in terror, letting out a whimper but unable to utter a word. Jack couldn't take it anymore; he wasn't going to let his sister take the blame.

'It's my fault! *I* forgot them, not Anne.' His father turned his head towards him, as if spotting new prey.

'You forgot them, eh…? I give you a roof over your head – and this is how you repay me?' Jack could have lied and said they'd run out, but what was the point? It wouldn't make any difference; there was no stemming his father's fury when it was in full flow. 'For one day of the year, you can't stop thinking about yourself, can you? You UNGRATEFUL …

LITTLE … SOD!' And he grabbed Jack's bandaged hand, twisting it.

Jack yelped in pain as his sister looked on helplessly. 'And what's this, hey…? Too busy daydreaming as usual?' And he applied more pressure. Jack could feel the blister on the back of his hand pop and tear, exposing the tender, raw skin underneath. Liquid spread out, dampening the bandage, and began oozing down his wrist.

Anne cried out, 'Father. No! Leave him alone!' He turned his attention back to her, amazed that she had dared raise her voice to him.

'And you, you knew about it, didn't you? You conniving bitch. And you thought that these would make it all right?' He picked up the vase of flowers and hurled it across the kitchen into a corner cupboard. It smashed in a fragrant shower of water and petals. Anne screamed and ran towards the broken vase.

'You drunken animal!' she shouted, as she crouched down in the corner to pick it up; seeing one of the only precious mementoes of her mother destroyed getting the better of her.

She sobbed as she collected the broken pieces in the lap of her apron.

'What did you just call me?' he said, getting up from the table and starting towards her.

The sight of his sister picking up the broken vase – surrounded by the flowers she had so carefully arranged, so distraught after all the effort she had gone to – hurt Jack more than his stinging hand. Spurred on by this, and the notion that it was all his fault, he lunged towards his father, grabbing his arm and trying to pull him back. But it was like trying to stop a raging bull. His father flung his arm back, knocking Jack onto the floor.

Plates and dishes fell to the floor with him, smashing on

the stone tiles. Jack staggered back up as his father grabbed hold of Anne's hair, trying to pull her up by it. She resisted, covering her head with both hands, cowering in anticipation of the blow she was about to receive. Just as her father drew his arm back, high into the air to strike, he lost his balance on the wet floor and his feet went out from under him. Crying out in surprise, he came crashing down, smashing his head with a sickening thud on the corner of the table. He let out a groan as he hit the floor. His head lolled to the side and started to seep blood as he came to rest – passed out in a sea of water and gravy – amongst a flotsam of food, broken crockery and flowers. A petal had somehow ended up on his mouth, and it fluttered up and down, indicating that, unfortunately, he was still breathing.

Jack had seen enough. His sister wasn't in any immediate danger, so he picked himself up and fled out of the back door, away from the madness. He ran and ran, across the meadow and into the spinney, until his lungs were bursting and his face was streaked with tears. Branches clawed at him as he hurtled through the wood, eventually slowing him down.

He collapsed at the far side of the spinney in the shadow of a large oak tree. The base of its trunk was hollow. Jack crawled inside and curled up into a ball. The familiar, earthy smell of its interior was comforting. In his haste, he'd dashed out of the house without any cider. He needed it to numb the pain; his hand was in agony now that the adrenaline had worn off. He thought of Daisy, and how much he had to see her.

Without cider, Jack normally found it impossible to sleep, but he must have rocked himself into an exhausted slumber and dozed off, for when he came to it was nearly dark. He was cold and desperately needed to pee, and for a minute he hadn't a clue where he was. Then the earthy smell hit him, and he could hear the sounds of the spinney.

He was cramped and aching, so he crawled out of the hole and stretched before urinating against a tree. He then paced around in the dusk, not wanting to go home yet. Thoughts like chalky phantoms returned to haunt him. He needed to see Daisy. For his own sanity and peace of mind he just needed to see her face, and couldn't go to bed till he did. He couldn't wait all weekend in the vain hope that she would be on the bus come Monday morning. What if she wasn't? So strong was the urge that he decided there and then to do something he was absolutely forbidden to do; he set off towards the village to find her.

CHAPTER 6

The Village

From birth, Jack had been kept away from the prying eyes of the world – a dirty secret, his father's cross to bear; a life spent in fear that one day there would be a stranger's knock on the door, bringing trouble, accusations and questions – but it had never come. In effect, Jack didn't exist, and his father had gone to great lengths to keep it that way: the boy had been schooled at home, the post box and the bin were placed strategically at the bottom of the drive, and save for a yearly dumping of coal there were no deliveries at all to the premises. Anne had been sworn to secrecy: 'Don't tell anyone about the baby or he'll be taken away!' He'd figured that if he could make it till Jack was sixteen it would be a lot easier, as school would no longer be an issue.

Over the years Jack *had* come across other people, but you could count those instances on one hand. He had bumped into other children from the village in the early days, during his forays into the surrounding countryside; the odd farmer too. But these accidental meetings were too brief and infrequent to have been of any consequence.

There was one time, when he was too young to know any better, he had spent a glorious afternoon playing in the local brook with some village children, catching fish with his hands and swimming under the bridge beneath the main road. They had never asked him where he lived, or even his name, but it was a memory he still cherished. It had never happened again, as he had received the worst beating of his young life when his father had found out. From that day on, Jack would always run away and hide when he heard other children. He would sit in the shadows, watching, curious, envious of their laughter and their company; aching to join in. So he had remained a rumour – like a large, black cat that was spotted from time to time, but no one really believed in.

Even though it was dark, Jack stuck to the fields. He could see the illuminated houses below. It was strange to think that Daisy was inside one of them. He had no idea where she lived, except that it was from this side of the village that she joined the bus queue. And it was only a small village: how hard could it be? As he reached the brook, he followed it to the bridge and climbed the bank onto the main road.

He remembered a gate he had noticed from the bus – about two hundred yards down on the right-hand side, before the crossroads. It always looked like a back way into the village, and this was what he headed for. He had to walk by the side of the road for a while as there was no path. This made him feel nervous and exposed, so he began to jog. His senses were on high alert as he listened for approaching cars and the faraway flash of headlights. It only took a minute or so to reach the gate, and he did so without a single car passing; then he slipped out of sight again. It was darker here away from the road, and he could just make out a footpath through an overgrown field. At the end of this path was another gate, known to the village children as 'the kissing gate'. Jack passed through it without delay.

Ahead in the gloaming he saw a yellow light across the

lane from the first house, causing his heart to flutter. He approached the small cottage and thought, could this be her house? Foolish, really. His nerves were already on edge when he heard a dog bark from within, making him jump out of his skin, and then a voice: 'Shut up, Bess!' as he hurried past. He almost lost his nerve and turned back. This was a bad idea.

Jack scurried past a couple more houses, both of which had their curtains drawn, and then he noticed some railings and a padlocked gate, guarding a small cemetery. In the moonlight, he saw a neat gravelled path surrounded by gravestones and marble slabs. Some had fresh flowers adorning them. There were crosses too, some older and more ornate, sticking awkwardly out of grass hummocks. He longed to go in to take a closer look, but didn't dare. Pulling himself away, he came to a corner where another small cottage stood. He gasped when he saw a woman at a lit window and ducked out of the way, careful to keep out of the orange glow of a street lamp. Was that her mum? he wondered. No, she was far too old.

He found himself on a bend facing a tall stone wall. To his left, there was a short, straight road of terraced houses, signposted Chapel Lane. It led directly to Main Street: Jack could see occasional cars at the bottom, swishing past. That way was too risky; he'd check down there on his way back, and only if he had no luck elsewhere.

Instead he turned right, following Church Lane. Before long there was the church itself, lurking in the dark. The sinister way in which its spire and lonely bell tower were silhouetted against the moon reminded him of Scooby Doo, and he half expected bats and creepy organ music.

The narrow lane began to curve round. It was hard not to feel closed in by the imposing wall, which was clearly guarding something. Then the wall stopped, parted by a large, metal gate with a sign that read 'The Manor'. Ah, that explains it, he thought. What if she lives in there? You couldn't see the house, but he couldn't imagine someone who lived in a manor catching a bus, so he carried on. Now he was getting his bearings he could sense that the road went round the Manor House and its gardens in a U shape, with Chapel Lane at one end and Church Lane at the other.

Straight ahead of him he could see, in exasperation, that the bottom of the lane also led back onto Main Street. There seemed to be no avoiding the fact that if he was going to continue with this crazy mission, he was going to have to walk down it. After some deliberation he cautiously approached, looking both ways. Fortunately the street was deserted. Opposite was another lane which he had never noticed before, with yet more houses. This was when the reality dawned on him – that trying to find Daisy was like trying to locate a queen bee in a beehive. He trudged up the lane anyway, just in case, and found that there were only five or six houses on it, all with drawn curtains and cars in their driveways; nothing more.

Returning to the corner of Main Street, with dwindling enthusiasm, Jack had to duck out of the way behind a garden wall as a man walked past with a dog. He had to lie on someone's lawn, agonisingly holding his breath, whilst the dog chose to piss against a lamp post just yards from him. When they were gone he let out a huge sigh of relief, thinking how too close for comfort that had been, and that this was madness.

For the second time Jack nearly turned for home, but looking down Main Street, he couldn't resist the pull of the larger residential street that he knew ran off it, before the bus stop. It had lots of houses, and surely would provide his best chance of finding her.

He kept to the shadows, dodging the street lights, and reached the corner of Roman Close – a cul-de-sac of fairly modern, large, detached houses. Being this close to so many people made Jack very uneasy. Under cover of darkness he sauntered from house to house, peering up at windows and feeling like some sort of Peeping Tom. There was definitely more activity down this street. People were visible in every other house doing something or other; closing curtains, or brushing their teeth behind frosted bathroom windows. But they all seemed to be adults.

Jack reached the last house with still no sign of Daisy. Downhearted and desperate for some cider, he began retracing his steps to Main Street. Suddenly, a light was turned on in an upstairs window. He dived behind a bush and peered up, not expecting anything at all, when there was an unmistakable flash of colour. Daisy! Her hair; it had to be! Jack was overcome with amazement and joy. Could it really be her, or was he just imagining things – as a mirage appears to a parched man in a desert? He rubbed his eyes, expecting her to have disappeared or to have morphed into someone else, but no: sure enough, there she was, staring out of the window into the night.

In her hand she held a silver brush. She brought it up to her head and ran it through her hair, which tumbled down her shoulders. Jack looked on, hypnotised by the movement of the brush as it moved through her locks. She did it in a distracted and almost solemn manner. It was hard to make out, but she looked sad and her face looked puffy – as if she'd been crying. She still looked pretty, though, and a lump appeared in his throat: he wanted to take care of her so much. His mind whirred with questions. Why wasn't she on the bus today? Was she ill? Did *her* dad beat her too? Then, to Jack's dismay, she put the brush down on the windowsill. And with one last look out into the night, she pulled the curtains closed.

The light in the bedroom went out and the room went dark. The show was over, and Jack became aware of his surroundings again. He was crouched in some bushes on a street – in the village he was forbidden to visit. Was he mad? It must be getting on for eleven o'clock too – when the house would be locked, and he would be shut out for the night. He bolted for home the way he had come, with the image of Daisy for company, spurred on by a successful outcome to a very risky mission. It was a happy end to a horrible day; he knew where she lived!

The door was still unlocked when he got home, and the house was silent. His eyes were getting accustomed to the dark when a chair scraped, startling him. Out of the shadows, a figure loomed. 'You're cutting it fine, aren't you?' It was his sister; she had been waiting for him. 'You know the rules, Jack. Please don't make any more trouble.' She locked the door behind him, relieved that he was back. 'How's your hand?' she asked, more softly.

'Sore.'

Not daring to put the noisy strip light on lest it should wake their father, Anne led Jack over to the sink by the window. She peeled off his bandage, and he grimaced in agony as it stuck to the tender, exposed flesh. She cleansed his wound and re-dressed it – chiding him for his protestations and calling him a baby. Jack secretly loved this; it was as close as he got to maternal tenderness or affection. He watched her throughout: she looked tired but otherwise OK. He longed to hug her to show his thanks, but they hadn't been that way since he was little; he didn't know how to anymore. 'Come on, get to bed,' she said.

CHAPTER 7

Static

When Jack entered the kitchen the next morning, his father was already seated at the table, slumped in his chair, nursing a mug of tea. He was looking slightly dazed and very sorry for himself. His hair was sticking up at the back because it hurt too much to comb it there. 'What are you looking at?' he growled, as a way of saying good morning. Jack could feel himself being watched as he went about making some breakfast.

It was the weekend, which always meant work, and Jack's father couldn't wait to get straight in with his tasks and insults. 'I want you to chip all the cement off those bricks from the greenhouses – they've been sitting there too long. You're getting lazier, you spend too much time daydreaming. I want them all cleaned up and stacked by the end of the weekend … and don't break any of them either, I've got plans for them.' Jack looked down at his bandaged hand as he buttered his toast, and groaned inwardly. There were hundreds of the bricks, covered in tarpaulin to protect them from the winter frosts. All had hardened cement attached to them, some more than others; it would probably take him all weekend.

It did, indeed, take him all weekend. Jack had toiled,

sometimes shirtless, under a hot sun as his sister brought him a bottle of cider now and then as refreshment. His father came over every so often to check on his progress, barking at him to make sure they were done properly. There was a knack to getting the cement off cleanly without breaking the bricks, but there was something satisfying about it. Jack was no stranger to work; it was all he'd ever known and he just got on with it. He enjoyed seeing the neatly stacked pile of bricks getting taller; high enough that he could sit in its shadow, out of the glare of the sun.

The other benefit of work, providing his father didn't keep bothering him, was that it kept Jack occupied and he could let his mind drift, his thoughts always of Daisy – picturing her face and wondering what she was doing. Now that he knew where she lived, the temptation to see her again was strong. It was too soon, though, and too much of a risk; it felt as if his father, who had been laying off the cider, was watching him.

At the end of Sunday night, Jack was well and truly done in. His back ached from being hunched over and his hands were in a state. Despite his best efforts, and wanting to prove something to his father, he had to admit defeat. There were still between fifty and a hundred bricks left. It was getting dark when his sister called him in. He fell into bed, utterly exhausted.

The next morning Jack couldn't stop yawning throughout breakfast. Afterwards, he stumbled bleary-eyed down to the cellar to get a couple of bottles of cider. The only words his father said to him as he left were, 'There's still some bricks left.' Jack passed them on his way out of the drive. They taunted him. He reached into his rucksack and opened a bottle.

He had been trying his utmost not to think about Daisy, or if she would be on the bus; he didn't know how he would handle the disappointment if she wasn't. The cider had done its job as he got on and sat in his usual seat; it had given him a heady buzz and woken him up – must have been a strong brew. He crossed his fingers, and kept them crossed all the way into the village.

Normally he would be looking out for her, but today he sat with his head down as the bus pulled to a halt, not daring to look up in case she wasn't there. Agonisingly, he listened to the rattling of change and the whirring of the ticket machine as people got on – until he just couldn't bear it any longer. He looked up, peering past the black dot and the passengers taking their seats. There at the front of the bus, thank the Lord, was Daisy.

As she began to walk down the aisle, he could tell straight away that she wasn't quite her usual self. She paused for a second by her old seat, which today was empty. Jack felt as if his whole life was held in the balance as she decided where to sit; as if his entire future depended on her choice. Then she looked up, catching him unawares, and continued to walk down the bus. But wait; was that a smile? The faint hint of a sad smile from her?

Once again, the scent of Daisy's perfume washed over him as she sat down; it felt as though he hadn't smelt it for weeks. As Jack observed her reflection in the window as usual, she started rummaging in her bag and pulled out her personal stereo. She pressed a button on it to eject a tape, checked it, then closed the machine again with a clunk. She then went to put the headphones over her ears, momentarily getting them tangled in her hair in the process. It dawned on him then that even if he spoke to her, she wouldn't be able to hear him anyway. As she pressed play Jack waited in consternation for the strange, tinny sounds to begin ... but they didn't. She pressed a few more buttons, and he watched with growing interest as she turned the stereo over, clicked open a compartment on the back and removed two batteries. As she did so, she fumbled one of them, and it bounced off her bag and onto the floor of the bus. It then rolled briefly along the floor before coming to a stop – directly against the toe of Jack's boot.

There was no avoiding it this time; he *had* to do something, but the old familiar dread had come back to haunt him. Daisy, meanwhile, had her head down and was searching on the floor in front of her. *Do something, you idiot! For once in your life, just do something!* Jack summoned up all the courage he had, and tentatively reached down to pick up the battery.

Daisy had given up looking on the floor and was rummaging in her bag again. Jack took a deep breath, slowly reached out his hand, and tapped her on the shoulder. The moment his fingertips made contact with her, there was a loud crack as a powerful bolt of static electricity ripped through them. 'Ow! Static!' they yelled in unison.

Daisy spun round, laughing. It was a wonderful sound to Jack as he shook his hand in pain. 'You zapped me!' she said.

You did, you idiot, Jack said to himself. You zapped her; your first contact with her and you give her an electric shock! 'Sorry,' he muttered through his embarrassment. 'Here.' He sounded a little like a caveman grunting as he offered the battery to her. It sat in the palm of his bandaged hand and he wished he'd used the other one.

She made as if to take it from him and then quickly drew her hand back. 'Are you sure you won't zap me again?' This drew a sheepish grin from Jack; her sureness in herself seemed to have a calming effect on him, making him feel more at ease.

She took the battery from him, fully turned round in her seat now. 'What did you do to your hand?'

'Oh, I, erm, burnt it at work,' he said, withdrawing it promptly and continuing to blush.

'Work?' she said, surprised. 'How old are you?'

'Sixteen.'

'Oh.' She sounded relieved. 'That's pretty young to be working. What is it, an apprenticeship or something?' Jack didn't know what an apprenticeship was, and was also starting to feel uncomfortable at giving out so much information about himself.

'Erm, no,' he replied, fidgeting in his seat. 'How old are *you*?' There; he'd asked his first question, and couldn't believe he'd done it. It was more to deflect attention away from himself than anything else.

'I'm seventeen,' she said. 'I'm at college ... my name's Daisy, by the way. What's yours?'

Jack thought long and hard before replying. And when he did so, it was as if he was crossing a line in the sand. 'I'm Jack.'

With introductions over, and both of them unsure of what to say next, Daisy turned around in her seat. She didn't put her headphones back on, Jack noted, and he was dying to say more; he wanted to know why she wasn't on the bus the other day – and why she looked so sad.

He was left feeling flummoxed yet exalted as he sat back in his seat. His heart was still pounding and he was buzzing from their brief conversation; she had spoken to him and he had actually replied, which felt both liberating and addictive.

When it was time to get off the bus, Jack pressed the buzzer and rose to get up, but lingered, taking his time. He made a big deal out of pulling his rucksack onto his back and then wished he hadn't; it clinked loudly as his bottles rolled around in it. He turned red again and prayed for it to subside as the bus approached his stop.

He looked at her out of the corner of his eye as he passed by her, willing himself to say something, when she spoke. 'Bye, Jack.'

'Oh, bye,' he replied, unable to look her in the face. If he had done, he would have noticed her bemused smile and then the curious tilt to her head as she watched him shuffle down the bus.

Who was this shy, slightly odd boy, with his mess of black hair and hooded blue eyes? He was sort of brooding – Brando-like – or was that just wishful thinking on her part? She had first noticed him some time ago now, and he was definitely handsome in his own way. She felt compelled to find out more about him.

As soon as the bus was a safe distance away, Jack let out a whoop of joy. She had said his name: 'Bye, Jack.' And for the first time in his life he felt as if he was somebody; as if he actually existed.

For the rest of that week, the only important minutes – the only ones that counted for anything – were those precious bus journeys. Nothing else mattered. Each day he made sure he sat at least a row behind anyone else, and would pray that no one else sat in front of him. Daisy did her bit too – always smiling and saying hello, then sitting down in her usual seat.

Unfortunately it was harder than they both thought to start up conversation again. It didn't help that she always had her back to him, but she didn't dare sit next to him in case she appeared too forward. She didn't put her headphones on anymore, just in case he said something, which was a massive compliment in itself – music was the most important thing in her life. Instead, she sat in hope from day to day, but, to her growing vexation, he never spoke a word.

Jack was even more frustrated. He watched her reflection as she stared out of the window, and ached to know what she was thinking. They still said goodbye to each other – Jack being brave enough to take the initiative with that at least – and

Daisy replied enthusiastically enough, but with an increasing edge of disappointment as the week went on.

After the initial excitement of making contact began to wear off, these mornings left Jack feeling despondent as another journey passed in silence. Once the bus was out of sight, he would hit another bottle of cider on the way to work, then feel depressed and listless all morning. When he was starting to think that this was it, that the spark was going to be snuffed out before it could grow, the hand of fate stepped in. It gave them a gentle nudge – as so often it does – blowing on the embers and making them glow.

On Friday morning, the bus was busier than normal – making Jack feel uneasy to begin with. There was a larger than normal queue in the village, and the bus was filling up fast. He made sure his rucksack was on the seat next to him, and for good measure leant forward on the seat in front of him, draping his arms over it to ward off any would-be occupants. To his annoyance and disgust, a sweaty, overweight man with a walking stick waddled up the bus, ignored Jack's arms, and sat down. The man took up most of the seat and obscured Jack's view. Jack hated him with all of his heart for potentially ruining his day.

He peered around the thick, hairy neck, huge back and rolls of fat to see where Daisy was, then realised she was standing right next to him. 'Budge up then,' she said, gesturing at his rucksack. She was being jostled by fellow passengers, who were trying to get past her. Jack quickly moved his bag and put it by his feet. She sat down, and they were both aware of their proximity as her warm thigh nestled unavoidably against his.

For a while Jack felt a bit shell-shocked. There had always been a physical barrier, a wall between them; now that barrier had been removed and they were thrust, unexpectedly, into each other's worlds. He longed for his cider. Daisy fidgeted and flicked her hair out of her collar, as was her habit, and fiddled with her bracelets. She clasped her hands together in an effort to make them stay still and said, 'So, how are you then?'

Jack turned to look at her, trying not to gasp. Up this close, her eyes were like two big, brown pools of chocolate, framed by long lashes. She had a button nose, dusted with a fine sprinkling of freckles, as if someone had seasoned it with one quick twist of a pepper mill. And as for those lips, those cherry lips… 'I'm fine, thanks,' he managed to croak; then cleared his throat.

'It's busy today, isn't it?' she said. 'The bus, I mean.'

'Yes.'

''Cause of market day in town, I suppose.'

'Er … yes,' said Jack again; not knowing it was market day as he'd never been into town.

'Still, at least it's Friday…'

'Yes,' said Jack, cursing himself. *Jesus, can't you say anything but yes?*

There was an awkward silence. Daisy noticed his bandaged hand and jumped upon the topic. 'So, how's your hand?' she said. He shoved it between his legs, still ashamed of how and why he did it.

'Oh it's better, thanks, a lot better – I just have to keep it covered up at work, that's all.'

'How did you do it? I mean, I know you did it at work.'

Jack was amazed that she remembered. 'Oh, I burnt it on an oven getting the sausage rolls out.'

'Is that what you do then, make sausage rolls?'

Jack felt ashamed at his lowly job; it sounded so pathetic. 'Well, it's not just sausage rolls … pies and things as well.' This didn't sound any better; it was as if he was trying to impress her. 'My father got me the job.'

'Oh, that was good of him. You must be close?' Jack didn't reply. When she could see he wasn't going to say anything else, she asked, 'So, what time do you finish for the day?'

Jack was horrified at the thought that they would catch the same bus in the evening, when he stank, so he lied.

'Er ... five-thirty.'

'Oh, that's a shame, that's a long day.'

The fat man in front was turning his head when Daisy spoke, as if he were listening to their conversation. Jack was oblivious, but it was starting to annoy Daisy. She was also mindful that Jack would be getting off the bus soon – and then it would be the weekend again. The lack of privacy and time was stifling. She felt under pressure. But there was something about the bewildered way that he looked at her with those blue eyes, like a lost little boy, that drove her on.

Out of desperation *and* out of character, she said, 'What are you doing this evening?' The fat man turned his head again and she scowled at him. 'Have you got anything planned?' she added, trying to make it sound more casual.

'Er, no,' said Jack. 'Have you?'

'No.'

The fat man suddenly whirled round, unable to help himself. 'Oh, for crying out loud, son, will you just put the poor girl out of her misery and ask her out?'

Jack and Daisy were both mortified at the intrusion. Daisy was furious and went on the offensive. 'Will you mind your own damn business?' she snapped – surprising Jack and the man with her feistiness. Jack slumped in his seat. People were starting to look over and he didn't like the attention; he had spent his whole life trying to be inconspicuous.

Daisy waited for all the busybodies to resume their dull, little lives, including the nosy walrus in front, whilst Jack kept his head down. Just then a thought came to her, and she reached down to rummage in her bag, coming back up with a notepad and pen. She opened up the notepad and began to write in neat, bubble-shaped writing. Jack watched, transfixed; everything she did was infinitely fascinating to him. She tilted the page towards him. There, in blue ink, were the words 'Do you know Bunny Wood?' Jack looked at her, confused; did he know it? It was practically his second home! He nodded in confirmation. She proceeded to scribble again. 'Can you meet me at the entrance tonight at 7?' Jack's stomach did cartwheels. He gulped, then looked at her again and nodded; but this time he grinned too, unable to hide his delight. Daisy smiled back, as if a shackle had been cast off.

CHAPTER 8

Bunny Wood

J ack had a bath and a shave before he went out that evening which, along with a bottle of cider, left him pink and flushed. Walking through the small parlour to the kitchen didn't help; it was always too warm during the summer months as the stove was perpetually lit. Without it they wouldn't have any hot water. He was trying to behave as normally as possible, but felt as if guilt was etched all over his face. As he left the house, both Anne and his father noticed his crimson countenance and the fact that he reeked of deodorant.

It was such a relief to get out into the fresh air, and Jack hoped that the breeze would cool him down. In order to calm his nerves, he cracked open another cider. Left alone with his roving mind, however, doubts crept in. What if she'd changed her mind? What if she didn't turn up? How would she even get there? Bunny Wood was two or three miles from the village.

Jack reached his stile and patted it before vaulting over. Once inside the wood he immediately felt at home. He followed an upper trail that ran parallel to the main track and also led down to the entrance. The branches overhanging it provided a leafy, shaded tunnel, giving welcome respite from the sun. At the end of the trail was a steep gradient with wooden steps, which Jack negotiated before coming out on the main path. His pulse quickened: he never usually came down here as it was too open; there was too much of a risk of bumping into people, and nowhere to hide. It was much lighter too, and he fought to control his escalating anxiety.

When Jack first laid eyes on Daisy, he stopped dead in his tracks. She was sitting on the large gate at the entrance to the wood with her back to him, silhouetted against a bright, azure sky. Her hair shone around the edges, rendered effulgent by the sun – glowing so brightly it hurt his eyes. He stood there and watched for a moment in rapture. Could this girl really be waiting for him?

He could see that she was wearing her headphones, and as a consequence, didn't hear him approach. Jack loitered behind her for a second, not knowing what to do, then cleared his throat and said, 'Hi.' Daisy still didn't hear him; she was too busy looking up the road, watching out for him.

Jack had no choice but to tap her on the shoulder, terrified of giving her another static shock. This didn't happen, but it was as if it had. When he touched her she jumped in surprise, gasped, and sprang off the gate. She landed on her feet and whirled round, whipping her headphones off and clutching her heart. 'Oh my God! You scared me to death. I thought you were the axe murderer!'

'The axe murderer?' said Jack, awkwardly.

'Yes, you know … the axe murderer who stalks the wood!' Jack was confused. 'Oh, never mind,' she said, waving her hand and regaining her composure. 'I'll tell you later.'

For generations village children had heard the legend of the axe murderer from their older brothers and sisters, and from their parents before them. The story varied from child to child, and generation to generation – like Chinese whispers. It was about an axe murderer who roamed the wood and hated children. Some said that he drove a pickup truck; that he loaded the children into the back of it, before chopping them up and eating them for dinner. Others said that he lived in the mine underneath the wood; and that the unpleasant smell that came out of the mineshaft was roasting flesh. Some children even claimed to have seen bones near the entrance to the mine, behind the large, rusty gates that guarded it. This had all passed Jack by, of course.

Daisy shimmied through a smaller pedestrian gate and joined Jack in the clearing. The reality hit that they barely knew each other, yet here they were; alone together for the first time. They looked uncertainly at one another, as Daisy clipped her Walkman onto the back of her jeans.

Jack noticed she was wearing a T-shirt with 'The Smiths' written on it above a picture of an actor he vaguely recognised off the telly. He was determined to try and make conversation, and, buoyed by the two bottles of cider, he asked 'Who are The Smiths?' Daisy looked at him with raised eyebrows. 'You don't know who The Smiths are?'

'Er, no,' he replied, wishing he hadn't said anything.

'You know, the band ... the best band in the world?' No response. 'Morrissey?'

'Oh, is that him?' He pointed to the picture on her T-shirt. Daisy burst out laughing.

'You're joking, aren't you?' Jack looked at his feet. 'You're not joking... Oh my God! What are you – an alien? That's Elvis – the king of rock and roll!'

It all came flooding back to him; he knew he'd seen him somewhere before. It was a black and white film on the telly about a prison, and the big, bold letters flashed before his eyes. 'Jailhouse Rock!' he said, grinning, pleased that he'd remembered and trying to pass it off as a joke. She studied him, unable to work him out.

'I never know when you're being serious,' she said.

They set off into the woods. Jack walked quickly, glad to be heading away from the entrance. His rucksack rattled on his back.

'Do you take that everywhere with you?' she said.

'Er, sort of.'

'What have you got in there, the Crown Jewels?'

'Oh, it's just cider.'

Daisy didn't know what to make of this. She supposed that it was normal for a teenage boy to have some cider with him on a night out; all the kids did it. But she thought she'd heard that clinking on the bus when Jack was on his way to work – and that seemed a bit excessive.

They walked in silence as midges danced about and the sun toyed with them, casting dappled light through the trees. It felt totally alien to Jack, and a bit rebellious, to be walking so brazenly down the main path of the wood. Every part of his being cried out against it. Daisy was totally oblivious to this, and despite her assured outward demeanour she, too, was suffering with first-date nerves. She felt uncharacteristically tongue-tied and kept having to fight the urge to giggle, which she was prone to do when she was nervous.

Keen to break the silence, Jack tried to start another conversation. But the best he could come up with was 'So, do you come here often?'

Daisy burst out laughing again.

'Wow, is that the chat-up line you use with all the girls?'

Jack blushed. Why was it that every time he tried to make conversation she ended up laughing? 'I mean, do you walk here often?'

'I know, I'm only joking,' she said and nudged him with her elbow, seeing that she had crushed his fragile confidence.

Her skin brushed against his as she did so. It felt electric. Jack couldn't believe how sure of herself she was.

'In all seriousness, yes, fairly often – it's one of my favourite walks, and my mum and dad's.'

'How did you get here?' asked Jack, still curious. Surely she couldn't have walked all the way from the village just for him.

'Oh, I drove.'

'You drive?' he said, in shock. 'What, do you have your own car?' He was starting to think he was way out of his depth; she came across as much older than him, much more mature – he felt like just a boy in comparison.

'No, I wish. Did you see the VW camper van out front?' Jack shook his head; he'd been too besotted with her to notice. 'Well, it used to be my parents' – embarrassing, I know. They used to go travelling in it; they were hippies – still are actually – well, Dad anyway,' she added, and laughed. 'Well it's mine and my sister's now, but she's too stuck up to drive it – which suits me! They've got a Montego now, an estate, but they won't let me drive that, nor my sister – to teach her a lesson for being a snob!'

Jack lost himself in his thoughts as they walked, thinking about Daisy and her sister, her mum and her dad – and how easy it was for her to talk about them. He felt unsure of himself again; the alcohol buzz was wearing off and he wanted another drink, but didn't want to appear desperate. He was determined to make it until they stopped for a bit. 'How about you?' Daisy asked, but Jack had lost the train of conversation.

'What? Do I drive?'

'No, I meant how did you get here? You came in a different way.'

'Oh! Yes, I came in through the side entrance.'

'You must live nearby then?'

This was getting difficult for Jack. 'Er, sort of I suppose.'

'Sort of, you suppose?' she repeated, turning to him in bemusement.

Unable to help himself any longer and desperate to change the subject, Jack said, 'Would you like some cider?' He stopped, swung his rucksack off his shoulder and began to unbuckle the straps.

'No, I'd better not; I'm driving,' replied Daisy. Jack looked disappointed. 'You go ahead though.'

Jack didn't need any further encouragement – and as Daisy watched, he deftly opened the bottle despite his bandaged hand.

He raised it to his lips and took a couple of long swigs. The sun shone through the bottle, turning the amber liquid golden. She noticed it wasn't a bottle of cider from the shops; it was smaller and there was no label on it. 'Where do you get that from?' she asked.

'Oh, we make it ourselves,' said Jack, taking another swig.

'Really? That's cool. Do you live on a farm or something then?'

'Er, not really,' he said, popping the stopper back on the bottle.

He felt a lot better already and announced unexpectedly, 'Come on, I've got something to show you!' before bounding off, a gundog eager to show its master something. Daisy had to trot to keep up with him.

They walked deeper into the woods for five minutes. Daisy was starting to get hot and tired. The swarms of midges – which at first had been a mere nuisance – were now a real pain in the arse. Her head and arms were itching as if she was being eaten alive. 'How much further?' she called.

'Oh, we're nearly there!' he said over his shoulder.

'Where are you taking me? You're not the axe murderer, are you?' She was joking, but she was beginning to wonder what she was doing out here in the middle of the wood, miles from home, with a boy she barely knew anything about. The only thing she had gleaned so far was that he made his own cider – and appeared to like it a little too much.

Jack reached a bend up ahead and stopped again. He hopped from foot to foot, as proud as punch and with a big grin on his face, waiting impatiently for her. When she caught up with him she also stopped abruptly and stared, open-mouthed.

In front of them, as far as the eye could see, was a vast carpet of bluebells – swathes of them; like a deep blue-violet enchanted sea – parted in the middle by the path. 'Wow!' said Daisy. 'How did you know?'

Jack beamed with pride as if he was personally responsible. 'The bluebells are always out in May!' This year's display seemed particularly magical; perhaps because, for once, he had someone to share it with.

They walked through the flowers in awe, both of them feeling an almost holy reverence for their surroundings. There was the chirp of birdsong and the flitting of butterflies – Brimstones, Cabbage Whites and Orange Tips – seeking the shafts of sunlight.

'You must know the wood well, Jack. I mean … to know about the bluebells and that.'

'Er, yes,' replied Jack cautiously. If only she knew how much time he'd spent there – and always alone. 'Have you seen the mine?' he asked, keen to get off the main path now that he'd shown her the bluebells.

'No. I've heard about it, though – you know, stories and that.'

'Come on, I'll show you!' And he veered off to the left, crouched down and squeezed through two thin wires that separated the main track from a bridle path. He held the wires open for Daisy, but she remained hesitantly on the other side.

'I don't know. Is it safe? I've heard that radiation comes out of it.'

This was another rumour passed around by the village children – that the mine was used to generate nuclear energy and gave off radioactive gases: a strange hum came from the mineshaft and its air vent, along with a weird smell. In truth, the mine belonged to British Gypsum and was used to mine the rock underneath the wood; it was perfectly harmless, although pretty spooky. 'Well it's never harmed me!' said Jack. Daisy was far from convinced.

She eventually gave in, thinking she must be mad, and slipped through the gap in the fence to join him on the muddy bridle path. They made their way over a stile and down a sloping path that headed directly away from the wood. Soon, on their left-hand side and protruding out of some overgrown grass, was a large, concrete circle that framed a round metal grille; the infamous air vent. It was about five feet across, and Jack made a beeline for it. He stepped up to stand on the deep, concrete lip. Daisy joined him on the edge, but kept her feet firmly on the ground.

She leant forward and peered down through the grille, but you couldn't see anything; it was just impenetrable black. She was struck, though, by the warm air that wafted out of it. It had an unnerving odour – not bad exactly, just stale and unnatural; somehow chemical. And then there was that humming – she could feel its vibration under her feet. 'Uh, I don't like it!' Daisy said – her active imagination conjuring up images of her hair and teeth falling out from nuclear radiation; too much Threads.

'It's fine,' said Jack. 'Look!' And he couldn't resist showing off by walking into the middle of the grille.

Daisy gasped.

'Jack, don't!' The metal bent under his feet as he stood there with his arms outstretched, grinning like a slightly unhinged teenage messiah.

He jumped back off and said, 'Come on, there's more. You've got to see the entrance!' And he set off again, in his element now, revelling in the novelty of having an audience.

'Oh, I'm not sure,' Daisy groaned, then shouted after him, 'What about the axe murderer?' But it was no use; he was gone. She scanned the long grass that surrounded her; it felt as if she was being watched. 'Wait for me!' she called, and hurried after him, clutching her Walkman.

She came out at the top of a sharp incline, where Jack was waiting for her. Down below was an old, overgrown road that led directly to the mine's rarely used back entrance. Local kids raced up and down it – and the steep banks on either side – at reckless speeds on their scramblers. There were often accidents, so the mine was locked and gated, and trespassing was strictly forbidden. Yet still they found their way in.

Jack and Daisy made their way carefully down the short hill. If you lost your footing, you could take a tumble all the way to the top lip of the mine entrance, and if you were very unfortunate, a possibly fatal one onto the concrete road below.

Despite her fear, Daisy had to admit she was enjoying herself – the feeling of danger, and the knowledge that she shouldn't really be there; it was an adventure. She wasn't an out-and-out tomboy, but had never been a girly-girl. Her dad was to blame for this. As he had been blessed with two daughters but no son, Daisy had borne the brunt of his frustrations, and had assumed a more boyish role. She had always been easily cajoled into a game of cricket or football on the beach, or a camping trip or fishing expedition with her dad. Her sister didn't seem to mind and Daisy enjoyed her father's company. As a result, she was equally content in boys' company as she was in girls'. In fact, she almost preferred it; they were simpler, less catty.

The roof of the mine entrance was no more than a concrete shelf, jutting out of the grassy bank. Below it were the two huge, iron gates that guarded the mine. Jack was quick to sit down, but Daisy stood on the ledge for a moment, admiring the view. Off to the west there was the main road, and just the other side of it the brickyard; another playground for Jack that he had only recently discovered. In the distance were the serpentine bends of a river – a tributary of the Trent. The water sparkled on the horizon, framed on either side by small trees that stretched away like fans. Further down the hill was the sleepy village of Bunny, with its chimney pots closely nestled together, its football pitch and school, all overseen by the church spire. Jack had never been there; the brickyard was as far as he'd travelled.

Daisy joined Jack, and they sat side by side with their legs dangling over the edge. It was a good ten feet or so down, but you could jump it if you were stupid enough. Some kids did; they dared each other and often ended up with sprained or even broken ankles as a result. Looking over the edge made Jack feel dizzy and his stomach spin. It was a dare for him just to sit there.

He fished the bottle of cider out of his rucksack and drained what was left of it in one go. Then, to Daisy's surprise, he immediately pulled out a second. Daisy looked longingly at it, wishing she'd brought a drink of her own. She'd had no idea they were going to be out this long; she'd had no preconceptions at all. Jack saw her looking. 'Are you sure you don't want some? I brought this one for you.' And he offered the stubby bottle, blushing.

Daisy deliberated. 'Oh, go on then. Just a bit. I am thirsty!'

To be able to share his cider with her filled Jack with joy. He watched as she raised it to her mouth. Her lips parted, revealing white teeth that the bottle clinked against. She took a good swig, and Jack looked on as some of it dribbled down her chin onto her pale throat. She stopped to wipe it away, laughing and a little embarrassed, before taking another quick swallow.

The cider wasn't what she was used to; it was flat for a start, and didn't taste of a great deal. It went straight to her head though. 'Whew! That stuff's lethal. What percent is it?' She passed the bottle back.

'How do you mean?' asked Jack distractedly; he was too busy staring at the top of the bottle in wonder. That bottle had just been between her lips and was now going between his.

'You know, how strong is it? What alcohol percent?'

'Oh … I don't know.'

'You don't know? Surely there must be a recipe you follow or something?'

'Not really, I just got shown and that was it. I think there was once, but it never got written down.' And he shrugged. Daisy looked at him, amazed. How could he drink so much of the stuff and not be pie-eyed?

'Well, I hope I don't get done for drink-driving. If I do I'll hold you personally responsible!' she said, nudging him again.

Just then, they heard a very faint chugging far off in the distance. A canal boat came into view, rippling the water. It looked tiny, silhouetted against the setting sun. 'It looks so peaceful, I've always wanted to do that – just go on a canal boat, following a river and stopping at pubs and things,' said Daisy.

Talking of pubs made her crave more of the cider. 'Here, can I have one more swig?' She pointed to the bottle. Jack handed it over gladly, and she took another slug before continuing, the cider loosening her tongue. 'It reminds me of a book my mum used to read to me when I was little; about two little bears that were the best of friends. They wanted to go on an adventure, so they made a raft out of banana crates and sailed away down rivers and streams till they reached the Panama Canal. I can still remember the pictures. There were jungles and monkeys and coloured birds in the trees. I just wanted to be there so badly…' She trailed off.

Listening to her brought a lump to Jack's throat; it reminded him of his own childhood books, such as *Where the Wild Things Are*, and also of his lifelong dream. Hearing her say it, it sounded so romantic – and it was as if she'd read his thoughts. Unable to help himself, he blurted out, 'That's what I'm going to do; sail to America.'

She regarded him closely, not knowing if he was being serious again or not.

'Yes, I'm sure we'd all like to do that.' He felt like screaming, 'No, really, that's what I'm going to do!' But he didn't; she would think he was mad or just making it up.

'Come on, I suppose we'd better be heading back,' she said; and the moment passed.

They trudged back up to the top of the bank, reluctantly so in Jack's case; he didn't want this evening to end. There was so much he still wanted to say.

It was a lot cooler inside the wood, darker too. Daisy regretted having worn a T-shirt. Her arms broke out in goose pimples, and she shivered as she rubbed them. Jack noticed this – he noticed everything about her – and wanted to put his arm around her, but wouldn't have dreamed of it. Instead, he did the next best thing, which he'd seen John Wayne do in the movies; he offered her his check shirt as he had a T-shirt on underneath.

Daisy was surprised at his chivalry. 'Are you sure?' she said. Jack nodded and eagerly handed it over. 'Here, swap,' she said, passing him her Walkman to put in his rucksack; it was getting on her nerves. Jack was overjoyed to be entrusted with it.

His shirt was too big for her and the sleeves hung below her hands as she walked, but this just made her look all the more adorable – younger and more vulnerable.

They passed through the bluebells, and were just rounding the corner on the other side when they were startled by a vehicle approaching rapidly from behind. Still slightly befuddled by the strong cider, Daisy panicked, letting her imagination get the better of her. 'Quick! Hide! It could be the axe murderer!' she cried, and grabbed Jack, dragging him into the undergrowth and a bed of stinging nettles.

A blue pickup truck hurtled past. At the wheel was a swarthy man with a manic look in his eye and unshaven, hollow cheeks. Daisy gasped. 'Oh my God, I told you it was him!' But Jack, despite the pain he was in, chuckled. 'What are you laughing at?' she said.

'That's the wood manager – he's always in here. He chops logs for people and that.'

Jack had watched him many times from the top trail. He didn't seem to like people being in the wood, and there was something a bit odd about him, but he seemed harmless enough.

'Oh,' said Daisy, feeling foolish as they pulled themselves out of the undergrowth. A gaggle of white dots had risen up on Jack's arm where he'd been stung. 'Here,' she said, picking up a good-sized dock leaf from the ground nearby. 'Rub it with this.' Jack took it from her, impressed.

By the time they reached the entrance of the wood a silent dusk had settled around them like a shroud. 'I'd better be getting back. Mum and Dad will be starting to worry. Do you want a lift?'

Jack wasn't expecting this. 'Er, no thanks, I'll just go back the way I came. It's quicker.'

'Oh, OK. If you're sure.' She sounded a bit put out. 'I'm a safe driver!'

'No, it's fine, really.' They both lingered a moment.

'Well, see you Monday, I guess,' Daisy said as she went through the gate.

'Yes,' Jack replied sadly, handing over her Walkman, glum at the thought of another weekend stretching ahead without her.

'Shit, no you won't. It's half-term next week; I'm not at college.' This was a sickening blow to Jack: a whole weekend was one thing, but a whole week without her? He'd go insane. 'I know! What are you doing tomorrow? Do you want to go into town?' she said.

Town, thought Jack, his head whirling with mixed emotions. He was elated at the offer, but why would anyone want to go into town? And what on earth would he say to his father? Weekends meant work; they always had done. He couldn't just disappear off for the day – not without an explanation, and certainly not on the bus. He was overcome with miserable frustration. The girl of his dreams, who pervaded his every waking thought, was asking him out: yes, him! And he couldn't go; he simply couldn't.

'I'm sorry, I can't tomorrow. I've got to help my father.'

'Oh, that's a shame,' said Daisy, trying her best to hide her disappointment. Was she being turned down? She had to know one way or the other – and right now; she was like that. 'Well, what about Monday then?' She mentally crossed her fingers.

'Er, well, I'll have to go to work.'

'No, you won't,' she said, smiling. 'It's a bank holiday!'

She was right; it was the last Monday in May – spring bank holiday. Jack suddenly brightened at the thought, and his mind began to tick over.

Bank holidays were a relatively new concept for Jack, and he still didn't quite understand them. He'd encountered them twice since going out to work, and both times they had caught him out; especially the first one.

It was a Monday morning not long ago, just after Easter, when he'd gone up the hill to catch his bus as usual. Much to his distress, the bus hadn't arrived. Worse still, neither had the next one. He had hit the cider hard and gone into one of his usual meltdowns. Unwilling to go back home to face his father, and in an act of rebellion against the strictures of his life, he had wandered off into the countryside. This was the day he'd ended up exploring the brickyard, which, for some reason, had been closed.

He'd spent most of the afternoon there, climbing on the stacks of bricks and timber, and sitting in the abandoned forklift trucks. He'd kept a close eye on the sun as it moved across the sky to tell roughly what the time was; an art he had perfected over the years. Another way he kept track of time was by the buses that ran past his house, more or less on the hour, every hour. Today this had been no use; he hadn't seen one all day, and couldn't understand why.

It was while Jack had been nosing about the yard that he'd peered into the window of a Portakabin, and his eyes had been drawn to a calendar on the wall above a desk. On it was a bronzed lady covered in a fine mist, with very few clothes on and her more than ample bosom clearly on display. Looking at it had made him feel peculiar, to say the least, and he'd eventually had to tear his gaze away. It was then that he'd noticed, purely by chance, a clock on the wall. This was a real stroke of luck, as it meant he would be able to go home at exactly the right time.

He had then returned to the Portakabin every half-hour or so to check the time – or at least that's what he'd told himself.

Returning home later that day, Jack's earlier bravado had disappeared as the alcohol had worn off. To his immense relief and amazement, everything was totally normal as if he'd spent the whole day at work. He'd had to suppress a smug smile at the dinner table that evening; it was as if he'd finally put one over on his old man. It had been the same the next day at work; he'd been expecting a rollicking or worse from Peasgood, but he too had seemed none the wiser. What *was* out of the ordinary was the buzz of gossip on the factory floor. People were saying 'What did you do with your bank holiday?' and 'What did you do yesterday?' It was as if they hadn't been at work either. The only other unusual thing had been when his boss had tossed him his pay packet at the end of the week. 'It's a day short. *You* don't get paid for bank holidays!'

The same thing had happened a month or so later, on a Monday again, at the beginning of May. This time, however, Jack hadn't been quite so freaked out, and had cottoned on fast. He was naive, but he wasn't stupid. His day had followed a similar pattern to the previous time; he had eaten his lunch sitting on top of the mine, drunk his cider, then headed over to the yard. He was starting to enjoy these unexpected bank holiday respites; they were a little bit of 'Jack time'. The only downside was not getting paid.

*****

The opportunity that Daisy was proposing, then, was too perfect to turn down. How could he say no? It would be risky and, admittedly, the thought of going into town filled him with dread, but he couldn't tell *her* that; he'd sound like a baby.

And if he *was* going to go into town for the first time it might as well be with Daisy. Perhaps it would be OK, more like an adventure. 'OK then!' he said, decided, and Daisy let out a sigh. 'Shall I meet you on the bus at the normal time?'

'No, I'll come and pick you up at nine if you want. I should have the van – that's if my sister hasn't suddenly decided to use it, that is.'

God, no, Jack thought; that's a terrible idea; she mustn't come to the house. 'Er, what about the crossroads?' he suggested. 'You can pick me up from there; it'll save you the trip.' It would also kill some time – he'd have to leave the house at ten to eight to pretend he was going to work.

'Well, OK then, nine o'clock at the crossroads if you'd prefer; but I really don't mind.'

Jack leant on the gate in a dreamlike stupor as she walked to her van. Suddenly she stopped and came trotting back, pulling off Jack's shirt. 'I nearly forgot!' she said, and passed it to him. The shirt felt warm in his hands. 'Thanks for that,' she said. 'Oh, and thanks for tonight as well – I really enjoyed it!' Jack beamed. Could this really be happening to him?

He heard her van start up, and some loud music come on. She reversed towards the gate. The van was blue and white and looked old-fashioned. It suited her. Jack had only ever been in his father's van, so that would be an adventure in itself. Then, with a spin of wheels in the gravel, she was off and away up the road, her music blaring and the red tail lights fading into the night.

Jack stood there for a bit, unable to move; tonight had been the best night of his life. And just when he thought it couldn't get any better, he put on his shirt and, oh God, it smelt of her – her perfume, her scent! The sweet musk enveloped him. He held the collar up to his nose and drank in a deep breath of it; it was divine. He set off for home, dashing up the steps in the wood, taking them two at a time. He vaulted his stile and bounded across the fields under a bright, starry sky, vowing never to wash his shirt again.

When Jack reached home, his father was already snoring in the living room. If he *had* been around, he'd probably have noticed what Anne noticed as she locked up behind him; the undeniable scent of a woman. It was somehow familiar too, awakening distant memories, as though she had smelt it before but not for many, many years. She looked after Jack's parting back in wonder – and also with growing anxiety. 'Well, I'll be,' she said out loud to the empty kitchen; she could see trouble ahead.

CHAPTER 9

The Shirt

'Get up! There's work to do!' Jack's father shouted from the corridor. Jack groaned. When was there *not* work to do? He was lolling in bed, replaying last night's events whilst they were still fresh in his mind.

Despite his father's orders, Jack took his time getting dressed. He went to pull on his check shirt then decided against it; it was already beginning to lose its scent. He wanted it to last all weekend, and so he tucked it back under his pillow where it had been all night.

When he wandered into the kitchen, what met him was a familiar scene that would have been comical if it hadn't been so repulsive. His father was sitting, straight-backed, in a chair, a large towel wrapped around his shoulders and a white expanse of hairy paunch protruding through it. His sister was standing behind him, a pair of scissors and a comb in her hands.

She was about to cut his hair; she cut Jack's hair too, and always had done – he had never been to a barber's in his life. But how she could actually bear to touch her father, and run her fingers through his hair after all he had put her through, astounded Jack.

They both looked up and stared, making Jack feel like a zoo

exhibit. The alarm on Anne's face turned to relief when she saw he wasn't wearing the previous night's shirt; his father had the usual expression of disdain on his face. He was clean shaven, an indication to Jack that he was still laying off the booze a bit.

It went in cycles like this with his father and alcohol: his body would reach saturation point, when he could no longer function. Then he would be clear for a few days, maybe a week at most, before it would start all over again. After all these years, Jack still didn't know which was worse. His father was definitely more violent when he was drunk, yet when his head was clearer, Jack had to be on his guard more; it was harder to be invisible. These brief days of sobriety didn't come around very often, and they always meant more work for Jack.

His father continued to scrutinise him, as if seeing him properly for the first time in a while. He barely recognised the boy; he'd grown up so much that he was almost a stranger – this unwanted offspring who was never meant to be. He was turning into a young man and it was going to get harder and harder to keep him from the world. Sooner or later he would be wanting to meet people – girls … troublesome girls who get pregnant, and nosey-parkers with their questions, wanting to know where he came from. The longer he could put that off the better, and he vowed (for the umpteenth time) to keep a closer eye on him – where he was going, and what he was up to.

Jack's onerous weekend task was to dig over the rectangular patch of land that had housed the greenhouses. This was no mean feat as it covered about thirty to forty square yards. The plan, according to his father, was to use part of the area as a new coal store, as the old one was on its last legs: it was beginning to leak. The rest of the ground was going to be laid to lawn, extending the wilderness that was adjacent to it.

Apparently this was going to have to be kept under control as well.

The soul-destroying aspect for Jack was that the plan would probably never reach fruition, or if it did it would take years. His father would succumb to the booze again, lose interest, and the weeds would grow back – returning to meadow, like the rest of the lawns.

Jack was set to work, his father instructing him where to start before heading off into his workshop. One of the machines buzzed angrily to life; he wouldn't be getting any help.

It had rained in the night and the earth smelt richly of it. The welcome moisture had softened the hard clay soil; just enough to get a spade through, but not so much that it would be too sticky. Jack had to turn the earth a spade's depth, going from side to side in five yard rows, working his way backwards. The soil was still full of lumps of crumbly red brick left over from the greenhouses. Some were quite large, and they jarred his spade, aggravating his healing blisters. He had to painstakingly remove the chunks as he went, chucking them into a wheelbarrow.

His mind drifted as he worked, and not for the first time he felt as if Daisy was with him, watching him. This was happening more and more often as he went about his everyday tasks – walking, dressing, bathing, or going to the toilet even. It was as if she was always there, observing him and judging his actions. It made him want to behave perfectly, and be a good person whom she would approve of.

Back in the house, Anne had work of her own. She swept up the last remnants of her father's hair, which she had watched turn from dark to grey over the years. Screwing her nose up, she held it at arm's length as she emptied it into the bin. This was the part that always made her feel squeamish.

After washing her hands, it was time to put a load of washing on. She looked out of the window and checked to see if Jack was busy before making her way to his bedroom. Jack had left his curtains closed and it was dark in his room. It smelt slightly unpleasant, as teenage boys' rooms often do; the main source of this was his work clothes, which he had left in a heap on the floor. She pulled back the curtains and opened one of the windows to let some fresh air in.

After scanning the room for more dirty clothes, a puzzled look fell across her face when she couldn't see what she had come in for. She looked in the chest of drawers, on the bed, under the bed – still nothing. Eventually she pulled back the bed cover and there, just peeking out from under the pillow, was what she was looking for – Jack's blue check shirt.

She pulled it out, glad to have found it but also curious about why he had hidden it. What had her little brother, whom she had raised herself, been up to? To confirm her suspicions, she raised the shirt to her nose and, sure enough, there was that faint trace of perfume. It wasn't as strong as the previous night, but was definitely still there. Again, it was hauntingly familiar. It made her head swim as she closed her eyes and inhaled deeply. It evoked memories of childhood, bittersweet memories – happy and comforting at first, then sad and lonely. And then it hit her with a sickening jolt; it was her mother's perfume. A bottle of it had stayed on her dresser for years after she had died, gathering dust, until it disappeared when her father moved rooms.

Tears unexpectedly welled up in her eyes, making them sting and quickly spill over. It was like a spring of sorrow that had been held back by a dam of suppression; once breached, once tapped into, it poured forth, hot and unrelenting. All the lost years, all the loneliness; her wasted life, Jack's wasted life; she missed her sister and mother so terribly it made her throat ache. Feelings that she had pushed deep inside a long, long time ago, or had been wrung out of her since, overwhelmed her.

Anne cried into the shirt for some time, dampening it with her tears. When she came round, she was shocked and surprised. She had always prided herself on being a strong woman; she'd had to be. She had been a little girl of four when sorrow had first come knocking and asked for a key; and when she lost her sister it had taken up permanent residency, inviting its brother, regret, in with it – like two interlopers in the mausoleum of her heart. They had set up a swing seat there, and had swung back and forth, like mocking twins, ever since.

She looked at the crumpled shirt in her hands, and knew it had to be washed straightaway. It posed too many problems and questions. Where had Jack picked up the smell of perfume? Could he have met a girl at work? He seemed too shy and innocent; he was still like a baby to her. Or had he found the perfume somewhere in the house – the same old bottle – somewhere that she didn't know about?

Either way, if their father smelt it, he would be thinking the same as her. What had Jack been up to? Who had he been speaking to? That, or he'd think Jack had turned into a 'poof'. To compound matters, surely, as Anne had, he would recognise the perfume. And if anything sent him over the edge into a spiral of drink and madness, it was the memory of his beloved wife Carla, who in death he had propelled to saint-like status.

Without a further thought, Anne dried her eyes and gathered up the dirty clothes. She loaded them all into the washing machine, lingering briefly over the shirt – as if its smell was a drug she needed another hit of. She pushed it in with the rest, then slammed the door behind it, putting powder into the drawer and turning the machine on. After a brief pause it whirred into life and started filling with water. Soapsuds appeared and the clothes began to spin. She stood there for a few moments, watching, as the blue shirt kept coming into view, tumbling round in circles like the unanswered questions in her mind.

Around midday Anne called Jack and her father in for lunch. They sat at the table in silence. She had prepared some homemade onion soup and cheese sandwiches which the men devoured.

Afterwards Jack got up from the table, placed his dishes in the sink and thanked his sister before heading down to the cellar. As he was filling a bottle of cider, he was dying to go to his bedroom to smell his shirt. He knew how ridiculous it was, but he couldn't help it. It was the next best thing to being with Daisy, and he'd been thinking about it on and off all morning. It took all his willpower, but somehow he managed to resist; it would give him something to look forward to at the end of the day, a prize to keep him going.

When he got back to the kitchen, his father eyed the bottle of cider. Jack noticed him licking his lips and his hand shaking on the table, and thought better of cracking the bottle open in front of him. Instead, he went to take it outside. 'There'd better be plenty of that left, you greedy little sod!' his father said.

Jack leant on his spade whilst drinking his cider in peace, surveying what he'd done so far. He'd probably done about a quarter of the job; he could have done more if it hadn't been for all the rubble. He took pride in his work and liked to do things properly. Despite this, his father always had something to moan about. The wheelbarrow was already half-full of broken brick fragments and would need emptying soon. Yes, this was going to be a long afternoon.

By five-thirty Jack had got well over halfway. He had planned to carry on for a few hours after dinner, but the call of his shirt was too strong for him to resist; it was driving him mad. He thought he might even wear it tonight; he intended on retracing the steps he had taken with Daisy in Bunny Wood to reminisce.

He bolted his dinner down – still in a good mood and buoyed on by what was waiting for him in his room. This didn't go unnoticed by his father, who was becoming increasingly irritable. By now, he would normally have had several bottles of cider. It was killing him; he was trembling like a coiled spring.

Jack left as soon as he could. When he entered his room he noticed his sister had had a bit of a tidy up. He went straight to his bed and pulled back his pillow. This was the moment he'd been waiting for all day...

To his utter dismay, there was nothing there. He frantically tore back the bedcover, but there was nothing there either. He dived to reach his arm down the back of the bed and grasped his hand about. Briefly, he thought he'd found what he was looking for, but only pulled out an old T-shirt. Where the hell was his shirt? He dropped to the floor to look under the bed – just as Anne had earlier – still nothing. 'What the hell?' he cried out loud. Then something dawned on him – hadn't he seen Anne hanging some washing out earlier on? His room had been emptied of dirty clothes ... but why would she go under his pillow? Surely she hadn't washed his shirt? That's why he'd hid it there in the first place – so that she wouldn't.

An unprecedented rage took over. It was as though a piece of his father that had laid dormant all these years had burst into life. He marched out of his room and back to the kitchen. Shocking his father and sister, he burst in with a wild look in his eye. 'Anne, where's my shirt?' he demanded.

'What shirt?' she asked, stalling.

'My blue check shirt; the one that was in my room!'

'Oh ... erm, I think I washed it. Why?'

'What did you bloody do that for, you stupid cow?' he spat, moving toward her.

Anne flinched as if she'd been slapped hard in the face. Jack had *never* spoken to her like that before and it cut her to the core; it sounded so like their father. What had got into him? She wished she'd never touched the damn shirt.

'I'm sorry, Jack. I didn't think it was important.'

Jack barely heard her; a fury like a thirsty hammer had seized him, and it wanted a drink. All he could think was that the one thing, the one *single* thing that he'd had to look forward to – that was 'his' and no one else's – had been taken away from him.

'Well you had no bloody right, did you?' he shouted, and raised his hand to strike her. Anne's knees buckled, as much in shock as from the physical threat. She bowed her head and raised her hands to cover it, just as she'd done a hundred times before. Seeing her like this, cowering with that hurt and fearful look on her face, was just enough to shock Jack out of his rage.

He saw them all as if looking down from above; him in the middle of the kitchen with his hand raised, and her hunched in the corner. Was he really responsible for that? And wait – was that a smirk on his father's face? Was he actually enjoying this? Would he have sat there and watched him hit her – just to show that he was no better than him? That he was just like him?

Jack lowered his hand and backed away. He looked at his sister, then back to his father with the smug look on his face. This made his anger boil up again – making him brave enough to shout as he backed out of the kitchen, 'I won't hide forever, you know!' before storming back to his room. The slam of his bedroom door shook the whole house, and the kitchen fell silent.

His father calmly got up from the table and padded down to the cellar to get his own cider. He sat back down at the table and cracked it open, as if in celebration. 'So,' he said to Anne, who was still shell-shocked, leaning against the cupboards, 'what was all that about?'

*****

Later that evening, Jack still hadn't left his room. Once his anger had dissipated he felt nothing but shame. This was nothing new; he'd always felt ashamed – ashamed of who he was, and that he wasn't good enough. But no, this was more than that. He had raised his hand to his sister, his dear sister, who had done nothing but take care of him her whole life. He kept picturing that look on her face; a look he had been responsible for. Everything he despised about his father, everything he represented, he had nearly gone and done. He writhed on his bed in anguish.

There was a soft knock at the door and his sister's voice: 'Can I come in?' Despite Jack's actions, Anne also felt guilty. He was right; she should never have touched the shirt – she had no right. That smell, that perfume, was obviously important to him for whatever reason (she could understand this now after her own episode this afternoon), and she had taken it away from him.

She walked into the room with a bottle of cider in her hand, but Jack found it hard to look at her. 'Here,' she said, offering the bottle as a peace-making gesture and sitting down on his bed.

He took it from her, his face streaked and full of remorse. 'I'm sorry, Anne,' he said quietly. And this nearly set him off again.

'It's OK, I'm sorry too.'

After a sip of cider, Jack said, 'What did he say?'

'What do you think? He wanted to know why you'd gone mad.'

'And what did you tell him?'

'I said I had no idea – and that I'd ask you when you calmed down.' This was the truth; Anne was fiercely loyal to her brother, even when he'd just raised his hand to her.

'And did he believe you?'

'I don't think so. When does he ever? He's probably waiting for an answer right now, that's if he's not fast asleep, drunk. I think he enjoyed our little show this afternoon.'

Jack shook his head in disgust.

Anne wanted to mention the smell on his shirt and where it had come from, but didn't know how to. And clearly Jack wasn't going to tell her himself. She was reticent by nature and felt especially awkward about this – in a way a mother and teenage son would, having their first talk about girls. She had her suspicions, though; she'd noticed him bathing more regularly and smelling of deodorant.

'Be careful, Jack,' was all she said; and then she got up to leave. That was as close as they would ever get to talking about 'the birds and the bees'. Not that she'd meant it in that way; she'd just meant that their father was onto him.

When she got to the door, Jack asked, 'So what are you going to tell him?'

'Don't worry. I'll think of something.'

The truth was, she already had, and she headed straight to the living room to get it over and done with.

Their father was watching telly, half-drunk, trying to answer the questions out loud on *Mastermind*. He looked up when she popped her head around the door, but she deliberately didn't go in. 'It was just some money, that's all, Father. He'd left the rest of his wages in his shirt after he'd given me his board …

you know what he's like with his money.' And before he could challenge her on it – or see her face properly to see if she was lying – she said, 'Anyway, goodnight,' and was gone again. He opened his mouth to call her back, when Magnus Magnusson spoke for him, distracting him: 'I've started, so I'll finish.' He turned his attention back to the telly, took another swig of cider and slumped back in his chair, not believing a word of it.

CHAPTER 10

Town

As Jack left the house, he said goodbye as if it was just another day, rather than one of the most significant occasions of his life so far. 'Town day' had arrived.

He walked up the lane as he normally did, but when he got to the top he turned right instead of left, skirted round the edge of the meadow and ducked into the spinney.

Once safely inside, he cracked open a bottle of cider to stroll with. The ground was glistening with dew, wetting his boots as he walked, and the call of an elusive spring cuckoo punctuated the air. It made him wish he was going somewhere like this with Daisy; somewhere that he felt comfortable and at home. For as much as he was looking forward to spending so much time with her, he couldn't shake the sense of foreboding that town induced. He sucked from his bottle to try and shake it from his mind, and thought instead of her face, her auburn hair, her smile, to allay his fears.

After finishing his cider in the spinney, a slow meander through the fields and a brief stop at the brook, Jack finally made his way to the bridge near the main road. He wasn't quite sure what time it was, but would rather be early than late in case he missed Daisy; that would be a disaster.

Disconcertingly, the main road was already busy with bank holiday traffic. Jack wasn't used to wandering about next to it in broad daylight, so decided to take a slight diversion by heading down a lay-by, screened by trees, that ran parallel to it.

The lay-by had a pub sitting at the bottom of it – an imposing, timber-framed building with lots of tall windows and a grey tile roof. A sign saying The Red Lion hung above the front door. Jack kept his head down as he walked past, then turned right and headed back towards the crossroads, passing a phone box on the way.

Once there, he didn't know what to do next; he couldn't just stand there for all the world to see. To his left, the main road stretched away up a hill to God knows where. By the side of it he spotted a bus shelter, which he decided to wait in. It was on the opposite side of the road to the village, and would allow him a clear view of Daisy approaching.

He cautiously peered inside the shelter. It was empty. The sun had warmed the wood, and it smelt like the lacquer his father used to stain doors and furniture with. As he sat and waited, cars in both directions continued to whoosh past in a blur of colours, with strangers' faces peering out. It made him feel uncomfortable and he wanted more cider, but he knew he had to make it last today.

He wasn't sure how long he sat there, eagerly watching the road out of the village. Every so often a car approached the crossroads, but time and time again it wasn't Daisy.

Just when he was starting to think she had changed her mind – or maybe her sister had taken the van – he heard a car approaching that sounded different to the others. He sat up, and coming into view was a light blue and white camper van, heading towards the crossroads. Jack quickly made his way to the corner of the main road to wait, feeling awkward.

On seeing him, Daisy waved before halting to look both

ways. Ringlets of hair swung from side to side as she leant over the steering wheel, biting her lip. She crossed over the main road, trundled past, then pulled up next to the phone box, music playing loudly.

Jack trotted up. The music got even louder as she opened the passenger door for him. 'Sorry I'm a bit late!' she called as she turned the volume down. Jack gingerly got in and sat down. The smell of Daisy filled the cabin, mixed in with mint from the gum she was chewing. He went to put his rucksack on the floor by his feet, but there wasn't much room; she already had her bag down there, and there was a litter of cassette tapes. 'Here, put it in the back – there's plenty of room in there!' she said, noticing his dilemma. 'You and that rucksack!' She grabbed it off him and tossed it into the rear of the van. 'Put your belt on then,' she said, before pulling off from the kerb. He hadn't uttered a word yet.

They headed back towards the village to follow the bus route into town. Daisy turned the music back up, but not so loud that they couldn't talk. It was as if she couldn't live without it; a bit like Jack and his cider. 'Have you been waiting long?' she asked.

'No, not really.'

'Ooh, that's where I live, down there!' she announced before he could say anything further. She slowed down and pointed out of her window.

'Oh, right,' he said, colouring slightly and making a show of craning his neck to look down the road she was indicating.

They passed through the village and out the other side. Daisy sped up, settling into her seat. 'So, are you ready for town then?' she asked. There was that word again: 'town'. Why did it fill him with such dread?

'Er, yes. I suppose,' Jack mumbled, trying to sound normal.

But it was no use; he couldn't relax properly without another drink. 'Do you mind if I grab my rucksack a minute?'

'No. Sure, go ahead,' she replied.

He undid his seat belt and reached into the back. It dawned on her what he was after when there was a loud clink. 'It's a bit early for that, isn't it?' she said, trying to sound light-hearted, but with a look of concern on her face as he opened a bottle. Jack smiled without answering and took a few small sips at first, conscious of her watching. When her attention returned to the road he took some larger gulps, relishing the head rush they brought. He offered her the cider. 'God, no!' she laughed. 'Not at this time in the morning. I'll wait until opening time, thanks!' She joked about it, not really knowing what else to do.

Jack sat with his rucksack cradled in his lap, sipping from his bottle every now and then. Everything looked so different from Daisy's van compared to the bus. The sun was shining, for the moment at least, and they both had their windows down. Daisy had a laid back attitude to driving, as if she was the only person on the road. She appeared more concerned with what song to play next, fiddling with the tape player whilst the van swerved from side to side. She kept on asking Jack if he 'knew this one' every time a different song came on, to which he shook his head and she tutted in response. At one point, she even leant across him to fish a pair of sunglasses out of the glove compartment. She did these things so casually, yet to Jack they meant the world.

Another time, she pressed eject on the tape player and asked him to pass her a tape from the floor that said 'Daisy's Mix No. 1' on it. He rummaged around until he found it, recognising her neat, bubble-shaped writing on the case. She inserted the tape, pressed play and turned the music up louder. A sweet, electric guitar melody rang out before the song kicked in, and when it did, Daisy was soon belting out the chorus of *Sweet*

Child O' Mine. It wasn't the kind of music Jack was used to, but it sounded amazing. They only had about five records in his house, and they were by the likes of Simon and Garfunkel and John Denver. He knew them all off by heart as his sister had listened to them over and over, especially when he was little. As the years had gone by she had played them less often; they reminded her too much of her mother and sister.

Daisy's household couldn't have been more different: music was her dad's profession for a start, and she lived and breathed it. Jack looked over at her, with her sunglasses on and tapping the steering wheel, her bangles halfway down her arms. The wind buffeted her hair as she chewed her gum, singing along in a carefree way, totally absorbed in the music. She looked like a movie star to him, stepped out of the screen and into his life, and he knew he was deeply and hopelessly in love. He stuck his head out of his window and the wind caught in his mouth, taking his breath away. He looked at himself in the reflection of the wing mirror. What he saw was a smiling, happy boy without a care in the world.

Unfortunately this feeling didn't last long. It began to wane when they passed the bus stop where he got off near work. These were still familiar surroundings for him and he was still on the outskirts of town; after this was uncharted territory. The traffic got heavier, the sky got darker, and his feeling of unease returned – along with his old companion, the black spot. His bottle of cider was long gone and he wasn't going to open his last one. He kicked his rucksack under his seat so he wouldn't see it and be tempted.

These were the days before Park and Ride, and before long they were stuck in traffic. They kept stopping and starting, edging forward and then stopping again – trapped and surrounded by cars and people. Jack was starting to feel suffocated. 'Where have all these people come from?' said

Daisy, exasperated. She had been hoping it would be quieter than usual thanks to the bank holiday. Her ankle was hurting from using the clutch so much.

Jack was trying not to look at all the miserable, red-faced people. Some were honking their horns, losing their temper, and gesturing rudely at other drivers. He vaguely heard Daisy muttering obscenities and getting a bit fractious herself, saying things such as, 'Well, thanks a lot, mate!' and, 'Go on then if you're going!'

Her earlier confidence seemed to have dwindled by the time they reached the city centre, where vehicles were now rushing by at an alarming speed. She'd even turned the music down and ditched her sunglasses so she could concentrate. After cautiously edging her way into the traffic, she tried to negotiate the van into the correct lane for the car park but no one was letting her in. Before long it was too late and they'd missed it. Daisy screamed in annoyance as they had to go all the way round the one-way system again. She was looking flustered and Jack could see two spots of colour on her cheeks. He felt sorry for her and wished there was something he could do, but was feeling increasingly alarmed. Why would anyone come here for pleasure? He didn't understand it. At the second attempt, Daisy managed to get herself into the right lane. 'Phew!' she said, and a smile returned to her face.

An electric blue sign on the exterior of the car park building advertised SPACES. 'Thank God for that!' said Daisy, as she steered the camper van under the metal-framed entrance, narrowly avoiding the 'Max. Headroom' sign. She came to an abrupt halt in front of a barrier. What now? thought Jack, panicking – is it closed or something?

He looked round, and there was already another car behind them. The black spot on his eye was starting to wink on and off like one of the traffic lights. Daisy calmly wound down her window and leant out to press a red button on a post. She let out a yelp as she did so, as she could only just reach it. A ticket appeared, which she popped into her mouth; the barrier shot up, and they were in. 'Here, hold this,' she said to Jack, passing him the ticket; it was damp at the edge and had her tooth indentations on it. He took it from her, silently marvelling again at how worldly-wise she was.

The interior of the car park was dark, meagrely lit by dim overhead lights set in a low ceiling. The roof of the van was only just clearing it, making Jack wince when he looked up; he kept anticipating a screech of metal and a shower of sparks.

'Keep your eyes peeled for a space,' Daisy said, as they followed an arrow up a ramp. The tyres of the van squealed as she steered it round the tight bend – one tyre bumping the kerb in the process. The next level was depressingly identical. And so was the next. There were lots of cars, no spaces and no people either; just a cave-like graveyard for motor vehicles. They went up and up, making Jack feel giddy and Daisy more exasperated, until finally on the sixth level she saw a space.

Typically, it was in an awkward spot, right next to a giant concrete post, but Daisy kept her composure, taking her time to slot in. She came to a halt and switched off the engine, blowing out a big sigh of relief.

She looked across at Jack for the first time in a while. He was looking … well, not too clever – pale, wide-eyed and traumatised, still clutching the stripy parking ticket (along with his rucksack) for dear life. Daisy burst out laughing. 'Come on, my driving's not that bad, is it?' She grabbed the ticket out of his hand and stuck it in her bag. Jack managed to raise a weak smile. He didn't feel well.

The prospect of stepping out of the van was like leaving behind the relative safety of a space capsule to explore a hostile alien planet. Would he be able to breathe out there?

His feet touched down tentatively as he closed the van door, whilst Daisy slammed hers with a loud, echoing clunk. She donned her denim jacket and slung her bag over her shoulder. 'Right, are we ready then?' she said, and gestured to Jack to follow her. He was leaning against the van as if it was a life raft, unwilling to leave it. 'Are you OK?' she asked; he was very quiet and also acting a little strange.

'Yes.' He reluctantly followed her as they set off across the car park.

They headed towards a sign saying 'Stairs and lifts this way'. Jack gulped in trepidation as Daisy pulled one of the double doors open. They were met by a tired-looking young couple with a screaming baby in a pushchair. The man had a fag in his mouth and the girl had one in her hand. Daisy stood aside, smiling politely, whilst Jack looked at the ground out of habit. Without a word of thanks, they were gone – leaving behind a lingering cloud of cigarette smoke, impossible not to breathe in. 'Lovely,' said Daisy, as they were left alone in a dingy, rank-smelling corridor.

Underneath the smell of cigarettes, Jack was hit with the unmistakable stench of piss; it was strong, like ammonia. The dark walls were covered in all manner of graffiti – swear words and rude pictures, both sprayed on and in marker pen. The walls got darker still as the two metal doors of the lift ahead clanged shut. To Jack's utter horror, it was impossible not to notice that someone had drawn a man's genitals, horizontally, on one of the lift doors, along with a woman's bush at the edge of the other one. Therefore, when the doors opened, and one slid behind the other to close again, the man's thing disappeared – sliding in and out of the woman's bush. It was as ingenious as it was revolting.

Jack went bright red; he had never felt so uncomfortable in his entire life. The normally unflappable Daisy also coloured

– at Jack's discomfort as much as anything else. It wasn't as though she could pretend she hadn't seen the drawing, and situations like this for teenagers, especially at the fragile beginning of a relationship, could cause irreparable damage. It was like treading in dog muck on your first date; how you handled it could make or break the relationship. Only parents could come close to inducing such cringe-worthy humiliation.

Daisy tried to pull herself together. 'Charming!' was all she could come up with. God, I'm turning into my mother, she thought as she stabbed the arrow button at the side of the lift. Then she turned to face Jack, but he wouldn't meet her gaze; he was looking at the stairwell in the corner. There was an awkward wait as the lift clunked and whirred, but did not arrive. 'Oh, come on!' said Daisy, tapping her foot impatiently.

Jack was getting more and more nervous at the groans and strains from deep within the lift shaft. 'Can't we just take the stairs?' he said, finding his voice.

He was desperate not to take the lift. He'd never actually been in one, but just knew he wouldn't like it. He'd heard stories on the news and seen films on telly where they'd broken down and people had got trapped in them. 'We're about six floors up,' said Daisy. 'It would take forever!' Just then, the lift clanged to a stop and the doors hissed open, prompting Jack to edge further away and nearer the stairs. 'Come on ... you're not scared, are you?' she said, taking a step towards him. As she did so, the doors began to close behind her, and she took a step backwards, still facing Jack, so that they opened again.

Jack looked beyond her, and the lift seemed like a monstrous, yellow mouth – opening and closing with that dreadful drawing on it – big enough to swallow them whole. She stretched towards him, keeping one foot near the lift door so it wouldn't close again, and held out her hand to him. 'Do you want me to hold your hand?' She said it playfully, as you would to a child, not really expecting anything of it. To Jack, though, the way she was standing there with her pursed lips, sweet face, and auburn curls framed by the lift represented all that was good and bad in the world. How could he resist her? And to her surprise he reached out his hand to hers, which felt warm and welcoming as she led him, for better or for worse, into the lift.

Once they were inside, the doors clanged closed. Jack tried to quell the rising panic that kicked in. Daisy pressed a button on the wall that said 'G' on it. The ground moved, making Jack stumble in surprise and want to throw up. Just to add to the rich potpourri of wonderful fragrances on offer – namely cigarette smoke and piss – the lift also smelt of stale beer. Jack noticed a couple of crushed empty cans in the corner. He tried to concentrate on the writing on one that said 'Special Brew', but this just made him feel worse. He closed his eyes and tried to think positive thoughts – like the feel of Daisy's hand and the smell of her perfume, which was competing with the rank smell of the lift.

Daisy looked up at him, wrinkling her nose and trying to hold her breath. Jack had his head pressed against the rear wall of the lift with his eyes closed. Beads of sweat had broken out over his forehead, and his hand was clammy. It dawned on her that he must be claustrophobic, and she wished he'd said something. She regretted making him take the lift and tried to take his mind off it.

'So, where shall we go first? I definitely want to go to Selectadisc – they've got a sale on today – and then Bankrupt Clothing; I could do with some new jeans. Then we can go to a pub if you like? There's one called The Dragon. All the college kids go there 'cause…' She trailed off as the lift stopped suddenly at another floor.

To Jack's alarm, more passengers got in, pushing him further into the corner. The smell and feel of them up close was invasive, hellish; he felt boxed in. He'd barely been listening to Daisy; he'd been doing his best to try not to be sick.

After what seemed like an eternity, with a jolt that made Jack open his eyes and grab the walls, the lift came to an abrupt halt again. They had reached the ground floor. As the doors opened they were met by another influx of people, all jostling for position. Some of them didn't even wait for the lift to empty first, and he and Daisy had to push their way out. As they did so, Jack could feel bodies rubbing and brushing against him, with their shopping bags rustling and crackling. Then they stepped away from the lift and the doors closed again, whisking everyone else away.

They were left in another dingy corridor, at the end of which Jack could see hordes of people scurrying past. There was the honking of traffic and the acrid smell of diesel fumes.

Before they knew it, more shoppers started to pile into the corridor to wait for the next lift up to the car park. That decided it – he just couldn't do it; he couldn't go out there. He'd seen enough. He needed a drink; God, how he needed a drink, and he reached for the strap of his rucksack … his rucksack that wasn't there as he'd left it in Daisy's van.

This provided the perfect excuse for him to scarper. 'My rucksack!' he said, turning to her. 'I left it in the van!' At that moment, the lift doors opened and even more people spilled out. That was it: Jack was off, making a dash for the stairs.

'Jack, wait!' cried Daisy, but he was gone. She knew she wouldn't catch him, so she darted back into the lift, just in time.

After a couple of annoying stops, Daisy reached the sixth floor and rushed out, expecting to see Jack waiting for her; but he wasn't. She waited at the top of the stairwell, not sure what to do. Surely he must have got up there first – he'd set off at such a pace; but then again, it *was* six floors up. She leant on the metal railings at the top of the stairs to peer down. To her disgust, she felt hardened lumps of chewing gum under her hands. She quickly wiped her fingers on her jacket. 'Jack!' she called. Her voice echoed down the stairwell but there was no reply. It occurred to her that he might already be at the van; knowing him, he was probably desperate to get his rucksack out so he could have a drink.

But when she pushed open the double doors to the car park, there was still no sign of Jack. Where had he got to? Perhaps he'd got off at the wrong level or something; he *had* been in a bit of a state. She thought about crossing the car park to go down the ramp to the next level, but what if she missed him coming back the other way? She remembered something her dad used to say to her when she was little and they were on days out in crowds. 'If you get lost, don't keep on wandering about, just stay at the last place you saw us.' Heeding this advice, she decided to sit in the van and wait; he'd soon turn up – he had to.

She unlocked the van and reached underneath the passenger seat to get his rucksack out. She was about to put some music on while she waited, then changed her mind; she could do with a bit of fresh air. She locked the van again and made her way over to sit on the thick wall at the edge of the car park.

This was something she had loved to do when she was younger, much to her parents' horror. It gave her a thrill to see all the people and cars down below looking so tiny. She used to wish she could fly like a bird to land on one of the buildings opposite. It looked as if the sky was brightening again – the sun was doing its best to come out. She felt better already, and was looking forward to her day out in town again. She looked down at the rucksack she was clutching and wished to hell Jack would hurry up. Where on earth had he got to?

Daisy's assumptions weren't far from the truth. Jack had indeed got off at the wrong level. He'd raced up the stairs, round and round, higher and higher, with the adrenaline initially pushing him on. But the further up he climbed the slower he went as the steep stairs began to take their toll. His heart was hammering in his chest, and he was beginning to feel dizzy from going round in circles. It was like being in a bad dream – all the stairwells looked and smelt the same. In his confusion he thought they'd parked on level five, so was blissfully relieved when he saw a big five on the wall.

He opened the doors and searched the rows of cars for Daisy's van. He figured he would wait for her whilst getting his breath back – not wanting to look like an even bigger idiot than he already did. To his alarm, he couldn't see the van anywhere, even though he was positive they'd parked near the centre: he could remember the concrete post.

This sent a fresh wave of anxiety over him. He felt disorientated, lost and alone, and stumbled around thinking crazy thoughts. Maybe he'd come back in through a different entrance from the one they'd left by? Or perhaps he'd been mistaken and it was level six, not level five. After circling the entire level in growing panic, he had no choice but to walk up the slope to the next floor.

Not being familiar with car parks, and without thinking, he staggered right up the middle of the ramp instead of keeping to the pedestrian kerb at the edge. As he reached the top, a car screeched up behind him and the driver honked his horn, making him jump out of the way. Its sound reverberated across the car park, and made Daisy look over. She saw Jack clinging onto the side barrier with a desperate look on his face. 'Jack!' she called. 'Over here!' He looked up at the sound of her voice. Daisy was coolly perched on a wall at the edge of the car park, her hair blowing gently in the breeze.

As he approached her, feeling foolish, his thoughts turned to his rucksack – and, more to the point, his remaining bottle of cider. Reading his mind, Daisy called in a sing-song voice, 'Here you go, here's your precious cider!' She smiled as she dangled the rucksack in the air. As he got nearer, she noticed how poorly he looked; his face was ashen. At the same moment Jack noticed where Daisy was sitting and how high up she was. His head started to swim. 'Come and sit down next to me; maybe you just need some fresh air,' she said, patting the wall next to her, like a siren drawing a sailor onto the rocks.

Daisy watched as he shuffled forward another couple of steps. The city appeared behind her – cranes and the tops of tall buildings – and in between nothing but a huge void, yawning hungrily. Then the other part of his fear took over, forcing him, willing him, closer to the edge and urging him to jump off. Instead of taking the bag from Daisy, he tottered straight past until he reached the wall next to her. 'Jack?' she said, turning to him; but he didn't hear: he was too crippled with fear.

Unable to help himself, Jack slowly turned his eyes downwards. His stomach cartwheeled as he registered the huge drop. It seemed like miles and miles, yet he could still see the cracks on the pavement. He imagined toppling forwards, hurtling towards the street below, falling and falling, the ground getting nearer and nearer – the cold certainty of it all – and there was nothing he could do. Nothing could change the fact that his head was going to burst open like a pumpkin on the pavement below. But just before that, he would feel his teeth briefly scraping on the concrete as his face was smashed to bits. This was the last thing Jack thought before a final wave of dizziness overwhelmed him, and he fainted clean away.

When he came to, the first thing he was aware of was a sharp, throbbing pain at the back of his head. Where was he? What had happened? The next thing he noticed was the smell;

the sweet, familiar scent – filling his nostrils, engulfing him. Then he was aware of something tickling his face, making it twitch, and a closeness, a heat – a warm glow against his skin. He kept his eyes closed for a moment, relishing the pleasantness of it all. Had he died and gone to heaven? It certainly felt like it – until the ache returned with a vengeance.

He opened his eyes and started. Daisy's face was inches from his, so close that her freckles had merged together. Her hair was brushing against him. 'Thank God!' she said, drawing back – much to Jack's disappointment.

'Here, drink this,' she said, and offered him his bottle of cider. 'I think some water would be more sensible, but you know – medicinal purposes and all that.'

Jack sat against the wall and drank. A family – a man, a woman and two young children – had stopped in the car park to watch. The children were fascinated but worried, whilst the adults had a look of concern, mingled with mild distaste, on their faces. Jack felt ashamed and hated them for staring. He must look a right state. What would his father have done if he could see him now, and all the attention he was drawing to himself?

'Are you going to be OK?' the man said to Daisy, rather than to Jack.

'Yes, we're fine now thanks, really.' The mother ushered them away, and they both heard her say, 'Now, children, let that be a lesson, that's what happens when you drink alcohol!'

Daisy and Jack looked at each other. 'What happened?' he managed to croak – even talking, moving his jaw, made the pain worse. He gently felt the back of his head with his hand. There was a considerable lump on it – but no blood of any consequence.

'You fainted. Why didn't you tell me you were scared of

heights?' Jack remembered being at the edge of the car park. It made his head throb even harder.

'I guess I didn't know.'

'You didn't know you suffered from vertigo?' she said in disbelief.

'What's vertigo?' he asked, thinking it must be a disease or something.

'Fear of heights, silly!'

'Oh.'

'Also, while we're at it, you didn't tell me you were claustrophobic either!' Jack *had* heard this word, but had never known what it meant.

'What's claustrophobic?' he asked; and Daisy groaned in despair. Was this that mock naivety again? She was sure he was winding her up, but he looked so earnest.

'Oh never mind!' she said, trying her best to be annoyed, but somehow finding him endearing instead. 'Just, in future – if there's anything you don't want to do, or don't like, please tell me first. OK?'

'OK,' said Jack, then paused before adding as an afterthought, 'I don't like town.'

CHAPTER 11

The Red Lion

With town now out of the question they headed home, both feeling a bit subdued to say the least. In the van on the way back, a slight atmosphere hung in the air. Daisy didn't even put any music on. She was feeling a little disgruntled that she hadn't had the opportunity to go to the record shops and the sales. The day had gone badly in general, which confused her: perhaps they just weren't suited to each other, and it wasn't meant to be. As for Jack, he felt as if he'd made a total fool of himself, and that the whole trip had been wasted because of him. He thought that being with Daisy he'd be able to handle town, to face his fears, but it had proved too much too soon. And so they drove in silence for a while, each lost in their own thoughts.

It was still fairly early by the time they reached the outskirts of Daisy's village. Jack was feeling better already – just being out in the countryside again – and he desperately wanted to make it up to her, but didn't know how. He couldn't go home yet as he was meant to be at work.

Neither of them said anything as they passed Daisy's close. They were rapidly running out of time: soon they would be arriving at the main road, and that would be it. Both of them were aware of this and both of them hated it. They stopped at the crossroads, and in another one of those defining moments where things could have gone either way, an opportunity presented itself – as there in front of them was the Red Lion. They turned to look at each other. Daisy said, 'Are you thinking what I'm thinking?'

Daisy had only been in the Red Lion once, and that was six years or so ago when her family had first moved to the area. Her dad had tried both nearby pubs and decided he preferred the Generous Briton in the centre of the village. She worked there now on Sunday lunchtimes as a waitress – serving food and washing up. Along with her pocket money, this funded her penchant for records and her weekly subscription to *NME*. This was all just as well; it would make it much more likely that she would get served, being a total stranger.

The car park was busy, and so was the large beer garden to the rear of the pub – bank holiday revellers enjoying a rare Monday off work. Jack's heart sank; all those people made him feel on edge. He had never been to a pub before, and being so close to home it didn't feel right. Daisy parked the van. It looked as if the sun had won the battle and was now firmly in charge of the day; dark clouds had been replaced by blue sky. Jack took a deep breath as he got out, desperate not to ruin this as well.

Much to his relief, Daisy said, 'Right, you go and find a spot in the garden and I'll go and get us some drinks.' He'd been dreading the prospect of having to go into the pub, but unbeknown to him, Daisy thought she stood more chance of being served on her own. 'Fingers crossed!' she said, doing just that behind her back as she bounced off across the car park.

Jack watched as she entered the pub through a side door before disappearing down a long corridor. The second she was gone he felt alone and on display. He rubbed the back of his head, where the pain seemed to have increased tenfold, and willed himself to get going.

He headed towards the beer garden, which was his idea of hell. There were people everywhere – families, children, dogs even – some of them lying on the grass, scattered about. He picked his way through them all, doing his best to remain inconspicuous and not to step on anyone. The beer garden went way back beyond the last tables, turning into a large expanse of grass surrounded by trees. One family had laid a picnic rug down, away from the crowds, in the shade of a large cherry tree in full blossom. It looked so much more appealing over there to Jack than stuck with everyone else.

He found a free bench and sat down. All around him people chatted, smoked and laughed; thankfully no one seemed to be paying any attention to him. He tried his best to relax as he waited for Daisy to return. He really hoped she got served as he was dying for a drink. She hadn't asked him what he wanted. He didn't know himself, but he hoped they had cider; he'd never tried pub cider before.

After about five minutes or so, with Jack feeling increasingly anxious, he finally saw Daisy. More importantly, she was clutching two pint glasses. She looked up, spotted Jack and raised the glasses triumphantly, which made him grin from ear to ear.

As he watched her edge her way through the tables, he couldn't believe this girl was actually coming to sit with him. It felt like a dream. She plonked the pints down on the table. Hers was a slightly different colour to his, but both were full of bubbles. 'Phew!' she said. 'That was a mission; it was busy in there.' She smelt of smoke. 'Well, cheers!' They both raised their glasses and she bumped hers against his.

Jack took his first swig of pub cider and baulked at the taste. What struck him the most was how fizzy it was, making it harsh on the throat. It tasted like flavoured, carbonated water compared to his cider. It was slightly sweeter too. 'What are you pulling a face at?' she said, laughing. 'You did want cider, didn't you?'

'Yes,' he replied, taking another swig, trying to get used to the taste. He had to stifle the urge to let out a big burp, it was so gassy. 'It's just different to my cider, that's all.'

'Ooh! You cider snob!' she teased, and Jack laughed.

'What have *you* got anyway?' he asked.

'Lager shandy. I'm thirsty *and* I'm driving, remember!'

They both sipped their drinks whilst furtively casting their eyes about; this was a novelty for both of them. To Daisy it felt like playing at being grown-ups, and also a little naughty, like bunking off school. 'So, how's your head?' she asked.

Jack put his hand up to feel the tender bump again, blushing at the memory. It was a miracle he hadn't split his head open, but the fact that his arm and shoulder were also sore probably meant they'd softened his fall. 'Oh it's not too bad,' he lied.

'You really have been in the wars, haven't you, what with your hand as well.' Jack looked at the back of his hand, where all that remained of the previous burn was a tight circle of new, pink skin, and shrugged by way of an answer.

'So, what is it exactly that you don't like about town...? Or were you joking?'

Jack took a gulp of his drink. 'Oh, I just don't go there much. I prefer the countryside, I suppose.'

'You soon get used to it, going to college every day and that.' He didn't reply again, and sensing it was a touchy subject Daisy dropped it.

She looked around, as if noticing everyone else for the first time. 'Do you want me to drop you home later? You can show me where you live,' she said.

Jack froze; this was the question he'd been dreading. He

stared intently into his rapidly emptying pint glass. Imagine turning up at his house with Daisy, even only going to the bottom of the lane?

'That's OK,' he said, after some deliberation. 'I can walk from here; it's not far.'

This wasn't the answer Daisy was after, and she studied him for a moment. Why was he so secretive about where he lived? And why did he find it so hard to look at her? It was a shame; he had such nice blue eyes.

'Oh I don't mind taking you,' she said, refusing to be put off. She was starting to suspect that Jack lived in one of the council houses halfway between the pub and Bunny Wood, and that maybe he was ashamed of this. But if he did live there, then surely he'd have gone to the same school as her, in East Leake. He must live further up on Bunny Hill Top, she thought, and so tried a different approach. 'Did you go to South Wolds school?'

This came totally out of the blue, and Jack was flummoxed. 'Hey?' he said.

'South Wolds... You didn't go to Harry Carlton, so you must have gone to South Wolds.' These were the two local comprehensive schools, and Bunny Hill Top bordered both the catchment areas.

Jack thought quickly. He'd heard of Harry Carlton school as his sister had gone there when he was little, and he passed it on the bus, but he'd never heard of South Wolds.

'Er, yes,' he said, lying through his teeth and hating himself for it.

'I thought so,' said Daisy. 'What was it like?'

'Er, you know...' He stalled; how the hell was he supposed to know what it was like? He looked around, feeling cornered, knowing he was digging a hole. He picked up his empty glass, desperate for another drink. 'OK, I suppose; boring really.'

Daisy seemed to be satisfied with this answer, her curiosity sated temporarily at least. 'Yeah, I know what you mean. I couldn't wait to finish school and go to college. It just got so dull... Did you make many friends?'

'Not really,' Jack said, as casually as he could.

'No, me neither, not really close ones anyway.'

Moving to a new secondary school had always felt like a distinct disadvantage to Daisy. She'd drifted through it, probably spending more time with boys in a matey way than girls, losing herself in her music along the way.

Her attention returned to the present and she noticed Jack fiddling with his empty glass. 'I suppose you want another cider then?' she said.

'Yes please,' he replied, glad the conversation was over.

'Considering you didn't like it, it didn't take you long to finish it!' Jack smiled.

They both stood up at the same time. Jack felt as though he should be going to fetch the drinks – in an old-fashioned, chivalrous way – but was still terrified at the idea.

'No, you sit down; I'll get them.'

'Are you sure?' he asked, feeling both useless and guilty.

'Yes, I know the way I suppose. You can pay this time, though!'

She was only joking, but it made Jack realise that she'd paid for the drinks before. He dived into his jeans pocket, pulled out a ten pound note that he'd stashed there earlier that morning, and passed it to her.

Daisy was about to set off when it occurred to her how peckish she was. It was lunchtime, and she didn't want her stomach growling in front of Jack. 'I've just thought, do you want something to eat – like a cob or something? I'm starving!'

Jack *was* hungry now she mentioned it, and he was going to say yes, but the image of eating in front of Daisy filled his head. It was another foible of his; he hated eating in front of other people – one of the reasons he never sat in the canteen at work. Eating was such a messy business; he could picture things stuck in his teeth and salad cream dripping down his chin. Not only that: he was always biting the side of his mouth. He should have been to the dentist – but of course he hadn't. As a result, his smallish mouth was crammed too full of teeth.

'Er, no. I'm OK, thanks,' he said. 'I'll have some crisps, though.'

'Oh, OK, if you're sure. What flavour do you want?'

'Salt and vinegar, please.'

'Ooh, a salt and vinegar man, eh? They're my dad's favourite too! OK, I'll be back in a minute.'

Before she left, Daisy looked up at the sky and removed her jacket. 'Phew! It's really starting to warm up now!' she said, popping it on her seat. And with that, she sashayed off through the crowds.

Jack watched her go, and couldn't help but admire the sway of her hips as she walked away in her tight, faded jeans. He wasn't the only one either; there were two middle-aged men with their backs to him at another table in front. He saw one of them look up as Daisy walked past, nudge his mate, then say something to him. They both laughed, and continued to stare at her as she made her way between the tables.

Jack was suddenly overwhelmed by loathing for them, and another emotion he'd never felt before – an alarming possessiveness. They were like thieves around a jewel, and his eyes bored angry holes into their backs. His leg tapped under the table as he seethed, trying to deal with this newfound feeling. He forced himself to look away, and took off his shirt; the afternoon really was hotting up.

Daisy soon reappeared, carrying a tray. As she approached the tables Jack's gaze went from her to the two men, and sure enough, when they spotted her they also looked up, watching her progress. Jack was overcome with hatred again; he could imagine their greedy, searching eyes, crawling all over her body like insects. He had a sudden and violent vision of going over there and setting about them – pummelling them with his fists, or smashing a glass and sticking the shards into their faces.

'Are you OK?' asked Daisy as she reached the table, snapping him out of his silent rage. 'You look like you want to kill someone!'

'Sorry,' he said, tearing his gaze away from the men and back to her. 'I was just thinking, that's all.'

'Thinking what?'

'Oh, nothing really, just … people.'

'Oookaay,' she said, seeing he wasn't going to say any more.

She removed the items from the tray. There were two fresh pints, some ready-salted crisps (she secretly wanted cheese and onion, but didn't want her breath to smell), Jack's crisps, and a small plate with a tasty-looking ham salad cob on it. She took the cob in both hands and took a large bite out of it. At first Jack tried not to look, in case she felt uncomfortable, but then he watched in growing admiration as she set about her meal with enthusiastic abandon. Why couldn't *he* be like that? At one point she offered him the cob through a mouthful of food. As he declined he shook his head in amusement, thinking how she was sometimes like a boy.

CHAPTER 12

Under the Cherry Tree

With the lunchtime rush over, the crowds thinned out as people left. Jack had one more pint, but not Daisy. The afternoon wore on and the sun continued to beat down, reddening Daisy's arms. They picked up their things and retired to the cool shade of the pretty pink cherry tree at the end of the beer garden – recently vacated by the family with the picnic rug. Jack was feeling dreamy and lazy, with an unexpected buzz from the pub cider; it must have been the bubbles. The horrors of town were long forgotten now, but something else was bugging him. This was the perfect opportunity, while they were alone and whilst he had the courage, to ask a question that he just had to know the answer to.

They sat in silence for a bit, cross-legged and opposite each other, amongst a litter of daisies and cherry blossom that had fallen like confetti. Daisy started picking the flowers and making a daisy chain, whilst Jack just picked at them. She'd always had an affinity with the little flower, being named after it – 'tiny and determined' was how she'd been described as a baby by her parents; not much had changed since.

She added her chain to her wrist with her other bracelets and held up her arm for Jack's recognition. He looked preoccupied. Daisy was wondering what with, when suddenly he spoke. 'Daisy?' It sounded loud and strange coming out of his mouth; was this the first time she'd heard him say her name? It gave her a little thrill, and she kind of liked it.

'Yes, *Jack*.'

There was a pause. 'Where were you that day you weren't on the bus?'

The question threw Daisy; it wasn't what she'd been expecting. She was secretly hoping for some hint about where he lived.

'When?' she asked, trying to cast her mind back.

'The other week; I think it was a Friday.' He knew exactly when it was, and when he said Friday, so did Daisy.

'Oh,' she said. Her brow furrowed and that sorrowful look came over her face, making Jack wish he'd never asked.

Daisy took a deep breath. 'It was my dad. He had one of his turns, but this time it was worse. He's got a dodgy heart, you see, something called "severe angina". It flares up every so often, even when he's not doing anything. He can just be sitting there and the pain comes on. It's awful to see.' She winced at the thought of it. 'He takes all sorts of tablets for it, beta blockers and stuff, but sometimes he forgets and my mum has to badger him about it. The doctor's told him several times to stop drinking and smoking because they aggravate it. He tries for a bit, but then just goes back to his old ways. He's been smoking all his life – so I guess it's hard to quit. It drives Mum mad … and me.'

She looked up at Jack with a sad smile; this was obviously hard for her to talk about and he wanted to comfort her. 'Anyway, last Thursday was the worst yet. He was in such pain and couldn't breathe very well either. It was that bad we thought he was having a heart attack.' Her voice trembled and she looked as if she was going to cry.

She fiddled with the straps on her bag, trying to compose herself. 'So we called an ambulance and they took him to hospital. They did loads of tests, and he had to stay there till Sunday. It turned out he *had* actually had a mild heart attack ... it's not fair, he's only forty-eight!' She threw her bag when she said this last bit, then her jacket on top of it, and plonked herself down on her back, using it as a pillow.

Jack was stunned. He'd never had to deal with anything like this before; he was ill- equipped for it, but desperate to do the right thing. He placed his rucksack and shirt next to hers and lay down beside her. As he looked across at her a tear welled up, making her eyelash look huge and wet. He wanted to dab it away with his thumb. It trickled out of the corner of her eye, cutting a path through her freckles.

At that moment, some stray blossom floated down and landed in her hair. Jack was struck by the contrast between the pale pink and the deep, russet red of her locks – and also how beautiful she was. God, he wanted to kiss her.

'I'm sorry,' was all he could say; and he truly was. He was sorry for Daisy – as she obviously loved her dad who was ill – whilst he didn't care about *his* father, who was right as rain despite trying to drink himself to death. It didn't seem right. He was also sorry for bringing up the subject; he felt, once again, that he'd ruined an otherwise pleasant afternoon.

'Don't be silly, it's not your fault,' she said. 'Besides, he seems to be doing better now. They changed his medication, which he's religiously taking for once, *and* he's quit drinking again. I think it's shocked him – and Mum, so he's taking it easy for a bit. I just hope he keeps it up this time. He's still having the odd fag, mind you, but at least he had a few days off them when he was in hospital.'

They lay there in silence for a while, side by side, until Jack's stomach let out an almighty growl that went on forever. He blushed, but Daisy burst out laughing. It restored a more jovial atmosphere if nothing else, albeit at Jack's expense.

'Anyway,' said Daisy. 'While we're at it, there's something I want to ask you too… Why are you so secretive about where you live?' Jack groaned inwardly. It was getting harder and harder to avoid the subject and he hated lying to her, but the lifelong fear gripped him, rendering him dumb. 'I mean, you know where *I* live. I hope you're not embarrassed or something 'cause if you are, that would be ridiculous – things like that don't mean anything to me. Trust me.'

Jack appreciated her kindness but still had to force himself to speak. 'It's not that… It's just…' He trailed off.

'Just what?' she cried, turning to him; she had just poured out her heart to him, and he wouldn't even tell her where he lived!

'Just complicated,' he said.

'Complicated *how?*'

'Well, it's my father… He's a bit … odd. He doesn't really like us mixing with other people.'

'Who's us?'

'Me and my sister.'

'Oh, I didn't realise you had a sister. How old is she?' Daisy asked, thinking maybe she had gone to school with her.

'Erm, I'm not sure.' Jack genuinely didn't know – birthdays had never been a big deal in their house; except for his father's, of course. He knew when his own was, give or take a few days, Anne had made sure of that, but he certainly couldn't say when hers was exactly.

Daisy looked puzzled. 'How can you not know how old your sister is?'

'Well, we've never really celebrated birthdays... I think she's twenty-something, maybe even thirty.'

This sounded totally bizarre to Daisy, and a little sad at the same time. 'Wow! Are you sure? That seems like a very big age gap – and she still lives at home?'

'Well, yes.' This hadn't occurred to him as noteworthy. 'Maybe she's twenty-eight,' he suggested, but he was just guessing and it showed.

'Surely she's old enough to make her own decisions about who she mixes with?' Jack didn't answer; he was busy staring up into the boughs of the tree.

Somehow they had slipped away from the subject of where he lived, so Daisy persisted. 'It's not like I have to drop you at your front door or anything. I can just stop somewhere nearby and you can point your house out to me.'

'The thing is, I can't go home yet anyway,' Jack said.

'Why not?'

'Because my father thinks I'm at work today, that's why.'

'Really? And why would he think that?'

'Because he doesn't know the factory closes on bank holidays – he thinks I'm there today. If I told him, he'd just make me stay at home and do jobs as usual – so I can't go home till about six o'clock.' He babbled this in one go without pausing for breath. It sounded odd to Daisy but sort of made sense; his dad was obviously one of those disciplinarian freaks.

'So, where do you want me to drop you in the meantime? I'll have to go soon. Don't tell me: Bunny Wood?'

'Er, yes, if you don't mind.'

'Well, you can point out your house on the way past, can't you?' she challenged, refusing to give up.

The question hung in the air, floating on the tension that had built up during their conversation. Jack looked miserable and Daisy felt as if she had been too hard on him. She was also aware that time was getting on; she'd promised her dad that she'd wash the cars for him during the afternoon and she didn't want to leave it like this. She wondered how she could cheer him up, and her thoughts turned to when she could see him again – and to what they could do. Town had been a disaster. What does he like? Cider, she thought, smiling; cider and woods … and a great idea came to her that would suit him down to the ground. She impulsively blurted it out.

'Hey, how'd you like to go camping this weekend?'

Jack turned to face her in surprise; he had been lost in dark thoughts, chasing the black spot on his eye through the cherry blossom.

'Camping?' he said, intrigued.

'Yes, me and my dad have been loads of times. I went with some friends last summer as well. There's a wood on the way to Wysall – it's perfect.'

Jack had never been camping before, but it was hard to get excited when all he could think about was how he could possibly get away with it.

'Do you mean, like, for the whole day?' he asked.

'Well, more like the evening really; it's more fun at night. We can make a fire to cook on and take a tape player and some cards to play with.' The more she thought about it, the more she was carried away by the idea. 'You can bring some cider!' she said. 'You'd love it!'

Jack reeled at the enormity of what she was saying. It sounded like the best thing ever, but what would he say to his father? 'Well, when?' he asked, still looking uncertain.

'I don't know. Friday night, say, and come back Saturday morning?'

'What, you mean for the whole night?' said Jack, gulping.

'Well, yes. That's what we normally do. Why?'

'But where would we sleep?'

'In a tent of course!'

It was then that she realised how forward she must sound, and mistook this as the reason for his uncertainty. She hadn't thought about the details, like the fact that they'd be spending the night alone in a tent together: she had just sort of come out and said it. She had been camping with boys before, but that was in a group with girls too; now, seeing his face, she was suddenly unsure. 'Well, that's if you want to. I mean, we don't have to, it was just an idea.'

Jack noticed her enthusiasm beginning to wane. 'I'd love to,' he said. 'It's just – I don't know what I'd say to my father; he'd never let me.'

'Say you're camping out with some mates, all the kids do it… Or, I don't know, if you really think he won't let you, why don't you just sneak out and go back early in the morning?'

Now *that* wasn't such a bad plan, thought Jack. Sure, it was risky as hell – but if he could get away with it, God, it would be worth the risk! He had some serious thinking to do, and, spurred on by this, his mood lightened. 'OK. Can I let you know on the bus tomorrow?'

Daisy did her best to hide her joy, thrilled that Jack was coming round to the idea – but he had clearly forgotten something. 'Oh, I'm not at college this week, remember; it's half term.'

Jack *had* clean forgotten, and it hit him hard. The more he saw her, the more he needed to see her; she was his pill to get him through the day. And worse, today was only Monday. How could she be so casual about it? Wasn't she dying inside like him?

Daisy could sense his disappointment and briefly thought about giving him her phone number, but then thought better of it. She hadn't mentioned anything about Jack to her parents yet, and if she had a boy ringing up about a proposed camping trip they would smell a rat; they were relaxed parents, but not *that* relaxed. 'I know, why don't I give you a ring in the week?' she said; that way she could do it secretly when they weren't about. 'What's your number?' And she reached into her bag, fishing out her notebook-cum-diary and searching for a pen.

'Oh, we don't have a phone,' said Jack.

Daisy looked up as if to say 'Oh, yeah!' But by the look on his face she could tell he wasn't joking. Her jaw dropped.

'Well, we do, but we're not allowed to use it. It's in my father's workshop – he uses it for his business and gets itemised bills every quarter to make sure we haven't touched it.'

Stranger and stranger, thought Daisy. What was this guy, some sort of paranoid dictator? She pondered this for a moment. 'Well, if I ring *you* it doesn't cost anything and he wouldn't even know – we'll just arrange a time so you can answer the phone.'

Jack looked unsure; he remembered the one time that he'd been caught touching the phone when he was younger…

He had been bagging up the wood shavings into bin liners (one of his regular jobs), and his curiosity had got the better of him. He had picked up the receiver and put it to his ear, fascinated by the buzzing sound it made. He was just about to turn the dial when his father had come charging into the workshop; Jack had forgotten about the electric bell that was attached to the phone.

When he saw the boy standing there with the phone to his ear, he hit the roof. Perhaps he had thought Jack was planning his escape – or even phoning the police. Jack had been dragged out by his ear and given another in a long line of hidings; he hadn't touched the phone since.

'I'm not sure,' he said, not wanting to risk it. 'Besides, I don't even know the number.'

'You don't know the number? You've got to be kidding me.'

Jack shook his head; he was starting to feel embarrassed. 'Well, I guess we're stuck till Friday then. I just hope you can come, that's all.' And she put her notebook and pen back in her bag.

'I'll go!' cried Jack suddenly, surprising her. He was sick of the deliberations, and of his father controlling his life. For better or for worse, he would find a way.

'Really? But what about your dad?'

'Don't worry, I'll think of something,' he replied, aware that all the alcohol on an empty stomach was playing a big part in making his decisions.

They packed up and headed back to Daisy's van. All the customers had left the tables now, leaving behind a sea of glasses, bottles, crisp packets and plates. A harassed-looking landlord was scurrying between them, clearing up as he went. He nodded a 'thank you' to Daisy as they passed, but gave Jack a curious look. Jack averted his gaze.

They reached the van and Daisy unlocked her door to get in. She wound down both the windows and began to fiddle with the stereo. Jack lingered, leaning against the van's hot exterior. He knew what was coming next and was unsure what to do about it. 'Come on then, get in!' Daisy called through the window.

He was in a real dilemma, at a crossroads in his life, with huge risks in every direction. He couldn't keep lying to her forever; he hated and resented it, *and* his bastard of a father. Look at Daisy: she could come and go as she pleased without any pressure, without hiding from the world. In contrast, he couldn't even go home because it wasn't the right bloody time!

Daisy gunned the engine. 'Jack?' she called, bobbing her head in time to the music. 'Come on, I've got to go!' Jack made his decision, and got in the van.

They turned right at the crossroads and headed up the main road. As they approached the council houses on the left,

Daisy braked and turned the music down, anticipating that Jack would say something, but he didn't. He was staring off into the distance, where his house had briefly come into view. His heart started to thump and he nearly chickened out – instinct telling him to lie – but he just couldn't do it anymore. 'That's it,' he said in a barely audible voice, pointing with a shaky finger. 'That's where I live.'

For sixteen years, he had lived an anonymous life; he didn't exist. If he'd got run over by a car or committed a crime, no one would have known where he lived, or where to look for his family. Up until now, that is. It was a relief, like the lifting of a heavy burden, but it also scared the hell out of him.

'What, the bungalow on the hill?' she asked. He nodded, struggling to comprehend what he'd just done. She studied his face to see if he was telling the truth or not. He looked drained.

Daisy slowed down again as they passed the bottom of the lane, trying to get a better view. Jack could almost feel his father's eyes boring into him, and wished she would speed up. 'You can see it better from the other side on your way back,' he said.

'Well, nice views!' she remarked as she accelerated again, leaving the house behind.

Daisy pulled into the gravelled area at the entrance to Bunny Wood. 'Well, I guess this is it till Friday?' she said.

'Yes.'

Friday seemed a long way away for both of them, and so they sat for a moment. Jack was secretly hoping that she might suggest they should meet up during the week; he was too shy to ask himself. She *was* thinking about it, but she figured her parents would begin to wonder where she kept on disappearing to, and why she'd suddenly taken such an interest in rambling. She would also need to use Claire, her friend from college, as a surrogate Friday night camping partner – she didn't want to use

127

her as an excuse mid-week as well. It was an unusual situation, but without a phone they really were stuck. It wasn't normally this hard with boys, but then again, Jack wasn't like any other boy she'd ever met.

'So, what time?' she asked. Jack hadn't quite figured out his plan, so this was a tough one. He normally went out for the evening at about six thirtyish, so he guessed it would be best if he stuck to his routine.

'Seven?' he suggested.

'OK. You still don't sound too sure.'

'No, seven's fine ... at the crossroads.'

Daisy had a sudden brainwave. 'I know. Why don't you give *me* a ring, but just let it ring once and then put the phone down? That way it still won't cost anything and won't arouse my parents' suspicion either. I'll listen out for it on Friday evening – but no later than six-fifteen, otherwise it'll be too late. If I haven't heard from you by then I'll know we're still on!' She got her notebook out again, pleased with her idea.

'What? Will that work?' asked Jack, still wary of going near the phone.

'Yes, trust me!' She began to scribble her number on a blank page, then ripped it out, folded it and handed it to him.

*****

As Daisy drove back down the hill, the bungalow was no easier to see, just a white blur through the poplars. It made her wonder about all that business with the phone. Who didn't have a phone in their house? And then there was all that stuff about Jack's family not celebrating their birthdays: that was downright weird.

She thought again how different he was to other boys she'd known – 'the strong, silent type', as her mum would say, but vulnerable at the same time. It gave her a buzz thinking about it, and she realised how bored she'd been before she had met him. He was her own little adventure, her own little secret.

Meanwhile, Jack still had at least an hour and a half to kill before he could return home. He'd clocked the time in Daisy's van before he got out, and it had only been quarter past four. He badly wished he had some cider – not that he needed it; he was feeling faint. Maybe it was the bump on his head, or maybe it was the fact that he hadn't eaten anything all day.

He ambled through the wood, thinking he'd head up to his stile to eat his sandwiches from his pack-up. He could pick up small sticks along the way, each one representing five minute intervals. This was another trick he'd learnt for when he wanted to keep track of time, but it was going to be difficult to concentrate today. His mind was reeling from the day's events. So much had happened – what with town, and then the pub, and her telling him about her dad being ill; most of all, though, revealing to Daisy where he lived. Had he done the right thing? What if she told her parents? He wished he'd told her not to now.

Then, to top it all off, there was the prospect of going camping. He had to figure out a way of making it happen, and he cheered up at the thought of it. To think that she had asked him *and* given him her phone number. Imagine spending the whole night with her!

As he sat on his stile Jack pulled out his pack-up, but on inspection didn't fancy it. The sandwiches were warm and crushed from where he had lain on his bag; so were his crisps. Oh well, it's nearly dinner time, he thought, and shoved it all back in his rucksack. He pulled out the precious piece of paper with Daisy's phone number on it to lovingly admire. He would store it in his tin when he got home, along with his other treasured items.

All in all it hadn't been a bad day, he supposed. He hadn't managed to get any of Daisy's scent on his shirt, which was a shame; but still, he'd managed to pull off another one of his bank holiday escapades. Everything had gone according to plan. He smiled to think that as far as his father knew he'd been at work for the whole day, while really he'd been spreading his wings. Or so he thought...

CHAPTER 13

Busted

Whilst Jack had been off gallivanting for the day, a drama had been unfolding at home.

That afternoon Anne had needed to do a bit of shopping – just a few bits for dinner – so after lunch she informed her father that she was nipping out. She headed up the hill to get the one o'clock bus; but to her surprise, it hadn't arrived. Unlike Jack, who didn't really think like anyone else, she turned round and inspected the timetable on the bus stop. It was then that she realised it was a bank holiday.

The timetable informed her that on Bank Holiday Mondays the buses ran a Sunday service, just from the village of East Leake (where she did her shopping). This was news to her, and she was amazed it had never cropped up before – but, then again, it wasn't as if she went shopping on any set days – and how many bank holidays were there a year?

Her musings turned to Jack. If there were no buses, how the hell had he got into work? Would the factory even be open? Surely he wouldn't have walked all the way to East Leake to catch a bus? He'd have had to walk all the way back again afterwards as well. Then she recalled him asking about bank holidays not so long ago. The little monkey! she thought.

She had no choice but to head back home, her dinner plans ruined. She was disconsolate as she walked down the hill, as she'd been looking forward to a break in the day's monotony – and for her own personal reasons too. As she headed up the lane and looked across the meadow, she noticed what a lovely afternoon it was. An idea came to her. Why didn't she cycle to the shops? She hadn't used her bike in years and it would do her good; she'd noticed of late that her hips and thighs were beginning to thicken and spread – nothing too drastic, a natural progression for a woman in her mid-twenties who led a pretty inactive life, consisting mainly of housework. This wouldn't usually have bothered her; who was going to look at *her*? She didn't go anywhere except to the shops. But she'd started to take notice of the butcher's son, who always made a point of serving her.

He must have been about her age but looked older; it was probably his hairstyle, which was old-fashioned and parted at the side. He always tried to engage her in conversation, even when there was a queue, holding her change back so he could talk to her a bit longer than necessary. She was flattered; it was probably the first male attention she'd ever received. She'd even started putting a clip in her hair, off to the side, while she was on the bus into the village. Never would she have dared to say anything to him, but she could still dream, couldn't she? She was still a woman, wasn't she?

She disentangled her old black bike from the shed. Her father (who'd been surprised by her return) was loitering at the doors of his workshop; she'd been hoping he was going to be inside. At first he stood staring, then he walked over – eyeing her suspiciously as he always did when anything out of the ordinary happened.

Under his disparaging glare, she proceeded to pump up the tyres of the bike. As she gave the first one a squeeze to see if it was firm enough, he spoke, startling her. 'What on earth are you doing? I thought you were going to the shops.'

Because her mind was on other things, she replied, 'Oh, the buses aren't running today 'cause it's a bank holiday, so I thought I'd cycle.' Instantly she realised her dreadful mistake. She carried on pumping up the tyres, keeping her head down, desperately hoping nothing had registered.

'Oh ... is that so?' her father said. Her stomach sank. She recognised that tone in his voice, and knew she'd sealed her brother's fate.

*****

As Jack sauntered up the drive at what he thought was his usual time (he was actually twenty minutes early), he was thinking how he couldn't wait to have a lie-down after dinner. He'd already decided he wasn't going to go out that evening; he felt slightly odd. The first thing he noticed that was out of the ordinary was Anne's bike parked under the kitchen window. He hadn't seen it in years. It didn't strike him as anything to worry about – just mildly interesting – and he made a mental note to ask her about it. He didn't get a chance, though, as his sister wasn't cooking dinner when he entered the kitchen: this *did* seem unusual. Instead, his father was hunched at the table, cradling a bottle of cider.

He'd been sitting there all afternoon, waiting for this moment, quietly seething and simmering. If there was one thing he couldn't abide, it was being made a fool of.

He sprung at Jack, taking him by surprise, ramming him against the door and knocking the wind out of him. Jack looked into the parlour for Anne, but she was nowhere to be seen; this only added to his fear and unease. 'Where the hell have you been?' his father hissed in his face, so close that Jack could smell his fetid breath and see his discoloured teeth.

'I've been at work, where do you think?'

Hearing the lie was just what his father wanted. It gave him satisfaction, and some sort of vindication, as he shoved Jack against the door again. 'No you haven't… You're a little LIAR! 'Where have you been?' And he started sniffing him like a dog.

Jack smelt of booze and cigarette smoke, but luckily not of Daisy; about the only thing that was in his favour.

'I told you, I've been at work!' Jack yelled back, making an effort to wrestle free. Now that he was over the initial shock, he felt indignant and repulsed at having this maniac in his face. But it was no use; his father had him pinned.

'No you haven't, 'cause I know the buses don't run today. You're a *FILTHY LITTLE LIAR!*'

How could he know that? thought Jack. How could he possibly have found out?

The bank holiday game was up, and Jack knew he'd been busted. But despite this, and despite his fear, there was no way he was about to tell his father where he'd been – and definitely not about Daisy.

Without an answer, his father continued to bash him against the door – as if he could beat it out of him. 'You're not going anywhere for the foreseeable future! I don't want you leaving this house except for work until I say you can again! Do you hear me? None of these evening jaunts, none of this disappearing off, you can stay here and work! While you're under my roof, you live by my rules! Do you understand?'

Jack thought of Daisy and the proposed camping trip, and he burned with rage. 'You can't do that! Not anymore. I'm sixteen; you can't stop me!' Spurred on by his anger, he gave his father an almighty shove.

The tussle was brief and one-sided. In his boozy and weakened state Jack was no match for his father, whose retribution was swift and exact. He landed a knock-out blow that made Jack see stars and go reeling against the door. As he slowly slumped down, for the second time that day and for the third time in his life, Jack lost consciousness.

He didn't hear his sister – who'd been banished to her room until Jack had been dealt with – come bursting in, screaming in distress. She had crept out and listened at the door when he'd come back, so she'd heard everything. In the end she couldn't take any more, knowing it was her slip of the tongue that had caused all this, and was ready to throw herself in front of the monster to protect her brother.

But it was all over. Jack was out for the count on the kitchen floor with his father standing over him. The scene was somehow reminiscent of that famous black and white photo of Muhammad Ali and Sonny Liston.

*****

Jack was standing in a town square amongst a huge crowd of people; he could hear their clamour and din and could smell their musty clothes as they pressed against him. There were old men in top hats and children in old-fashioned dress.

Suddenly a clock rang out, loud and clear across the square, and a hush fell over the crowd. As the chimes fell silent, the last one reverberating on the air, the clip-clop of hooves on cobblestones could be heard. Everyone pushed forward, jostling and fighting for position. It made Jack feel trapped. People were craning their necks, trying to see. Children were being hoisted onto their parents' shoulders, and Jack had to stand on tiptoe to see what all the fuss was about.

Over their heads, through the tall hats and tobacco smoke,

Jack made out a girl on horseback entering the square. She was riding side-saddle and had auburn hair. It was *his* girl ... it was Daisy; and he gasped. Her hair was longer, much longer, and it fell over her breasts, covering them. She was naked.

At first he stood there in awe, the same as everyone else; startled and amazed at her beauty. She looked so confident, so proud and sure of herself. His feelings turned to jealousy at the realisation that all these other people were staring too, feasting their eyes on her nakedness. He was overcome with rage, and began lashing out at the men around him, trying to pull them away. A circle formed around him, an angry mob. They set about him with their sticks and canes; kicking him and holding him down. He thrashed but couldn't get free, while the rest of the crowd carried on staring at the mesmerising spectacle in front of them.

*****

He woke up struggling in bed. His shoulders were being shaken and someone was saying, 'Jack, wake up!' He opened his eyes, but it hurt and he winced. It was dark in his room and there was someone sitting on his bed, holding his arms.

'Daisy?' he said, delirious and disorientated. Where was he? What time was it?

'Jack, it's me.' He recognised his sister's voice, his nurse; she was peering at him with a worried look on her face. He couldn't see properly out of one of his eyes; it wouldn't open fully. His head felt as if it had been used as a punch bag, as did the rest of his body.

'Bastard,' he said, remembering.

'You're awake. I was worried – here, have some water,' Anne said.

He leant forward with his arms still down and drank from

the glass. Anne watched him, thinking, Daisy … so that's her name, is it? So it's true, there is a girl. She couldn't believe it, and wasn't sure how it made her feel.

The water tasted good and cool. Jack's throat was parched – and once he started he couldn't stop.

'Steady!' his sister cried, as it cascaded down his chin and onto the bed.

Once he had drained the glass, Anne tearfully informed him how their father had found out about the buses, and how sorry she was. Jack didn't blame her; it wasn't her that had given him a black eye, was it?

It was a real corker too – as he discovered when he managed to make his way to the bathroom. It was his right eye, or was it his left? He couldn't make it out in the mirror. It was swollen, tender to the touch, and an angry black and purple. His immediate thoughts were of Daisy and what she would think; he looked a real sight – she couldn't see him like this. Then, he realised that she wouldn't anyway; he wasn't going to see her all week – and that was even worse.

He went straight back to bed, not even bothering to eat; it was too late now. While he'd been gone, Anne had put some aspirin next to the bed with a fresh glass of water – not cider, he noted. He took them gratefully and lay back, hoping they would make the pain subside. Slowly but surely everything came back to him – the cherry tree, the camping, her phone number. Oh, God! Where was it? And he sat up, causing a bolt of pain to shoot through his head. After frantically searching through his jeans pockets, he found the bit of paper. He didn't even put it in his tin, but clutched it in his hand all night.

The next morning Anne had to wake him, otherwise he simply wouldn't have got up. Going into work was the last thing he wanted to do, but not going wasn't an option; his father wouldn't have allowed it. Besides, he'd already missed a day's wages because of the bank holiday, and this forced him out of bed. His head still ached, but not quite as much as the previous night. The bruise above his eye, though, had got worse. It was darker and seemed to be spreading.

If Jack was supposed to keep a low profile and go unnoticed, his father was playing a dangerous game. The bus driver noticed the lad's eye straightaway. Other people on the bus noticed it too, as did Jack's co-workers; and so did Peasgood.

Surprisingly, nobody said a thing. That's the thing with a black eye; it almost always looks as if it's the recipient's fault, as if they deserved it. 'What sort of unsavoury character gets mixed up in something like that?' This was particularly so in Jack's case because, to the casual observer, he came across as stand-offish, surly even.

The black eye made Jack feel like this as well, as he knew people were staring; it made him feel ashamed, as though it was a punishment – as if he were a branded criminal. When he went to check on its progress at lunchtime, he was thankful again that Daisy wouldn't see it – at least until the swelling had gone down.

The week dragged on, and every evening Jack dutifully got on with the tasks his father set him. There were always a million jobs to do. The lawns needed mowing, the foundations of the new coal store needed digging and laying, cider had to be made, logs needed chopping; it was never-ending. But what choice did he have except getting on with it? He was trapped; he couldn't leave as he didn't have enough money yet – and this made him more determined than ever to go into work to earn more. He couldn't go to the authorities either. Where could he say he'd come from? What story could he tell?

The only positive was Jack's desire to fight back, physically. Even if he couldn't overpower his father just yet, he was determined to put up a better defence in future. He started doing press-ups in his room when he got home from work. At first his head pounded and throbbed, and his arms shook in protest. It wasn't that he was weak, far from it; he was used to hard graft; but his body wasn't used to this specific form of exercise. He could only manage a dozen or so before he had to give up, and the next morning his chest ached from the muscles he hadn't used before. Ignoring this, he gritted his teeth and did another set before work, pushing himself harder.

Then one evening, mid-week, when he was building the wall for the coal store and his father wasn't about, he tried curling the bricks as if they were weights. He enjoyed seeing how they made the muscles in his arm tense and contract. The only problem was, they weren't quite heavy enough. After scouting about, he soon found some old ones that were caked in cement on all sides – proper lumps that were a lot heavier. He secretly snuck a couple back to his room and stashed them under his bed.

These, too, became part of his daily workout; it was as if he had his own gym in there. What else did he have to do? He felt like a prisoner who spent his days cooped up in a cell doing press-ups and chin-ups. He conjured up images of Sylvester Stallone in *Rocky IV* preparing to fight the Russian, likening the encounter to him and his father, and using it as motivation.

It became a routine, and by the end of the week he was doing twenty press-ups in the morning and twenty at night. He began studying his body in the mirror in the bathroom from under his one puffy eyelid (which helped to enhance his 'underdog boxer' look) to see if it was making a difference yet. This was his way of getting through – trying to keep his mind off Daisy and how much he missed her, especially with their camping trip looming.

That Friday evening, when he got home from work and had to go and make the call, Jack didn't think he'd ever hated his father so much. First, he had to check he was in the living room watching telly and then – without wasting any more time – headed straight back out to the workshop. His sister watched him with a bemused look, wondering what he was up to; he hadn't been down to the cellar for his cider yet.

Jack's heart was beating fast as he slipped inside the workshop. He lifted the receiver, flinching as he heard the bell ding in the yard. He'd already memorised the number and quickly dialled it. He let the phone ring once, just as Daisy had instructed, then put it back down as gently as possible, dashing out of the workshop. Mission accomplished.

Jack knew he couldn't go camping – he'd known since he woke up that bank holiday night with a sore head, so he was resigned to it. Daisy, however, was not. She had been hoping, praying, and missing Jack terribly all week, and looking forward to their trip more than anything in her life. She'd got everything organised, everything packed, and had used the excuse that she was going with her college friend, Claire. She honestly thought everything was going ahead; surely he wouldn't ring this late, would he? So when the phone rang at just gone six that Friday evening, she could have cried. It only lasted a fraction of a second – the briefest, most innocuous of dings; a mere trifle that conveyed a world of disappointment.

She couldn't believe it at first, and slunk back to her room where she sank onto her bed; her bed that was littered with tapes she was getting ready for that night – all immaterial now. She lay there for a while, staring blankly at the ceiling. And when it got to seven o'clock and she still hadn't come out, her mum called her.

'Daisy, you're going to be late! Do you want a lift?' She didn't answer. What would she say? 'Daisy!'

Daisy appeared forlornly on the landing.

'What's up?' asked her mum.

'We're not going now. Claire called off.'

'Oh, when? I didn't hear the phone go.'

'No, I rang her to remind her about something and she said she couldn't make it. We're going next week instead.' Maybe if she said it, it would come true.

Her mum looked at her strangely and said, 'Oh, that's a shame. Bit late notice! Well, never mind, at least you're going next week. Not the end of the world!'

Not the end of the world! Daisy was dying. She moped on her bed for the rest of the weekend, listening to music – choosing the most depressing songs she could find. She'd staked everything on the camping trip; it had been the only thing keeping her going all week, and made not seeing Jack in the mornings just about bearable. If she'd known this was going to happen, she'd at least have caught the same bus into town as him one day. As it was, they were screwed for the whole weekend. Monday couldn't come soon enough.

*****

Jack felt a little apprehensive when he caught the bus on Monday morning. Any closeness that he and Daisy had developed – any progress they had made – seemed to count for nothing. It had been a week since they'd seen each other, but it felt more like a month. At first they could barely look at each other, both feeling shy and awkward. It was as if the day they'd spent together had never happened.

And then Daisy noticed Jack's black eye. By now it was an unpleasant, faded, brown colour with a yellowish tinge round the edges – as if someone had drawn it with a felt tip pen. She gasped. 'Oh my God, Jack, what happened to your eye?' He'd almost forgotten about it; it was no big deal anymore, old news – especially since the swelling had gone down. But now she'd noticed it, he felt self-conscious again.

To his surprise, Daisy placed her cool hand on his face, turning it towards her. She inspected the bruise closely as her scent came off her in waves. God, he'd missed that smell – he'd missed it so much. Tenderly, she put her hand up to touch his eye. Jesus, thought Jack, I could get used to this; perhaps I should get black eyes more often.

'Please tell me this isn't why you couldn't come camping!' she said. Jack shrugged. 'It is, isn't it? Oh God! Did he do this to you?' Again Jack didn't say anything. 'He did, didn't he?' She put her hand to her mouth. 'The bastard! You ought to report him!'

'It's nothing, really,' he replied, not wanting a song and dance made out of it – certainly not on the bus.

'It's not nothing!'

'Daisy, please keep your voice down,' he pleaded.

She carried on regardless, unable to help herself, albeit at a slightly lower volume. 'It's child abuse is what it is, and if *you* don't report him I will! I mean, the phone's one thing – but this! What did your mum say?'

This was the first time Daisy had asked about, or even mentioned, his mother, and he didn't know what to say. He would have to tell her eventually, but this just wasn't the right moment; he didn't want the brief time they had together to be taken up with such a sombre subject. So instead he lied, and hated himself for it.

'Nothing really.'

'*Nothing!*' she cried, as Jack shot her another look. 'What sort of a mother is that? Who stands by while her son gets beaten by his dad?' This hurt Jack more than she could have imagined. His mother wasn't there to defend herself – she was an unknown entity, an enigma; something that was hidden away, deep inside.

'Please, Daisy, can we just drop it?' She sat back with her arms folded, staring straight ahead. It was hard for her to let it go, and Jack recognised this. He was always surprised at the feistiness that could spring up out of her. Perhaps it wasn't ideal on the bus, but he couldn't help but love her all the more for it; he wished he could be more like her. She would always stick up for herself and fight her corner; it was an inspiration to him.

'I just don't like bullies, that's all!' she said, which seemed to draw the matter to an end.

Keen to change the subject, and also a little curious, Jack asked, 'What did you tell your parents ... you know, about not going camping?'

'Oh, I just said Claire couldn't make it. It *was* a bit dodgy, though, what with it being the last minute. *And* the fact she hadn't even rung up!'

'Who's Claire?'

'My friend from college.'

'You didn't tell her about me, did you?' said Jack, sitting up in his seat.

'No, I just used her as an excuse! I hadn't even seen her all week – so don't flatter yourself! What's the big deal anyway?'

'Nothing,' he said, sitting back.

After a pause, Daisy said, 'I *did* tell my mum we were going next Friday instead.' She looked across at him coyly.

'Who? Us?' he said in alarm.

'No! Me and Claire, silly. Why are you so jumpy?'

'I'm not,' Jack said. Daisy put it down to the black eye and his father, who really did seem to put the fear of God into him.

'So, what do you think? Do you reckon you'll be able to

go this Friday?' She felt like a dog with a bone, doing all the chasing again.

'Erm, I'm not sure. He's not letting me out at all at the minute.'

'Oh … so you're grounded then. For how long?' she said, disappointed.

'What's grounded?'

'It means you're not allowed out.' Was he being serious?

'Oh, right. Well, I don't know. Till he says so, I suppose; but it can't be much longer – it's already been over a week.'

'Well, I guess we've got no choice but to play it by ear,' sighed Daisy – still hopeful.

'Suppose so,' replied Jack, not knowing what that meant either.

They spent the rest of the week getting to know each other again, but even more so. Nothing too deep; there was a limit to what you could talk about on a crowded bus with other people listening in. Daisy rattled on endlessly about music, whilst Jack listened, enthralled. It was always about music with her – it was her whole world; she'd been mad on it from the age of six or seven.

Daisy's father had been a big influence on her choice of artists, but over the years she'd gradually developed her own tastes. In the last few months alone, her world had been rocked by a trio of life-changing albums. The Stone Roses' debut album had been released in March; a mixture of The Byrds' jangly guitars, Simon and Garfunkel harmonies and contemporary indie cool. It was like pure sunshine dripping out of the speakers, and had been the soundtrack of her spring. This had been closely followed by the Pixies' *Doolittle* album in April; she'd never heard anything like it before. To top things off, The Cure's majestic masterpiece *Disintegration* had been released in May. This stunning trio had been more than enough to keep her occupied, and in a world of her own, these past few months.

*****

As the week went on, their expectations grew. Daisy was always keen to ask Jack how things were going at home. Things had settled back to normal, or what counted as normal. Jack had kept his head down (he still hadn't been out) and just got on with his work. Knowing he was desperate to go out on Friday night, he'd been a paragon of obedience – it was like earning brownie points from his tormentor. Jack had an agenda, though, and on Wednesday evening he thought he would test the water.

After dinner, he grabbed a couple of bottles of cider, popped them in his rucksack and loitered by the back door. He still refused to ask if he could go out; he was too proud for that, even he had his limits. His sister, however, noticing his intention, took the initiative for him. She still felt guilty, and if anyone was going to get shouted at she would rather it was her.

She looked over from the sink and said, 'Father?' He looked up from his cider, wondering why she was bothering him. Anne gestured towards Jack. He considered for a moment, then grunted his assent. 'Don't go far, though!' he barked. Jack slipped out, not needing to be told twice.

He ran up the lane, punching the air with joy, feeling as if he'd been let out of prison. He couldn't wait to tell Daisy the next day.

CHAPTER 14

Camping

By the time Friday evening rolled around, Jack's father seemed to be descending into one of his periods of drunkenness, which was good news. It meant that, for the time being, Jack was able to slip under the radar again – or at least stay on the periphery of it.

Yes, the old man was satisfied that he'd taught the boy a lesson – thus underestimating his tenacity and latent Machiavellianism, both of which had surprised Jack himself. Earlier that day, he had thrown caution to the wind and confirmed to Daisy (much to her glee) that he would be going camping with her that evening. He still had her parting words ringing in his ears: 'You'd better not let me down again, buster!'

It was with this warning in mind that he had no choice but to draw his unwitting sister into his plans. On returning home from work, he beckoned her into his bedroom before dinner, whilst their father was still watching telly. This was highly unusual, and Anne couldn't imagine what he wanted. When he told her what he was planning to do, she turned pale and, at first, refused point blank to have anything to do with it.

She told him he must be mad, and to think of the consequences should their father find out – for both their sakes. She said that he'd got a nerve involving her, and asked how he could spring something like this on her at such short notice. Jack's guilt at making her complicit was far outweighed by his need to see Daisy, and he pleaded with Anne to help him. She could see how desperate he was, and the hangdog look on his face – together with the remnants of his black eye – eventually swayed her. 'I just hope she's worth it,' she said.

Jack sat at the dinner table, fidgeting and restless because he hadn't had a drink all day. He was as jumpy as a jar of crickets, which made Anne even more nervous; she kept flicking her eyes from him to her father. When it was over, Jack went straight down to the cellar to grab a couple of bottles of cider. This was normal behaviour and a normal evening's supply, but what his father didn't know was that Jack had been stockpiling them all week. He'd not allowed himself more than two bottles a day. It had practically killed him.

Once in his room, he reached under his bed and pulled out six more bottles, giving him eight in total. He hoped it would be enough – he daren't take any more out; his rucksack would be bursting at the seams.

After his workout routine, Jack sprayed himself with as much deodorant as he dared and then dressed, putting on his favourite check shirt. Next, he downed his first cider of the day (practically in one) and it went straight to his head – good; that was the idea. The time had come, and he looked at the window, hoping to God his sister wouldn't forget. He didn't know why he hadn't thought of leaving the window open before – he'd never had anyone to sneak off and be with; that was probably why.

The cider sloshed in his stomach as he headed down the corridor. He hoped he hadn't overdone it – drinking it so quickly on top of exercise. The final hurdle was to get out the front door with his full rucksack without his father noticing.

Fortunately he was already back in the lounge watching telly – too loudly as usual. Jack tiptoed past, trying not to make the floorboards creak.

He hurried through the parlour to the kitchen, where his sister was pretending to wash up. She glanced over at Jack, looking more terrified than he did. She'd been going over the plan in her head: ply her father with as much cider as she could, but make sure he still makes it to bed, lock up as normal (pretending Jack's already home), then open the bedroom window once he'd gone to sleep; simple. Simple, that is, unless she couldn't get him to bed, simple, that is, unless he asked if Jack was back, or, even worse, decided to check up on him. In sixteen years he'd never done that; even so, she shuddered to think of the consequences if he did.

Anne dried her hands on her apron, taken aback as she was so often these days at how he was growing up. 'You stink, Jack,' she warned him – meaning he had put on too much deodorant again.

'You won't forget, will you?' he said, his voice shaking with nerves. She looked at him without answering. How could she forget? This was as dangerous for her as it was for him. They stood there awkwardly, not knowing what to say. Jack noticed a strange look on his sister's face, as if she was going to cry. There was fear there, no question, but something else as well. Suddenly, and to Jack's surprise, she hugged him fiercely, hissing in his ear, 'Take care.' After all the years of longing for maternal arms around him and a benevolent bosom to rest his head on, he didn't know what to do – so he just stood there, his arms pinned against his sides.

She let go again almost as abruptly, embarrassed. 'You too,' was all he could manage to say. And he gave her a purposeful look, pitying the night she had ahead of her, and mindful of what he was asking of her.

Anne opened the door and let Jack out. She felt as she had done on that first day he'd gone to work – it seemed like another big step; he would be going further afield, broadening his horizons and forging relationships. She closed the door behind him, leaning against it for a while, breathing heavily.

At last he was out in the open, beneath the brilliant, evening sunshine; the culmination of almost two weeks of planning. The scene was set – everything was perfect. Jack crossed the lane and entered the meadow, where the crickets chirped around his feet, then headed towards the spinney. Once out of sight, he would pass straight through it, before walking to the crossroads.

He swung his rucksack off his back and pulled out a bottle to enjoy on the way. As he walked, and the farther he got from the house, the more relaxed and happier he felt. And the more he drank, the more he thought that tonight could actually be *the* night when he'd finally get to kiss Daisy – something that had been constantly playing on his mind. Yes, that would be his goal – to kiss her!

Jack popped out onto the main road at the bridge over the brook and headed down the lay-by. As he rounded the corner near the pub, he saw Daisy already at the crossroads. She was standing with a huge, camping-style rucksack at her feet. When she heard a familiar clinking from behind, she turned and waved. Jack waved back. Why did he always appear from an unexpected direction? Daisy wondered.

She walked towards him, struggling with the rucksack. He took it from her, and again his chivalry didn't go unnoticed. The rucksack had a metal frame attached to it with a rolled-up sleeping bag tucked into it, and all manner of bits and pieces hanging off it.

Jack pulled his own rucksack off his back. It looked pathetic in comparison. There was nothing in it except cider, a solitary tin of baked beans and a toothbrush; it hadn't occurred to him to bring anything else. As if reading his mind, Daisy said, 'Don't worry, I've brought everything but the kitchen sink! My mum wanted to drop me off when she saw what I was taking and I nearly died. I think she thought I was going for the weekend or something and I had to talk her out of it. Can you imagine?' And she laughed that easy laugh of hers.

Jack didn't think he had ever seen her looking so alluring – and that was saying something. She was wearing a blue-green lumberjack shirt, similar to his, over a white vest, and her trademark faded blue jeans. Her hair was tied back and her lips looked even redder, even fuller than usual – or was it his imagination? God, he wanted to kiss her. Easy, boy, easy, he told himself, you've got all night! He watched as she hoisted his rucksack onto her back, when suddenly she let out a groan. 'Oh shit! Oh shit, oh shit, oh shit!'

'What?' said Jack, thinking something terrible had happened, but also finding it amusing to hear a girl swear like that.

'You know what I've forgotten?'

'What?' he asked, perplexed.

'The most important thing! Well ... after matches and a tent, I suppose. *The tape player!*'

'Oh!'

'I can't believe it! How could I forget it!' She had been *so* looking forward to listening to music later, and had packed some special tapes and everything. 'Oh well,' she sighed. 'It's too late to go back now.' She looked so gutted that Jack was worried it was going to ruin their evening.

He tried to get the giant rucksack onto his back, but struggled as the straps were too tight. 'Here, let me help,' she said, and came over to stand in front of him. Her face was inches from his as she adjusted the straps. Now! thought Jack.

Do it now! But he froze; he just couldn't. She patted the straps and said, 'Right, are we set then?' Back to her normal self.

'Nearly,' he replied. 'Wait a minute!' And he turned her around so he could get a bottle of cider out of his bag. 'Now we are!' He cracked open the bottle, taking a swig as they set off.

They headed east away from the crossroads, following a sign that said 'Wysall 2½ miles'. As they passed the Red Lion, they glanced at each other and shared a smile, remembering their afternoon there. Soon they were heading down a winding country lane, banked on both sides by ditches and low hedges that afforded views of open fields.

Daisy set off at quite a purposeful pace as if she was on some sort of Girl Guide hiking expedition. Jack cut a comical figure struggling to keep up. He felt like Saucepan Man out of *The Folk of The Faraway Tree* as he rattled along. After a while he slowed to his own pace, wanting to enjoy the scenery around him. He swigged from his cider as he walked, trying to ignore the heavy pack on his back.

It was a perfect summer's evening; a veritable symphony of sights, smells and sounds. From somewhere in the distance a tractor droned and insects buzzed busily in the hedgerows. The sun was a ball of butter in the sky, dripping over the gently sloping fields of rapeseed and corn. The rape fields were mottled now. Most of their vivid yellow flowers had turned to seed and given way to green, as though a giant paint roller had run out of paint. They were still exuding their pungent, heady bouquet, though, carried on a warm breeze across the lane. Jack imbibed it indulgently. God, he felt good – the troubles of home clean forgotten. He felt ebullient, as if a giddy bubble of happiness was building up inside him in anticipation of the evening ahead; if he wasn't careful, it would burst out of his mouth and he would shout hysterically in sheer abandonment.

Because he'd been dawdling Daisy was already quite a way ahead, and he quickened his pace to catch her up. If only it wasn't for this damn pack. Jesus, what had she put in it? He was too proud to shout to her to wait, so he gritted his teeth and soldiered on. He tried to find something to concentrate on, and his eyes were drawn to the comely curves of Daisy's denim-clad bum. It seemed to oscillate to a tune of its own and he tried to look away, aware that he was staring, but his eyes kept getting pulled back against his will – as if it was a magnet.

He couldn't take it any longer and jogged to catch up with her. Daisy noticed his reddened face, and realised she'd been walking too fast. It was a habit she'd got into from her camping expeditions with her dad – they always marched quickly as if they were soldiers: 'Hup-two! Hup-two!' It crossed her mind that they probably wouldn't be doing that anymore.

After about fifteen minutes they passed the first house they had seen so far. There had been no cars either. 'How much further is it?' Jack asked, breathing hard.

'Oh not far now.' There was colour in her cheeks too. 'About half a mile or so – there's three woods close together. The first one, if you can call it a wood, is just coming up on your left.' She pointed to it. 'But it's more of a spinney really, like the one near your house. The trees are too sparse in there and too widely spaced for camping – you certainly couldn't light a fire. The next one is the one we're camping in. It's a lot bigger – denser and darker.'

She made it sound appealing, but Jack was fearful at the prospect of lighting a fire, especially in a wood. What if the wood caught fire? He kept his reservations to himself; he didn't want to sound like a scaredy-cat. 'The next one's a bit too far and too close to a farmhouse anyway; these are private woods, remember, not like Bunny Wood. You're not *actually* supposed to be there.' This gave Jack another flutter of trepidation; it conjured up images of angry, red-faced farmers with shotguns and wild dogs lying in wait for them.

They carried on walking, and soon came across a gated lane, guarded by a cattle grid. It led up to the first wood, which sat on the horizon. Jack offered Daisy what was left of his cider. 'No thanks, I'll dehydrate. I've got some water in my rucksack.' Jack wondered as he finished the rest of it if she'd be drinking water all night; he hoped not. It somehow made him feel closer to her when she drank; he wanted her to feel how he felt. 'Anyway, I'm not drinking that stuff again; I've brought my own for later!' she laughed.

Before long their chosen wood appeared, luscious but foreboding, across several fields. Jack imagined the secret coolness beneath that thick canopy. It still looked a bit of a trek away, but at least it was a safe distance from the road or any houses. There was a gate and cattle grid, as before, but no real lane; so much the better. They climbed over the gate, Daisy going first and negotiating it with ease. She touched down on the other side and stood with her feet apart on the cattle grid.

Jack went over next, but not quite so easily – the weight and bulk of the rucksack almost carrying him over in one go. Daisy giggled and put a hot, sticky palm on his arm to steady him. She held onto him as they traversed the cattle grid. He loved every minute of it.

They were on the edge of a large cornfield, surrounded by a high hedge. Close up, the corn was not so straw coloured. It was greener and less ripe, but still smelt dry. Before going any further, they paused whilst Daisy took off her shirt; she was already too hot. Jack followed suit, but to do so he had to take off the heavy pack first. He did so with great relief as, despite the padded straps, it was beginning to dig into his arms and shoulders.

As she went to tie her shirt around her waist, Jack couldn't help but notice the way her vest was tucked tightly into her jeans, accentuating her chest, and he fumbled as he tied his own shirt. Jesus, why did he feel so guilty all of a sudden? Unbeknown to Jack, Daisy did her own bit of checking out. Jack was also wearing a vest; it was the first time she had seen him in one, and she liked what she saw. He was wiry – slim, with broad shoulders, a flat stomach and well-defined arms, a result of chopping endless logs since he was young; she noticed the way the veins in them stood out compared to hers.

They made their way around the edge of the cornfield. It was tiring work on the hard, uneven ground and it was also dusty and hot; the high hedge had cut out the breeze. The evening sun continued to beat down on them and they couldn't wait to get inside the wood. After about ten minutes they got to the other side of the field, where they were then met with a barbed-wire fence. That wasn't their biggest problem: between them and the wood, was a field of giant beanstalks – taller than a man – with pale green pods bursting with mottled black beans. Daisy gasped. It must have been planted since the previous summer. There was no way around; the field was huge and banked on both sides by high hedges.

'Is there no other way?' asked Jack.

'No, and even if there was it would take about four times as long – the wood's on the other side!'

Jack took the pack off his back again and lifted it over the barbed wire fence, straining as he put it down. Daisy did the same with hers. He held the barbed wire apart for her so she could get through. As she did so, some of her hair got tangled and she yelped. Jack had to free it for her, handling the tresses as if they were precious spun gold. Daisy held the fence apart for him in turn, and he got a scratch on his shoulder for his troubles. Next they were faced with the beanstalks, which looked even taller close up, and seemed to be waiting for them in a sinister manner.

Despite his uncertainty, Jack went first as he thought it was his duty. He pushed aside the tall stalks, carefully at first, trying his best not to damage them. At the same time he tried to carve a path for Daisy to follow. It was like exploring a jungle, but instead of being exciting, it was just unpleasant. It was hot, humid and dark, and the coarse stalks scratched at him. They went on forever, and as he had feared, it wasn't long before the old claustrophobic feelings began to gnaw away at him. He tried to ignore them, but after a while he wasn't even sure if he was going in the right direction; if you looked to the side for even a second it became disorientating.

For Daisy's sake he was trying not to panic – at least he could still hear her behind him. He pressed on more urgently, not caring if he damaged the crops anymore, just wanting to get the hell out of there. Visions filled his head of being found in there days later, a gibbering wreck, and he thrashed forward for what felt like an eternity. The dust coming off the stalks was going up his nose and down his throat. And just when he thought he was going to lose it entirely, the field began to thin out and it became noticeably lighter. They stumbled, crashing out of the beanstalks like two wild animals into the daylight on the other side.

Jack threw off the rucksack and bent over with his hands on his knees. He was aware of Daisy close to him doing exactly the same – and for a few moments there was no sound but their heavy breathing.

Then Daisy burst out laughing.

'What?' said Jack.

'Your face! You've got this black powder all over it from the beanstalks!' She barely had any on her – just a bit on her arms and shoulders. 'Here, wait a minute,' she said, sensing his discomfort, and started unzipping the rucksack.

She pulled out a flannel, along with a large bottle of water, which she had stowed at the top of the rucksack – she really *had* thought of everything. She took a long swig from the bottle before offering it to Jack. For once water was more appealing than cider. He took a swig himself before passing it back.

She dampened the flannel with the water, told him to close his eyes, then proceeded to wipe his face gently, but with enough roughness to clean it. She wiped his forehead, his eyelids (taking extra care around his bruised eye), his cheeks and his chin; he surrendered to the firmness of her hand. It took him back to his childhood, and how Anne used to do exactly the same thing to him at bath time. 'There!' she said, and he opened his eyes.

Her large doe eyes were looking directly into his. Normally he looked away if their eyes met, but this time he held her gaze – just for a second or two – and something passed between them. He could see the fine dust that had settled on *her* face too – and her lips, her inviting lips. Perhaps this was it, the moment he'd been waiting for. He yearned for it; his beating heart was standing up on its hind legs, fists wrapped around the bars of its cage, throwing itself against the sides and clamouring for it. She wanted it too, but wanted him to make the first move … but he didn't; he couldn't; he didn't know how. And the moment was gone.

Daisy turned, slightly disappointed and sensing a missed opportunity. She leant against a fence post, drank from the bottle again, then tipped some of the water over her forehead to try and rinse away some of the grime. Jack watched as it cascaded down her face, throat and chest, dampening her vest and making it cling to the swell of her bosom. His eyes travelled down lower, searching, unable to help himself. He noticed her belt buckle and the way it gathered her jeans, forming a perfect V-shape between her legs. He wanted to touch her there. Oh God! What was coming over him? It was ever since he'd had that bloody dream!

He was disgusted at himself; ashamed at the way he was taking pleasure in looking at her, and he tore his gaze away. He was no better than those filthy animals at the pub or the crowd of people in his dream.

'More?' she said, offering him the bottle of water again.

'No, I'm fine thanks,' he replied. They stood side by side then and turned together, as if noticing the wood for the first time.

There was nothing now but a wooden fence and a ditch in between them and their destination. As Jack surveyed the scene, he fully expected the familiar black spot to be in his vision, but to his surprise it wasn't there. The wood stretched away to their left and right, and from this distance it looked dark inside, secret and inviting. They could make out the gnarls and twists of the faded brown tree trunks nearest to them, but the further they tried to see into the wood the closer together the trees got, until they all blended into one mass. Deep inside, there were no shafts of sunlight penetrating the overhead canopy at all.

After climbing over the final fence, they stood at the ditch. 'Well, here goes,' said Jack, and he jumped it easily in one go. Daisy then passed him the rucksacks, the large one second and with some effort, then made to jump the ditch herself. She only just made it – and if Jack hadn't shot his hand out to catch her she would have tumbled on her backside with her legs in the air.

'Phew! Thanks! That would have been embarrassing!' she said, blushing, which somehow made her more tangible to Jack – less of an enigma.

They donned their packs again and then they were in the wood, Daisy leading the way. It was like entering a totally different world; going from a hot, bright room into a cool, dark one. The air smelt sweetly aromatic of dry bark, mixed in with the musty smell of damp earth, protected under a carpet of leaves. This was a proper wild wood. There were no footpaths and the terrain was more difficult to negotiate, especially with a giant rucksack on your back. They heard the snap and crackle of every twig and leaf, the creaking of the trees, every bird tweet. The distant drone of the tractor was long gone.

At first they jumped at every noise, feeling like interlopers. Jack broke the silence first. 'Where are we going to camp?' he whispered.

'Further in on the other side, away from the road because of the fire.'

'OK.'

'Jack?'

'What?'

'Why are we whispering?' They burst out laughing.

'Who owns these woods anyway?' Jack asked as he ducked under a large branch.

'A farmer from Ruddington, I think, but someone local looks after them for him.'

Jack followed Daisy, both of them hunched over, as she held branches back for him. 'We're looking for a clear patch of ground,' she said over her shoulder, 'but with lots of leaves above to hide most of the smoke – sort of like a cave.'

From time to time he looked behind him as they made their way through the wood. It had a different personality to Bunny Wood, which was hard to explain. The trees appeared to close up behind them, enveloping them in their bewitching bosom. He liked its secrecy; it was as if it was theirs and no one else's – no one was going to come strolling through at any minute with a dog.

Daisy seemed to know the wood well. It made Jack wonder how many times she had been there … and with whom. That old green-eyed monster briefly reared its ugly head at the thought of her sharing it with someone else – maybe with other boys. It was a black thought, and he couldn't help asking, 'So, how many times have you camped here?'

'Oh, three or four times, I suppose – twice with my dad and a couple of times with friends.' She didn't volunteer any more information, leaving Jack to ponder. 'I think we're nearly there,' she said, veering abruptly off to the left. 'Yes, this is it!' And sure enough there was a small clearing.

The ground was already flattened and it looked as if someone had made a fire there not that long ago. 'Probably kids from the village,' said Daisy. 'It saves us a job.'

Jack put the rucksack down and stretched his aching back.

As they sat down Jack reached for a bottle of cider, prompting Daisy to pull out some of her own. He was curious to see what she'd brought; it was a four-pack of Strongbow, and he watched as she popped her first can open. They drank together, surveying the surrounding wood in silence, before smiling at each other nervously.

'Right! What time is it?' said Daisy, looking at a small plastic watch hidden amongst her bracelets. 'God, it's eight o'clock already!' It seemed much later; the light in the wood – or lack of it – was deceptive. 'OK, we'd better get a move on. We'll put up the tent whilst it's still light, and then we'd better make the fire – but we won't light it till later 'cause of the smoke – we'll have to collect a load of wood first anyway. Then we can make something to eat.' Jack smiled as he listened to her; he was already feeling woozy from the cider.

Daisy started to unpack her rucksack. Jack was intrigued by

what else she'd got stowed in there. First she pulled out a torch, then a large, metal grill thing, then another bottle of water, then a rubber-headed mallet. No wonder it weighed so much, he thought, as he continued to watch. There were pots, pans, food parcels and tins – even plastic plates and cutlery. Finally she found what she was looking for – a tight, green bag with a drawstring. 'Tent!' she said, placing it next to her.

They flattened a large area of ground, removing as many twigs and stones as possible. It was a good job Daisy knew what she was doing as Jack wouldn't have known where to begin, what with all the zips, flaps, drawstrings and pegs. He just did what he was told, holding the tent this way and that when instructed. 'Sorry, am I being too bossy?' she asked at one point, pausing for a sip of cider.

'No,' he replied, secretly enjoying it.

When it was done, it was satisfying for Jack to see the sturdy finished article. He popped his head inside to take a look. The tent had that strange stale smell that all tents have, and was bigger than he had imagined. It gave him an odd feeling to think that they would be sleeping in there together.

'Right, wood next. What me and Dad normally do is make three piles. I get bunches of dry twigs for kindling to get it going and medium-sized ones to feed it with, while he goes and gets the bigger logs for later – so you can be Dad!'

'Righto, boss!' replied Jack, and he saluted her; he was having the time of his life. He threw his bottle onto the rucksack and, losing his inhibitions, set off through the wood making Tarzan noises. Behind him he could hear Daisy giggling as she set off in a different direction. It pleased him to have made her laugh.

Jack didn't stray too far at first as he didn't want to lose his bearings in the unfamiliar wood. He searched the ground for dead, dry logs, knowing from the incinerator at home that green ones were no good. He soon returned with a good armful at the same time as Daisy, whose face was flushed from the work. They smiled at each other before setting off again. This time he ventured further as it was becoming harder to find suitable logs in the dwindling light. Along the way, he made mental notes of certain vantage points so that he didn't get lost. When he returned again, Daisy wasn't there; and he missed her already. He then set off for the third time, gaining confidence and straying even further from camp. He went so far that he could see the edge of the wood: it looked like broad daylight out there in comparison, even though it was nearly sunset.

Back at base, Daisy was trying to keep herself busy by tying strips of newspaper into knots and stacking them in a circular pile. She hated being on her own like this – the times when her dad disappeared to collect logs. She always got this irrational fear of being alone in the wood, and chided herself for being such a chicken. Yet she would torture herself further, letting her imagination run away with her. This she did now, looking about her and seeing how the dark had crept in; you couldn't see further than ten feet away. She needed to pee. Where was Jack? He'd been gone for ages. Why was he taking so long? What if he'd got lost?

She heard a branch snap off to her right and it made her jump. 'Jack? Is that you?' she called. Perhaps he was playing a trick on her. But she instantly quashed this thought; he wasn't like that, he was too kind. So what was that noise? And where was the bloody torch? Suddenly she heard a crashing sound close by, and stood startled, frozen in fear. She grabbed a large log in panic just as Jack came bursting back into the clearing. He was clutching what looked like the whole forest in his arms – enough to last for a week.

Daisy was so relieved to see him that she dropped the log

she was holding and rushed over to give him a big hug, which made him drop all the branches at their feet in surprise.

She felt warm and small, almost childlike, as her chest heaved against his. He had never known such a feeling – he felt like her protector. He couldn't believe how much she could change; she was like a chameleon – forever shifting and changing colour. One minute she was fiery, confident and beguiling, the next she was a tomboy, a mate and companion. Now she was a lost little girl – fragile and clinging.

Much to Jack's dismay, she let go; he could have stayed like that forever. 'Sorry … I thought you'd got lost!' she said, feeling foolish at the state she'd got herself into. Look at me, she thought; the experienced camper reduced to a silly girl the minute I'm left alone. She was still brooding as they began to build the fire. Jack continued to think about how Daisy's body had felt when it was pressed against him; so warm and helpless.

When they'd built a good wigwam of smaller twigs, Daisy said, 'I think we'd better light this, we won't be able to see soon.' She shone the torch into the rucksack till she found some matches. 'Right, do you want to do the honours?'

'No, no. You do it.' Jack wasn't allowed matches and didn't trust himself with them. He was nervous about the fire being lit at all. But Daisy insisted.

'No, you do it, I've done it loads of times… Besides, I've got some drinking to do!' And she sat cross-legged in mock stubbornness as she cracked open another can of cider.

Not wanting to chicken out in front of her, Jack hunched over the fire and tentatively struck a match. The sudden flare in the darkness hurt both their eyes and left an image on them when they looked away. 'Aah, I love the smell of matches,' said Daisy. 'I used to light them just so I could smell them.' Jack shielded the match with a shaking hand and touched it to the splayed, fanned end of a newspaper stick. As it began to take flame he felt a mixture of fear and exhilaration. Under Daisy's instruction, he took more newspaper, lit it, then used it to light different points around the fire. The flames quickly took hold, lighting up the clearing. At first it looked as if the fire wouldn't spread to the twigs, but Daisy stepped in to lend a hand, and slowly but surely they started to crackle.

Between them, they placed the medium-sized branches on, trying not to burn their hands in the process. Soon they had a huge, orange pyramid of flame. 'God, I hope it doesn't carry on like this!' Jack cried, unable to hide his alarm.

'Don't worry. It'll die down in a minute when we put the bigger logs on,' said Daisy.

And she was right. They carefully put on some larger logs, which flattened the fire, creating a better surface to cook on. They moved back a couple of feet as the fire got hotter, reddening their arms and faces. 'A real team effort!' said Daisy. They clinked their can and bottle together.

Jack lay propped on one elbow – enjoying the fire's glow and prodding it occasionally with a stick. He felt dreamy, drunk and blissfully happy as he watched Daisy busying herself with their meal. He so wanted to kiss her, and remembered the goal he'd set himself – perhaps if he could get a bit more drunk he'd have the courage. She pulled out a can opener and a tin of baked beans which she passed to him to open. He was glad to help. Then she produced a plastic tub that contained four fat sausages, a knob of butter (still in its foil), and half a loaf of sliced bread. Jack grinned as he opened the beans, thinking how the rucksack seemed to be bottomless; it was like Doctor Who's Tardis!

'What are you laughing at?' asked Daisy, noticing his mirth.

'Nothing. I just can't believe the amount of stuff you've brought.'

'Oh, there's more yet!' As well as the plastic plates and cutlery, there were also two matching plastic mugs and some teabags and biscuits. 'For tea in the morning,' she said, holding them up. Next she pulled out some metal tongs for turning the food over with, then some soap, a toothbrush and toothpaste, a small towel and lastly some loo roll. Jack found it absolutely hysterical. 'That reminds me,' she said. 'I really do need to go for a pee.'

This was a new quandary for Jack – he was always a bit embarrassed around toilet habits at the best of times, never mind in front of Daisy. What if he needed a crap? This was a terrifying thought, but Daisy clearly didn't seem embarrassed at all. Perhaps it was the cider – she was on her third can. As if to confirm this, she staggered as she got up and wandered off with the loo roll, saying, 'Back in a minute. And no peeking either!' The image of her undoing her jeans and pulling down her knickers, out there in the darkness, suddenly struck Jack as erotic. What's wrong with me? he thought as he cracked open another bottle.

When she returned, Daisy made a point of washing her hands before handing Jack the grill; a rectangular, metal stand with four foldaway legs. He placed it carefully over the fire, and Daisy put the pan of beans and the sausages on it. 'Can you keep an eye on the sausages, please? Or the bangers as Dad would call them!' And she passed him the tongs. From somewhere, Lord knows where, she produced a wooden spoon, and instructed Jack to stir the beans so they wouldn't catch. She took another swig of cider, and proceeded to butter the bread. Under Jack's watchful eye, the sausages slowly turned black and crispy until Daisy was satisfied they were done. She spooned the beans onto their plates and put the sausages between the buttered bread. 'There you go: sausage sandwich and beans – not bad eh? I hope you're hungry!'

Because it was dark, and because of the alcohol, Jack felt less awkward about eating in front of Daisy, but he still turned away in case he bit the side of his mouth. His hunger soon got the better of him, though; the sandwich tasted too good – salty from the melted butter – and he mopped at his beans enthusiastically.

'Is it OK?' she asked, getting an age-old satisfaction from seeing a man eat.

'Umm,' said Jack, through a mouthful of sandwich. 'I don't suppose you've got any ketchup in your rucksack, have you?' he joked. Daisy gave him a smack, but thought how nice it was to see his true personality coming out. She remembered how shy he'd been at first, barely able to speak.

'Do you want some more bread?'

'No thanks.' He was done – he wanted to leave room for cider.

When they had finished eating they cleared everything up, which Daisy insisted on so that they didn't have to deal with it in the morning. Jack stuck more logs on the fire to stoke it up a bit whilst Daisy rummaged in the pockets of her rucksack again. What now? thought Jack; all he wanted was for her to come and lie next to him. There was one thing on his mind – and that was to kiss her.

To his amazement, she pulled a cigarette packet out – she was full of surprises this evening. He didn't know how to feel about it. 'I didn't know you smoked.'

'Oh, I don't,' she replied. 'Only when I'm camping: it's a tradition. Look, I've only got two – one for me and one for you!' She showed him the pack. 'It's my dad's fault. After supper when we were camping, the first thing he would do was light a cigarette and make a big deal out of it, saying how good it tastes after a meal and all that. Anyway, one time when I was about fourteen, he let me have a puff, and then again the next year too. Then when I was sixteen, he let me have one for myself. It's awful really, I know. My mum would go absolutely spare if she knew, so it's our little secret. Now I just sort of carry on the tradition when *I* go camping.'

She took the two cigarettes out of the packet and offered one to him. He'd never seen a cigarette close up and didn't trust them. 'Erm, no thanks. I'd better not.' He was worried he'd make an idiot out of himself and start coughing. And what if he hated it? 'I'll try a bit of yours,' he suggested, not wanting to appear boring.

Daisy put the cigarette between her lips, then struck a match and lit it. The end glowed orange as she took a drag, exhaling the smoke and shaking the match out with her other hand – effortlessly cool. Jack watched, fascinated. 'God, what I'd give for some music now!' she said as she offered him the cigarette. He took it from her, not knowing what to do with it and feeling foolish; he couldn't look cool like her. He took a quick, trial puff and the smoke caught in his throat. Just as he'd dreaded, it made him cough and splutter. He passed it back, decidedly un-impressed.

Daisy settled down next to Jack so their heads were near each other. The fire was at its best now. They talked and drank, and talked and drank some more. Daisy spoke of her past, of growing up and of college, and Jack asked after her dad and how he was doing – feeling rude not to have done so earlier. Apparently he was doing OK – taking it easy. Jack listened, captivated, as she talked, his eyes fixed on her mouth as she spoke. She was so close he could almost feel her breath, and he waited for the right moment to stretch over and put his lips on hers. He kept playing the scene over. Should he do it quickly or slowly? Should he ask her first or surprise her? His stomach churned just thinking about it.

Soon Jack was doing plenty of talking himself; he'd never talked so much in his life. He spoke of America, his dream of going to live there, and of his dream house made of white clapboard, with a veranda and porch swing. It sounded more sincere to Daisy this time, as though he actually meant it, which confused her – how could he possibly think of going to America? She steered the conversation to a less serious topic by proposing a game of 'Confessions' – something she had done when she'd been camping with kids from school. She had an ulterior motive: there was something she'd wanted to confess to Jack all evening, and now the alcohol was getting the better of her.

'Go on then, you first!' she said. 'And it's got to be something good, something embarrassing!'

Jack felt she had put him on the spot, and didn't know what to say; his whole life had been an embarrassment. He thought about confessing to the dream he'd had about her, but decided against it. She'd probably think he was some sort of weird pervert. Then he considered revealing that his mum had died when he was little, but that seemed too gloomy – he was enjoying himself too much to change the mood. In the end, he decided to tell her about his secret tin with his map and the large wad of notes, proudly stating how much he had saved.

'Oh, that's boring!' she teased him drunkenly.

'Well, sorry. I don't know,' said Jack; his life *was* boring, except for her. 'You go.'

'Well…' She paused, still not knowing whether she was doing the right thing. She kept hearing Blanche Dubois' voice in her head out of *A Streetcar Named Desire* – something about a woman's charm being fifty per cent illusion. She'd always taken this as meaning not that you should play hard to get, exactly, but that you should try to keep some mystery about you: don't put all your cards on the table. 'You know that day on the bus when I dropped the battery out of my Walkman?' Jack hung on her every word as she stopped to bite her lip, suddenly shy. 'I can't believe I'm telling you this,' she said, shaking her head. 'Well … I sort of did it on purpose.'

'How do you mean?' asked Jack, not quite following.

'I dropped it on purpose, hoping you'd pick it up.' She buried her head in her elbow, cringing.

'Really?' he said, grinning from ear to ear.

'Well, yes. You hadn't picked up my NUS card when I dropped it before, so I tried again.' Oh my God, what am I saying? she thought. It's all coming out now – there's no stopping me; my mouth's like a runaway train! I should never drink. She yawned as if the confession had exhausted her.

Jack turned to lie on his back, watching the smoke from the fire as it drifted up into the darkness. He let this new information sink in. He couldn't believe she'd done those things on purpose. 'What does NUS mean, by the way?' he asked, still looking upwards – he'd always meant to ask her… 'Daisy?' he said, turning towards her. But her eyes were closed and she was breathing deeply; fast asleep. 'Damn it,' he said. He watched her for a while. Bless her, he thought – I love you. Completely overcome with tiredness himself, Jack followed her into an alcohol-induced slumber.

*****

When he awoke in the morning Jack felt cold and stiff. He had no idea why this was, or indeed where he was. He had a dull headache and his mouth was dry – but that was nothing new. He felt a cover, half on, half off him, and tried to pull it back around him for warmth, but it was trapped under something. He opened his eyes and squinted at the bright morning light. The first thing he saw was the remains of the fire, and then the clearing in the wood. It all came back to him. But where was Daisy? He turned around, grimacing as he did so, and there she was behind him, lying under a blue sleeping bag that had been unzipped. All that he could see of her was one outstretched arm and her untied hair, which spilled across it like deep red wine.

He noticed the plastic watch on her wrist, and panicked as reality hit; he was in a wood, miles from home – and it was morning! *Oh my God! What time is it?* And he got up, then walked round so he could see the watch properly. He feared the worst, but thankfully it was still early – only six o'clock. His father never got up before eight at the weekend, but he was still cutting it fine.

They really should have planned this better and brought an alarm clock, he fretted as he paced the clearing. Still, it had been worth the risk. Or had it? Last night's events came back to him, and he couldn't help but feel disappointed – he had never got to kiss her. Here they were, all alone for the whole night, and they had just fallen asleep. When would he get another chance like that? A frown knitted his brow as he kicked a twig into the ashes.

There was a groan from under the sleeping bag. 'Morning. Ooh, my head!'

'Morning,' said Jack, brightening at the sound of Daisy's voice.

She poked her head out. Her eyes were half-closed, and her face was puffy and lined from sleep. 'Oh, don't look at me!' she cried, burying her head back inside. Jack laughed; she still looked beautiful to him. Then she popped her head out again, like a puzzled tortoise, wondering why she was on the other side of the fire. She saw the flattened ground next to her and the unzipped sleeping bag. 'Oh, sorry,' she said, remembering. 'I woke up in the night and needed the loo again – it was freezing and the fire had gone out… I hope you didn't mind.' Didn't mind? thought Jack. He only wished he'd been more aware of it – and he rued another missed opportunity.

'We'd better get packed up,' he said. 'I really need to get back.'

They set about tidying the campsite, making sure they took all their rubbish with them. They did it quickly and in silence, save for Daisy bemoaning the fact they didn't have time to make a cup of tea; she felt parched from the smoke and alcohol. It was another tradition, to have a cup of tea in the morning, but water would have to do today. When it came to dismantling their unused tent, they both gave each other a similar look, as if to say, 'Well, what a waste of time that was.' Once they were done, they washed their hands and faces with cold water and brushed their teeth, before setting off for home.

The bean field was easier to traverse on the way back, as they followed the tunnel they had made through it the previous night; but they did feel a bit guilty about the mild destruction they had left in their wake. Before long they found themselves back on the road, and checked the time on Daisy's watch again. It was just gone seven and Jack still had three-quarters of an hour's walk home. He quickened his pace. Daisy could see the change in him. She could sense the return of his desperation; could see it in his face. She resented the hold his father had over him.

Daisy didn't want the camping trip to end this way: they had barely had a chance to speak a word – she felt as if they had unfinished business. 'What are you doing later?' she asked, trying to keep up.

Jack hadn't thought about later; his mind was firmly on the present and on trying to get home before his father got up. He had planned to stay up all night (last night) and return in the early hours of the morning – not like this. 'I don't know. It depends on what happens when I get back … work probably.'

Daisy looked glum – his *bloody* father again. 'Could you get away for a bit this afternoon? Surely you must get a break at some point.'

'I could try,' he replied, but without much hope.

'Shall we say three o'clock, under the bridge by the brook?'

'OK, I'll try … but I really can't promise.' He didn't want to let her down again, or for her to think he wasn't interested.

'If you don't show, I'll know why,' Daisy said diplomatically; but she couldn't help wondering why it had to be so complicated. Why can't I just ring him up like I would a normal boy and say 'Hi! Are you coming out to play?'

They reached the crossroads and swapped rucksacks. It was half past seven and the pressure was mounting. 'I've really got to dash!' Jack said, giving her one last desperate look before jogging off at an alarming pace. 'Sorry!' he called over his shoulder.

Daisy watched him go. 'Not even a peck on the cheek,' she said with exaggerated pathos to an imaginary audience. 'Good luck!' she shouted. She really pitied him – *her* parents couldn't have been more different.

*****

As Jack neared home, and the hill got steeper, his legs started to burn and his chest stung. For once he stuck to the main road – there wasn't time to go cross country; besides, there weren't any cars about at this time on a Saturday morning. He reached the corner of the lane and slowed to a walk. If the worst comes to the worst, he thought, and my father is already up, I'll just say I went for an early morning walk – he can't prove otherwise, can he?

Jack crept through a gap in the hedge and into the front garden. Keeping low, he headed round the back of the house to his bedroom. He thanked his lucky stars when he saw that his window was still ajar and that the curtains were closed. Quietly, he took the latch off and peered in – half-expecting his father's hand to come out of the darkness and grab him by the throat. His room was empty and undisturbed; his bed was still made too. Seeing everything like this brought home to him the risk he had taken. He climbed inside, threw his rucksack on the floor and sank into bed with his clothes on, utterly exhausted.

CHAPTER 15

A Near Miss

When Jack got back, his sister was at the kitchen table, a lukewarm cup of tea in her hands, gnawing at her nails. She'd barely slept a wink as she'd been on tenterhooks, listening out for the sound of him returning; a feat easier said than done with the cacophonous snoring of her father reverberating around the bungalow.

Sick of lying awake and worrying, she'd got up at around six o'clock and tiptoed down the corridor in a slow-motion game of hopscotch, avoiding the noisiest floorboards. Perhaps she'd dozed off at some point during the night and not heard him come back.

Jack's bed was empty, the window was still ajar and the curtain was fluttering in the breeze. I could wring his neck, she thought, before pulling the door gently closed behind her.

Sitting in the kitchen, she kept her ears open in the vain hope that she would hear him return in time. But all she heard were the hum of the strip light, the whirring of the old fridge and the traitorous ticking of the kitchen clock, which seemed to get louder and louder with every passing minute – as if it was in cahoots with their father: 'Wake up, master, wake up! The sun is up, and look who's not in his bed!'

As the hands crept past seven-thirty, she cursed Jack again for the risk he had taken and the hell he was inviting upon them both. She thought back to the previous night and what she had gone through for him. After plying their father with cider all evening – enough to fell an elephant – she had slipped something extra into the last one. When she was sure he was too far gone to notice, she crumbled one of her sleeping pills (which she only used on those nights when the past came back to haunt her) into his bottle. She watched it sink to the bottom, where it settled with the rest of the sediment – a trait of the naturally cloudy homemade brew.

To her immense relief he drank it undetected, but it had been touch and go for a while, and she thought she'd overdone it when he started to nod off in his chair. In a high state of alarm, she shouted at him and gave him a few whacks of encouragement before shepherding him, stumbling and muttering, to his bed.

It was seven forty-one exactly when she finally heard a noise from Jack's room: not the sound of him climbing through the window that she'd been expecting, but the groan of bedsprings as he settled into his bed. Her heart leapt, as she thought it was her father waking up and getting out of bed. When she realised it was Jack, she said a little prayer, also making a mental note to give him a piece of her mind for cutting it so fine. She briefly considered going straight to his room right there and then: 'You're not having a lie-in if that's what you think!' But then again, their father wasn't up and about yet, so she decided to wait – let him get a bit of sleep; he was probably going to need it.

It was gone nine o'clock before their father got up, and this didn't bode well. The sleeping pill had obviously had more of an effect than she'd intended. When he stumbled into the kitchen, looking dishevelled and with a dull headache, the day went rapidly downhill.

*****

Anne said good morning and brought him a mug of tea as he sat down at the kitchen table. He felt … well, how would you describe it? … woolly. He had a headache, and couldn't understand why he'd slept for so long. He found he couldn't remember going to bed. Even by *his* standards he knew he'd drunk a lot, but he could still remember watching telly and Anne being there. He didn't seem to remember that good-for-nothing boy coming back, mind you. And why wasn't that lazy sod up now? It dawned on him that he'd got a load of furniture to collect for stripping: the tank was already full with doors and the van was full of logs.

He sipped the hot and welcome tea in brooding silence and it began to revitalise him. A nagging suspicion that the wool was being pulled over his eyes began to grow. He thought of that business with the shirt not so long ago, then the bank holiday incident, then the blurriness of last night. It was just a hunch, but he felt that something was going on. He didn't trust the pair of them anymore; not one bit.

He regarded Anne as she put his breakfast in front of him – tinned tomatoes with cheese melted into them, carefully seasoned with salt and black pepper. He picked up his knife and fork to eat, then bent down, took a sniff of the plate and shoved it back across the table in disgust. 'This plate stinks!' he barked. 'It smells like wet dogs!'

Anne scurried over to take the plate away before his breakfast got cold. It was one of his pet hates – when crockery had that dirty, stale egg smell that was sometimes impossible to avoid. Sometimes she washed and rewashed in hot, soapy water, before rinsing then drying with a clean tea towel – but still it came back to haunt her. She brought him another plate, sniffing it herself obsessively before doing so. 'And where's that good-for-nothing boy? Why isn't he up? There's work to do!'

'I'll go and wake him now, Father,' she said, hurrying off down the corridor.

She knocked on Jack's door. 'Jack, wake up, it's gone nine o'clock!' But there was no answer. She tried again, more urgently, beginning to lose her temper herself. She turned the handle and opened the door to his room. A lozenge of light lay slanted across his bed from the gap in the curtains, and his unruly mop of black hair was poking out from under his duvet.

There was movement as he began to stir ... and then the smell hit her – smoke; so strong and acrid it permeated the whole room. She could almost taste it in her mouth: it was as if he'd actually had a campfire in there. She rushed over, shook him awake and pulled back the covers. Jack was still fully dressed as he sat bolt upright in shock; the smell was even worse on his clothes and hair.

'Jack, it stinks of smoke in here!' she hissed. 'Father will smell it. Get your clothes off, now.' She knelt on his bed to open the curtains and windows. The room flooded with light. Jack's face was deathly pale from being woken up so suddenly. 'Go and wash your hair, quickly, and get some new clothes on too. Father wants you – there's work to do. It's late and he's in a foul mood!'

Jack climbed out of bed, and as he shuffled off to the bathroom his sister pulled him back. 'Jack, clothes!' He stripped down to his underpants in front of her, cupping his hands over the front of his too-tight briefs. Anne tutted as if to say, 'God, it's nothing I haven't seen before!' – she *had* raised him from a baby, after all; but she couldn't help but notice that he really was in need of some bigger pants.

She pushed the door closed behind him and proceeded to strip his bed. Jack was washing his hair when there was a loud shout in the corridor. 'What are you two up to?' They both froze – Jack with shampoo dripping into his eyes, stinging them, and Anne with her arms full of washing.

'I'm on the toilet!' yelled Jack – still not happy at being woken up.

'And I'm stripping Jack's bed!' called Anne. Silence...

'I want you up that yard in two minutes flat – or else! Watch that mouth of yours too! And bring me a cup of coffee!'

By the time Jack had towelled his hair dry, Anne had sneaked the incriminating clothes and bed sheets into the washing machine. She also had two mugs of coffee ready – one for Jack and one for their father. Jack would have preferred tea, but he didn't feel in a position to argue. She pushed the mugs into his hands, making eye contact with him only once to gesture towards the door – desperate for him not to antagonise their father anymore. He stepped out into the bright morning sun, wincing like a mole that had burrowed its way into the light.

Carefully, he made his way up the steps to the caustic tank. His father was waiting for him, in his boiler suit, wellies and maroon rubber gloves that reached up to his elbows. This was a familiar routine and one of Jack's most hated jobs. His father used the tank to strip doors and furniture, before restoring them in his workshop. Jack's task was to ensure every last scrap of paint was removed before a final sanding and varnishing. Even though the doors had been soaked, it was still painstaking work that involved scraping, scouring and sanding, and sometimes flakes of paint stuck under his nails, making them bleed.

Placing the coffee well out of the way of the tank, Jack put on a pair of gloves similar to his father's. Together, they reached into the murky depths and Jack braced himself for the smell. The tank was supposed to have a cover on it when it wasn't in use, but half the time his father forgot – or didn't bother. As a result, all sorts of debris fell into it, such as leaves and branches, small creatures too. They were forever dredging birds and rodents – once a stray cat – out of the tank. Anne had cried for days when this happened. Jack secretly thought his father had got a sick satisfaction out of it. Perhaps that was why he never put the cover on unless it rained heavily.

Jack nearly retched as, one by one, they pulled out the submerged doors. His father had to root around for the final one with his pole – a purpose-built tool with a hook on the end of it. Jack could tell by looking at the three doors, dripping blackly, that they could have done with another day in the tank at least. He stared at them miserably, still half-asleep. It was going to take most of the day to clean them up, which made him think of his proposed rendezvous with Daisy.

His father swallowed his rapidly cooling coffee in one go before throwing the dregs onto the floor. He picked up the hose and turned on the tap. The hose hissed, spluttered and juddered into life, and he stood by the first door with it, putting his thumb over the end to increase the pressure. Then he turned abruptly and blasted Jack in the face with icy water. Jack's breath caught in his throat and he gasped in shock. When his hair and face were drenched, his father turned the hose back to the door. 'Are we awake now?' he said, laughing.

Jack burned with anger, shame and hatred – wanting to kill him; to turn and run away there and then. If he didn't leave soon, he *was* going to kill him; pure and simple. He removed the cumbersome gloves and threw them on the floor, swallowing his anger – as he always did – and picked up the scraper. Shivering in the shade, he scraped at the stubborn flakes of paint on the first pine door, eager to get it over and done with. His father hosed down the rest of the doors, satisfied he had regained some sort of control. Jack wished he would piss off and leave him in peace.

When his father had finished, he said, 'Right, make sure you do a proper job. I don't want a scrap of paint left on them. I've got wood to unload that needs chopping later.' Jack groaned; it was as if his father knew he wanted to go out.

Jack watched him open the back doors of his van and slide out the first of many semi-circular lumps of wood; cross sections of large tree bases that had been sawn in two. By the time he had removed the last one, he was panting for breath and sweating profusely. He noticed Jack looking over. 'What are you staring at?' he snarled; all the exertion had made his dull headache roar and he needed a sit-down.

Jack looked dejectedly at the pile of logs, then at the retreating figure of his father as he sloped back into the house. Lazy bastard, he thought – but he was glad he'd gone, and he moved the door he was working on into the welcome warmth of the sun. He took off his T-shirt, still wet from the spraying, and hung it up to dry. The sun felt good on his back. After half an hour he had managed to get one side of the first door done. He quickly turned it around to set about the other side. As he worked, he willed his brain to come up with some excuse for leaving the house later.

It was noon, and Jack was well into the second door when he was distracted by something out of the corner of his eye. His sister was by the back door, spinning lettuce, which had always made him laugh. She had a little wire salad strainer that she put the lettuce into once it was washed. She clipped the lid shut then swung the contraption in a circular motion with one arm, faster and faster, as if she was trying to take off. The lettuce was probably part of lunch, and he realised that he hadn't had anything to eat since the previous night. He hadn't had any cider either, which was odd now he thought about it.

When Anne had finished trying to fly, she looked up and saw Jack, scrubbing away. Her heart went out to him. 'Are you coming in for lunch soon?' she called, but despite his stomach's protests, he shook his head – he simply didn't have time to stop. Daisy was more important. Anne looked confused; it wasn't like Jack to refuse food. 'Do you want a bottle of cider then?' she called, thinking he must be thirsty. Jack nodded, barely stopping what he was doing.

He was still scraping away at full pelt when she returned. As he took the bottle from her, she saw that one of his nails was bleeding. 'Slow down, Jack – and be more careful; you're bleeding!' she implored him. Jack hadn't even noticed. He thanked her for the cider, took a long swig, then carried on scraping away at the doors.

It was gone two o'clock, and Jack was sanding the remains of some stubborn bumps on the third door, when his father appeared again. Although he would never have said so, he was astounded at the speed at which Jack had managed to get them done.

He turned the doors over, thinking that Jack must surely have skipped bits, but his disappointed grunt indicated that they passed inspection. 'Right, I've got to collect a load more furniture from a house clearance in Bulwell. I want all those logs chopped by the time I get back – and when I do, the van will need unloading.'

Jack slowed down, only a little: had his father said he was 'going out' to Bulwell? He was feeling giddy from a lack of food, so perhaps his mind was playing tricks on him. But no, sure enough, his father was making sure the back doors of his van were closed properly, fishing out his keys and getting in the driver's seat. It wasn't until Jack heard the engine cough and turn over that he truly started to believe. His father didn't leave the premises that often, so this was an absolute stroke of luck. Jack looked up to the heavens in thanks. Judging by the sun's position he figured it couldn't be much later than two, and as he watched the van disappear in a cloud of exhaust fumes he whooped for joy. He looked at the stack of logs, reckoning he could easily get them chopped in three-quarters of an hour if he cracked on. If there were any left he could do them when he got back. He guessed his father would be gone for at least an hour and a half to two hours; Bulwell was on the other side of town. And it was a Saturday – so the traffic would be bad.

Jack's triceps ached with the repeated effort of scraping and sanding, but there was no time to linger; this opportunity, this piece of good fortune was too good to be true. He raced down to the stack of logs and carried the top one back up to the yard. He placed it on the chopping block – a huge, solid round of oak about a foot deep – then rushed over to grab the axe.

He briefly steadied himself before swinging the heavy axe high above his head. The momentum, coupled with the exertion, made him dizzy. As he brought it back down, he lost his balance and missed his intended target. The axe glanced off the log and narrowly missed his foot, hitting the concrete in a shower of sparks. Anne, who had been bringing some lunch out to him, shrieked in alarm, which in turn made Jack yell in surprise.

'Jack! Stop, please!' she cried, rushing over. He leant on the axe, breathing heavily, suddenly aware of how foolish he'd been and what a near miss he'd had. The axe was kept razor-sharp by their father, and he'd nearly taken his toes off with it. 'What's got into you?' Anne said, glaring at him as he hung his head in shame. 'Is it 'cause you're mad at him? If it is, then running yourself into the ground and chopping your foot off isn't going to help, is it?'

Jack shook his head. 'It's not that at all.'

'Well, what is it then? Tell me!'

How *could* he tell her? Especially after he'd been out for the whole night. She wouldn't understand: she didn't know what it was like to *have* to see someone, to need someone like he needed Daisy. 'I have to go out at three,' he said, unable to look at her.

Anne didn't say anything in return, and Jack didn't need to say anything more: she knew exactly where he wanted to go. He was clearly besotted with this girl, which would explain his frantic behaviour today. But these crazy chances he was taking... What if their father hadn't gone out? What then? Despite what Jack thought, she *did* know what it was like to have to see somebody. She, too, had begun to rely more and more on her trips to the shops to see her admirer. She knew how to contain it, though, to keep it hidden – it was something shiny to get out and polish when no one else was around; a bit like Jack and his secret tin. Jack was younger, though … and impulsive.

'You can't keep doing this,' she said; but he didn't answer. I knew she wouldn't understand, he thought. 'Here, please, sit down a minute and eat your sandwich.' She passed him the plate and a fresh bottle.

Jack sat in the shade, and his sister studied him as he tore into the sandwich. She noticed how wiry he was getting and how defined his muscles were becoming from the hard work. His face was changing as well: it had become more angular, his cheekbones higher. The hooded, pale blue eyes were more intense, and there was something in his mannerisms too. It dawned on her then, with dismay, that he was starting to look like his mother; her sister. She would have been about the same age when … when it happened; and hazy recollections of that dreadful time came back to her. It was all such a blur, as though she'd sleepwalked through it. She remembered there was trouble with a boy, and then her sister getting fat, becoming withdrawn and hiding away in her room – telling her to go away. And then *she* went and the baby came…

A lump appeared in her throat. God, was it really all that time ago? It was a lifetime – and yet she still missed her terribly, worse than her mother. She was only young then, but her sister – they'd had a life together, well, nine years or so anyway. And she'd never even got the chance to meet Jack; not really. She would have been so proud of him. A tear rolled down her cheek. Jack looked up and saw it.

'What's the matter?' he said.

'Nothing, really … it's nothing,' Anne replied, trying to compose herself. 'It's just that … you're growing up so fast, that's all.' She pulled a tissue out of her apron pocket to blow her nose. Jack wasn't convinced. He thought of Daisy and how she always spoke her mind.

'Is it about our mum?' Anne looked up in shock. He hadn't spoken those words for years – not since he was little. A fresh wave of anguish washed over her. How could she tell him? How could she ever tell him they didn't have the same parents? It was too painful to tell the truth: silence had always been the simpler option, and it still was now. Jack sensed this, and being met with the same stony response after all this time made him see red.

He put down his plate and bottle, picked up the axe and began chopping again with a renewed ferocity and concentration. Taking his frustration out on the logs, he easily cleaved them into wedges with a practised arm, sending them flying in the process. Anne walked away, upset. There was something about him that she couldn't quite put her finger on. She didn't like this newfound temper for a start; he was quick to anger – and where did he get that from, she wondered?

Jack didn't see her return at ten to three, and only just heard her calling. 'It's nearly three o'clock! You'll be late!' He snapped out of his trance. In his fury he'd lost track of time, but he'd managed to chop about two-thirds of the logs. The rest could wait: he'd do them when he got back. She held out his dry T-shirt to him, and he grabbed it, shouting, 'Thanks!' as he ran past. She shook her head at him running down the drive, trying to pull his T-shirt on at the same time. 'Yep, I hope she's worth it,' she said again, but to herself this time. 'And I sure as hell hope she feels the same way too.'

CHAPTER 16

The Babbling Brook (Unfinished Business)

Daisy sat amongst the dandelions on the bank of the brook, below the road, in the shadow of the bridge. It was cool out of the sun and her arms and legs felt a bit goose-pimply, so she hugged them to keep warm. She briefly regretted her choice of attire: a short-sleeved white cotton blouse tied at the waist, exposing her midriff, and cut-off denim shorts – like her namesake Daisy Duke. She was feeling a bit overdressed for a simple walk by the brook, but she had wanted to dress nicely for Jack. He had never seen her legs before and she stretched them out again in front of her. They looked too pale and short to her in the pumps she was wearing. She didn't know what was coming over her: she had never felt like this before, but he made her want to dress more like a girl – to wear nail polish and dresses. Maybe it was because she hadn't managed to entice a kiss from him yet. She'd even decided to stop wearing her bangles and bracelets; it seemed as though it was time to do away with childish things.

After a lie-in, she had spent a long time getting ready. She had showered and shaved her legs, then tried on different outfits before deciding – and then changing her mind again. She had braided her hair into a plait, finishing it with a pretty clip at the front, then tentatively applied some make-up; not too much but just enough. With her hair tied back and her denim shorts, this unintentionally enhanced her gamine qualities – her large eyes and slim hips.

As she sat there, she felt as if she were on a first date all over again. There were butterflies in her stomach. Perhaps it was because there was a weight of expectation. How long had she been sitting there? Time played tricks on these lazy summer afternoons. She looked at her watch: it was ten past three. She had been there for nearly a quarter of an hour. Tendrils of doubt crept in. What if he couldn't come? She didn't want to acknowledge this thought, but he *had* said he couldn't promise. What if something had happened at home again? She already despised his father, despite never having met him. I'll give it until at least three-thirty, she said to herself, knowing that she'd probably wait even longer just in case. It occurred to her that they hadn't specified which side of the road to meet on. What if he was on the other side? She picked up a dandelion and put it to her lips, blowing on it and making a wish. The fine down floated like a miniature parachute, drifting upwards on the still air.

At that moment, a mop of familiar black hair appeared and Jack's worried face peered over the bridge. When he saw her sitting on the bank, there was the ringing of bells in the cloisters of his heart. He broke into a broad grin. Could this heavenly creature really be waiting for him? She looked good enough to eat *and* drink, effervescing with beauty like a shaken can of cherryade. She smiled back in relief when she saw him, but still tried to play it cool. 'About time!' she called. 'I was starting to get cold!'

'Well you're on the wrong side!' he cried as she climbed up to meet him. He took her hand and pulled her into the golden afternoon sun. 'Come on, let's go and catch some fish!' They ran hand in hand across the main road. Wow, this has moved on a stage, thought Daisy. It felt exhilarating, but natural at the same time. They climbed over a stile and passed a field with a pony in it, before heading down the sloping bank to the babbling brook. 'Come on, we need to find some clearer water!' Jack said, as he led Daisy further downstream.

Through the overhanging branches, the sun cast a dappled yellow light on the brook. Shoals of minnows and sticklebacks clung to the edges of the banks and stone loaches darted about. They carried on walking until they reached the shallowest part, where the water was stillest. Every stone and reed was perfectly visible on the river bed, as if under a magnifying glass. The only movement on the water was where it parted in ripples around large stepping stones, or where pond skaters whizzed over the surface in their own little ballet.

'Right, come on then, we're going in!' said Jack. He was in his element again, and sat down to take off his socks and shoes.

'You can't be serious!' Daisy said.

'Yes!' He rolled up his trousers to his knees. Daisy stood next to him with her hands on her hips, still undecided. After some deliberation, she put a hand on Jack's shoulder for support and proceeded to remove her pumps. Jack, who had been too excited to notice, turned his head and noticed her shorts properly for the first time. He gulped at all the flesh on display: the fine down on her bare stomach, her smooth, creamy thighs – the colour of pale honey and only inches from his face – right down to her feet. He stared at her dainty toes in fascination – as if he'd never seen anyone else's feet before. Well, he hadn't come to think of it, apart from his father's and sister's.

They made their way to the edge of the brook. Daisy held onto Jack in case she made a fool out of herself by falling in. There was a strange sensation as they paddled: if they stood still for a moment, it felt as if their feet were being sucked under in quicksand. The stones were slippery underfoot, but the water that clouded and muddied up around their ankles, cool at first, soon began to feel warm.

'Right, we've got to be really quiet and move as slowly as possible,' said Jack.

'What are we hoping to catch? Salmon?' said Daisy sarcastically.

'No, bullheads. You'll see!' He crouched down at the first large stone he came to and carefully turned it over. They peered underneath but there was nothing there: Daisy didn't even know what she was looking for. He put it back, then edged further downstream.

Daisy followed, and they came to two more large stones, side by side. 'Right, you do that one and I'll do this one.' They rolled back their stones together. Jack groaned in disappointment, but Daisy gasped. Under her stone were not one, but two odd-looking black fish. They were about the size of her finger, with tapering bodies and bulbous black heads.

'Ugh!' she said. 'I'm not sure if I like them.'

'They go to sleep, but you still have to be really quick to catch one,' Jack said, moving into position.

'But why would you *want* to catch one? It's not like catching a prize trout!'

'Because … you have to catch these with your hands, and it requires great skill,' he said with a smile on his face. Daisy snorted as Jack cupped his hands over the surface of the water. With lightning speed, he thrust them in and back out again. To Daisy's amazement, there, flapping about in his dripping hands, was one of the black fish. 'Yes!' cried Jack. 'Here, do you want to hold it?'

'No, I don't!' she shrieked, laughing, squeamish at the thought. That was the one thing she hadn't liked about going fishing with her dad (apart from the smell): the landing of the fish. She didn't like the way they jumped and flapped about.

Jack teased her, walking towards her with his catch as she stepped backwards, trying to get away from him. Then she lost her footing and yelped, grabbing Jack's arm to stop herself from falling in. He dropped the fish in surprise and it splashed back into the water, hurrying off to join its friends. Just when it looked as though she was going to pull Jack in too, they managed to gain a foothold and did a bizarre little dance, before tottering to a standstill. They stood with Jack's arm around the small of her back, ankle deep in the middle of the brook.

All of a sudden they were aware of how their bodies were pressed waist to waist, and their eyes met before gazing down at each other's lips. Her scent of white musk and Parma Violets seemed to be enveloping him – to be everywhere as their hearts thudded against each other. Time stood still for a moment, until she placed her hands on either side of his face and gently pulled him towards her. The last thing he saw was her eyes closing, so he immediately did the same. The sun beat down on his eyelids – turning the world a strawberry milkshake pink.

As her lips met his, the touch was so sensitive, so powerful that he felt as if he was going to faint. He could taste her lipstick and feel the gentle urgency of her tongue, parting his lips and exploring him like a foreign being. She pressed herself more tightly to him and he became aware of the swell of her chest, rising and falling, hot against him through the thin material of her blouse. Her lips became moister and her breathing became heavier. Then, just when he thought he couldn't take it anymore – that he was going to explode – it was suddenly over. She pulled her lips away and giggled, hiding her face in his neck, which tickled him and set him laughing too.

They clung to each other, as Jack's old friend the sun smiled down. Little fish darted around them, forgotten now and no longer important, in the warm yellow waters. A dragonfly hovered by and stopped to look at them – laughing like idiots; like young, innocent fools in love. And if Jack had been struck down dead at that moment, he wouldn't have cared.

CHAPTER 17

In-Between Days

That sunny day at the brook was a watershed moment (no pun intended) for Jack and Daisy. Their fates were sealed with a kiss. It wasn't spoken, but they were now – in Daisy's eyes at least – officially 'going out' or 'an item'. This was confirmed, as were all important events in her life, by an entry in her notebook with the date next to it. She still didn't tell her parents about Jack, as she knew how funny he was about where he lived. Besides, they would only have made a big fuss, him being her first proper boyfriend – and so would her sister, Lily. They would ask too many questions and want to meet him; she didn't think Jack was ready for that yet.

Parents know more than we think, and some subtle shifts in Daisy's behaviour hadn't gone unnoticed; neither had her slight change in attire, which was now less 'band T-shirts and boots' and more … feminine. That, and the permanent dreamy look on her face, gave Daisy's mum and dad the sneaking suspicion she was seeing someone – most likely a boy from college.

Jack, not being familiar with the protocols of courtship, wasn't aware they were now 'going out', or what even constituted 'going out'. All he did know was that he had practically floated home that afternoon; he had just kissed a girl! And not just any girl, but Daisy – the object of his desire, the thief of his heart; John Wayne would have been proud. He got back in time to finish chopping those logs before his father returned; he could have chopped a whole forest down the way he felt that day.

Over the next few weeks the days got longer and the nights got shorter, as June somersaulted towards the summer solstice. That contrary mistress the weather had other ideas, however. She threw a tantrum and wept for a week, blowing and cooling things down – perhaps sensing that Wimbledon was around the corner. But as everyone on the bus kept saying, 'Ooh, we're due some rain – the garden needs it,' and 'Our lawn is parched!' Unfortunately this inclement weather further limited Jack and Daisy's already brief opportunities to see each other. They always had their mornings on the bus together, but it was never long enough. There was never time to say everything they wanted to say, and before they knew it, they arrived at Jack's stop, where another mind-numbing day of drudgery awaited.

On top of this, Daisy had a fortnight of exams, which she couldn't care a toss about but was supposed to be revising for in the evenings. This she attempted to do, whilst listening to music. As a result, she often became distracted, wondering what Jack was up to, wishing she could play him the song she was listening to. It was then that the idea of making him a compilation tape of her favourite songs came to her, and the revision took a back seat as she began to compile a list.

But where do I start? she thought. How can I possibly cram a lifetime of music onto one tape? This was a big deal to her and was going to require some research, so she began to probe Jack on his musical tastes every morning. She was astounded at his lack of musical knowledge, which was limited to about five LPs from the '60s and '70s. But then again, so much the better: he was a blank canvas and she saw it as her job to educate him – a task she set about, to Jack's amusement, with relish and gusto.

The upside of Daisy and Jack not being able to spend much time together was that it kept their burgeoning relationship fresh. The highlight of the week was Wednesday nights, when Daisy's parents went out for the evening to play cards (at least that's what they said they were doing; they normally came back drunk). They'd devised a series of secret rings on the telephone for when they'd set up a meeting. Nothing meant 'all clear – still on', one ring meant 'not possible – mission aborted' and two rings meant 'meet me at the phone box as soon as possible'. This was added to as their relationship developed.

One of the few places they could meet was the Red Lion – or at least its garden. And it was whilst they were standing under the cherry tree, sheltering from the falling drizzle, that Jack decided to tell Daisy about his mum. The rain had pummelled away any last remaining petals of blossom, but they still liked it under there; it was well away from the pub, and all of their most significant confessions thus far seemed to have come out there.

Telling her was no small feat, as he'd never spoken of it to anyone before. Daisy was stunned. She wished he'd told her sooner – on their camping trip, for example. She was racked with guilt, recalling that day on the bus that she'd first seen his black eye. There'd she'd been – in inimitable Daisy Jones style – railing on about what a poor mother Jack must have, when all the while… God, it did explain a few things, though, such as how his father got away with what he did. Daisy held him close and called him a 'poor lamb', and it was her eyes that were wet with tears when they eventually pulled apart.

The big news in Daisy's house was that her dad, Jim, had decided to retire early, or 'semi-retire', because of his recent heart scare. He was co-owner of a company that made and supplied guitar amps – something he'd got into during his earlier days as a roadie. Over the years it had made him a very good living, as well as involving him in the things he enjoyed: music and people. It had begun as a bit of a hobby, a tinkering really, into a successful international business. Now he was in a position to take more of a back seat role, still doing the odd bit of consultancy to justify his 'dividends' to the board. As he put it, 'Your mum and I would like to make the most of the time I have left,' (a morbid sentiment in Daisy's opinion), 'by travelling and seeing the world – you and your sister are old enough to look after yourselves now.'

It was because of this new situation that Daisy, ever the wily opportunist, saw a chance for spending more time with Jack. Holding hands and pecks on the cheek in a pub garden was all very romantic, but it never seemed the right moment to recapture the spontaneous passion they had felt that day at the brook. In fact, their public rendezvous more often than not left them feeling similarly frustrated. Daisy began to hatch a plan, and the next morning she proposed it.

Midsummer Night was approaching, and what with Daisy's parents being ex-hippies, the summer solstice and Midsummer Eve had always been a big deal in their house. They weren't as important as Christmas, say, but were equally as important as Bonfire Night and Halloween – if not more so. They had always marked these occasions by going to festivals or holding their own gatherings with like-minded friends. They would light a bonfire and drunkenly do the 'dance of the merry peasants' whilst wearing garlands and wreaths – all very embarrassing, especially as the girls got older.

It turned out that Jim's retirement coincided with the midsummer festivities, so Daisy's parents had decided to celebrate by doing 'the big one', Stonehenge, and making a mini-break out of it. Daisy was told that her sister was going to be left in charge of her, but better still, Lily had informed Daisy that she was going to her own party that Friday night. This would conveniently leave Daisy with the house to herself – and on Midsummer Eve no less.

Daisy wasn't the only one who had been doing some scheming. Anne's trips to the shops in East Leake were becoming ever more frequent. She always went on her pushbike now, weather permitting, and usually after making the excuse that she'd forgotten something or other. There was more colour in her cheeks and her shoulders weren't so hunched. On one occasion Jack even heard her humming to herself. All this didn't go unnoticed by their father, who was unusually quiet, brooding and menacing.

With Jack and Anne now having something in common outside their home, they spoke to each other more. From time to time she lingered in his room when bringing in washing, as if she wanted to say something important. One night she plucked up the courage and told Jack that, spurred on by him, she too had met someone; nothing serious, just someone to talk to – a man. Jack couldn't believe it. He was thrilled for her and proud that he, her baby brother, had had some kind of influence on her. 'Well, make sure you don't tell him where you live!' he said; and she laughed. Their shared secret brought them even closer. She felt more and more that she should tell him the truth about his mother and where he'd come from, but feared the consequences. She was loath to shatter the period of peace and quiet that had settled over the house.

The following Wednesday night in the pub garden, Daisy presented Jack with the tape she had made for him. She had planned to unveil it on Midsummer Night, but buoyed on by the excitement of her parents going away and the return of the sunshine, she couldn't wait any longer. She had agonised over it for hours; re-taping some songs, replacing them with others, and changing the order of play.

On the spine of the case, in black transfer stickers, it said: 'Daisy's Greatest Hits Vol. 1'. 'I couldn't fit them all on, so I might have to make you a second volume!' she confessed. She had made a cover for the tape out of a colourful Garfield cartoon strip. To her, it was the ultimate personalised gift. Jack didn't know what to say; he was overwhelmed by the time and effort she had put into it. 'Well, go on, open it then!' she said. Jack prised open the case and slid out the tape. Behind it was a little note in Daisy's familiar writing: 'To Jack, all my favourite songs. Love from Daisy x.'

'Why Daisy x?' he asked.

'Seriously?' she replied. Jack blushed. Was he being stupid again? 'It's a kiss – an x stands for a kiss! Everybody knows that!'

'Oh!' he said, and beamed.

It was the most precious thing he'd ever received, which in turn made him feel ridiculously emotional. She had neatly written the track listing on the inside cover along with the artists' names. Most of them didn't mean anything to him – they were just random names, like The Cure, Kate Bush, Blondie, Pixies for Christ's sake! Was that a joke? It went on... Madonna (he had actually heard of her), The Smiths and The Stone Roses – he'd seen those names on Daisy's T-shirts. 'Ooh … Simon and Garfunkel, I know them!' he cried, pleased with himself.

'I know, that's what I thought,' she said, glad that he'd noticed. 'That's why I put a couple on there – Scarborough Fair's my favourite!'

You'd be hard put to find a more random and eclectic bunch of songs on one tape. They were, nevertheless, most of her favourite songs – some influenced by her parents admittedly, but only a handful. A lot of the songs conveyed subtle messages and expressed how she felt, such as *True Colors* and *Buzzin' Fly*. Others, not so subtle, like *Ask* by The Smiths and *Push It* by Salt 'n' Pepa – which she'd debated over for ages in case he thought she was a slut! The rest were just favourite current tunes. The full track listing was as follows:

Side A

Buzzin' Fly (live version '68) – Tim Buckley
There She Goes – The La's
Feels Like Heaven – Fiction Factory
Push It – Salt 'n' Pepa
Ask – The Smiths
Waterfall – The Stone Roses
Love Me Do – The Beatles
The Caterpillar – The Cure
Walk The Line – Johnny Cash
Because The Night – Patti Smith Group
The Chauffeur – Duran Duran
Feelin' Groovy – Simon and Garfunkel

Side B

Sweet Child O' Mine – Guns 'n' Roses
She Sells Sanctuary – The Cult
Debaser – Pixies
Denis – Blondie
Crazy For You – Madonna
Sally Cinnamon – The Stone Roses
Scarborough Fair – Simon and Garfunkel
True Colors – Cyndi Lauper
Only You – Yazoo
Shelter From The Storm – Bob Dylan
Ceremony – New Order
Under The Ivy – Kate Bush

As Jack was reading it, his elation was shattered by a sobering thought. 'Daisy, you know I don't have a tape player?' he said.

'I thought you might say that,' she replied, and pulled her red, slim-line personal stereo out of a carrier bag. Again, this was a pretty big deal – it was her most treasured possession. She used it at night in bed when it was too late to have music on loud, when she was sunbathing in the garden, and when she was at college or on the bus. She couldn't live without it, but she did have an old one too that was big and clunky with some old-fashioned headphones. The sound wasn't so good but it wasn't the end of the world; it was a sacrifice she was willing to make. She passed it over to Jack. 'Please look after it.' Jack was speechless: he knew how much Daisy's music meant to her. He carefully transferred the tape and stereo into his rucksack. When they parted that evening, both of them wishing tomorrow would disappear so it would be Friday, Daisy said, 'Now, make sure you listen to the tape tonight – and all the way through as well! I'll be quizzing you on it tomorrow.'

Jack went straight to his room that evening, like a smuggler returning to his den with a sack of precious booty. He pulled the tape and the stereo out in wonder. It was as if he'd brought a piece of Daisy back into his house, and into his room with him. He read the note she'd written again, loving how she'd put 'love from Daisy' with a kiss after it. He smelt it, and it did indeed have a faint trace of her musky scent on it.

After brushing his teeth, he lay there in the dark with his headphones on and pressed play. Sweet, rich music filled his ears; and his life would never be the same again. That tape and those songs would forever remind him of that time – of those long days and short nights. It was a whole new experience for him, and transported him to another world, another planet even – one where only he and Daisy existed. For an hour and a half, the music washed over him in waves. He'd never felt such powerful surges of emotion; save when meeting Daisy herself.

Throughout, he smiled and he cried tears of joy that trickled down his cheeks in the dark: such is the power of music. It enhanced his dreams and fantasies that had previously been silent. Now they had a soundtrack. And all the while Daisy was there with him on his journey, hovering above his bed. She was celestial, her hair all aglow and her big, brown eyes wide, warm and watching, as she raised a hand to her full lips and blew him a kiss.

*****

The next afternoon, after making sure her master had been fed and watered, Anne informed him that she had to nip to the village for 'a few bits'. Normally, around this time of day when he'd had a few ciders, he'd nod off in front of the telly. He didn't say anything in reply, pretending to be ensconced in the news, but he immediately sobered up. There was something familiar about all this; a pattern was developing. It reminded him of the trouble with that boy all those years ago, and that little whore of a sister of hers…

Way back then, not having a phone in the house had seriously increased the girls' isolation. They were never the most sociable of children in the first place – always on the edge, just watching. When their mother became ill, a painful and protracted affair for all of them, their father had hit the bottle hard; even more so after she'd died.

They'd always been one of those families that came and went as they pleased, only turning up at school for the bare minimum of time. This was partly because of their father's scorn of the education system and also because of where they lived. Any excuse and they didn't go in, especially during the winter when the sloping lane was impossible to traverse. As they didn't have a phone, eventually people stopped bothering, unwilling to make the journey just on the off chance. Naturally, this was more of a problem for the eldest – being a fourteen-year-old girl. She had met a boy, a farm boy, and now she'd left school she had no other way of seeing him. There had been rows, and she'd started sneaking off to the phone box to set up meetings – just as Jack would later.

It felt like that now; he'd got a sense for this kind of thing. He sat in his chair and listened to the back door closing, waiting for about ten minutes before getting in his van and setting off. He didn't want Anne to see him but didn't want to lose her either. As he approached the crossroads, he looked left towards the phone box before turning right. That was where he'd caught her sister on that fateful night. Flashbacks tormented him. He'd driven her back to the house and thrashed her. Tearing her room apart, he'd found a diary, with all the depths of her hatred for him laid bare in black and white. More to the point, and catastrophically for her, it was where he'd discovered she was sexually active. Yes, at the age of fourteen. He'd hit the roof and called her every name under the sun. She'd also given away the boy's name and where he lived, which he'd probably have beaten out of her anyway.

He'd driven straight round to the house with the sole purpose of breaking the poor lad's neck, but this hadn't gone entirely according to plan. First, he'd had his hand slammed in the front door (Anne could remember him returning clutching his wounded hand), and then he'd been escorted off the farm with a shotgun pointing at him. Needless to say, he'd taken it out on the girl instead – oh, he'd done that all right…

He drove through the village, trying to banish these

unwelcome recollections. There was no sign of Anne and he hoped he hadn't lost her. But then he spotted her on the long stretch of straight road, some way ahead. She must have ridden like the clappers, he thought. He noticed her stopping just before the first houses of East Leake, and he had to pull into a field entrance, obscured from view. What he couldn't see was Anne fishing a make-up purse with a mirror from her bag. She pulled out a clip which she put in her hair, and applied a discreet bit of blusher and lipstick before setting off again – all of which she would remove again on the way home.

After waiting impatiently for about five minutes, her father pulled back onto the road and headed into East Leake. It was then that he saw her again, and he couldn't believe his eyes. Her bike was leaning against the butcher's shop window and she was in the doorway, not even inside, talking to a young man in a white coat. He had no choice but to drive on by. The butcher's son looked up briefly to see if it was a customer he recognised; he didn't – it was just an unshaven old man in a dirty white van who meant nothing to him.

He parked in the Co-op car park and leant against the steering wheel, breathing heavily, not quite knowing what to do next. Did it mean anything? Was she just chatting before getting some meat? Intuition said no. He'd felt this way before and he'd been right then.

He headed back to the T-junction near the butcher's, but her bike was already gone. He panicked, looking left, and glimpsed them again – with the young man pushing her bike. They were holding hands too, he noticed, as they disappeared into the park. His disbelief grew. He had to find somewhere to turn round. He'd become obsessed; he needed to know what was going on – to see it with his own eyes – as a jealous, spurned husband would who had discovered his wife's affair. As he slowly drove past the park, he spotted them, sitting together on a park bench. They were laughing and talking, as brazen as you like, while some litter swirled around a bin next to them – like a scene from a Carla Lane sitcom.

Well I never, he thought as he drove home, and he let out an unhinged laugh. His knuckles were clenched white on the steering wheel; he still couldn't believe what he'd seen. It's always the quiet ones, eh? God alone knew how long this had been going on behind his back. This could only bring trouble; bad trouble. It could bring the whole house of cards crashing down. She had to be stopped. The younger him would have gone flying straight in; full of rage and unable to help himself. But he was older now, not as physically strong, yet a little bit wiser – he'd made that mistake before, and look how it had cost him. No, he'd bide his time and wait for an opportunity; when that bastard boy wasn't around: he was getting too strong now. She'd get her comeuppance, though; he'd make sure of that.

CHAPTER 18

A Midsummer Night's Pageant Play
Act I – Daisy's House

Midsummer Eve finally arrived. Much to the annoyance of Jack's father (in light of his recent discovery), Jack had spent the previous evening in his room. He'd listened to his tape over and over again, and already knew most of the songs by heart. His favourite so far was *The Caterpillar* by The Cure; it summed up exactly how he felt about Daisy, and described her to a tee. He'd barely slept as he'd been far too excited: he'd just lain there, listening to the birds and watching it get light from about four o'clock. Throughout the week he'd been stockpiling cider again. His father, on the other hand, had been hitting the bottle hard, waiting for an opportunity to strike.

Jack left for the night without any ceremony. He and his sister had arranged to leave his window open again, but she'd pleaded with him not to return so late this time; it was too risky. Their father was in the living room out of earshot when they said goodbye, and Anne was just as nervous as she had been before. Jack got the sense that she badly wanted to tell him something again: he could tell by the way she was drawing it out. But she didn't … and the moment was gone. As she watched him leave, she felt conflicting emotions – of worry, but also of happiness for him. There was also a little twinge of envy; that he could get to spend all that time with someone he loved, whilst she was stuck at home.

It was a beautiful summer night as Jack set off, cross country, towards the village. Midsummer Eve, the best night of the whole summer – and he'd never felt so alive. The spinney seemed to be full of mischief and magic this evening, feeding his imagination – nymphs, fairies, sprites and Pan, that god of nature and the wild, chasing them all and playing his flute.

Jack's head was whirling, just like Anne's but with a different mixture of emotions. He'd never been inside another person's house in his entire life, and he didn't know what to expect or how he was going to react. As if in answer, the black dot (which had been keeping a low profile) flickered just out of reach in the corner of his vision. He pulled out a bottle of cider in retaliation and took long draughts from it: 'Be gone!'

He headed into the village the back way, through the kissing gate, and retraced his steps from that first night. This time it was broad daylight, and he felt dangerously exposed, even more so as he arrived at the unavoidable stretch of Main Street. It was a small village and everyone knew each other, yet here he was – a complete stranger – marching down the street in full view. If only he could make himself invisible.

Walking quickly, he soon rounded the corner into Daisy's close – but this was even worse. There was activity everywhere: the hissing of sprinklers, the clip of shears, the drone of lawnmowers and the smoky haze of barbecues from back gardens. It all sung of summer. Everything was neat and perfect, just like the people playing out their lives of suburban normality – a world away from the one that Jack had grown up in.

He reached Daisy's drive without attracting too much

attention, but that didn't dispel the uncomfortable feeling of being watched. Daisy had gone to great lengths to explain exactly which house it was, and Jack had pretended to listen. She'd also said there would be a wreath on the porch door, so he couldn't miss it – and there it was. He was just about to crunch down the driveway when he saw a twitch at an upstairs curtain. It was the same window he'd seen her at before, but under very different circumstances.

Daisy had been looking out for him, and as she ran down the stairs her stomach did giddy cartwheels. She looked stunning, radiant – her face tanned and flushed with excitement – as she opened the porch door; she'd been lying in the back garden all day, working on her tan.

It was a hot and sticky evening, and she'd opted for a red and white gingham-check summer dress, tied at the back with a bow. She'd painted her nails a ruby red (with nail polish covertly borrowed from her sister), including her toenails, which had taken ages as she hadn't had much practice. They looked resplendent in white, strappy sandals. This was all in the hope of giving off an air of casual beauty: that her chosen man might say, 'You look nice!' Well, it had the desired effect. Jack was once again bowled over by this wildflower, this caterpillar girl who never ceased to amaze him. 'Hello you!' she said.

All Jack could manage in return was, 'Wow!'

'Do you like the wreath?' she asked. 'Here, smell it!' Jack did, and it smelt incredible. 'That's honeysuckle, St John's wort, Alba rose and tobacco plant – I made it myself. Mum normally does it but obviously she's not here.' Saying this made her blush.

'Wow,' was all Jack could say again.

'It's tradition. We do it every year for Midsummer Eve… Anyway, come in. Welcome to the Jones household!' She gave a little bow. Jack took a deep breath and squeezed past her into the porch. He drank in her familiar scent: it was calming but arousing at the same time. She pulled the wreath off the porch door and brought it inside, closing the inner door behind her.

Jack found himself in a large, cool hallway. It was the strangest of sensations, being in someone else's house. He was as jumpy as a kitten in a new home; all of his senses seemed on red alert; he wanted to sniff everything, explore everywhere and get his bearings. He felt like a wine taster sampling the air... There was furniture polish, overripe bananas and the undeniable smell of stale tobacco. 'Is your dad still smoking?' It was the first real thing that he'd said, and it struck Daisy as funny.

'Yes, unfortunately. He still has the odd one but not in the house. Mum makes him go out the back. God, can you smell it?' Jack nodded, and she was amazed. A clock hanging on the wall tick-tocked, seeming too loud in the empty stillness of the hallway. 'Come on, put your bag down and I'll show you around.'

Reluctantly, Jack surrendered his rucksack, and she hung it at the bottom of the stairs. He looked up to the landing. Living in a bungalow, stairs were a novelty to him, and he wondered where they led to: what rooms, what secrets. He noticed a shoe rack where all the shoes were neatly lined up in pairs; there were different sizes and different shoes – men's, women's, trainers, boots. Jack took his time, not wanting to miss anything. Daisy waited, watching him in curiosity; you'd think he'd never been in anyone's house before.

The first door he passed led into a spacious lounge. Jack surveyed it from the doorway. It all looked so neat – with matching sofas, a clean, plush carpet and ethnic-style rugs and lamps. There was a large, modern television in a cabinet with a video player underneath it – something he'd never seen in real life. On a coffee table were not one, but two remote controls. Jack couldn't imagine having a remote control for your telly, let alone for a video player. He also noticed there were lots of exotic-looking house plants. The only plant in *his* house was a sprawling spider plant that resided in a ceramic bowl in the parlour. His sister was the only one who ever bothered with it. She watered it regularly, and had even taken a cutting from it, which she had grown into a smaller version in her bedroom.

On the far wall of the lounge was a dresser. It had a fruit bowl on it and photos in frames of what he presumed were Daisy's family. 'It's OK, you *can* go in,' she said.

'Won't your parents mind?' he asked.

'Don't be daft! They're probably sloshed, watching a play somewhere in Somerset by now. And Lily won't be back till late – that's if she comes back at all! So you can relax,' she said, patting his shoulder.

Jack looked down at his scruffy boots, and felt as though he should take them off before entering. This was something he didn't usually have to worry about at home; he didn't even have a carpet in his bedroom. He prised off his boots, thankful that he was wearing clean socks without any holes in them. The carpet felt springy and luxurious underfoot. Daisy watched as he tiptoed over to the dresser. He made a beeline for the photos, eager to know what Daisy's parents looked like and where she came from. He'd never seen a photo of his own mother – he'd never seen any family photos at all; for some reason they were banned in his house.

There were individual and family portraits of Daisy, her parents and her sister from throughout the years. Jack's eyes grew wide in childlike wonder. It was all so much to take in. Daisy's mum had her daughter's auburn hair and similar features; the full lips and large eyes. She had once been a very attractive woman, but her face was drawn now, as if her husband's illness had taken more of a toll on her than it had on him.

Her dad, in comparison, looked slightly younger – he

was much fuller of face, carrying some weight, and had mischievous, twinkly eyes. Perhaps he'd enjoyed life a bit *too* much and that's why he was ill now. He always appeared to be laughing, and he'd had various beards, moustaches and hairstyles over the years – most of them long. In some photos he'd got his hair scraped back in a ponytail. Her sister looked two or three years older than Daisy and more like her dad, with lighter, sandier hair. Not as pretty as Daisy, but then Jack would say that. She had a knowing smile too – as though she was older than her years.

Jack's eyes were drawn to a school photo of Daisy in uniform. Her hair was in bunches and she was smiling happily to reveal train track braces on her teeth. Daisy noticed his gaze and slammed the photo face down in mortification, lest the illusion of womanhood be shattered; she didn't want Jack to see her as the frumpy young girl she had been only a few years before. Jack was unperturbed and reached for another photo. This was of a whole class of children of primary school age, both boys and girls, all grinning. They were looking towards the camera with tanned faces – their hands placed on their knees in front of them. It took Jack a while to find Daisy, but there she was on the front row, beaming, shoulder to shoulder with her classmates. It made Jack feel sad. He wished he'd known her then, and wished he knew what it felt like to be surrounded by other children. He wanted to ask her, but felt too ashamed to admit the truth.

Daisy sensed a change in him, an air of melancholy, and so she pulled him away. 'Come on, that's enough photos.' Jack took one last, lingering look at Daisy's mother as she dragged him out of the room. 'I think it's time for a drink, don't you?' she said, sashaying off down the hallway ahead of him. Jack stopped to pick up his boots, then followed the swish of her cotton dress that clung to her hips.

He passed another room on the left, briefly seeing a dining table and chairs, before entering a large, bright kitchen. Again, it was all clean and tidy with modern appliances, but lived in – a family kitchen with a cat calendar on the wall that had dates circled on it: 'Aunt Jean's birthday' … 'Dad's hospital appointment – 10.15' and so on. There was a table at one end near some patio doors that provided access to a large back garden. Daisy went over to a tall fridge with more photos stuck to it – some of family, some of cats – and with various, yellow Post-it notes on it, such as 'Bins out Friday' … 'Cancel milk Saturday?' The top half of the fridge was well stocked with food (nothing like Jack's at home) and the bottom half turned out to be a freezer. She opened one of the frosty-looking drawers and pulled out an ice cube tray that smoked in the warm kitchen. It stuck to her hands, and she dropped it on the side yelling, 'Ouch!' as if she'd been bitten.

Jack leant against a counter, still clutching his boots, and watched her, fascinated. It was a real pleasure to see her pottering about in her own home, especially in a dress. She walked over to a high cupboard and stretched on tiptoe to reach some glass tumblers. The hem of her dress rose to reveal the back of her knees, and her calf muscles tensed and relaxed again. She put the glasses on the side next to the ice cube tray, which she casually bashed on the counter a few times to dislodge some ice. The ice clunked into the glasses, and when they were two-thirds full she picked them up in one hand. 'Right, follow me!' she said, smiling at Jack. She stopped to pull his boots out of his grasp, throwing them towards the patio doors.

She led him into the room they had passed, a dining room with a solid wooden counter in the corner. Behind it were mirrors and shelves stocked with different types of alcohol – mainly spirits. There was a bucket on the counter with a pair of metal tongs and some plastic straws and stirrers sticking out of it. Jack was amazed by it all. 'I know,' said Daisy, seeing the look on his face. 'It's their own little bar, Dad's plaything – he's a frustrated landlord! They've always liked a drink, both of them – *and* entertaining. So ... what can I get you, sir?' She slipped behind the counter and leant on it playfully like a barmaid.

'Oh, er, no ... I'm fine, thanks, I'll just stick to my cider.'

'Oh, come on! Let me make you one of my famous G and Ts. I've been making Mum hers for years.'

'OK,' said Jack, not wanting to ruin the moment. 'Are you sure your parents won't mind?' He couldn't get used to this sense of freedom.

'Oh, they won't even know ... as long as we don't drink too much of the same thing ... Now, let me see,' she muttered, putting one finger against her lips and running the other hand across various bottles. 'Gordon's, Tanqueray, Bombay...' It was all gobbledygook to Jack. 'We'll start with Tanqueray first – it's a special occasion.' She carefully measured out two capfuls into each glass, and the neat alcohol made the ice crack and snap. She replaced the gin on the shelf before ducking below the counter, coming back up with two bottles of tonic. Swiftly, she dispensed with the yellow caps using a metal bottle opener attached to the bar. She caught both the caps in her hand and popped them in a pocket on the front of her dress. 'Evidence,' she whispered, giving him a mischievous look. Using both hands, she filled each glass with tonic. The sparkling liquid tumbled over the ice, making Jack's mouth water. Then she stuck a straw into each glass. 'Just one more thing, you can't have a gin and tonic without lemon!' And she placed the drinks, along with the empty bottles, onto a tray.

'Evidence?' said Jack, quickly catching on.

'Evidence,' she confirmed, as though they were some sort of double act. She floated back into the kitchen with the tray and Jack followed her. He *was* enjoying himself, but he really wished he could put his boots back on; it just felt unnatural without them.

The drinks were finished off with wedges of lemon that hissed when they were popped into the glasses. Daisy clinked her tumbler against his, saying 'Cheers!' The sun streamed in through the back window as they leant against the counters and finally got to taste their drinks. They sipped them through straws as their eyes flickered over each other, taking one another in. Jack savoured his first gin and tonic, which was fizzy, citrusy and refreshing, all at the same time. He had to restrain himself from draining the glass in one go. 'Wow! I could get used to these — it's like lemonade!' he said, pausing for breath.

'Yes, adult lemonade!' she replied. 'They're deceiving, though, so watch out — they can knock you for six! Come on, let's go outside.'

Act II – Honeysuckle Cottage

They walked past the kitchen table to the patio doors at the end. Daisy slid them wide open. She held his drink for him whilst he put his boots back on. They ventured out onto wooden decking that was awash with evening sun, and also home to patio furniture and container plants. From next door could be heard the resonant buzz of someone mowing their lawn. It sounded too loud and invasive this close. Jack shielded his eyes against the glare. His gaze was met with a large, private back garden that seemed to go on forever.

The middle of it was laid to an immaculate lawn, full of long, slanting shadows and with trimmed, curved edges. It was the flowers that bordered it, though, that really caught his eye. There were swooping sprays of different colours, all of varying heights. Towering hollyhocks and foxgloves presided at the back, whilst sweet peas tumbled over trellises in between them. Hot-pink coneflowers rubbed shoulders with blood-red penstemon in the middle, and sun-kissed marigolds, nasturtiums and cranes bill geranium all vied for attention at the front. Someone had spent a lot of time on this garden; it was almost too much to take in. Jack felt as though he'd stumbled into the Garden of Eden – spoilt only by the noise of the mower. 'Now this is Mum's department – it's her passion!' Daisy said, fighting to be heard.

As Jack's eyes became more accustomed to the light, he could see as far as the bottom of the garden. One corner was dominated by a small weeping willow, whilst the other was home to a little wooden house, or painted shed. It was entirely covered in a climbing plant with creamy white flowers. 'What's that?' he asked, intrigued.

'That's Mum's summerhouse – her hippy retreat. She goes in there to meditate – or, as Dad says, to get some peace and quiet! Come on, I'll show you.'

They made their way down the garden, both sipping their drinks: Jack's had nearly gone already, much to his dismay. He took it all in – the neatness and order, the smells, the buzzing insects hovering over the painter's palette of colourful flowers; so different from his garden at home. They passed a mature buddleia that was living up to its name 'the butterfly bush'. Its dripping purple cones were alive with the things – restlessly hopping about, clearly in heaven.

As they neared the bottom of the garden the lawnmower stopped abruptly, which was a blessing. For Jack, it had been too much of a reminder of the outside world and people, and more to the point, how close they were. The scent of flowers was even stronger down here, filling the air. One scent was particularly fragrant and familiar. 'What is that smell?' he asked.

'That's probably the honeysuckle. You smelt it in the wreath, remember? Isn't it amazing? You wait till later on tonight – it gets even stronger in the evening when it cools down. It's like a storage radiator that soaks up the sun during the day and then releases its scent at night. This is Mum's sensory garden as she calls it, her own area of calm. She loves the sound of the breeze through the willow tree – when you close your eyes it sounds like running water. There's jasmine and nicotiana too,' she said, pointing them out, 'and the Alba rose – all of which smell amazing. In fact, and this is really embarrassing,' she paused to drain the last of her drink before continuing, 'that's what our middle names are.'

'What? Jasmine and Nicotiana?'

'Not quite,' she replied. 'Although I wish mine was Jasmine – I'd prefer that. No, it's Lonicera, which is the Latin for honeysuckle, and is just, well, cringeworthy! That's what you get for having flower-loving hippies for parents, I guess. Still, it's got to be better than Nicotiana – which is my sister's, and is the Latin for tobacco plant. I think it was a drug-induced joke of my dad's – her first name is Lily, so he calls her Fag-Ash Lil!' She snorted with laughter.

Daisy could tell by Jack's face that he was struggling to keep up and that she was waffling: she blamed the gin and tonic. He was, but he was also impressed at her knowledge: some of her mother's influence must have rubbed off on her. There was so much more to her than met the eye. 'What's your middle name?' she asked, drawing him back into the conversation.

'Oh, erm, I don't have one actually, It's just … Jack.' This sounded so sad to Daisy – that his parents or parent hadn't even cared enough to give him a middle name. It made her want to kiss him softly on the lips.

The summerhouse was larger up close than it had looked from the top of the garden and had a fairy-tale quality about it.

The flowers of the plant it was covered in were multi-coloured as well, not just white, with flecks of yellow and pink in them. Above the door was a wooden sign that said 'Honeysuckle Cottage' with a heart below it. They had to duck their heads to enter. Inside, there was a wicker mat on the floor and a matching chest with three large candles on it. The wooden slats on the roof let in thin strips of sunlight, and also that sweet smell from the honeysuckle. He felt as though he could stay in there forever.

They spent the early evening in the comparative coolness of Honeysuckle Cottage, seeking refuge from the hot sun. Whilst Daisy was returning to the house to refresh their drinks, a pretty tabby cat with striking green eyes appeared. It wandered over to Jack as he sat in the doorway and proceeded to purr – revving like an engine as it rubbed and nuzzled itself against him. Jack stroked and fussed it; it was such a treat for him to be able to pet an animal as he'd never been allowed one. The cat rolled on its back with its legs in the air, encouraging him to rub its stripy tummy. When he did, it clawed at him – but in a playful way.

Daisy returned, carrying two drinks and a tape player. She also had Jack's rucksack strapped to her back like a parachute. It was little things like this that killed him, and he laughed out loud. 'I see you've met Sookie then?' she said. 'Look at her, the little tart! She's never normally that friendly – she must like you.' And when Daisy bent down to fuss her, the cat trotted off. 'See?' Jack smiled as she passed him his rucksack. 'I hope you've brought your tape with you!' she said.

'Of course I have; I can't stop listening to it!' he replied, fishing it out of his bag.

She plugged the tape player into a socket inside the summerhouse. 'Mum likes to listen to panpipe music while she's meditating,' Daisy explained.

They listened to Jack's tape, enthusing over each song and exchanging their ideas about them. Daisy was in heaven, and so was he. She made intermittent trips to the house for more drinks and Jack offered to help, but she was happy to play the hostess. He was content to watch her coming and going; letting the music wash over him as the alcohol buzz kicked in. Sometimes she pecked him on the forehead or cheek before leaving, her lips lingering longer each time. Jack held her, not wanting to let her go. Then she'd totter away on increasingly wobbly feet.

After a lengthier absence than normal, Daisy returned with the wreath of flowers placed cockeyed on her head and with her hair down, the combination giving her the appearance of an irresistible Ophelia. On a tray she was carrying two glasses of a pink concoction she drunkenly declared was a 'gin daisy' and a load of snacks to eat. This wasn't a bad thing – as they both needed something to soak up the booze. Jack didn't know if it was because he wasn't used to drinking spirits, or just because he'd become immune to his cider, but he felt a lot drunker than usual. He longed to kiss her properly again, as he had that day at the brook.

As the evening wore on, they made their way outside, stumbling onto the lawn as the sun was setting. It had nearly disappeared entirely; just the top of an orange ball peeping over the fence – an over-eager extra in the play, refusing to leave the stage. They danced round and round, holding hands like the owl and the pussycat, under a peregrine moon, spurred on by the music and the alcohol. They kept on spinning until the wreath flew off Daisy's head and she collapsed, giggling in a heap, whilst Jack got his breath back. She lay on her back with her knees up, kicking off her sandals and letting the grass tickle the soles of her feet. Staring up at the sky, Daisy tried to concentrate on shapes in the clouds to stop her head from spinning. As Jack looked on, she picked up the wreath and laid it onto her chest where it rose and fell. Then she began to pull rose petals off it, scattering them about her and chanting, 'Rose leaves, rose leaves, rose leaves I strew, he that will love me come after me now.'

So lost in her drunken reverie was she that she didn't notice her dress slipping down the length of her thighs towards her hips. From where Jack was standing, in an instant, he saw everything; her slim legs that were golden from the sun and the heavenly hollows of her inner thighs. Nestling in between them, in this secret, tea-coloured valley, was the cloven white mound of her knickers. His whole body ached with desire. Blood coursed through his veins and he saw colours and shapes, as if he was about to swoon. He thought he was going to be struck blind right there and then for looking. And then just as quickly it was over. Daisy regained her composure and flattened her dress, totally oblivious to what Jack had witnessed.

He threw himself down next to her – exhausted, guilt-ridden and confused – in the large shadow of the weeping willow. They rolled under its secret skirts together. The hanging leaves brushed against them as they lay face to face with locked hands and touching knees. Jack noticed the inviting, shadowy gap between her dress and the swell of her chest. She studied his face – wondering if he was feeling the same way as her. 'I can't believe how light it is; it must be half nine at least,' she said, unwilling to unlock hands to look at her watch. Jack was still in shock and just 'hmphed' in reply. She shifted closer till their faces were inches apart. 'You know … there's an old Swedish proverb that says Midsummer Night isn't long, but it sets many cradles rocking.' Jack still didn't answer; his eyes were fixed on her lips. God, how many hints can a girl give? she thought, before placing his hand on her hip and her own hands behind his neck, pulling him towards her.

They kissed, softly at first and unsure. Jack could feel the waistband of her underwear through the thin material of her dress, reminding him of what was underneath and driving him mad. Their kissing became more urgent as their hands explored each other. She clambered over him, lingering on top as she rolled across him – feeling his need and confirming hers. She knew the time had come, and without another word she led Jack by the hand from under the willow tree and back into Honeysuckle Cottage.

It was dark inside at first, save for the moonlight that shone through the window. Daisy took the candles off the chest, reached inside and pulled out a blanket. She passed it to Jack, kissed him and murmured to him to lie on the floor. He did as she said, and by the light of the moon he watched her, transfixed and shaking. Daisy reached behind her and did that curious thing girls do; where they unclip their bra and somehow manage to pull it through the arm of their dress. Throwing it on the floor, she reached under her dress to slip off her knickers. They whispered down her legs. She came to Jack then, still in her summer dress, and sat on top of him under the blanket, pulling it around her shoulders as her hair hung in his face. She was right about the honeysuckle – the smell seemed to have increased tenfold, to be everywhere, permeating through the roof slats and trapped in the expectant dusk...

And this is where the curtains close on this scene; let's leave our two lovers in peace. All of this was new to Daisy and Jack, but they found their way – as the young always do. Like a magical mystery tour to an unknown destination; that's how it struck them; colourful and explosive, with bombs going off along the way, both of pain and, ultimately, sweet pleasure.

Let's pan away over the countryside, about two miles away, to a very different scene at Jack's home. As usual, his sister was having a torrid time of it. She was used to being alone with her father whilst Jack was out, but tonight she had never felt more isolated and vulnerable. You're just being irrational, she told herself, a feeling brought on by the added stress of having to leave Jack's window open again. It wasn't just this, though – it was because he was acting oddly, well, more oddly than usual – and she'd lived with him long enough to know his habits. Normally by now he would be almost blind drunk, lost in some television programme or other, occasionally conversing with the screen. Tonight, however, he didn't even seem halfway gone, and this was bad news.

Now that she thought about it, he'd been in a strange mood all week and had barely spoken to her. Instead, he'd watched her in disdain as if he was suspicious of something. This particular evening the silence made her feel uncomfortable, and so she kept disappearing – hardly able to be in his company at all. She did odd jobs to keep out of the way, such as washing, ironing and putting a new brew of cider on. She went for one of her night-time jogs around the top garden – something she'd started doing recently, ever since she'd met her beau. It was always in secret and in the dark before she locked up for the night, so no one would see her flushed and sweaty face. She was determined she wasn't going to become a lonely old spinster just because of *him*.

Meanwhile, her father had been watching her, still semi-sober, as she brought him more cider. He knew she was fidgety and restless. Well, good – let her squirm. He was also aware that the bastard boy wasn't back yet. Well, good again – tonight he'd be locked out to teach him a lesson. Secretly, he'd been pouring away half his cider into a plastic jug hidden the other side of his armchair. He wasn't going to waste good cider – it would go back into the keg later – but tonight he wanted his wits about him.

After returning from outside, Anne mopped her brow as she regained her composure in the kitchen. She looked at the clock: five to eleven. She was dog tired and wanted to go to bed. He must be gone by now, she thought. When she went to check, to her utter dismay he wasn't; he was still sitting there, fully awake, watching telly. He sensed her disappointment, enjoying it as he ignored her. She took away another empty bottle and went back to the kitchen in an increasing state of distress.

This could go on all night, she fretted; he must know that Jack hasn't come back yet, or maybe he thinks he's already in his room. It's not as if Jack normally announces when he's back – he just goes straight to bed. But what about the window? Last time he'd been plastered *and* she'd given him the sleeping tablet. She didn't see any other choice but to do it again. This time it was even more risky as he didn't seem anywhere near as drunk. What if he noticed it? This didn't bear thinking about.

It's funny how history repeats itself. Here she was – all these years later – doing to him what he'd done to her; returning the favour, so to speak. When he hadn't wanted her to know what was going on, he'd slipped *her* a 'soporific' night after night in her hot bedtime milk. She placed the doctored bottle on the floor by his armchair, trying her best to sound casual. 'Right, I'm going to bed now, I'm tired. I'll lock up, so… Goodnight. I'll see you in the morning.'

As she was leaving to close the door behind her, he shouted, making her jump. 'Bring me the key when you've done it!' It was the first thing he'd said to her all night, and it set her nerves jangling. He never normally asked for the key – it just got left in the back door; he had to suspect that Jack wasn't back. She locked the door and brought the key back to him. Somehow, this made her feel more trapped than ever. She said goodnight again with a slight tremble in her voice, closing the door behind her.

Once in her room, she got undressed with jittery hands that fumbled at her zips and buttons. She put on her nightdress and went to the bathroom to brush her teeth, all the while debating what to do about the window. She decided to risk doing it now, getting it over and done with whilst she was up and about. As she spat in the basin there was blood in the toothpaste from where she had scrubbed too hard. She washed away the pink foam and slipped out of the bathroom, down the corridor, to Jack's room.

Her father sat there for a few moments, feeling tired himself. There was part of him that couldn't even be bothered to deal with her tonight – perhaps it could wait. She needed teaching a lesson, mind you, and whilst he was still seething. He needed to know what she'd been up to, what she'd been saying, and how long it had been carrying on for. Just thinking about it made his blood boil. But he was surprised at his deliberation. What had got into him? What had happened to his rage? Tonight was the perfect opportunity, especially while *he* was not around – something else that never used to bother him. He reached to pick up his bottle and looked at it. Should he neck it in one go or just pour it away? Sometimes the cider helped when you were going to dish out a beating.

As he turned the bottle over in his large, rough hands, he noticed that the cider looked cloudier than usual. It must be getting stale, or air had got into the keg or something – but this looked *really* cloudy. He popped open the top and sniffed the cider before taking a tentative swig. He pulled a face when he did so; it tasted bad all right – but not in an 'off' way; just bitter, with a nasty aftertaste. He inspected it more closely and held it up to the light. Sure enough, there at the bottom, mixed in with the sediment, were small white crystals of powder. 'You bitch!' he said out loud as the revelation sank in. He recalled a couple of Fridays ago when he couldn't remember going to bed, and had then woken up late with that splitting headache. 'So, this is what it's come to, eh?' Sneaking off to talk to men like a whore is one thing, but drugging your own father as well?

He crept into the hallway and headed straight towards Anne's room, wanting to surprise her and throttle her within an inch of her life. When he opened her door, the light was on but she wasn't in there, which was odd. He went to the bathroom and did the same, slowly opening the door. She wasn't in there either. This fanned the flames of his anger further. Where was that bitch? Perhaps she'd snuck out. Perhaps that was her plan all along – to drug him to sleep so she could sneak out to see this man. But then he realised he had the key, so she couldn't have done. Just then he thought he heard a noise from further down the corridor, coming from … from *his* room – the boy's. The room that he avoided going in because it brought back dreadful, nightmarish memories. What was she doing in there? What if she was in there for protection? Or worse, what if … what if they were … ugh! He shuddered at the disgusting thought. He faced his fears, and for a large man crept stealthily down the corridor towards Jack's room.

Even though she knew Jack wasn't there, Anne was still dismayed at seeing his empty bed. A full and low moon shone in as she tiptoed over to close the curtains and open a window. She flinched as the frame made a horrible, jarring sound. Suddenly, she froze. What was that noise? Something in the corridor? She felt fear in her guts like knotted twine. Or was it her imagination? It had happened at the same time as she'd opened the window, so she couldn't be sure.

Perspiration stood out on her lips and forehead as she put the window on the second latch. She left the curtain slightly open so she could see her way out of the room. She was about halfway across when, to her horror, the door handle began to turn. As the door opened, meagre light from the hallway slanted in, casting a rectangle onto the wooden floor. It was filled with the large shadow of a man.

He took in the scene – not knowing what to expect. Anne was frozen to the spot, her eyes wide in fear. The curtain was fluttering in the breeze, which confirmed his suspicions. He moved towards her, and Anne backed away. She looked round, searching for an exit, and also saw the open window. Glancing back at him, with that madness in his eyes and his arms outstretched, she made a snap decision. If she didn't get out she was going to die. The window represented freedom, maybe forever: she could feel the breeze of it on her back, calling her. She looked down at her bare feet and then, without a further thought, picked up the hem of her nightdress and flew at the window like a wraith.

Act IV – Underneath the Covers

Daisy and Jack had fallen into a dreamy and contented sleep, the kind you only get after love-making. They had drifted off snuggled in each other's arms, warm and safe underneath the blanket, like two warm eggs in a nest. As Daisy slowly came to, she was disorientated – fuzzy from the alcohol and aching from lying on the wooden floor. It was then that she realised, in alarm, where they were – but with no idea how long they'd been asleep. The light was confusing: it was that time of year when it barely seemed to get dark at all, especially when there was a full moon. 'Oh my God, what time is it?' she said, sitting up and looking at her watch. It was eleven forty-five, and her sister could be back at any time – if she wasn't already. Panic set in.

'Jack, wake up!' she cried, patting his chest. He groggily

came round, also not knowing where he was at first. His arm had gone dead as Daisy had been lying on it and his back was sore. It felt kind of chafed … and then it all came back to him. A smile crept over his face: he wanted to lie there forever. But Daisy had other ideas. He watched through bleary eyes in the murky half-light as she slipped her underwear back on under her dress; it reminded him of what had happened; he still couldn't believe it. Then she threw his shirt and jeans at him. 'Come on, lazy bones! We need to tidy up!' She crouched down to do up her sandals.

They emerged into the moonlit back garden and quickly gathered up their things. 'What about the tape player?' asked Jack.

'Oh, that can wait till morning. Leave it in the cottage.'

As they scurried towards the yellow lights of the house, clutching their belongings, a phone started to ring. 'Shit, that'll be Mum!' cried Daisy, speeding up as she made for the patio doors.

She ran into the kitchen, throwing the stuff she was carrying onto the table before snatching up the receiver. 'Hello!' she said, out of breath, and then, 'Hi, Mum.' She glanced at Jack, who was shielding his eyes from the bright overhead lights. 'No, I was just upstairs getting ready for bed when I heard the phone.' And she looked at the kitchen clock for confirmation of the time. 'Er, no she's asleep … I know. Well, I think she was tired – or drunk.' Daisy listened to her mum for a bit and gave some impatient 'yes and nos' – yes she'd remembered to water the garden, no they hadn't forgotten to feed the cat. She took the phone away from her ear for a bit, holding it towards Jack as if to say, 'Are you listening to this?' Her mum gibbered on loudly, with shouts from her dad in the background – it sounded as if they were enjoying themselves. Daisy put the phone back to her ear. 'Tell him to stay off the fags and go easy on the booze! OK, I'll tell her… Yes, love you too … *and* Dad – see you tomorrow!' She put the phone down, smiling.

After tidying up the kitchen and bar area, they loitered at the bottom of the stairs for a moment, canoodling. It really was time for Jack to go. He was determined to get back at a reasonable hour this time, but neither he nor Daisy could bear the thought of parting, not after what they had shared. Suddenly there was the sound of a car pulling up outside; its headlights shone through the top windows in the front door, lighting up the hallway. Daisy looked at Jack in panic as they listened, rooted to the spot. A car door opened, high-spirited voices said their goodbyes, then the door slammed closed again. 'Quick! Upstairs! It's my sister!'

They just managed to dart into her bedroom before the front door opened. They stood with their backs against the bedroom door, held their breath and listened. Daisy could dimly make out Jack's face. He looked so terrified that it was almost comical. 'It's OK,' she whispered, trying to suppress her giggles. 'She won't come in here; she'll probably be drunk.'

'Daisy?' There was the sound of footsteps on the stairs.

'Under the bed! I'll pretend I'm asleep!' She shoved Jack under the bed before diving into it, pulling the covers up to her chin. The bed sagged until it was millimetres from Jack's nose. They heard Daisy's sister trip on the top step and swear. Her footsteps stopped outside Daisy's door.

'Daisy, are you awake?' Daisy didn't answer, hoping she'd go away … but then the doorknob turned and the door slowly opened. Jesus, thought Daisy. When does she ever come into my room?

From under the bed, amongst the dust and boxes, Jack saw a strip of light in the doorway and a bare foot appear. Lily spoke again, slurring her words. 'Daisy, are you awake?'

This time Daisy did answer. She peered out from under the

duvet, doing her best to sound irritable and tired. 'Well I wasn't but I am now.' She half-yawned, half-spoke.

'Oh sorry. I was just checking you were OK ... you left all the lights on downstairs.' Jack was trying not to breathe loudly but it was agony – the dust was tickling his nose.

'Well I left them on for you, didn't I?'

'Oh, OK... Well, as long as you're all right ... I'm sure there was something I was going to say, but I've forgotten...' Daisy could have killed her. 'Oh well, never mind... Night, then.'

'Night,' said Daisy, and Lily closed the door.

Jack exhaled, when suddenly the door reopened. He held his breath again. 'What now?' Daisy groaned.

'Did Mum and Dad phone?'

'*Yes!*' Daisy snapped, without elaborating.

'Oh, OK then – no need to get your knickers in a twist... Night. See you in the morning.' She closed the door again. They heard her walk away, then stop. 'Oh, I know what it was!' she called. 'Whose is that rucksack downstairs?' They both froze, wide-eyed in the dark.

They'd left Jack's rucksack hanging on the banister, and if she looked in it they were doomed; it was stuffed full of cider bottles. 'Er ... it's Claire's, she ... popped round earlier,' said Daisy. She braced herself for the response, and hoped to God that Lily wouldn't go back downstairs.

'Oh, right ... funny bag for a girl!' she slurred; then toddled off to her bedroom, closing the door behind her. She still hadn't turned the downstairs lights off – or brushed her teeth.

'Dirty cow,' Daisy said, loud enough for Jack to hear her. He started snorting in fits of suppressed laughter, which encouraged her further. 'Funny bag for a girl,' she said, mimicking her sister. That was it ... he was gone; he couldn't stop laughing, as much in relief as anything else. He sneezed because of the dust, then banged his head on the wooden slats under the bed. This set Daisy off, and she burst into fits of laughter as well; he felt the bed shaking as she convulsed in hysterics, and tears streamed down his cheeks.

When they were back under control, Jack crept out from under the bed and Daisy lifted back the covers to let him in. They cuddled and it felt hot in there with their clothes on. The whole room was warm, now he thought about it – so different from his own. To be safe in the cocoon of her bed, underneath the covers, was the most luxurious feeling he'd ever known. But to think that someone else was in the house as well was madness. 'We're going to have to wait till she's properly asleep before we can let you out,' Daisy whispered. That was OK by him; he was drinking in her musky perfume and already beginning to nod off. Daisy sensed this. 'You can't go to sleep! It's too risky… Talk to me or something.' She nudged him, trying to keep him awake.

'What about?' he said, nuzzling into her neck.

'I don't know… Tell me something about yourself that I don't know.'

'Like what?'

'I don't know … like what happened to your mum. I mean, how old were you? That's if you don't mind talking about it.'

Jack wanted to talk about it. He felt so close to Daisy, especially after tonight – he *wanted* to tell her things.

'Well, I can't remember her at all – so I must have been a baby when she died… I can only ever remember my sister being there.'

'Well, haven't you asked *her* what happened?'

'I did try when I was younger, but then I sort of gave up… She doesn't really like to talk about it.'

'But that's crazy!' Daisy said, a little louder now. 'I know it must be upsetting for her, but you deserve to know where you came from. I mean, what was your mum's name? What did she look like? What hospital were you born in?'

This was quickly becoming too much for Jack; he tried not to think about or deal with these things – there was no point as it just upset him. 'I honestly don't know. I've never even seen a picture of her.'

Daisy couldn't believe what she was hearing. 'That's just not fair: you must demand to know!' she said, sitting up on her elbow to look at him. 'What about your father?'

Jack huffed; it was no good asking *him* anything. Besides, all these questions were starting to make him feel depressed.

'And what about when you started school, what did *they* say?'…

Oh dear, here it was again; the biggie – the one he'd managed to get away with so far. He didn't want to lie to her anymore; he loved her too much and they'd gone too far. Yet still he deliberated before taking the plunge, knowing that this was it – the final secret he'd been holding back. What if she thought he was a freak? What if she didn't want anything more to do with him when she knew how he'd lived? He'd already lied to her about it as well – something he deeply regretted now. 'I've never been to school, Daisy,' he said, then turned away.

Daisy sat bolt upright. Did he just say what she thought he'd said? She looked at him for confirmation. The stony, faraway look on his face and the moisture in his eyes told her that he had; he certainly wasn't joking, that was for sure. She tried to get her head around the enormity of it. I mean, how was it even possible? Who *was* this boy in her bed whom she'd just lost her virginity to? She realised that, even now, she barely knew anything about him.

Daisy considered herself a liberal girl, a free spirit – she'd inherited that from her parents – but this was something else. What was she getting herself into? She lay down behind him again, letting what he'd said sink in. She thought about the intimacy they'd shared and how she'd given herself to him – and so freely in the end. Like Jack, she knew she'd come too far to turn back and that she couldn't renege on him – not now, not like this; and she knew what to do. 'My poor baby,' she said, cuddling into his back and slipping her arm around him. And when she did, it made everything all right again; any remaining doubts were vanquished. 'Jack, I want you to tell me everything.'

They stayed up all night, with Jack lying on his back, staring at the ceiling, and Daisy on her side facing him. He talked and she listened. There was so much to say, yet nothing to tell; he'd never been anywhere, never done anything – he could only tell her the things he *hadn't* done. He'd never been to school or mixed with other children. He'd never paid a visit to a doctor or a dentist, nor had any sort of immunisation or injections. He'd never been to a swimming pool, never been to the cinema and never been on holiday – so he'd never seen the sea.

He talked lovingly about the rambling garden and surrounding countryside that had been his playground, his whole world – his eyes lighting up as he did so. How he'd played Robin Hood in the spinney with a bow and arrow that he'd made himself, and spent summers catching crickets in glass bottles, watching them get drunk on the cider residue. How he'd carved tunnels through the long grass of the meadow, imagining he was in the trenches during wartime and that he was hiding out from the enemy; pretending the farm trucks that sometimes trundled up the lane were German army vehicles. He'd had the childhood that every boy dreamed of, yet none of them would have wanted. He'd watched endless telly and read countless books – these, along with his sister's schooling, had been his education. The warm parlour had been his classroom, where Anne had patiently sat in the rocking chair, teaching him basic maths and literacy. He enjoyed reading and writing, but the maths he struggled with: numbers just didn't interest him and he always got distracted.

He talked about the cider and the huge part it had played in their lives; and about his sister – how sad she was sometimes; and about his father – how controlling he was. He spoke about the day he had played with the children at the brook and the beating he'd got when his father had found out. How his father had said that if the 'authorities' had got hold of him they'd have taken him away and locked him up forever. Daisy was horrified at this and her lips thinned in suppressed anger; but once he had started he couldn't stop. He'd never had anyone to tell before.

He described the trauma of his first day at work; the shock of going on the bus and being surrounded by other people for the first time in his life. He spoke about the things he didn't understand – why his father had made the decision not to let him go to school. This had never been explained to him, it just ... *was*. And that's the thing – when you don't know any different, even the strangest situation just becomes normal. When he finally finished, having got it all out of his system, he made Daisy swear not to tell her parents or *anyone* what he'd said.

The more Daisy heard, the sadder and angrier she felt. Jack had spent his whole life as an outsider, almost a prisoner, at the whim of a monster. So many things made sense now – like what had happened in town that day. It also explained why he'd acted so oddly when he'd arrived at her house. And no wonder he'd been so reluctant to say where he'd lived – he must have been terrified. That's what angered her the most; that he'd spent a lifetime living in fear lest the so-called 'authorities' had got hold of him, as if he was to blame or something. He wasn't to blame, none of this was his fault; he was the victim.

But for what reason? What possible explanation could justify it all? All this secrecy, suffering and misery – there had to be more to it; and he had a right to know.

As dawn broke, Daisy turned Jack to face her and made him look into her eyes properly – something he still found it hard to do. She held his hands and gave him a pep talk, telling him that things were going to be different from now on. He didn't have to live in the shadows, and she was going to show him all the things he'd always wanted to see. At home, he'd got to start standing up for himself, and not let his father push him around; he was sixteen now, he could go where and when he liked. He'd also got to demand some answers to questions about his mother. 'Don't take no for an answer,' she said – his sister must know something; ask *her*. And do some digging: there must be some evidence somewhere: a birth certificate, photos ... something.

CHAPTER 19

A Photograph

It was five-thirty in the morning when Daisy snuck her paramour out of the house and onto the sleepy street. Despite being late home again, Jack insisted on retrieving his tape from the summerhouse so that he could listen to it on the way back. He lingered for a moment when he opened the door of Honeysuckle Cottage and surveyed the scene inside. The smell of the honeysuckle hit him straightaway, and even though it was not as strong as the previous night, it still made his stomach spin and his loins stir. That scent would always remind him of the magical Midsummer Night.

'Hey, you didn't miss much by the way,' Daisy said before they parted, and Jack looked at her, not quite following. 'School. It's not all it's cracked up to be.'

Jack set off for home with Daisy's words of encouragement for company. She was right: things *would* be different from now on. He felt different somehow – more like a man. There was a swagger to his walk as he sang along to his tape; but he was still careful to go the back way through the village and to keep to the fields.

On reaching home, Jack cut across the lane to sneak into the garden, shoving the stereo into his bag as he did so. As the music disappeared, so did some of his courage. Seeing the house cast a pall over him; it seemed to represent his father – as if his presence and personality had been woven into the very fabric of the building. It felt as if the two bay windows were watching him as he scurried across the front lawn.

He was glad to be free from their gaze when he reached the side of the property; the sooner he got back inside the better. But as Jack rounded the corner to his bedroom, he stopped dead in his tracks. He couldn't believe it: the window was closed. Panic set in – confusion: surely Anne couldn't have forgotten, could she? What was he supposed to do now? What if she'd been caught? Jack's fear for his own safety turned into fear for hers, followed by the guilt that his selfishness might have brought harm to her.

Just then, a movement further up the garden caught his eye. There, over by the huge incinerator tank, with his back to Jack and poking the remains of a fire, was his father. Jack gasped. So intent had he been on returning to his room that he hadn't registered the smell of smoke. What the hell was he doing up? Jack crept up behind the van and peered around it to take a closer look. His father was staring into the fire, his hair sticking up at all angles and wearing a dirty coat and wellies. His pyjama bottoms were just visible in the gap between them.

It wasn't unusual for there to be a fire – this happened every few weeks or so – but not at this time in the morning. His father was never up and about at this time; especially not at the weekend. Something must have happened … and Jack dreaded to think what.

He was unsure what to do, but he knew one thing – he had to get to his sister. He had to find out what had occurred, so he'd know what excuse to come up with. Part of him still held onto the hope that he could pretend he had been locked out. He tiptoed as quickly as he could across the gravel between the van and the house. 'Please don't be locked, please don't be locked,' he said to himself, before gently trying the latch on the back door… It wasn't.

Having managed to enter the house without his father detecting him, Jack expected Anne to be sitting at the kitchen table – probably nursing a new bruise that would be entirely *his* fault. But she wasn't; the kitchen was empty. At least that was something; but it *was* a bit strange. She was always up if their father was awake: he couldn't function in the morning before a cup of tea had been made for him. The cellar door was closed, so she couldn't be down there, and she wasn't in the parlour either. As he crept into the corridor, it struck him how deathly quiet the house was. He knocked on the bathroom door. There was no answer, but he pushed the door open just to make sure. There were pools of water and towels on the floor, but that was it. It wouldn't have been left in this state if his sister was up and about.

Genuine concern began to gnaw at Jack as he made his way towards Anne's bedroom. What if she wasn't even able to get up? He didn't think he'd be able to bear it. His sister's bedroom was somewhere he seldom ventured; he couldn't even remember the last time he'd been in there. It was on the right-hand side, halfway down a short hallway that led to a rarely used and old-fashioned front porch. Before Jack's time the room had belonged to his father, but when his wife had passed away he couldn't bear to sleep there on his own; it had too many memories. So he had swapped with Anne.

Jack tapped on the door and whispered, 'Anne.' He feared the worst, expecting a groan in response; but there was nothing. He hissed again, louder this time. But still nothing. He took a deep breath, turned the handle and slowly pushed open the door. The room smelt of dust, and the air was thick with it, as if things had been moved about. As he peered around the door, he braced himself to see her curled up in bed, battered, bruised and fast asleep…

There was an empty double bed, a bare bedside cabinet, a bare dressing table and an empty bookcase, cleared of all her books. The top of Anne's chest of drawers had also been cleared, leaving a shape in the dust where her record player used to sit. The chair, which would normally have had some clothes neatly folded on it, was bare too – and there were no shoes tucked underneath.

He ran to the wardrobe and flung it open. A musty smell hit him: it too was empty. What the hell was going on here? Could she have left them – left *him* – without a word of goodbye? Had their father kicked her out because of *him?* The thought made him wobble and he had to sit down. Was that possible? Or worse, what if he'd done something really bad this time? What if he'd gone too far? Jack shuddered at the thought; then anger welled up inside him. Fear and desperation were replaced by hatred as fury took hold of him. What had he done? *What had that bastard done?*

Jack stormed through the house and out of the back door. He marched straight up the garden, past the rhubarb patch, to his father. *'Where is she?'* he shouted – any fear for himself forgotten. His father slowly turned to face him, unaffected by the fury in Jack's voice.

'Ah, you're back.' His eyes were glassy, while his face was red, filthy with soot and patchy with long, grey stubble. Jack shrank back: he looked like a raving lunatic.

'Where is she?' he demanded again, trying not to be bullied, just as Daisy had instructed.

'She? Who's *she*, the cat's mother?'

'You know damn well who I mean. Where's Anne?'

'Oh her… She's gone, left us … snuck out in the night … found herself a fella, so it seems.' He seemed to be speaking in riddles in a detached voice, and with a slight lisp too. It made it hard for Jack to understand what he was saying. 'They're all the same … good for nothing, conniving bitches. They all leave in the end, they always do…' He paused for effect, then delivered the final blow. 'Just like yours will leave you.'

This was what he did: he pushed buttons, twisted the knife – seeing how far he could go. And it worked. It hit Jack like a slap in the face. To hear him spout his filth about Anne – his sister – the woman who had raised him from birth – was one thing; but to hear him talking about his precious Daisy in the same breath – and making his seedy assumptions… This sent Jack into a renewed fury, and he started towards his father as the aggressor for the first time in his life. He wanted to hurt him, and to hurt him badly.

But his father had other ideas. Quick as lightning, he thrust out the wooden pole that he'd been poking the fire with. The tip of it glowed red hot, inches from Jack's face. 'Get back, you dog!' The smoke stung Jack's eyes, making him retreat. 'Now listen here,' his father hissed, advancing. 'Things are going to be different round here from now on. It's just you and me now. Forget her, she's gone – we don't need her anymore. We're going to get this place fixed up and finished off and *you're* gonna help me … and there's going to be no more sneaking in and out like a thief…' He didn't have the chance to finish, as Jack suddenly tumbled backwards into the rhubarb patch.

Seeing an opportunity to get the upper hand, his father pounced. Using the pole as a weapon, he held it under Jack's chin and applied pressure. Jack clutched at it with both hands – one of which was dangerously close to the hot end. His father's face was inches from his own, his eyes bulbous, bloodshot and crazy. The wood bit into Jack's throat and giant rhubarb leaves flapped about his head as they struggled; their thick, maroon stalks snapped and cracked in his ears, spraying his face with pink juice. Even though Jack was physically aware of these things, his mind drifted elsewhere. He conjured up Daisy's voice for strength, and she spoke to him calmly, telling him to be brave and to stand up for himself. She talked about all the things they were going to do together. He was not going to be dictated to anymore, and certainly not about her. Nothing on this earth was going to stop him from seeing her.

Jack raised his knees and kicked upwards with all his might – straight into his father's stomach and chest. His father yelped with surprise as the air was knocked out of him. He fell backwards, yet still refused to relinquish his vice-like grip on the wooden pole. Jack held on to it too, and the momentum sent him somersaulting over his father's head. They both scrambled to their feet in a cloud of ash and dust – twisting and tussling for control of the stick.

His father was shaky on his feet, and as they struggled Jack felt him weakening. He sensed his moment and took it. Charging with all his might, and using the pole for purchase, he forced his father backwards, slamming him into the incinerator. The sharp metal edge rammed into the bottom of his back, causing his spine to arch and his legs to shoot forwards. He would have toppled backwards head first into the incinerator if he hadn't put his hand out to stop himself. As he did so, he scorched it in the glowing remains of the fire, and cried out in agony before finally letting go of the pole. Jack grabbed it, and watched as his father slumped to the floor, clutching his hand. He was beaten, and he knew it.

Jack could have delivered the knock-out blow. He could have bashed his father senseless – with or without the stick; but he didn't. He'd never been able to hit his father, and he still couldn't. He looked down at him instead, seeing his chest and shoulders heaving from the exertion and how he was sweating; a broken man. But after all the years of bullying, beatings and victimisation, Jack didn't derive one iota of pleasure from it – not one. In fact, he pitied him; and even felt a trace of guilt.

Jack's hands were shaking as he threw down the pole. His father refused to look at him – his pride wouldn't allow it. So, with trembling knees, Jack crouched down to his level, and in his bravest voice said, 'You're right … things *are* going to be different around here.' His father's eyes flickered up towards him – just for a millisecond; but that was enough. In that instant Jack saw something in his father's face he had never seen before … fear. There and then, there was a subtle yet seismic shift in the balance of power.

Back in the house, the empty kitchen screamed at Jack. His sister wasn't there to give him one of those sad, sympathetic smiles or to gently soothe his wounds. Could it really be true? Could she have left them and gone off with this man she'd only just met? Perhaps she'd been seeing him for longer than she'd let on, and Jack had been too wrapped up in Daisy to notice. He felt confused. He couldn't blame her for going; who could? But without saying goodbye? And what about all the questions he'd wanted to ask her? Who'd answer them now – his father? After what had just happened, he'd take his secrets to the grave.

With a heavy heart, Jack made his way to his room. Once there, he pulled Daisy's stereo out of his rucksack to return it to his secret tin. As he reached under the bed, something struck him as unusual. He'd got into the habit of putting his heavy exercise bricks on top of the loose floorboard; there was quite a wad of money in his tin now – not to mention Daisy's phone number. Today, the bricks weren't in the right place, and he could have sworn they had been the previous night. Don't tell me that bastard has been in here too! he thought.

Plonking the tin on his bed, Jack held his breath as he lifted the lid. To his relief, the familiar map was still there, neatly covering his money. He decided to count the money anyway just to make sure. Underneath the map, to Jack's astonishment, was a photograph. How on earth had that got in there? With trembling hands, he picked it up.

It was of a woman with a scarf on her head, a young girl with mousy brown hair sitting on her knee. The woman was thin and pale. She was trying her best to smile for the camera, but it was her eyes that gave the game away – they were those of a condemned woman. There was no doubting the similarity between the woman and the girl, and there was no doubting the resemblance between the girl and his sister. So this must have been Anne when she was little, which meant … and he didn't dare believe it was true. Could he really be looking at a picture of his mother after all these years? A lump appeared in his throat, and he had to fight back tears. Unused to photos, he turned it over as if he would be able to see her from the back, then felt foolish at the blankness that greeted him. There was, however, some writing in the bottom right-hand corner. It said 'Love, Carla.' Carla – that name again. Was that his mother's name? Had she written this? Was he looking at his dear, long-lost mother's handwriting?

It was a day of questions: too many questions and not enough answers. How did the photo get there in the first place? It definitely hadn't been there the previous day when he'd put his wages away. The only possible explanation was that his sister must have put it in there – which meant that she must have known about his tin all along, which also meant she knew of his plans to leave for America, yet she'd never said anything. It would also suggest that she knew *she* was going to leave as well. Perhaps she'd found the tin and it had spurred her on – not wanting to be left behind. Had she left it for him as a goodbye gift – or a message so he would finally know who his mother was? If so, then this was a sign – a sign that she had left for good. In turn, this made him feel abandoned and hurt. How could she?

But the more Jack thought about it, and when he saw beyond his initial selfishness, he realised it had to be a good thing – a positive thing. She had met someone and had a chance of being truly happy. He'd be leaving soon anyway, and now he wouldn't have to deal with the terrible guilt of leaving her behind. Let's face it, she'd done it; she'd got away, and put one over on the old bastard. No longer would she have to serve him, to cook and clean for him, and to get nothing but a beating in return.

Jack held the prized photo in one hand as he clenched the other into a fist. A cautious smile appeared on his face. In the last twenty-four hours he had experienced every emotion under the sun. It was overwhelming, and this time the tears did spill. But they were triumphant tears, and they were for his sister. This was a happy ending he could truly cherish and believe in.

CHAPTER 20

A Period of Adjustment

The following week was a little strange, to say the least. It was like when something bad happens in your life – something big, life-changing and catastrophic. You wake up in the morning and there is still that blissful period between sleep and consciousness where everything is all right, everything is normal – and then the sickening reality hits you. For Jack it felt as if he was waking into a nightmare instead of waking up from one.

He slept for most of the weekend – a luxury he'd never managed to indulge in before, and one that his father wouldn't have normally allowed. Sleeping was bliss; it made everything go away – the fact that his sister had gone and the agony of not being able to see Daisy. They'd parted in a hurry and hadn't made any further plans to meet; it was the same old familiar frustration. With no plans to see her, sleeping was the best option. It made the time go quicker and kept him out of *his* way too. Jack couldn't bear the thought of seeing his father – not yet anyway – and he managed to avoid him for the whole weekend. It wasn't because he was afraid of him, far from it; it was because he was still too angry with him. There were no two ways about it – he solely blamed his father for Anne's leaving.

Once, when he knew his father had gone to bed, Jack crept into Anne's room again. The emptiness struck him, how everything had disappeared. Surely she couldn't have taken it all with her; even her spider plant had gone. His father must have cleared it all out. It was as if he was trying to erase the memory of her – as if she'd never existed. Jack resented him even more for that. It was the books that bothered him the most. Those were the books that he'd grown up with, that had fed his imagination: Roald Dahl, Enid Blyton. They had taken him to faraway places and given him the company of friends when he'd had no real ones. He still had the books he'd learnt to read from in his own room but this was cold comfort. It made him wish he'd taken a closer look at that fire.

He searched the room again, but more thoroughly this time, hoping to find something she might have left behind; maybe even another clue. Under her bed, to his surprise, there *was* something his father had missed. It wasn't of much significance, but would come in useful over the next few weeks – her alarm clock. It must have been knocked off and rolled underneath. Well, at least that was something he had of hers. He also had the treasured photograph, which he couldn't wait to show to Daisy.

Daisy was desperate to see Jack too, and eager to know what had transpired when he'd got back home. She worried about him, especially after what he'd told her; it would have been a relief just to know that he was all right. She also had some exciting news of her own.

It was Anne's alarm clock that woke Jack on the Monday morning – the sound was shrill and foreign in his ear; usually Anne woke him up with a cup of tea. He shuffled bleary-eyed into the bathroom to have a bath. Afterwards he couldn't find his work clothes, so he stomped down the corridor in his underpants and poked his head around the parlour door. He still expected his sister to be in there – or pottering about in the kitchen. She wasn't. And it hit him hard: she'd been there every day of his life. It just wasn't right without her.

He found his work clothes, neatly ironed, in the washing basket next to the ironing board. Bless her, he thought. He put the kettle on, gave the stove a poke and chucked a log on it before going to get dressed. The kitchen was quiet as he prepared his breakfast. At least his father was still in bed; normally he'd have been up by this time. It occurred to Jack that he was going to have to make his own pack-up; that would be a first. Already he was noticing all the little things Anne did that had been taken for granted. After breakfast he set about making his sandwiches. He failed to find the cling film she used to wrap them in, and had to use foil instead.

Before leaving for work, Jack deliberated over something else as he washed his breakfast pots, then came to a surprising decision: he put the kettle on again and made his father a mug of tea, leaving it outside his door and saying simply, 'Tea'. He couldn't quite put his finger on what had compelled him to do this. Was it a peace offering of sorts? Did he feel sorry for him? Was he unwittingly adopting some of his absent sister's roles? He bloody well hoped not, and went to brush his teeth without waiting for a reply.

By the time he'd finished, the tea hadn't been touched. Jack shook his head before returning to his room. He packed Daisy's stereo and the photograph into his rucksack before heading back down the corridor. The tea was still sitting there, getting cold. Sod him, he thought, ungrateful bastard! It wasn't until he was leaving that he heard his father's door open. It closed a few seconds later, and for reasons Jack couldn't explain, this made him smile.

As the bus pulled into the village Jack was fidgeting in his seat – as excited as a child on Christmas morning. Even after all this time (a whole two months!) he still got butterflies at the thought of seeing Daisy. It felt as if he hadn't seen her for two weeks, never mind two days.

Daisy clutched at his hands and started babbling straightaway, all too aware of the limited time they had. Some days she wished the sodding bus would break down so they could spend some extra time together. 'I've got some really exciting news!' she gushed, before pausing suddenly to kiss him on the cheek. 'Sorry, I had to do that, God I've missed you… Anyway, where was I?' She was like a whirlwind, and Jack was swept up in her storm as usual. 'Oh yes, well Mum and Dad came back and they had an amazing time and it seems to have done Dad the world of good. You know, to get some fresh air and relax now he's finished work and everything, well get this…' She gripped Jack's hand harder. 'They're going away again on Monday next week – and this time for a whole week! Can you believe it?' She practically squealed the last few words.

'Really?' said Jack.

'Yes, really! I mean they sort of wanted me and Lily to go with them – they're going to the Lake District and we've never been before. We've always stuck to Wales, Norfolk and Cornwall for holidays, but we made out that we were too old for family holidays now. I mean, can you imagine? We also said someone would have to feed the cat! They've become obsessed with this film called *Withnail and I* which came out the other year. It's set in the Lake District, and you can go for walks and take photos and see some of the places it was filmed and that. Sounds a bit dull to me, but there you go! So, what do you think?'

'Yes, it sounds great,' Jack replied, still not quite getting the big deal.

'Well, don't sound too enthusiastic,' she said, sitting back in her seat.

'Sorry. I just don't see how it's going to change things much, especially if your sister's still around – I suppose it means we can meet up in the evening more often.'

'Yes, she'll still be *around*,' said Daisy, turning to face him again, 'but she works during the day from Tuesday till Saturday and she's never back till about five-thirty. We'll have the house to ourselves for the whole week, *and* she goes out most evenings!'

'Yes, but how's that going to help if you're at college and I'm at work?'

'I'm not at college all next week – this is my last full week. I've got a few study periods after that and then I break up for the whole summer!'

'Well, what about me? I'll still be at work.'

'You? Well, you're just going to have to get some time off, or call in sick or something.'

'I can't do that!' he said, flustered. 'I might lose my job or my boss might ring my father – I don't think he likes me anyway.'

'You're entitled to holiday. Everybody who works full time is. Have you had any holiday since you started?'

'Er, no.' It had never occurred to him.

'Well, there you go then! Ask for some time off.'

There was silence for a while. It wasn't quite as simple as all that: Jack was secretly terrified of his boss, and didn't fancy the idea of talking to him one bit.

As if sensing his reluctance, Daisy tried to entice him further. 'Just think of all the things we could do.' She leant into him, placing her hand on his thigh.

Oh God, please don't do that, thought Jack. He could

smell her, and it was like catnip to him – it made him want to drool, roll over and go doolally.

'We could…' What's she going to say, please don't say that – not now. 'We could watch movies together, go to the seaside, anything you've ever wanted to do.' She made it sound so good. 'Anyway, think about it.' Oh, he would – he would *certainly* think about it…

So lost were they, snuggled together in the dreamy possibilities that the following week offered, that before they knew it, it was nearly time for Jack to get off at his stop. Daisy became aware of this first. 'Anyway, God, I forgot to ask – what happened when you got back home? I take it your dad didn't know you'd stayed out again?' He hated it when she called him Dad – it was like, for a second, he didn't actually know who she was talking about.

'Oh, yeah – he knew all right.'

'What?' said Daisy, wide-eyed. 'How did he find out?'

'He was awake when I got back and my window was closed.'

'Oh my God! What did he say? Did he hit you?' She looked Jack up and down in alarm.

'He didn't say anything really. There was a bit of a fight, that's all.'

'A bit of a fight…? Well, what happened? And what about your sister? Please don't tell me he took it out on her?' She almost felt as if she knew Anne, even though she'd never met her.

'Oh, she's gone. She left in the night,' Jack said sadly; and saying it out loud made it really hit home.

'*Gone!*' Daisy's voice was getting louder and louder, and people were beginning to stare. But Jack didn't have time to explain: the bus was already slowing down at his stop. She felt like clinging onto him, not letting him go. 'Jack, you've got to meet me tonight – I need to know everything,' she implored.

His home life was a soap opera that she'd become addicted to. 'Meet me at the Red Lion, you've got to!'

'But…'

She stopped him by pressing her lips onto his. 'Seven o'clock,' she said, pushing him out of his seat. And that was it; he had to go.

He looked up at her, in a bit of a daze as the bus pulled away. She kissed her hand, putting it up against the glass. Jack waved back, trying his best to smile as the prospect of work hit him. He hadn't even told her about the photograph.

Work dragged as it always did, and he mulled over what Daisy had said about asking his boss for time off. It would mean visiting his office where he sat, red-faced and beady-eyed. Jack only went there once a week to get his wages and he hated doing that.

He knew his sister wasn't going to be there when he got home, and so he tried not to think about it. It wasn't until he opened the back door that the reality bit, and bit hard. In fact it chomped and chewed: it was the lack of activity, the inertia, the silence – none of the usual sounds and smells of dinner. There were dirty plates and cups on the draining board: evidence that his father had been up and about.

Jack needed a drink for the first time that day. This was incredible: he hadn't even thought about cider until that moment. Today had been the first day since he'd commenced work that he'd not actually taken any with him. He headed down to the cellar for a bottle, then stood in the empty kitchen, swigging from it. In the living room, there were the sounds of a tennis match on the television – his father had the volume up loud as usual. It was Wimbledon fortnight, his father's favourite two weeks of the year; and today was the first Monday.

His father, having been a keen tennis player himself when

he was younger, got totally engrossed in the tournament. Jack saw more emotion from him during this fortnight than at any other time. He sat in his chair and sometimes swished an imaginary racquet or stretched for an imaginary ball, living every minute of it. Sometimes he laughed or cheered, rising up out of his seat as he got caught up in the action. When Jack was little he'd sat and watched it himself, trying to remain inconspicuous on the living room floor, curious to know what all the fuss was about. What was animating this ogre so? What was giving him such pleasure?

Jack had gradually got wrapped up in the action too, noticing how the pristine green courts slowly turned bald as the fortnight went on. He had enjoyed the sound of the ball being struck and the epic battles between McEnroe and Borg that seemed to have been played out in a dust bowl. Then there was the ginger-haired German boy who'd won aged just seventeen years. It was the way he dived for the ball and threw himself theatrically about the court that struck a chord with Jack. He had fantasised about doing the same himself one day, and had tried it out on the front lawn that summer. Once the usual British no-hopers had gone out, Becker became his father's favourite too. This further aroused Jack's suspicions that his father did indeed have German roots and was secretly a Nazi.

*****

Earlier that morning, his father had retrieved the unexpected cup of tea and returned to bed. He'd intended to get up and make a new start. He was going to dig out his old plans for the loft conversion and set about making a list of materials required. But instead he was plagued by the familiar listlessness and depression that had been building of late, exacerbated by the weekend's events. He felt old, he didn't have any energy –

and his hand was sore from that blasted fire. What had he got to get up for? It was the small things that got him through the day – cider obviously, but also a well-cooked meal, a casserole or a decent sandwich. He also liked the feeling of being in control. All of this had been taken away from him; and it was that loss of control that hit him the hardest. The situation was also (although he would never admit it) of his own making.

He eventually surfaced at about eleven o'clock, his stomach getting the better of him. After making his way to the kitchen, he peered into random cupboards and the fridge for the first time in years. He hadn't a clue where anything was, but he wasn't a bad cook – he was actually a very good one. When he and Carla had first married, it was *he* who had taught *her* the art of cooking a good meal, although mainly for selfish reasons: he couldn't abide bland, badly cooked food. Being an only child, he was used to being spoilt.

He spied some eggs: they would do – some perfectly cooked poached eggs on toast. They'd make him feel a lot better; not like those bullets that no-good daughter dished up. In fact, it would make a change. He was looking forward to cooking his own breakfast just how he liked it for once. Now, where was the vinegar for the poaching liquor?

A full half an hour or so later he sat down to eat, pleased with himself. He didn't need her; he didn't need anybody. After spending a goodly amount of time on the toilet post-breakfast, he retrieved his first bottle of cider from the cellar. Then he wandered through to the lounge and turned on the telly – those loft plans could wait for a bit. To his pleasant surprise the Wimbledon coverage had just started. He'd totally forgotten about it. The tall Swede, Edberg, who'd won the previous year, was opening on Centre Court against a chap he'd never heard of. The courts looked in mint condition and there was something familiar and soothing about them. The sky over SW19, in comparison, looked ominously overcast as he settled into his chair.

*****

Unlike his father, Jack did know where most things were kept; he'd spent hours on the kitchen floor as a child or at the table watching his sister. But food itself – or more to the point, cooking it – had never interested him; it was just fuel. He knew what he liked, what he didn't, and also when he was hungry – and he was hungry now. On that first Monday, he'd gone for the simplest thing he could think of: beans on toast. His father, still watching the tennis, was distracted by the sounds of cupboards opening and plates rattling. Unable to help himself, and like a bear drawn to a picnic, he lurched his way into the kitchen – thinking that perhaps by some miracle *she*'d come back.

Jack hadn't seen his father in days, and was again taken aback by his unprecedented state of dishevelment. He looked as if he hadn't bathed for weeks. His hair needed cutting and he was pretty much sporting a full beard. The most striking aspect of his appearance was his eyes: they had a haunted quality about them – as though he carried a heavy burden. He watched Jack from the doorway.

Normally this would have intimidated Jack, but not anymore. It was just plain annoying. He wanted to turn round and scream, 'WHAT?'

Jack carried on preparing his dinner. His father seemed to be taking a keen interest. Perhaps the old bugger was waiting to see if he was going to be made anything, thought Jack. Well, he could think again, a cup of tea was one thing, but he wasn't going to set a precedent by making him dinner as well. He could sod off! When it became apparent that Jack wasn't going to play, his father headed down to the cellar for another bottle of cider. He then sloped off back to the living room, muttering, 'Cider needs making and the stove's gone out.' These were the first words he'd spoken to Jack since the fight. Oh, so I'm allowed matches now, am I? thought Jack.

This was how it continued during that first tentative week after Anne left. Each continued to weigh the other up, observing from a distance to see how the other was coping and what roles he'd adopt. The departure of a quiet and unassuming woman had had a considerable impact on the household. A third of the unit had gone and the dynamics had changed dramatically. She was the fulcrum, the placatory piggy in the middle. She greased the cogs and kept things running smoothly – or as smoothly as possible.

As Jack headed out for the evening, he announced his intentions through the living room door, stressing that he'd be back later.

His father was in a worse temper now. The novelty of preparing his own food had vanished. He was hungry, yet couldn't be bothered. Knowing that Jack was probably sneaking off to see a 'bit of skirt' made it even worse. Still, it had to happen sooner or later: at least he wasn't a queer. But that wasn't what ate away at him. What had he told this girl? Or worse, what had *she* told her family? This was a real concern. There would be questions – and he felt that familiar shrink-wrap of terror and recriminations.

He got up and followed Jack into the kitchen. Jack heard him stomping behind him and his heckles went up. Here we go, he thought – I knew this wouldn't last. 'Just tell me one thing,' his father slurred, swaying and holding the cider bottle in front of him as if for protection. 'Tell me you haven't been stupid enough to tell her where you live!'

'No, of course not!' Jack replied, almost too quickly.

His father glared at him, trying to work out if he was telling the truth. 'Well you'd better not!' he warned, swigging from his bottle. 'And stay away from the village too!' Look at him, thought Jack – still giving me orders when he can barely stand up. He turned away, having heard enough, but his father was on a roll. 'And I don't ever want to see her anywhere near this place either, or so help me God!' He let the veiled, but somewhat hollow, threat hang in the air, then shuffled off.

Before leaving, Jack nipped up to the yard to grab some logs. He was on his way back when something poking out of the junk shed caught his eye. It was the wheel of his sister's bike, and it tugged at his heartstrings to see it. It looked so sad and forlorn and reminded him of her; she'd used the bike so much in the weeks before she'd left. An idea suddenly came to him, and after he'd dumped the logs he returned to the shed to pull it out. The seat looked a bit low, but the main thing was that the bike worked: it had two brakes, three gears and two good tyres – supposedly.

He crept across the gravel driveway with it, past the kitchen window and into the lane. He took one last look behind him before clumsily straddling it, trying to get his balance. Jack hadn't ridden a bike in years; he'd never been allowed one of his own, and had only ridden his sister's when he was big enough, cycling up and down the drive on those rare occasions his father went out. He pushed off up the lane, wobbling and trying to keep upright. The pot-holes didn't help, but they say that you never forget how to ride a bike. Sure enough, after a few tentative moments, he started to get the hang of it again. Crouching low, he freewheeled back down the lane, all the way to the bottom. He looked up and down the main road to make sure no one saw him leaving, then set off down the hill.

Instantly, he began to pick up an alarming speed. He applied the brakes, but too hard, and they squealed as the bike wobbled from side to side. He'd forgotten to change gear as well, so when he tried to pedal it was like pedalling fresh air. But once the road levelled out, and the giddy feeling in his stomach subsided, his initial terror turned to exhilaration. The wind rushed in his ears and face, blowing his hair back, and he whooped for joy. He felt a new sense of freedom – and not just because of the bike; his father knew exactly where he was going tonight, and there was nothing he could do about it.

Jack reached the pub in no time at all. Daisy was already sitting on a bench in the garden. She thought she was seeing things when he wobbled into the car park on an old-fashioned bike, and couldn't stop laughing as he jumped off before he'd even come to a halt. He wasn't wearing his rucksack either, she noticed. 'You don't see many like that anymore!' she teased as he leant the bike against a bench. The thing was, she knew Jack wouldn't give a toss whether the bike was cool or modern or not. It wouldn't even have occurred to him, and that was what was so endearing about him. Besides, the more she thought about it, she was sure that Morrissey rode one just like it in one of The Smiths' videos – which actually *did* make it cool. She couldn't imagine where he'd got it from.

After Daisy had been to get their drinks, they got straight down to business: she'd been waiting all day to hear what had gone on. She listened intently, and with growing horror, as Jack relayed the story about the fight. He spoke calmly, as if it was the most normal thing in the world for your father to hold a burning wooden pole to your throat and try to throttle you with it. She was shocked by the violence of it all, and hung on his every word.

Jack went on to tell her about his sister leaving, and as he did so, a frown came over his face and he kept reaching for his drink. He stalled, searching for the right words, losing his train of thought at times – especially when he described her empty bedroom. Daisy really felt for him. It had obviously hit him hard – and it would: Anne was like a mother to him. She tried to imagine how *she*'d feel if her mum just upped and left, but couldn't – it was too horrible. She squeezed his hand and rubbed his shoulder, leaning across to kiss him from time to time. Jack loved the attention. Eventually he got round to telling her about the photograph, which he produced from his shirt pocket and laid on the table as his trump card.

Daisy came round to his side of the bench, and they huddled together as they examined it. She searched for a family resemblance whilst trying to get her head around the enormity of it – that after sixteen years, Jack was looking at a photo of his mother for the first time. Quite clearly that was what it was, and that was his sister when she was younger. The writing on the back must have been written by his mother to his father. She looked poorly – not on death's door yet, but sort of sallow and hollow-cheeked. So the cancer theory must have been right – it must have got her in the end. Daisy held Jack tighter and said, 'Well, I guess this has answered a few questions.'

When Daisy went to get the next round of drinks, Jack heard distant laughter coming from the bar as she came back out through the door. She shook her head when she sat down. 'Wow, they think they're so funny!'

'Who?'

'The landlord and the regulars at the bar – they think they know me now – just 'cause they've seen me a few times. They keep calling me 'darling' and 'sweetheart'. Uggh!'

'What were they laughing at?' asked Jack, feeling a slight twinge of jealousy.

'Oh, nothing, they were just being idiots, that's all.'

'Well, like what?' he persisted – a touch of irrational paranoia creeping in.

'Nothing much… Just saying things like, "Ooh, where's

your boyfriend?" and "Why isn't your boyfriend coming in to get the drinks?"'

Jack was really pissed off. It was like when they'd first come to the pub: he'd felt he should have been the one getting the drinks because he was the man. And now look what had happened.

Daisy wished she hadn't said anything, as she could see Jack was brooding about it. She tried to lighten the mood. 'So, then, what are we going to do next week? What would you like to do?'

'Er, I don't know... Haven't really thought about it,' he mumbled.

'Haven't really thought about it? God, I can't *stop* thinking about it! Ooh, that reminds me: did you ask for some time off today?'

'Er, no ... not yet.'

Daisy groaned. 'Oh you've got to, sooner rather than later – the more warning you give the better.'

'But I don't know what to say.'

'Well, just say you need some time off. I dunno ... say it's for a funeral or something – that way he can't refuse!'

*****

They called it a night when the brooding sky that had been threatening rain all evening eventually delivered. Under the patter of raindrops, they shared a lingering kiss before parting. Daisy made Jack promise that he'd ask for some time off the next day. She also told him to make a list of things he wanted to do the next week, and she would too, so they could condense their thoughts into a definitive wish list. Daisy loved making lists – favourite songs, favourite bands, favourite films or albums she wanted to buy.

It was a damn sight harder cycling home for Jack than it had been cycling to the pub. The wind was against him and it was mostly uphill, getting steeper the nearer to home he got. On the last stretch, the steepest bit, he had to admit defeat and get off to push: his thighs were on fire. The door was still unlocked, which was something at least. There was no sign of his father, and the house was in darkness. He had to turn the kitchen light on so he could see to lock the back door. It felt strange doing it himself.

As Jack surveyed the kitchen, a bluebottle buzzed about, knocking into the strip light. That would be dead by now if Anne was still around, he thought. She hated flies and chased them, batting them with a tea towel and not stopping till she'd killed them. It annoyed him to see more dirty pans and plates on the draining board. Lazy sod, thought Jack – guessing this was going to be another of his jobs as well. But it could wait till the morning. He turned the light off and went to bed.

CHAPTER 21
The Wish List

The next day at work (after another gentle hint from Daisy on the bus), Jack made his way upstairs to Peasgood's office. He felt as though he was being watched by his fellow workers even more than usual as he climbed the stairs. His boss's name was engraved importantly on his door: **'JOHN PEASGOOD'** – a name associated in the East Midlands with pies, pasties, and sausage rolls. He emerged from time to time to strut the balcony high above the packaging floor, his beady eyes striking fear into his workers in the process. It was with a trembling hand that Jack knocked on his door. 'Come in!' Peasgood barked in his reedy, Scottish voice. Jack gulped.

He was sitting behind his desk in his white coat – despite the fact that he didn't do any menial work. Originally he'd been a butcher, and had the ruddy pallor typical of one, as if he'd spent too many years in cold rooms. With his prematurely white hair, which also sprouted out of his ears and nose, and the loose, crimson skin at his neck flapping over his collar, he resembled an overgrown leghorn chicken.

He was surprised to see Jack as it wasn't payday, and he wasn't entirely pleased about it either. There was something odd about the boy and, as with Jack's father, he was a reminder of an incident he'd rather forget. 'Yes, what is it?' he snapped.

'I … I … was just wondering if…' Jack floundered, not knowing how to word it, 'if there was the possibility of … of, if maybe…'

'For Christ's sake, lad, spit it out and stop blathering!' interrupted Peasgood.

'If maybe I could have some time off next week.' Peasgood didn't look too happy about this unexpected request. Time off meant the extra work of reorganising rotas and shifts. Statutory holiday entitlement for his legitimate, full-time workers was one thing – a necessary evil designed by this Tory government to bleed small businesses dry; and this from a cabinet that claimed to be championing the entrepreneur – the self-made man. But this boy wasn't entitled to anything: he was a walking, breathing embodiment of blackmail – and if there was any way he could exploit this unfortunate situation to his own ends, he was bloody well going to.

'Time off. What for?'

'There's this funeral,' Jack said, taking Daisy's lead. Peasgood pricked up his ears at the word 'funeral', and leaned forward on his desk. Maybe the old man had carked it and taken their secret to the grave. That would leave him with the great satisfaction of relieving the boy of his post once and for all, and finally putting the whole sorry business behind him. Shame though, the lad *was* a good worker, one of his best – he couldn't deny that.

'And whose funeral might that be? Anyone we know?' He hung on the answer, but Jack was a bit stumped. He hadn't expecting to have to come up with any details: he hadn't thought that far ahead.

'Erm, it's my aunt,' he said. 'Aunt Kath.' He blushed at the lie. His boss slumped back in his chair, disappointed.

'What day?' he said.

'Sorry?' said Jack.

'What day is it, the funeral?' Jack hadn't thought of this either, and panicked.

'Er, Tuesday.' It was the first day that sprang to mind.

Peasgood pondered for a moment. He couldn't really refuse the lad a day off for a funeral; he might blow the whistle on him. Perhaps that's what this was – a test devised by the boy's blasted uncle. After some deliberation, which seemed to last forever, he said, 'Tuesday it is, then … and it goes without saying, you don't get paid.'

Jack was pleased with himself over his little achievement and couldn't wait to tell Daisy. Daisy, however, wasn't quite so impressed, but tried her best to hide her disappointment. 'One day? Couldn't you have said the funeral was up north or something?' She'd been working frantically on her list, which had spiralled out of all control into about twenty activities. How were they meant to fit them all in? Remembering Jack had got his list too, she'd whittled it down to a more realistic five suggestions.

They met again on the Wednesday evening with great anticipation – both excited about seeing each other's ideas. For a change of scenery, they went for a walk in the spinney, where Jack was keen to show her the famous crab apple tree. It was a good opportunity to check on the apples, which were already in abundance but still tiny and hard. The tree reminded him of Anne, and it made him feel sad to think that they wouldn't be picking the fruit together this year. They'd spent some of their nicest times together there, alone, away from their father. She'd become a young girl again, and they'd have crab apple fights.

They sat at the base of the huge, hollowed-out oak tree. Daisy couldn't resist venturing inside it and sat, cross-legged and elfin, framed by the oval cavity. It didn't go unnoticed that Jack would normally have cracked open a bottle of cider by now, but he didn't have his rucksack with him again. She considered this a step forward, but decided not to draw attention to it. They pulled out their lists and eagerly exchanged them:

JACK'S LIST – *bike ride, go to the seaside, go to the cinema, play tennis, go to America together!*
DAISY'S LIST – *Swimming. Go into town (Loughborough). Strawberry picking. Picnic. Movie Marathon. X*

Jack felt deflated when he read Daisy's choices. Most of them seemed to involve people and public places. He didn't even know what a movie marathon was – did it involve jogging? And town again – *really?* In contrast, Daisy was quite pleased and impressed with Jack's list. There were some really good ideas that sounded like fun, especially the cinema – which she hadn't been to for ages. She laughed when she read the last one and said, 'I can't promise for sure that we'll make it to America next week!' Jack had put it down because he'd run out of ideas, but as a subtle reminder too.

There was silence for a while as they digested each other's lists, thinking of the possible permutations. 'So, what do you think?' Daisy said.

'Erm, yes, great.' Jack tried his best to sound enthusiastic, but failed. Daisy had been expecting this, as on paper some of her ideas didn't exactly look like Jack's cup of tea. She'd known she was probably going to have to sell some of them to him. As she'd compiled her list, she'd joked to herself that it was her job to ease Jack gently into the real world. She'd looked at the week, and the list in particular, as part of his rehabilitation. It was as if she was in a movie about an alien who'd landed from another planet, and she'd been given the sole responsibility of introducing him to society.

Well, here goes, she thought. 'You said you'd never been swimming – not properly in a real pool anyway – so I thought that would be a good idea. I know this amazing outdoor one at a place called Stanford Hall. We're all members there so it won't even cost anything, and it's perfect on a sunny day … that's if we get one. It's set in the grounds of this big old house, so I thought we could take a picnic and make a day of it… Oh my God!' she said suddenly, scanning Jack's list again. 'Now I think of it, it's got tennis courts too! We could cycle up there, it's not far at all – this is too good to be true; that's four items off our lists in one go!' Her enthusiasm was infectious, and Jack soon started warming to the idea; but there was still that issue of town looming.

'I'm still not sure about town, Daisy. You know I don't like it.'

She took his hand – she'd been waiting for this. 'This time will be different, I promise – you've just got to trust me. We'll go to Loughborough instead, which is a lot smaller, sort of like a university town – not a big city like Nottingham. We'll go on the bus too, so no multi-storey car parks or lifts or anything like that.' Jack shuddered at the memory. 'Most of the students will have broken up for the summer, so it'll be fairly quiet – especially on a Tuesday. We can go to a pub and the record shops and we're *also* going to get you some new clothes!' She was beginning to realise that Jack always wore the same shirt, and his jeans were – how could she put it? Not exactly fashionable.

Jack looked horrified at the prospect; he still hadn't been into a shop. She appeared to have it all planned out, though. 'Just trust me,' she repeated. 'Come to think of it,' she said, glancing at his list again, 'we could even go to the cinema on the Monday night: that's in Loughborough too. It's in the market square, which'll be even quieter at night so you can get used to it… God, I can't wait!' Daisy squealed, her excitement getting the better of her.

She threw her arms around Jack and kissed him, making them both topple backwards into the dry, brown leaves under the oak tree. He could smell the earth mixed in with her scent. It was a heady combination. They rolled around for a bit, giggling and petting, but that was as far as it went – much to Jack's dismay; she was more interested in talking about the next week.

Having dissected the lists further, they made a rough plan – dependent on the weather of course. It wasn't long before Daisy announced that she had to go, as her parents would be back soon. She was going to go home and type up a proper 'itinerary' on her mum's typewriter.

*****

When Daisy got home, she was surprised to see her parents' car in the drive. That was strange; they were back from cards early. Whoops! she thought; they'd probably ask her where she'd been – and twice already that week. She tried to let herself in undetected and tiptoe upstairs to avoid any awkward questions. 'Is that you, love?' her mum called. Shit, thought Daisy – I'm going to have to go in and talk to them.

Her mum, Carol, was on her own, sitting with her feet up and sipping a G and T as she watched telly. Daisy tried to control the conversation from the off. 'Hi, Mum. You're back early. Where's Dad?'

'Oh, he was worn out so we called it a night.'

'Worn out? How come? He hasn't been overdoing it, has he?' Daisy asked, concerned.

'Well … yes and no. I think that round of golf today really took it out of him.'

'Golf! Dad?' said Daisy. 'Since when has he played golf? I thought it was – and I quote – "a pointless, pompous and elitist pastime for the idle rich".' Carol laughed, thinking when did *she* get so grown up?

'Yes, I know. You don't need to tell me… Bob talked him into it – it's what you do when you're retired, apparently. Anyway, where have you been?'

'Oh, just for a walk.'

'Oh right. You seem to be doing a lot of walking lately… What's his name?'

'Mum!' said Daisy, blushing; it was the first time her mum had voiced her suspicions. Daisy didn't answer the question, though. She felt as if she would be betraying Jack by speaking his name.

'Well…? Honestly, Daisy, I don't know what all the secrecy's about!'

'He's just a boy from college, that's all,' Daisy said, trying her best to make it sound unimportant. Carol slapped her knee and sipped at her gin and tonic in a celebratory manner.

'I knew it!' she said; she loved being right and couldn't wait to tell her husband. 'Well, I hope walking's all you've been doing, young lady.'

'Mum!' cried Daisy, squirming now.

'It's just that you've got a leaf in your hair and your lipstick's smudged, that's all. What did you do, fall over?' God, she was enjoying this! But Daisy wasn't – and she beat a hasty retreat to find a mirror. Carol sat back with a smile on her face, secretly pleased that her youngest had admitted to having a boyfriend; she'd been a tomboy for so long.

*****

262

Jack and his father settled into some sort of routine as the first week without Anne progressed. Boundaries were established. His father begrudgingly accepted the fact that Jack was seeing a girl, and Jack continued to leave his father a cup of tea outside his door every morning. He was sure he even heard a 'hmmph' towards the end of the week. Was that a 'thanks'? Mainly, though, they kept out of each other's way. His father got up late and proceeded to make some breakfast-cum-lunch from whatever he could find. Then he started on the cider at around twelvish before plonking himself in front of Wimbledon for the rest of the day. The curse of the Wimbledon weather had struck again – delaying matches and forcing the BBC to show repeats, some of which were actually more entertaining than the current matches. On a brighter note, Boris Becker was steadily progressing through the tournament.

Predictably, it wasn't long before the food began to run out. They never kept much in at the best of times, even less when Anne had been popping to the shops almost every day. As a result, it was becoming harder and harder to find ingredients to scrape a meal together. It had turned into a bit of a stand-off – who could last the longest? What new and inventive ideas could they come up with to feed themselves? Old tins of Spam and jam sandwiches became the order of the day, and jacket potatoes became a luxury item. There was still some stuff in the freezer, such as mince and the odd leg of lamb, but his father couldn't be bothered to plan that far ahead. Jack sometimes caught him running a warm tap over an unidentifiable lump of brown meat. Someone was going to have to go shopping before they became malnourished, got scurvy or poisoned themselves.

It wasn't just food either; it was simple things like the toilet roll running out. Jack secretly pilfered a few from the staff toilets at work and brought them home in his rucksack. He kept one hidden in his room for emergencies; his father would have to bloody well go out and buy some.

Shopping wasn't the only issue that needed addressing. At some point the laundry was going to become a big problem, more so for Jack than his father – who seemed content to slob around in the same set of clothes every day. Jack, in stark contrast, needed his work clothes washing, and also liked to smell clean for Daisy. They took it in turns, when the other one wasn't around, to circle the washing machine and eye it suspiciously. They turned a few dials and opened the little drawer to peer in at the mysterious blue gunk inside. Nervously, they even prodded a few buttons, then jumped back in alarm when the machine sprung to life, hissing and whirring. It was quickly turned off, each of them beating a hasty retreat, hoping the other would work out how to use it first.

Daisy spent the rest of the week working on the itinerary, whilst also keeping a close eye on the weather forecast. She'd set about the task with military precision, and an eye to detail that Napoleon Bonaparte himself would have been proud of. There were even contingency plans in the case of adverse weather. She proudly presented it to Jack on Friday night at the pub. They perused it over a couple of chip cobs – the first hot meal Jack had eaten in days.

Afterwards, Daisy dropped a bit of a bombshell. She'd totally forgotten she was supposed to be going to her aunt's fiftieth birthday bash in Cambridgeshire that weekend; her mum had reminded her earlier. Daisy felt she couldn't refuse. It was doubly annoying that she was going to miss her shift at the pub on Sunday as well. She'd been counting on the money as she suspected their plans could be expensive. Understandably, Jack was gutted by the news.

With Daisy out of bounds for the rest of the weekend,

he reluctantly threw himself into some chores. Nothing had changed, save for the fact that his work had transferred from outdoors to indoors – washing up, vacuuming, keeping the stove going; he really was turning into his sister! He set about making a fresh batch of cider, even though there was plenty left. Jack had been drinking so much less of late. He'd got used to the pub cider now, and was even starting to prefer it. Their homebrew tasted coarse and flavourless in comparison.

On Sunday, both the laundry and shopping situation came to a head. His father stumbled into the kitchen at around midday to find something to eat, but the cupboards were literally bare. He slammed them shut and got a bottle of cider instead, which helped to dull the appetite. When he went to watch the tennis, he discovered it was middle Sunday and there was no play. This sent him into a fit of rage and he hurled his cider bottle across the room – at which point Jack made himself scarce. From the safety of his bedroom, he heard his father run a bath and splash around for a bit. Fifteen minutes later he stomped up the drive, minus his beard and clutching his bloodied handkerchief to his face. He got into his van and drove off. This was the first time Jack had seen his father leave the house since Anne had gone.

Jack went into the bathroom, dying for a pee. Whilst negotiating the puddles of water left on the floor, he saw his father hadn't emptied the bathtub. It was still full of filthy water; and there were things floating in it. On closer inspection he discovered it was a shoal of his father's giant Y-fronts. These had once been white, but were now grey – and had all manner of stains on them which made Jack feel like retching. Enough was enough: he'd got to get that washing machine working; he needed his work clothes the next day.

After one last failed attempt at using the blasted machine, Jack carried his clothes to the kitchen sink instead; he'd seen his sister do this before. He turned on the hot tap, but there wasn't any hot water as his father had used it all. He chucked in some washing powder anyway, then stirred his clothes around with an old wooden spoon before trying to rinse them in cold water. They were still dripping wet and slimy with soap as he chucked them into the washing basket. The rest of his clothes he shoved into two carrier bags; he had a plan for them.

He was hanging his sopping laundry on the line when his father's van pulled up. Jack watched him with interest as he opened the van doors, then carried bags of shopping into the house – a sight Jack had never thought he would see. When he went back inside himself, the shopping was all over the kitchen floor and his father was making himself a fat ham sandwich. He shoved it into his mouth, chewed noisily, and from what Jack could make out, said, 'This lot needs putting away and *you* owe me forty quid!'

CHAPTER 22

A Night at the Pictures

As Jim reversed their heavily laden Montego estate out of the drive on the following Monday morning, Carol was feeling a little bit tearful. She was having what her husband would call 'one of her moments' and she didn't know what had brought it on. Was it the sight of their two grown-up daughters waving them off from the doorway as if *they* were the parents? Where did all the time go? They used to have family holidays together – beach holidays in Cornwall, setting off at the crack of dawn, crammed into the camper van. The girls would be sleepy on their duvets in the back, so they'd put music on to wake them up and soon they'd all be joining in – especially Daisy. Carol smiled as she pictured them running around naked on the beach when they were little. There were walking holidays in Wales too, when they always seemed to have bad luck with the weather. The girls spent most of their time in brightly coloured anoraks and wellies, or playing board games inside. None of that mattered, though; it just added to the fun. All that had mattered was that they were all together – now it was just her and Jim.

She was also having second thoughts about leaving them on their own for a whole week. They'd never done it before, and it was a long time. What if something happened? A myriad of possibilities went through her mind, both trivial and tragic. What if one of them had a car accident or something? God, perish the thought. Why was she thinking like this? 'Do you think we're doing the right thing, leaving two teenage girls on their own for a week?' she said, as they waved one last time and drove off.

'Well, what's the worst they're gonna do – smoke a bit of pot and play their music too loud?' replied Jim, laid back as ever. Sometimes he was so laid back it drove Carol mad.

'Smoke a bit of pot? This isn't the sixties!'

'Well, what do you think they're going to do? Throw a party and trash the place? They're sensible girls – Lily's going steady with someone and Daisy, well, she's still my innocent little tomboy.' He smiled to himself, knowing this would wind her up. Men! thought Carol; they can be so naive sometimes. Lily may be going steady with someone, but she's no shrinking wallflower – in fact, she can be a right little tart when she wants to be. As for Daisy, I swear he still thinks she's twelve years old. I'm not sure about the 'innocent' anymore either. Carol could remember being seventeen herself, and she also recalled the leaf in Daisy's hair earlier that week – something she'd neglected to tell her husband about. Perhaps if she had, he wouldn't be quite so lackadaisical about leaving them to their own devices.

*****

That evening at seven o'clock, Daisy picked Jack up from the crossroads. She wished she could have picked him up from his house – it was ridiculous. He was jigging from foot to foot and was wearing, she noticed, his ubiquitous blue check shirt. This was looking a little creased, even though he'd tried to iron it, as he'd wanted to look smart for the occasion. His rucksack was back too – another sign that he was nervous. Daisy gave him a kiss, trying to make him feel at ease. She had make-up on and her hair was tied loosely in a low, off-centre ponytail that hung over her shoulder. It must be so much fun being a girl, Jack thought. 'You don't mind if I have a cider do you?' he asked straightaway, rummaging in his bag.

'No, go ahead,' she said, not knowing why he still asked. 'Hey, guess what?' She put her hand on his knee. 'Monday nights are half-price for students, so I'll be able to use my NUS card!' Daisy loved to feel she was getting a bargain – a trait she'd got from her dad.

'Cool.' Jack felt slightly better after a few swigs of cider, and forced himself to talk so he didn't have to listen to the voice in his head. 'So, what are we going to see?' he asked.

'*Indiana Jones and The Last Crusade*,' she replied, pulling a face. 'It was the only thing on worth watching. The *Echo* gave it a really good review anyway.' This was fine by Jack. He'd loved the first two films. The outbuildings and sheds back home had been perfect for acting out scenes from the films when he was younger.

The journey only took about twenty minutes, but the nearer they got to town and the more built up it became, the quieter Jack was. Daisy kept on looking across at him, but he was staring out of the window, waiting for his old acquaintance, the black spot, to arrive. She sensed his anxiety – and it started to make her feel tense too. Oh please, please don't let this be like last time, she prayed to herself; she'd been so excited and so looking forward to it.

Daisy pulled into a side street full of shops and parked cars. She spotted a space and parked the van. 'See, that was easier!' she said. Jack was pale and clutching his rucksack, but she chose to ignore it. 'Right, are we ready then?'

They got out of the van – Jack hesitantly so, as he surveyed his surroundings. The air was warm and humid, and this place felt different to Nottingham somehow – not that he'd got beyond the car park that time. It was on a much smaller scale; there was hardly anyone about.

Daisy came round to his side as he was reaching in for his rucksack. 'You can't drink cider in the cinema; they'll chuck you out!'

'Oh, right,' he replied, looking disappointed. 'I'll still take my rucksack anyway.' As he went to put it on his back, Daisy stopped him. There was then a brief, but gentle, tug of war, before Daisy stood on his toes and looked up into his eyes. 'Leave it here, Jack, please, for me?' She kissed him lightly on the lips. It made Jack's head swim and he acquiesced; he could never resist her.

She dragged him away from the van and down the street. Jack gave himself a pep talk – telling himself to relax, and that he could do this. He felt Daisy's fingers intertwined in his, and he caught their reflection in a shop window. They looked like a proper couple. He told himself how lucky he was to be walking down the street with this beautiful girl.

The street opened out onto a large square full of closed shops. There were more people here and lots of pigeons, but before Jack had time to get too stressed out they were at the steps of the cinema. He looked up, and there in big, red writing were the words 'INDIANA JONES AND THE LAST CRUSADE 19:30 PG'.

The Curzon was an old-fashioned cinema with a huge, high-ceilinged foyer. It was cool inside, fairly quiet too. The foyer was dominated to the rear by a grand staircase that looked to Jack like something out of an old film. There were some game machines, huge stands with movie posters on them, and a pool table where some youths were playing. Their laughter and the sound of the balls echoed across the hall. The youths made Jack feel on edge. He wasn't used to coming across boys of his own age, and not with his girl on his arm.

Daisy, who was totally oblivious to all this, led Jack over to a long, brightly lit counter. Behind it, an old man in a shirt and bow tie stood at a till. There was an enticing array of sweets and chocolate bars on show at the front, together with a huge glass box full of popcorn, which smelt sweet and buttery. To the back there were tubs of ice cream, cans of pop and a curious machine full of crushed blue ice that churned constantly. It was mesmerising, and reminded Jack of *Charlie and the Chocolate Factory*.

Daisy let go of his hand, and he hung back as she dealt with everything. She showed the man her NUS card, and he looked at them for a moment before printing two tickets. 'Anything to eat or drink?' he asked. Daisy turned to Jack and he shook his head – he didn't really have a sweet tooth.

'Popcorn?' she said. He shrugged, feeling foolish as he'd never had popcorn before. Despairing, Daisy turned back. 'We'll have a medium popcorn and a large Fanta, please.' The man eyed Jack as he shovelled the popcorn into a carton, and Jack looked away. He filled a large plastic cup from another machine, then squeaked a lid and straw onto it. After giving Daisy her change, he said, 'Cinema three, up the stairs.' She thanked him.

As they headed towards the stairs, Jack slipped his hand in his pocket, pulled out a ten pound note and offered it to Daisy. 'Here you go,' he said.

'God, you don't need to give me that much. We'll go halves – I think it's best if we do that all week.'

'No, I want to pay,' said Jack, as if he wanted to make up for being useless at everything else.

'Well, if you insist,' Daisy said, relenting, 'but we'll even it out later in the week.' He tried to give her the money but her hands were full. 'Here, stick it in my pocket,' she said, offering her hip to him. Her black jeans were skin-tight, and Jack struggled to get his hand in. He tried to force it in harder but it went in *too* far; he could feel the heat of her hip and thigh. He blushed an alarming shade of red and tried to pull his hand free, but it got stuck again on the way out. Daisy giggled, as he was tickling her. The youths around the pool table looked up at the sound of her laughter and Jack hung his head. Way to go, Jack, he said to himself.

As they ascended the staircase together, Jack felt as though he was somewhere really special, and his self-consciousness was replaced by excitement. They reached the deserted landing, which was plush, deep burgundy in colour, and dimly lit by wall lights, making it feel secretive. They headed down the corridor, past more movie posters and doors, to the digital sign that said 'Screen 3'. 'Well, here we go then!' said Daisy, and pushed the double doors open with her hip.

Jack's heart fluttered in anticipation. The room was dark – so dark it was almost impossible to see. They shuffled forwards, and were startled by a member of staff in uniform who appeared out of the shadows. 'Tickets please,' she said. Daisy gave Jack the popcorn and Fanta to hold whilst she gave the usherette the tickets. She ripped them in half and handed them back. Daisy kept the stubs as a memento and stuck them in her diary later that night; she always did things like that. 'This way please.' The usherette turned on a torch to show them to their seats; these seemed like flapping, velvety mouths to Jack: you had to prise open the jaws of them and quickly sit down before they bit you.

When their eyes had become accustomed to the darkness, they looked around and noticed that the cinema was barely half full. Jack began to relax a little. They were just tucking into their popcorn when a rectangular light lit up the biggest pair of curtains Jack had ever seen at the front of the theatre. The curtains parted to reveal a huge screen, and you could hear the crackle of the projector as the film classification came up. The screen came brightly to life, hurting their eyes at first. They sat through three adverts – one for a local Indian restaurant called Koh-i-Noor, one for a local hardware store called Putts and one for ice cream, where people with impossibly white teeth were splashing about in a swimming pool. Jack was mesmerised – he couldn't believe how big everything was or how loud; the sound seemed to be everywhere around him, and right in his ears.

As the film started, Daisy offered Jack the drink. He took it from her and slurped through the straw, his eyes glued to the screen. To his disappointment, the film ended abruptly after about three minutes. He stopped slurping and looked across at Daisy, dumbfounded, the straw still in his mouth. His face was priceless, and Daisy burst out laughing. 'It's a trailer, you ninny!' she whispered.

'Oh.' He had no idea what a trailer was, but wasn't going to say so. There were a few more of them, which became a bit disconcerting, as he didn't know whether he was watching the real film or not. Some of them had loud bangs and explosions in them, making him jump; and again Daisy had to stifle her laughter.

The film began for real, and it did exactly what films should do – it transported them to a magical place. The people around them didn't exist. It was the second – no, third most incredible experience of Jack's young life. He was completely blown away by it. When the credits started rolling at the end, he sat there in stunned silence, staring at the screen. Then the lights came up, and they were suddenly back in the cinema again.

He was still in a daze as they walked hand in hand down the

cinema steps and into the town square. It had been raining; the air was heavy with the smell of wet pavement and the concrete was dark with it. 'So?' said Daisy. 'What did you think?'

'Wow! That was amazing!'

'Yes, it was a lot better than I was expecting.' She was getting a little too old for Indiana Jones films; *Rumble Fish* was more her kind of thing. But River Phoenix had been an unexpected surprise as the 'young Indy'; she had a bit of a crush on him. They discussed the film all the way back to the van – particularly the funny bits – stopping now and again to gesticulate and to get their point across.

'Hey, are you hungry?' Daisy asked as they climbed into the van.

'I'm starving. Why?'

'Right, McDonald's it is then!' Jack had seen adverts for McDonald's on the telly, but inevitably had never been to one. Daisy chose the new drive-thru on the edge of town, so they didn't have to sit inside.

They ate in the car park like a pair of normal teenagers out on a date. Burgers, it turned out, weren't the easiest things to eat, though. Jack kept turning to the window so he could wipe his mouth with a napkin. The food didn't last long; it was salty and addictive – a quick fix. Jack cracked open a bottle of cider afterwards, whilst Daisy popped some chewing gum into her mouth before starting the van again.

On the way back, she put some music on loud. Jack couldn't have felt more different than when they'd been driving in. He wound down the window and stuck his head out. Behind him he saw the glowing orange lights of the town, nestled together in a valley and fading in the distance. They represented some sort of victory, and he drank from his bottle, letting the music wash over him. He could hear Daisy happily singing her head off as usual. God, I love you, he thought.

As they climbed the hill to Jack's house, he couldn't see through the impenetrable hedges if any lights were still on. This made him feel sad either way. Tonight had lit a fire in him and he didn't want to lose the feeling. He didn't want to go back to how things had been before – and he certainly didn't want to go back to his house, bereft of life. Daisy pulled into the entrance to Bunny Wood and turned the van round. 'What time is it?' he asked, not really wanting to know the answer.

'It's nearly ten-thirty,' Daisy replied as she killed the engine. Jack groaned; he was going to have to go soon or he'd be locked out. It was infuriating – Daisy had no curfew all week. It didn't matter what time she went back, yet here he was, still trapped by the gatekeeper who was controlling his life. Something had to change, and the look on Daisy's face echoed his feelings.

Through Jack's open window they could see the wood, delicious and inviting. It was so tempting to go for a moonlit stroll, but they just didn't have time.

Instead, Daisy took her gum out and put it in some paper before placing it in the ashtray. 'Come here, you.' She leant across to kiss him, minty from the gum and with salt on her lips from the French fries. She didn't mess about. It was a big kiss, straight for the jugular, setting Jack's pulse racing. He placed his hand at the nape of her neck, underneath her ponytail, where her hair was gathered – one of his favourite places. All their frustrations and passion poured out then; both of them wanting more.

She kissed up and down Jack's neck and behind his ear, her breath so sensitive it was driving him mad. His other hand explored underneath her T-shirt. For the first time, he tentatively ventured towards the cup of her bra. Her breast felt full, exquisite and warm in his palm. He half-expected to get slapped away, but on the contrary it made her kisses more urgent. Her breathing became heavier and hotter in his ear, which encouraged him further still, and he sought out the bud of her nipple. He felt it hardening through her bra … and then a car drove past, slowing down to honk its horn at them. Someone shouted obscene encouragement out of the window, just for good measure, laughing as they went by.

It snapped Jack and Daisy right out of their moment – like the proverbial bucket of cold water being thrown over them. They were suddenly aware of themselves again – embarrassed and surprised at how swiftly things had escalated. 'You'd better go, Jack,' Daisy said, trying to compose herself. 'It's getting on.' Right then, Jack wouldn't have cared if he *had* been locked out. He tried to kiss her again, but she stopped him gently by putting her thumb on his lips and giving him a firm peck that signified it was over. 'Tomorrow,' she whispered. 'Just one more night, and then we've got the whole house to ourselves.'

They had both fantasised about what they'd done on Midsummer Night in the days following it, of course they had – what they could remember of it, anyway. But as the weeks had gone on, and having no further opportunity to follow it up, they had begun to feel as if it had never happened. Now Daisy had started something – and tomorrow couldn't come soon enough.

Jack got out of the van and slammed the door. 'Hey, mister, didn't you enjoy tonight?' she reprimanded him through the window. He instantly felt guilty; he was being ungrateful.

'God, sorry, Daisy, yes of course I did – it's been amazing – and thanks for taking me.'

'You're welcome,' she replied. 'And that's just the start – we've got the whole week! I'll see you in the morning… Oh, and don't forget to bring some money: we're taking you shopping, remember!'

Daisy drove off feeling pretty pleased with herself. That's stage one over, she thought – roll on the rest of the week! As Jack trudged home, he too pondered the week ahead. And for once the thought of town didn't fill him with the usual dread; not after that night.

CHAPTER 23

Salad Days

The next morning Jack couldn't get his head around the fact that he wouldn't be going into work. He wondered who'd be doing his jobs. As he made his father a cup of tea, he fretted about the prospect of getting off the bus in the village. He didn't like the thought of it one bit – and he had those two bags of washing he wanted to take to with him as well. These would draw even more attention to him. He decided there and then to go on the bike. His father was still in bed, so what did it matter? He wouldn't see him leave and he wouldn't miss the bike either. He'd better get his skates on if he didn't want the bus passing him on the main road.

Earlier, he'd taken fifty pounds out of his savings tin. It seemed a hell of a lot of precious money, but he still didn't know if it would be enough; he wasn't sure exactly what Daisy had got in mind. He'd also taken a long, loving look at his mother's photograph, which had become a daily habit. He packed a couple of bottles of cider, guessing he might need them. With his rucksack on his back, and a carrier bag of clothes perched on each handle bar, he set off down the hill.

These were the salad days for our Jack: the heady, innocent days of youth and summer, married with a newfound air of sanguinity and freedom; all brought about by being in love and being loved back equally – when love was visceral, intuitive and unconditional. It wasn't governed by age, weight, height, salary or social status – a luxury that belongs exclusively to the young. Everything was new. Life was an adventure and life was for living. OK, his sister had left and he missed her terribly – but no more so than any normal sixteen-year-old boy would if his mother walked out on him; he'd felt hurt and abandoned at first, but not for long. He had his own stuff going on – and that stuff happened to be a certain Miss Daisy Jones.

He pedalled as fast as he dared with the bags on his bike. Now he knew how Anne must have felt when she brought shopping back from the village. He'd just made it over the main road near the crossroads when he saw the bus go past. It was strange not to be on it. He imagined there were two of him, and his normal self was still sitting on the bus going to work and looking out of the window. Jack felt sorry for that boy but happy for himself.

After hoisting his bike over the kissing gate (an obstacle he had overlooked), he took his usual route to Daisy's, via Church Lane. But when he saw the main street looming up ahead he came to a halt, reluctant to go down it. He scanned the paths and driveways to his right, thinking there must be a back way of cutting across to her house. Sure enough, there was an overgrown path that he'd never noticed before – purely because he'd never been looking. It was quite well hidden, a cut-through, and people obviously walked their dogs down it, apparent from the amount of dog mess he had to avoid. The path was enclosed on both sides by high fences, and at the bottom of it was a clearer purpose-built jitty. This ran in both directions, also parallel to high fences. If he'd got his bearings right, this had to be the back of the gardens on Daisy's row.

Jack parked his bike against the fence, stood on one of

the struts and peeped cautiously over – but it wasn't Daisy's garden. He made his way along a bit further, peering over at random intervals and trying to gauge how far along Daisy's house was. Before long, he was met by the familiar sight of Honeysuckle Cottage and the weeping willow. In the distance were the decking, the patio doors and the kitchen window. Bingo!

Daisy hadn't slept well; she'd been too revved up from the success of the night out and from their moment in the van. The buzz had continued to course through her – making her long for the next day. Not only that, but it was too humid in her room – it always was in the summer. There'd been no air, even with the window open, and as a result she'd struggled to wake up; if it wasn't for meeting Jack, she probably wouldn't have got up at all. She showered and dressed, still half asleep, then picked at some toast and drank two cups of coffee.

She was just dumping her second cup in the sink when something caught her eye; a movement at the bottom of the garden. To her amazement, a carrier bag had just been chucked over the fence. She thought she was seeing things and rubbed the sleep from her eyes, but then another one appeared. It landed on the grass and some clothes spilled out of it. As she looked on, two arms appeared, and then a bike, which was carefully lowered down. It was followed by a head. 'Jack!' she laughed to herself, as he climbed the fence into the garden. Trust him to make an entrance: he couldn't just use the front door like any normal human being, could he?

She watched him as he approached the house, furtively looking from side to side as if he intended to rob the place. He was so funny sometimes. She knocked on the window and waved. Jack looked startled at first, but grinned when he saw her and raised the carrier bags in greeting. What on earth was he carrying them for? Was he planning on moving in for the week? Just then, the cat appeared, trotting up to him and rubbing around his legs. Jack bent down to fuss her and Daisy shook her head in wonder.

She met Jack at the patio doors and opened them up for him. The cat brushed past his legs and followed him in before heading straight for her food bowl. 'Something wrong with the front door?' she asked. He grinned sheepishly back.

'I found a back way.'

'Yes, I can see that! Anyway, I thought you were coming on the bus … and what's with the clothes?'

'Oh, I thought I'd come on the bike instead, and these, well, they need washing. Would you mind?' He held them up. 'It's just that … I don't know how to work our machine.'

'You're joking. What about your dad?'

'Oh, I don't think he knows either.'

Daisy couldn't believe what she was hearing. 'Come on, I'll show you,' she sighed, as she beckoned him into the kitchen.

Jack followed her. He hadn't been in her house since Midsummer Night, and that seemed ages ago. He was struck by the cleanliness and order again, especially compared to the squalor of his own house since Anne had left. Daisy showed him how to use a washing machine and where to put the powder and softener. She explained which setting was best for what, and that it was important to spin the washing afterwards. Then she unloaded the dirty laundry into the machine. Some of his work clothes had been in there since the weekend. Daisy turned up her nose and said 'Phew!' as she held them at arm's length. Jack blushed. He went even redder when she pulled out some of his small, battered underpants – complete with threadbare elastic. She held them up for inspection. 'I think we need to get you some new underwear today too!'

Daisy nipped upstairs to brush her teeth whilst Jack stayed in the kitchen petting the cat. After a few minutes, curiosity got the better of him and he had a little wander. First he peered into the dining room with the bar, and then the lounge with the photographs. Memories of that night came flooding back, but it felt different this time – he felt a lot more at ease. He looked longingly up the stairs, where he could hear Daisy banging about. He was dying to see her room again; last time had all been a mad rush, *and* it had been dark.

When Daisy was ready, they walked to the bus stop near the crossroads and caught the bus into Loughborough. It stopped often on the way, getting fuller and fuller, but this didn't bother Jack too much. He was used to buses now – and he had Daisy with him; he told himself it was just like going to work. They got off at the last stop, the bus station in the centre of town. It made a nice change to be getting off a bus at the same time as Daisy for once.

Town was busy – a marked difference to the previous night. Jack had a few moments of panic, but Daisy pulled him along, talking to keep him occupied. When she told him she wanted to go to 'The Left Legged Pineapple', he thought she was joking. She repeated it, confirming that he had indeed heard her correctly.

'It's the coolest record shop in the world! All the Indie kids go there. It sells new *and* second hand albums – you'll love it!' she enthused.

She was after an album that had just been released and that she'd been saving up for – *Tranzophobia* – the debut album by Mega City Four, a band she'd been following from the beginning. This didn't mean a thing to Jack, but clearly did to a lot of other people; when they got to the shop the album cover was plastered all over the windows, together with huge posters of the band. Daisy grabbed Jack's arm, letting out a squeal of excitement.

The Left Legged Pineapple was a unique little place – a

Mecca for music aficionados. It had painted yellow window frames on the outside with the shop's purple logo written above them. Inside, there were two small rooms. When Jack and Daisy entered, various cool cats – most of them with earphones draped around their necks – looked up briefly. They went back to thumbing their way through the thousands of LPs on offer whilst nodding their heads to the loud music that was playing.

Jack had never been inside a real shop, and had certainly never seen anything like this. Daisy knew exactly where to find the album she was after, and soon extracted it from among the others. She pulled out the inner sleeve and smelt it with a dreamy look on her face before sliding it back in again. 'God, I love the smell of a brand new record!' she exclaimed. This was like her church. Browsing for music was her favourite pastime, and she spent a further ten minutes or so earmarking future purchases. It was all a bit overwhelming for Jack and he just followed her around.

She finally took her purchase up to the counter where she was served by a man in his twenties with a ponytail and earring. 'Good choice,' he said, acknowledging the album.

'Really? I've been dying for it to come out!' Daisy said, clearly pleased.

'Yes, it's wicked – worth all the hype… Here, do you want a free poster? We're giving them away as a promotion – we've got loads of them.'

Daisy was made up. 'Wow, yes please!' He rolled the poster up and secured it with tape before popping it into a record bag with the album. Daisy turned around and beamed at Jack, who was starting to feel like a bit of a spare part and a tiny bit jealous. She had such an easy way with people – men in particular – who seemed only too happy to go out of their way to please her (not that she was aware of this).

They walked out of the shop, Daisy proudly clutching her yellow bag with the eye-catching purple logo on it. That was half the attraction: just to be seen around town with the bag automatically meant you were cool.

'Right, that's *my* shopping done – now it's your turn!' she said. Now that the moment had arrived, Jack was having serious misgivings about going into shops and looking at clothes. The embarrassment of having to try them on, then take them up to the counter in front of everyone was playing on his mind. It was such an alien concept, something that other people did – people on telly, behind a glass screen; not him.

'Could we just go for a bit of a walk first? I'm not quite ready yet.' He secretly wanted a drink, but Daisy suspected this; she wasn't stupid. She considered being firm with him and refusing, but in the end compromised by dragging him into an alleyway.

After Jack had necked half a bottle of cider, they headed back into town. The market square was full of shoppers and office workers rushing about. Jack gulped at the sight of it. Daisy proceeded to drag him in and out of various men's clothes shops. She knew exactly where to go, and she did all the looking too – pulling items off racks and holding them up against him. Jack stood there as if it wasn't happening to him, as if he was just a bystander, until he was sent in and out of changing rooms. Sometimes he got a 'thumbs up'; sometimes a laugh and a shake of the head – he endured it all silently.

The lowest point was when Daisy remembered they had to get him some new underwear. Jack was hoping she'd forgotten. She insisted on him getting boxer shorts; something he'd never worn. His humiliation was complete when she asked him in front of everybody what size to get –to which he mumbled, 'I don't know, medium I guess.' He drew the line at taking them up to the counter, as he was too embarrassed, and Daisy had to buy them for him. This didn't seem to bother her at all.

By the time it was over Jack's head was in a spin and he needed another drink. They headed to the pub clutching their bags. Daisy was thrilled to bits as she had bagged some real bargains. Jack wasn't so impressed; he couldn't believe how much money they'd spent. Daisy had even had to lend him a tenner as she couldn't let him pass up a pair of black Converse boots – not at that price! They were marked down because they had a couple of eyelets missing. They'd also bought a white under T-shirt, a shirt, some black drainpipes and some second-hand Levi's – timelessly classic in their shape. Some of the boys had started to wear flares as the baggy fashion was coming in, but Daisy wasn't sure about them. She definitely couldn't imagine Jack in them either. And all of this for sixty quid!

Jack got his first real smell of a pub at the Three Nuns. It was miles from his home, and he felt comfortably anonymous there. A haze of blue cigarette smoke hung from the low, beamed ceiling of the bar, and the rich, sweet scent of ale was strong from the drip trays. Mingled with this was the unique and appealing smell of lunchtime pub food: the tang of salt and vinegar from chips, and raw onion from cobs – it was an enticing mix and Jack loved it. Even though it was early on a Tuesday lunchtime, the pub had a good smattering of customers, both young and old; students who lived in the town (or hadn't gone home for the summer) and pensioners playing dominoes.

Jack felt self-conscious under the harmless interest of some old-timers as they approached the bar. Daisy was a little concerned that they wouldn't get served, but a cheerful landlady immediately made them feel at ease. She welcomed them with a big smile. 'What can I get you, loves?'

They carried their drinks to a snug corner near a window.

'So, what do you think then? Your first time inside a pub,' Daisy whispered. Jack looked around before answering. No one was paying them any attention. This was the thing he'd learnt that day about town: not everyone *was* watching you all the time, you just blended in.

'Yes, I love it!' he replied, taking a much-needed mouthful of cider.

'Are you hungry?' she asked, thinking that she was always asking him this – but the smell of the food was getting to her.

'Yes, I am a bit.'

'Same here. I don't know how much money we've got, though.' And she emptied her pockets on to the table. Jack was totally broke, but Daisy took full responsibility for that. They counted her money, and once they'd set aside their bus fare, they only had enough left for either another pint and a half or a couple of cobs. They looked at each other and grinned, both knowing what the other was thinking. 'Let's get another round of drinks; we can make some lunch at home,' Daisy said. 'You're a bad influence on me, you know!'

They sipped their drinks and went through their purchases. To Daisy's pleasant surprise, Jack offered to fetch their second round of drinks: a huge step forward. She watched him make his way to the bar from over the top of her record, like a teacher with a clipboard watching her protégé. She smiled to herself at his progress, then went back to reading the lyric sheet.

After another hour, when they'd run out of drinks and money, they made their way to the bus station. The booze had gone to their heads, especially Daisy's. She had that alcoholic glow where your cheeks feel warm and your throat looks flushed. Everything was suddenly right with the world – everything was perfect. They'd both got a taste for it now, and planned to keep on drinking when they got home.

When they arrived back in the village, Jack insisted on going the back way to her house again. 'I'm not climbing over a fence into my own garden!' Daisy said.

'OK, I'll race you then!' challenged Jack, and they both shot off in different directions. He had slightly underestimated the time it would take to negotiate the overgrown path and back fence whilst clutching four shopping bags, and despite a valiant effort, including a commando roll when he landed on the grass in Daisy's garden, she still beat him easily.

She was unlocking the patio door and laughing as he approached, out of breath. 'I won!' she teased. Jack smiled, gracious in defeat, as he put his bags down on the decking to get his breath back.

Daisy watched him fondly from the doorway. 'Hey, what do I get for winning?' she said. Jack shrugged. 'How about a kiss?' He leant forward to peck her on the cheek but she pulled back. 'Hey, that's not a kiss!' And she put her arms around his neck and pulled him towards her. The kiss was seductive, slow and alcoholic. Afterwards she held his gaze for a moment before letting him in, as if it was a promise of things to come.

Wow, thought Jack. I'm not even in the house yet!

Daisy set about preparing some food whilst Jack cracked open a bottle of cider. They ate their lunch in a sophisticated manner out on the patio, feeling like proper grown-ups. When they'd finished, they headed to the bar in the dining room. Daisy made them a couple of gin and tonics to take upstairs. Daisy led the way and Jack followed, clutching his bags and trying his best to do the gentlemanly thing by keeping his eyes away from her bum. He recalled the last time he had gone up these stairs; he had sprinted up them for dear life.

They reached the carpeted landing, and it was as if he was

seeing it all for the first time. There was a washing basket, and a plant on a window ledge that he hadn't noticed before. There were more doors than he remembered as well; he wasn't sure which one was Daisy's. Then there they were, standing outside her room. She put her hand on the handle, trying to turn it whilst holding two drinks and a record bag. This was the moment Jack had been waiting for all day. He was finally going to enter the 'inner sanctum' – and in broad daylight too! She slowly pushed open the door…

CHAPTER 24
The Warm Room

There it was in all its glory; the beating heart, the engine room; an Aladdin's cave of secret treasures. It was larger than Jack remembered, a lot bigger than his bedroom at home. The walls were covered in posters of bands, album covers and movie stars – some of whom he now recognised, such as The Smiths, The Cure, Patti Smith and The Stone Roses. There was a black and white film poster of a moody looking guy with muscles, with the banner 'A Streetcar named Desire' across the top. Another one was of an old guy with glasses whom he'd seen before on one of her T-shirts. He was standing with a woman – apparently called Annie Hall. There were magazine and newspaper covers stuck to the walls too, mostly the *NME*. He noticed there were piles of these dotted around the room. There was a chest of drawers with a mirror on it, and mysterious bottles, canisters and pots surrounding it like an alchemist's potions.

To Jack's amazement there was a TV and a modern music system as well. It looked like some sort of magic box from the future, with not one but two tape decks. There was a built-in wardrobe with a full-length mirror, and shelves groaning under the weight of hundreds of records, tapes and books. In the middle of it all, like an island, was the majesty of her bed. It was neatly made up with a flowery print cover and matching pillows. In pride of place, tucked in, was a small, faded orange teddy bear, wearing a little blue waistcoat. Jack was drawn to it, as it looked somehow innocent and childlike in comparison with the rest of the room.

'Well, come in then!' said Daisy. Jack was standing slack-jawed in the doorway. It was all too much to take in, and he shuffled into the room, not wanting to disturb anything.

'What shall I do with these?' he asked, indicating his bags.

'Oh, just plonk them down anywhere.' He put them by the door and Daisy offered him his drink. He stood there sipping it as she went over to the window, where there was a tall fan on a stand. It was then that he noticed how hot it was. She opened the window and turned the fan on; it hummed and rotated but gave little relief.

He was still hovering by the door when she turned back to him. 'Well, sit down then, make yourself at home, *you're making me nervous!*' She said the last bit in a New York accent. Jack didn't know where to sit, so he perched on the edge of her bed as if it was going to explode. Daisy went over to her hi-fi and lifted the lid. She lovingly pulled out her new record, which she'd been dying to play, blew off the dust and put it on the turntable. The first song began, and bars of red lights danced up and down on the front of the stereo in time to it. The music was fast and frenetic, but the singing was melodic and harmonious – unlike anything he'd ever heard before. Daisy nodded her head in time, pleased with it.

She came and sat down next to him on the bed, and they sipped at their drinks without speaking. It was one of those rare moments when even Daisy felt shy. Here they were at last, alone in her bedroom, with no one else in the house. It was exactly what they'd both been yearning for, yet that put them under a sort of pressure. Jack noticed the awkwardness and initiated conversation for a change, asking about the posters on the walls. This got them going, and they talked more freely until their drinks ran out. 'Right, I'm going to make us some cocktails!' Daisy said; and she disappeared downstairs.

While she was gone, Jack feasted his eyes on the room again. He noticed things he hadn't seen before, like an acoustic guitar leaning in the corner. Did she play the guitar? It made him realise there were still so many things he didn't know about her. He lay back on her bed and smelt her pillow, picking up the threadbare teddy. Lucky thing, he thought, holding it out in front of him and imagining all the nights it had spent in Daisy's arms. It *was* cute, though – it had a button for an eye and had lost most of its stuffing.

Daisy returned clutching two drinks and Jack sat up quickly, still holding the bear. 'Isn't he adorable? I've had him since I was born. His name's Denim. He's been stitched up so many times – I cried for days when he lost his eye! Here, try this,' she said, passing Jack his drink. It was fizzy and cloudy, with ice and lime in it. 'This is called a Moscow Mule.'

It tasted fiery: hot and pleasantly refreshing. 'Whew! What's in it?'

'It's vodka, lime and ginger beer – that's the kick.'

Jack was impressed. 'How do you know all these drinks?'

'Oh years of practice, I suppose. Dad's always wanted a pub. Like I said before – he's a frustrated landlord and I'm just a frustrated cocktail girl! You wait, next I'll make you a White Russian. It's Mum's favourite!'

It was after the seriously potent White Russians that things started to get a little … strange – but in a good way. The music got louder as Daisy changed records at will – The Smiths, Happy Mondays, Pixies – all the usual suspects. Then she put on *Girls Just Want to Have Fun* by Cyndi Lauper, and danced around the room to it, encouraging Jack to join her. After this, she decided to put on a compilation tape, as it was becoming too disruptive to constantly change records.

The drinks kept coming, their dancing got flirtier and their tongues got looser (in more ways than one), until Daisy asked Jack to try on his new clothes for her. He reluctantly left the room, swaying slightly and taking his bags with him, before returning a few seconds later. 'Er, Daisy, where's the bathroom?' And she laughed, following him out. She showed him where it was, and he instantly shut the door on her.

'Oh, I'll go and make some more drinks then, shall I?' she said, with mock affront. 'And don't forget the boxer shorts!' She tottered down the stairs, smiling to herself.

When Jack returned to her room she was still gone. His new clothes felt odd. It was so long since he'd had some that he barely recognised himself when he looked in her full-length mirror. They'd certainly take some getting used to. Oddest of all was his new underwear: it almost felt as if he wasn't wearing any. Compared to his underpants, everything felt ... well, loose and free; he wasn't sure if he liked it. He stood with his legs apart and jiggled himself about experimentally while looking in the mirror. Just at that point Daisy walked back in the room. 'Everything all right?' she asked in amusement.

'Yes, fine!' he said, as he spun round.

She put the drinks on her dresser and eyed him up and down. The clothes suited him but something wasn't quite right. A few minor alterations were needed – a few tweaks. She walked over to him and started unbuttoning his shirt, instructing him to untuck it and to take his belt off too. He did as she said, and when she reached the bottom button she opened up his shirt to reveal his pale, defined chest and stomach. She slid her hands around to the sides, and as she did so she felt his stomach tremble. She hooked her thumbs into the gap between his jeans and his skin and tugged them down, just a little, to sit on his hips. This revealed the waistband of his boxer shorts, and she stood back for a moment to check him out. Yep, now he was beginning to look the part.

She had another idea, and walked over to the dresser, pausing to sip her drink first; she was enjoying this. She grabbed a can of hair mousse, shook the can and sprayed it into her hand, filling her palm with the foam. As she approached him with it, she noticed the look of fright on his face. 'Don't worry, nearly done!' she reassured him. She smoothed his hair back at the sides, then moulded it into a quiff at the front before spraying it in place with some hair spray. She stood back again to admire her handiwork. With his hair back, his high cheekbones were accentuated; he looked like a model to her and sexy as hell. Daisy came over to him, kissed him, and said, 'Just one more thing and then we're done, I promise!' Jack groaned as she scurried out of the room.

She returned with a spare pair of her mum's black-framed reading glasses, and when Jack saw them it dawned on him what she was up to. He looked up at a poster of her beloved Morrissey, and then back to her. 'Daisy, no!' he protested.

'Please!' she said, approaching him – and he backed away as if she was wielding a knife.

'No, I'll look stupid.'

'You won't, you'll look gorgeous!' she giggled. He held her wrists as she tried to put them on him and they had a bit of a play tussle. 'Come on, just for a minute, it's only a bit of fun!' Jack gave in – he always did. The transformation was complete. 'Wow!' she exclaimed, and steered him in front of the mirror. He thought he looked foolish and his eyes felt funny.

At that moment, a song by Madonna started playing. 'Oh my God! I haven't heard this for ages – I used to love Madonna!' Daisy said, and this gave her another idea. Next thing Jack knew, she was rolling up her vest to reveal her stomach, turning up her jeans and tying her hair up in a ribbon. She put on some dangly earrings and made a beauty spot on her upper lip with an eyeliner pencil. He removed the glasses so he could see her better. She rewound the tape, then began dancing around the room to *Into the Groove*, dressed as Madonna, circa *Desperately Seeking Susan*. She even mimicked her in the film by standing in front of the fan with her arms above her head. Jack just laughed at it all; he had no idea what she was doing but could watch her for hours – she was as mad as rhubarb and as creamy as custard.

The drink was strong in Daisy now and she danced with carefree abandon – free of inhibitions and living out her fantasies, just like in the song. And she was good – the music was hypnotic and so were her movements. Jack was entranced. The thin straps of her vest had slipped off her shoulders, revealing her bra, and her face was flushed. She came towards him, kissing and touching him briefly, before moving away again when he wanted more.

When the song finished she came to rest against him, her chest rising and falling against his. She ran her hands underneath his shirt again, but this time pushed it off and onto the floor. Her hands glided over the contours of his back, exploring him with an electric touch. She looked up at him, her eyes never leaving his, as she reached down, crossing her arms and pulling her vest over her head. Quickly, she pressed herself to him, feeling a fleeting moment of self-consciousness in her semi-nakedness. He felt her breasts shift against him through the silky material of her bra; her skin was sticky and hot. His mouth moved over her bare shoulder and across the musk-scented hollow of her collarbone to her neck. She shivered with feeling, then unexpectedly pulled herself away.

Jack watched as she walked over to the window and closed the curtains. It was still relatively light in the room, so when she turned to face him he could see everything. She started to undo her jeans, each button popping open one by one – agonisingly slow. They slipped down her hips, and she stepped out of them to reveal matching pink pants, the same as her bra – French cut with white lace trim. Reaching up, she took the ribbon out of her hair and shook it loose. She stood there, seemingly unabashed now in her underwear, as the fan gently rippled her hair. It was the single most beautiful thing he had ever seen in his life. Here she was – his caterpillar girl, shedding her skin and moving towards him, flitting about him like one of the butterflies in her garden, and glowing like a fairy in a fairy-tale. She dusted him with kisses, light as air, as she undid the top button of his jeans. He pulled them off and she led him towards her bed, where they slid beneath the covers, as the music played on in the warm room.

It was different from the last time; their needs were different. It was faster, more frantic – like the album Daisy had bought. They knew from experience what was at the end of it and they both wanted to get there as soon as possible, going about it almost savagely, a pair of cannibals in the sticky summer heat. Daisy was distantly aware that *Gimme! Gimme! Gimme!* by Abba was playing on the stereo – and as the music crescendoed so did her urgency. She grabbed the back of Jack's hair, which was damp with perspiration, put her lips to his ear and cried, 'Say my name, Jack, oh God, say my name!'

Afterwards, when their breathing was returning to normal, the music came to an end and the tape clicked off. They lay there on their backs, staring at the ceiling, in that blissful state of post-coital nirvana when they say people are at their most truthful. 'Daisy?' said Jack.

'Umm.'

'You *will* come to America with me, won't you? Say you will.'

There was a pause, and then she replied, 'Yes, if it'll shut you up.' Her eyelids were heavy. The sandman was trying to take her.

'Really?' he cried, propping himself up on one elbow to look at her; but her eyes were closed. 'You really mean it?'

'Sure, why not...? We could go to Las Vegas and get married in a chapel.' She rolled away from him, her voice slurry with sleep. She had said it flippantly, but to Jack it sounded like the most romantic notion he'd ever heard. His mind raced with the possibilities as he lay down again.

'I love you, Daisy.' It was the first time either of them had uttered those words to the other. Unfortunately, for such an auspicious moment, it was somewhat wasted on her.

'I love you too,' she managed to whisper, before adding 'pour some sugar on me, baby.' And then fell fast asleep...

Daisy was brought back around by a voice calling her name. It pervaded her dreams where she lay happily anchored, pulling her to the surface. 'Daisy!' Was she still dreaming or was she awake? *'DAISY!'* It became louder, more persistent, and she dozily recognised it. She then realised that she *was* awake and...

'Oh shit! It's my sister!' she cried, sitting bolt upright in bed, waking Jack up. The duvet slipped down, and he was greeted with a side view of one of Daisy's pert breasts. It was a wonderful sight to behold, but only lasted a second before she clutched the cover to her chest – thus regaining her modesty. Her eyes were wide with the sudden gravity of the situation. Here she was, naked in bed with a boy, in her parents' house in the middle of the day. God, what time was it anyway? She looked at the clock by her bed and it was nearly six. Jesus, how did that happen? And her sister was what ... on the stairs?

Outside her door? About to come in? How was she meant to get Jack out? Again, her sister's voice yelled '*DAISY!*', getting angrier.

When Daisy answered, her voice was croaky. 'Yes?'

'Oh, finally!' Lily replied. 'Can I have a word with you please?'

Why does she sound like my mother? thought Daisy. 'Just a minute!' she called. 'Shit, where are my knickers?' And she groped around under the covers, amid an unfamiliar mass of limbs. She located them with one of her feet and hooked them up, still clutching the cover to her chest with her other hand. 'Turn around!' she hissed to Jack, as she needed both hands to put her pants back on. Making sure he was facing the other way, she jumped out of bed and grabbed her vest. God knows where her bra had gone.

When she found her jeans and wiggled into them, she caught her reflection in the mirror. Her hair was all over the place – more like a nest than hair – as if she'd just spent the afternoon having mad, drunken sex or something. She patted it down and padded barefoot to the door. When she reached it, she turned around and put her fingers to her lips, giving Jack a 'Sshh!' gesture. She opened the door a crack, but there was no one there … so she opened it further and looked out. 'I'm downstairs!' her sister yelled. Daisy walked out onto the landing. Lily was standing at the bottom of the stairs with one hand on the banister and one hand on her hip, looking up at her.

'Oh. Hi,' said Daisy. Lily beckoned her with one finger and walked off towards the kitchen.

Daisy gulped and headed downstairs. She was trying to piece together events, but everything was fuzzy. What evidence had they left? She couldn't recall tidying up … and then she remembered the cocktails. *Shit!* she thought, desperately trying to think of an excuse. Sure enough, her sister was standing in the dining room next to the bar. She had her hands on her hips and was looking displeased, as if she actually *was* their mother. On the bar were spirit bottles, empty mixer bottles and pools of ice.

'Bit early for a party isn't it…? Got guests, have we?'

'Er, yes. Claire came round earlier – we had a few drinks.' Lily gave her a look that said: 'Yeah, right!'

Look at her getting all high and mighty, Daisy thought – as if she's some kind of angel and never raided the bar before! Lily marched past her and into the kitchen. Daisy followed her in, and saw the washing machine with its door open. Shit! Jack's washing; she'd forgotten all about it.

Her sister knelt down by the washing basket in front of the machine, pulled out a pair of Jack's underpants and held them up. 'And what about these?' she said. 'I suppose they're Claire's as well, are they? Or has a twelve-year-old boy moved in?' For once Daisy was stumped – there was no way out of this one.

She opened her mouth to speak when something over Lily's shoulder, through the kitchen window, caught her eye. With no explanation forthcoming, her sister went on. 'Look, I know you've got a boyfriend, Daisy, and so do Mum and Dad – so you might as well just admit it…' But Daisy wasn't listening; she was too busy watching, in amazement, the sight of Jack sprinting down the garden with his shirt tails flapping out behind him. He grabbed his bike, chucked it over the fence, and then vaulted it himself. Her sister's voice swam back into focus: '…you're seventeen after all, but that doesn't mean you can go trashing the place as soon as Mum and Dad go away. *Or* do washing for every waif and stray in the area either! And that reminds me,' she said, turning round and pointing outside. 'Whose is that old bike at the bottom of the gard–?' She trailed off when she saw there was nothing there.

Daisy had to bite her bottom lip and cover her mouth so her sister didn't see her laughing. 'What bike?'

*****

Jack pedalled home as fast as he could; he was late. Desperately, he tried to make it all the way up the hill on the bike but the blasted gears wouldn't work properly as usual. He had to give in and push when the after-effects of the alcohol conspired against him too. He walked the bike into the lane, ditched it in the hedge at the bottom of the garden, and continued up to the house. As he approached, keeping low beneath the hedge, he realised he was wearing a new shirt and jeans. This would look highly suspicious, and so he took the shirt off and tied it round his waist. He'd have to risk the jeans and hope that his father didn't notice them – or better still wasn't even in the kitchen.

He was … and Jack was struck by an unfamiliar and not unpleasant smell when he entered the house; it reminded him of the pub earlier. It was the smell of fish and chips, doused in salt and vinegar; and there was his father, tucking into them at the table. He briefly looked up when Jack came in, and then looked at the clock. 'The bus broke down so I had to walk the last bit,' Jack said, by way of explanation. He certainly looked the part as he was flustered, his bare chest hot and sweaty. His father didn't say anything in return; he just went back to his fish and chips with a smug look on his face.

The fish and chips were still in their paper wrapper. They looked good. This was a new development in the war on dinnertime, Jack thought to himself. He had to admire the old dog's tactics, and wished he'd thought of it himself. His father didn't seem to notice Jack's new attire as he passed on through to the parlour. It was as if he'd gone from one extreme to the other; from scrutinising Jack's every move to acting as if he was invisible.

It was hot and muggy in his room, and he opened a window to let in some air. He untied his shirt, took off his jeans and threw himself back on his bed in his new boxer shorts. Oh boy! What a day, what an afternoon! *And* he'd got away with it. He thought of what had happened while it was still fresh in his mind, and of the hot slickness of Daisy's body; he could still smell faint traces of her on him...

*****

He was awoken some time later by the crack of thunder and the heavy drum of summer rain through his open window. It was dark and his stomach growled, reminding him he hadn't had any dinner. It was too late to make anything now. He went to the bathroom to brush his teeth instead. His father had left the light on, so there was the first of the annual influx of daddy longlegs in there. God knows where they came from every year. He batted them away, whilst urinating to a generous applause from the toilet bowl and brushing his teeth at the same time.

Jack struggled to get back to sleep. He wondered what Daisy was doing and regretted leaving without saying goodbye; he missed her. He wondered where his sister was and what she was doing. Could *she* hear the rain too? His thoughts turned to the next day, and he groaned when he remembered he was back at the factory. Still, at least the rain couldn't ruin any of his and Daisy's plans for tomorrow – they had none ... or so he thought.

CHAPTER 25
Stanford Hall

Jack trudged over the fields to the bus stop under a hot sun. He was in a foul mood and not just because of the cloudless, blue sky. Where had that come from? He didn't have any clean work clothes, as he'd left most of them at Daisy's – along with his rucksack and the rest of his new clothes. This prompted him to reflect on what her sister had wanted; she hadn't sounded too happy. He hoped Daisy hadn't got into trouble – or, worse still, that her sister hadn't told her parents about him. It felt strange without his rucksack; he couldn't remember going to work without it. He was carrying his pack-up in a plastic bag instead.

As the bus pulled into the village, Jack couldn't help but look down Daisy's close, in the vain hope of seeing her house or maybe even Daisy herself. At exactly the same time, Daisy was walking down the other side of Main Street, seriously regretting her choice of footwear. She'd left the house in a rush and had grabbed the nearest thing she could find: flip-flops. She, too, was not in the best of moods; she'd already slept through the alarm that she'd set in the hope of contacting Jack before he left for work. She also still felt rough from the previous day's exploits. Hazy recollections of the afternoon kept coming back to her. What annoyed her the most was that both times they'd had sex she'd been drunk, and it was all a bit of a blur. She vaguely remembered agreeing to go to America with him; they really had got to control their drinking!

Jack was still looking behind him when the bus pulled to a stop. Imagine his surprise when he turned back around and was met with the sight of Daisy's auburn hair through his window. He couldn't believe his eyes – and sat up out of his seat, overcome with pure joy. What on earth was *she* doing queuing for the bus?

She walked down the aisle looking a little worse for wear, dressed in an oversized hooded top and shorts. Her hair was a mess, and as she sat next to him he noticed she wasn't wearing any make-up either. It was a while since he'd seen her without any; she looked impossibly young and fresh faced. 'Don't look at me!' she said. Unable to help himself, Jack broke into a grin. How could he *not* look at her? He wanted to eat her up – to consume her there and then.

'Daisy, what on earth are you doing? Coming to work with me?' he asked, perplexed.

'You're not *going* to work,' she replied, turning to face him. 'You can't. Look at it out there!' And she pointed out of the window, indicating the sunshine.

'But, I've got to. I don't have a choice … I'll lose my job!'

'You won't lose your job.'

'I will! And anyway, what about the itinerary?'

'To hell with the itinerary!' she cried. 'It's changed. We've got to make the most of today. I've been studying the weather report on Ceefax *and* on the news and it says that today's the best day; it all goes downhill from tomorrow.'

Jack considered this new information. 'I don't know, Daisy, I want to – you know I do – but … it's my boss. He didn't seem happy about me having one day off, never mind two.'

'Oh don't worry about Peabody. I'll deal with him!'

'It's Peasgood,' interjected Jack.

'Yeah, whatever. Well, I'll just give him a ring and tell him you're still grieving after the funeral and are too upset to come in.'

'You wouldn't?'

'I would!' she replied; and then more softly, 'If it meant I was going to get to spend the day with you.' She tucked her arm through his and leant into him, as she knew she had to work quickly; they were nearing the next stop in East Leake – after that it would be too late to get off and walk back. 'Please Jack … for me?' she cooed. Jack's resistance was crumbling by the second; he was such a fool for her. She batted her doe eyes and long lashes at him before putting her hands together in mock supplication. That was it; he was sold. They got off together at the next stop. And I'm supposed to be a bad influence on her? Jack thought.

They headed back to Daisy's on foot, which was a good twenty-minute walk. It was hot, and Jack asked her why she was still wearing the big hooded top. She opened it up to show him she was still wearing a pyjama T-shirt and shorts set. 'It's my dad's – I kind of left the house in a rush.'

'Well, at least I know what you wear in bed now!' he joked, taking her hand. 'So what are we going to do today? Go to the seaside?' He hoped this was the case.

'No, it's probably too late for that now. We can go to Stanford Hall instead, though; it's the perfect day for swimming.'

Jack felt a momentary wave of panic. For all he'd known he was going to work when he got up that morning. 'Swimming? But I don't have any swimming trunks or anything!'

'Oh, you can borrow some of my dad's; he's got loads of shorts. They might be a bit big round the waist but you'll be able to tie them tighter!' She smirked, as if there was something amusing about this.

When they reached Daisy's house their first job was to phone Jack's work. He still thought this was a bad idea.

'What's your work number?' asked Daisy.

'I've no idea,' he shrugged.

'No, course not, silly me,' she said, remembering that he didn't even have access to a phone. She grabbed a Yellow Pages and proceeded to thumb through it, finding the number under Wholesale Food Suppliers. 'Right, here goes then!' Daisy began dialling the number before she lost her nerve.

Jack sat on the bottom step of the stairs with his head in his hands. He couldn't believe she was actually going to go through with this, and could barely take the tension. He looked up, surprised, when he heard her speak in a posh, authoritative voice that he'd never heard before. 'Ah yes, could I speak to Mr Peasbody please?'

Jack slapped his forehead, hissing '*Mr Peasgood!*' before putting his head back in his hands; he knew this was a dreadful mistake.

'Yes, Mr Peasgood, sorry,' she said, correcting herself. She covered the mouthpiece with her hand and whispered, 'She's putting me through!' Jack couldn't take much more of it. He could picture the phone ringing on Peasgood's desk, and his gnarly red hand reaching out to pick it up. After a few seconds Daisy said, 'Ah, Mr Peasgood, it's Anne Hemsley here – I'm phoning on behalf of my younger brother, Jack Hemsley. I'm afraid Jack won't be able to come into work today. He's still grieving after the funeral yesterday, you see, and he's far too upset – it's hit him hard.' Where was she coming up with this stuff? thought Jack. She appeared to listen as Peasgood said something. Jack could imagine his reedy voice with the Scottish lilt to it. It seemed totally surreal that Daisy was having a conversation with his boss. 'Yes, well, it can't be helped, and all being well he'll be back in tomorrow as usual … so, apologies again for the inconvenience and, er … good day!' She put the phone down, letting out a whoosh of air in relief and bursting out laughing. Jack couldn't believe her audacity; she really was something.

'See, I told you to leave him to me!' she said, pulling Jack to his feet and putting her arms around his waist. 'He was a pussycat!' And she dotted his face with celebratory kisses – driving him mad already, and it wasn't even nine o'clock. Just when he was starting to enjoy it, she pushed him away. 'Right, no time for this – we've got work to do. First we've got to make a picnic and then we've got to find the tennis racquets and get our swimming stuff ready. We need to crack on if we want to make the most of the day.'

Jack helped her get the picnic stuff ready, adding his pack-up to it to save time. He also made a big bottle of squash (at Daisy's request), as she informed him that it was going to be an alcohol-free day. At least that's what she wanted – whether they'd pull it off was another matter. She located the tennis gear in the garage: two racquets in sleeves and a tube of balls.

They went upstairs, and Daisy grabbed a couple of towels from an airing cupboard before giving them Jack to hold, telling him to wait. She went through another door off the landing, into what Jack presumed was her parents' room, and returned with two pairs of swimming shorts; both of which looked too big. One pair was Bermuda-style – dark grey with fluorescent pink and yellow patterns on them – and the other was a more sensible dark blue. 'Here, try these on and see which fit you best. They're all I could find – he must have taken some away with him. At least these should be smaller as they're older; he's put some weight on recently!'

Then they were in her room again – her warm room; the

scene of yesterday's debauchery. He sat down on her bed, which today wasn't so neatly made. Daisy yanked open a series of drawers in her dresser, pulling out a few items of clothing and leaving the drawers open. 'Right, I'm going to get changed.' she said. 'Try on your shorts and I'll be back in a minute.' Jack reluctantly did as he was told, and was unsurprised to discover that the garish ones fitted best. Even they were too loose for comfort, despite the string being pulled as tight as it would go. He walked over to look at himself in the wardrobe mirror and groaned; he looked ridiculous.

On his way back he noticed Daisy's top drawer was still open. It was full of underwear, and he felt himself drawn to it. There were pants and bras of every colour and material imaginable. Plain ones, coloured ones, patterned and striped ones – like a giant drawer of dolly mixture. Cotton ones, lacy ones, satin and silky ones – he ran his fingers through them all. Just then he heard the bathroom door, and shot backwards in surprise, flushing crimson.

Daisy knocked on the door. 'Can I come in? Are you decent?'

'Er, just a minute!' Jack cried in a panic. He quickly pulled down the shorts before grabbing his boxers. He pulled them on, and then his jeans, whilst hopping about on one leg. 'OK!' he called, and she breezed in wearing a short denim skirt, a vest and some pumps. She noticed Jack looked a bit flustered.

'Are you OK?' she said.

'Yes, fine.'

'Did you try them on?'

'What!' he replied in alarm.

'Dad's shorts, did they fit?'

'Oh, the shorts – yes, they're fine, thanks.'

'Ookaay,' Daisy said, looking bemused.

For the first time they actually left through the front door together. As Daisy locked it she looked up and noticed her bedroom window was ajar. 'Damn! I'd better close that window – here, can you put this stuff in the van, please?' She handed him the picnic bag and van keys. Jack put everything in the back and wound down the windows to let out some of the heat. When Daisy came back, she said, 'That reminds me, how *did* you make your great escape the other day?' Jack looked up and pointed to the sloping porch roof that was directly beneath her window. 'I thought so,' she said.

After choosing their music for the drive (Daisy went with a '60s compilation for a change), they set off. Jack felt a childish sense of excitement. It was such a novelty for him; as if they were going on a proper day out. It sure as hell beat going to work.

They drove towards East Leake, then headed out of the village on a small, winding country road. Summer was in full swing and the hedgerows were tall with cow parsley and red campion. As Jack settled into the journey he couldn't help but notice Daisy's legs as she drove, how they scissored up and down as she worked the pedals. The denim skirt (which she'd borrowed from her sister) wasn't particularly suitable for driving in. It had already ridden up to reveal a more than decent amount of creamy thigh. He swore she did these things on purpose to torment him, and he couldn't help but wonder what type of pants she was wearing. He imagined they were pale pastel blue, and cotton.

Before long they joined a main road. They'd barely been travelling ten minutes when there was a sign for Stanford Hall pointing to the left. Daisy indicated and began to slow down. Jack couldn't believe that they were there already, and felt disappointed. They drove through a large, but modest, entrance with waist-high black metal gates and a gatekeeper's cottage, before entering the grounds.

Stanford Hall was an eighteenth century manor house that had been transformed during the 1920s and '30s by its owner at the time. It had its own cricket pitch, an outdoor swimming pool, a pitch and putt golf course and two tennis courts, all of which were now accessible to the public through much sought-after season tickets. To Jack, the grounds looked like those of a grand stately home – an impression that was enhanced by the surprise appearance of regal peacocks, which strutted in and out of the shadows of numerous trees.

There were plenty of empty parking bays near the high, curving, outer stone walls of the swimming pool. Daisy chose one in the shade and pulled in. 'It doesn't look busy at all yet; that's good,' she said. They stepped out of the van to find the air was warm and humid. After making sure they'd got their passes, Daisy locked up, and they made their way towards the imposing entrance steps, with double doors at the top. Jack felt jittery. Here he was, in a new and extreme situation, stone cold sober.

They pulled open the doors and were met with a breath-taking and idyllic scene. Daisy had seen it all before, but Jack was gobsmacked. The pool was a perfect aquamarine blue, dappled with golden reflections from the sun. It was set within thick stone walls covered with ivy that had little steps here and there leading up to various suntraps and rockeries. There were caves underneath them, and stone fountains on pedestals. It had the feel of an ancient, outdoor Roman bath. Directly in front of them were three ominous-looking stone diving platforms of various heights. They curved upwards, overhanging the water like three huge dinosaur ribs, with steps all the way to the top. The middle one was the tallest, and so high it made Jack dizzy just to look at it. Its steps seemed to lead all the way up into the azure sky, as if you could walk off the edge of it onto a wispy cloud – or perhaps even into heaven itself.

At that moment there was a loud *boinging* sound followed by a large splash. An elderly, pot-bellied gentleman had launched himself into the pool off a springboard that continued to bend up and down for some time afterwards. He broke the perfect, mirrored, blue surface of the water, splintering the golden cracks that looked like shimmering snake skin. The water looked refreshing and inviting – the perfect antidote to the heat.

A brown man in a vest and shorts, who had been perched on a stool near the entrance, stood up. He put his newspaper down and asked to see their tickets in a foreign accent. Daisy's was pink and Jack's was blue: apparently Jack was James Jones for the day. The man thanked them and handed back their passes before returning to his stool and newspaper. His movements were slow and languid – no one was in a rush here.

'Right, I'm going to get changed, I'll see you in a minute,' said Daisy. Jack automatically followed her, but she stopped and he bumped into her. 'This is the ladies', Jack, you can't come in here! You're over there!' she laughed, pointing to the other changing rooms. The attendant briefly looked up from his newspaper in mild amusement.

'Oh!' said Jack, feeling foolish and a little alone as he made his way with his head down to get changed. The men's changing rooms were large and cool with wall-to-wall stone tiles. They were also empty, thank God – or so he thought. As he made his way over the slippery floor he heard the sound of running water, and looked through to another room as he passed it, then wished he hadn't. There was a large, hairy man, totally naked and covered in soap lather, standing under an open shower. Jack had never seen a naked adult in his life; he turned away in disgust and scurried past.

There were no cubicles, so he hurriedly got undressed and put on his shorts, pulling the drawstring as tight as he could. He packed the rest of his clothes into his rucksack, but didn't know what to do with it as there were no lockers. He tucked it under a wooden bench.

When he ventured back outside, the sun was bright and Daisy was waiting for him. It hadn't taken her long to get changed as she'd already had her swimming costume on under her clothes. She stood a little self-consciously by the smallest diving platform, looking an absolute knockout in a black bikini with her hair tied up in a ponytail. It left Jack speechless, but he was also a bit shocked to see her dressed like that in front of complete strangers. He couldn't help but feel a little envious: it was as if everyone was looking at her in her bra and pants, and *he'd* only got to see her like that the previous day!

He walked over and she took his hand. 'Are you OK?'

'Yes, fine,' he replied, feeling anything but.

'Good. Right, I'm going to jump in off here – I always do it. It's the only way. I find it too cold going in bit by bit. Are you coming?'

Jack looked up at the curved stone steps. It was the smallest platform and barely five feet high, but he still didn't fancy it at all. He wasn't used to deep water, as he'd only ever swum in the brook. 'No, you go ahead – I'll watch!'

As Jack made his way round the side of the pool, he passed a large, old-fashioned mangle lurking in the shadows and an ornamental bird bath. Everything struck him as quite bizarre. He was about a third of the way along the pool when he heard Daisy shout him from the top of the diving platform. She squeezed her nose together with her fingers, then jumped, letting out a shriek on the way down. The water cascaded over the side of the pool as she disappeared under the water, before bobbing back up again, laughing. It looked like fun. 'It's amazing!' she called. 'Come on, jump in!'

Jack dipped a toe in the water. It was freezing. He made his way further along the pool, to where the water looked shallower. 'Come on!' she goaded him. What the hell, he thought, and jumped in. The water was icy at first and took his breath away. His shorts came down a bit as well, and he had to yank them back up. His feet hit the bottom and he sprang back up to discover that, to his relief, he could stand. And the water wasn't too bad once you were in. Daisy swam down to join him. She was a strong swimmer with a purposeful, measured stroke.

Everything was great for a while, as they pretty much had the shallow end to themselves. There were only about half a dozen other swimmers – mostly older people in swimming caps – doing lengths in a very serious manner. Jack practised his basic stroke across the width of the pool, whilst Daisy swam up and down the length of it. From time to time she got out to jump off one of the diving boards or to dive off the springboard. Eventually Jack agreed to jump off the springboard: he certainly wasn't going to use any of those diving platforms. When he was catapulted into the deep end, to his horror his shorts nearly came off. Desperately he scrabbled them back up his legs, hoping no one had noticed. I'm not doing that again, he thought, and doggy-paddled back to the shallow end.

Slowly but surely the pool began to fill up as more and more people piled in – drawn to it like animals to a watering hole. Jack became withdrawn, sticking to the shallow end, but Daisy continued to use the diving boards. It was on one of these excursions that Jack noticed a trio of boys of about their age had stopped to talk to her. They gathered around her with their trendy haircuts and cool shorts, all of them sporty-looking and tanned. And there *she* was in nothing but her bikini.

He felt a twinge of possessiveness as they chatted to her

and she spoke animatedly back, sometimes laughing. As he watched, he felt himself being overcome with feelings of hatred for them, but then hated himself even more. Daisy pointed at him at one point, and they all looked over. He felt paranoid; like a freak, a special case – lurking in the shallows in his stupid oversized shorts.

Daisy dived off the springboard (under the boys' appreciative gazes, Jack noted) and began to swim down the pool towards him. The boys climbed the highest diving board and jumped off it – whooping, being boisterous and showing off. Daisy floated on her back for a moment to watch them, smiling and laughing, before swimming over to Jack. She was proud to be seen with him, and came straight up for a kiss; but Jack pulled himself away – he couldn't help it. He'd let his jealousy get the better of him; he was its hopeless slave and it was his unforgiving master. 'Hey, what's wrong, mister?' she said, hurt by his surprise rejection.

'Nothing,' he muttered.

'Well, why won't you let me kiss you then?' She tried again, but he resisted.

'Who are they?' he asked, gesturing with his head.

'Them? Oh they're friends from school; I haven't seen them in ages. They were in my year.'

'What were you talking about?'

'Why?'

'I saw you looking over.'

'Well, they were just asking who I was with and I said "my boyfriend". Is that OK?' She wasn't mad with him – she was just puzzled. Being referred to as her boyfriend soothed Jack somewhat. She tried to kiss him again. 'Well, is it?' He still turned his face away but without much conviction, and it suddenly dawned on her what was wrong with him. She gasped 'Oh my God, Jack! Don't tell me you're jealous?' Jack brooded. 'You are! Of them?' She couldn't believe it. 'You stupid thing!' And she came towards him, wrapping herself around him, not letting him get away this time. She was as slippery as an eel and trapped him with her thighs, showering him with reassuring kisses and pressing herself against him. It wasn't long before nature took its course, and he was trying to pull himself away for very different reasons.

The problem was, after the previous afternoon, he couldn't help but associate her with sex. Just the thought of her was enough to make him twitchy. The feel of her writhing against him in a bikini in a public place was a recipe for disaster. 'What now?' she asked as he pushed her away – but she knew.

'Nothing,' he said, embarrassed. 'You've just got to stop, that's all. People are watching!'

Daisy pouted, pretending to be put out. 'Spoilsport,' she said. Just then a small boy in goggles surfaced between them, kicking and splashing. 'I suppose we'd better get out then?'

'Yes, suppose so.' She started to move off, but Jack didn't follow.

'Well, come on then!'

'You go, I'll be out in a minute,' he said, not looking at her. She gave him an amused smile and swam to the steps at the edge of the pool. Jack concentrated on a spot high up on the rockery, refusing to look at her, knowing she would be pulling herself out of the pool, dripping wet. He desperately needed things down below to subside, but it was as if a giant pair of hands had his head in a clamp, turning it against his will...

There was no way on earth he couldn't look, and the last thing he needed to see right then was Daisy in that bikini as she squeaked away, leaving wet footprints on the hot concrete. Jack cursed himself, and stood trapped in the shallow end. He tried to think of anything except what he'd just seen – horrible things, depressing things. He thought about the fact that his sister hadn't tried to contact him, and how much that hurt. She was probably running around on a beach somewhere with her new man and a dog; she'd always wanted a dog. Then he thought of the unique and deathly stench of the bathroom after his father's daily evacuations, the fumes of which could singe the wings off a daddy longlegs. This did the trick, and he was able to make his way out of the pool.

Jack walked to the changing rooms with his head down, conscious that the boys were looking at him in his idiotic shorts. Daisy was waiting for him again when he came back out. She'd left her wet hair down and neatly combed it straight. He'd never seen it like that before. 'All right?' she asked.

'Yes, fine thanks,' said Jack, without meeting her gaze.

They headed out through the double doors and went to put their swimming stuff in the van. All the parking spaces were full now, and there were bikes chained up too. 'We can walk to the tennis courts,' said Daisy, and passed Jack the racquets. She grabbed the picnic stuff and pulled out the squash bottle to take a long swig before offering it to him. On the way to the courts they debated whether to have their picnic before or after they played tennis. They were both hungry so decided to have it before: what was it about swimming that always made you hungry? Off to their left they passed the crowded pitch and putt golf course. It looked like fun. Jack thought he might like to try it one day. Everyone looked a bit hot and bothered, though, especially those waiting for their turn.

In the background was the grand sight of the red-brick hall. The path curved round to it, but they veered off across a huge, shadowy expanse of grass, populated by large trees. They passed a thatched pavilion and then a shaded, whitewashed toilet block surrounded by yew and pine trees, behind which the tennis courts were hidden. To their dismay, both courts were already occupied – one by a couple and the other with four people who were trying to play doubles. Still, they were going to have their picnic first; perhaps one of the courts would be free by the time they finished.

Daisy laid down a rug in the shade of a large yew tree. She set the picnic stuff out, dishing it all up and playing 'Mum'. She'd put on a good spread: there were sandwiches, pork pie, sausage rolls, crisps, and even yoghurts for dessert. The only thing missing, thought Jack, was a bottle of cider to wash it down with; he could have murdered one. As he watched Daisy, he couldn't help but notice that she didn't appear to be wearing a bra, and he tried not to stare. He also noticed that she didn't seem to be able to get comfortable; she kept kneeling or sitting awkwardly with her legs to the side. Probably the pine cones, he thought; he could feel them sticking into him too. They must have rolled down and gathered there from a nearby tree.

They ate their picnic in a comfortable silence. Jack was becoming more at ease eating in front of her. Daisy was also getting used to his familiar winces of pain and his eyes watering whenever he bit the side of his mouth, and would put her hand on his back and rub it in sympathy. As they ate, they watched the people playing tennis. The couple weren't bad, and their ball made a satisfying *thwack* as it echoed off the surrounding trees. Before long, the group on the nearest court looked as if they'd had enough – the heat getting the better of them. They packed up their stuff and left the court, chatting, sweaty and red-faced. Jack and Daisy looked at each other; they'd better make their move before someone else came along. They tidied away the picnic, and grabbed their racquets and balls.

A tennis court was a lot bigger in real life than it looked on the telly, and the net seemed higher too. They slid their racquets out of their sleeves; they were lightweight with large heads, not like the wooden ones Jack had messed about with at home. They began to play, or at least tried to play, but could barely get a rally going. One of them would either miss the ball completely or whack it into the net or out of court. Having the couple on the other court next to them made them feel even more useless. Thankfully, after about ten minutes they too had had enough and left, nodding goodbye as they walked past.

With the courts to themselves, they could relax more and actually speak to each other. 'God, they make it look so easy on telly!' Daisy said.

'I know!' replied Jack, hitting another ball hopelessly out of court. He was already starting to get too hot, and he took his top off to tie it around his waist. They persevered, but without making much progress. Having played before, Daisy improved more quickly than Jack – and more often than not it was he who messed up the rally, much to his annoyance.

Truth be told, they were both struggling to concentrate for their own private reasons, and it wasn't just the heat. Jack was distracted by Daisy's breasts jiggling about as she ran for the ball in her bra-less vest. And as for Daisy, well, she didn't know if it was the heat acting like an aphrodisiac, the warm breeze blowing up her skirt or the sight of Jack with no top on, but she too had only one thing on her mind – and it wasn't tennis. It wasn't just now either; she'd felt the same since the previous afternoon. An unusual feeling had come over her. It was as though a light had been turned on in a walk-in wardrobe, and she wanted to try on all the shoes.

After Jack had missed another ball and yelled in frustration, she came to the net and smiled at him. 'Shall we call it a day? It's too hot for this!'

'Yes, I suppose so,' he said, disappointed. He'd really been looking forward to playing on a proper court, and hadn't expected it to be so hard. They collected up the balls and headed back to the welcome shade of the yew tree. Daisy reached into the rucksack for the squash and they both took another much-needed swig. She watched Jack as he drank – just as he'd watched her that night when they went camping. Some drink spilled down his hard body, which was already covered in a sheen of perspiration, and she followed its trail to the button of his jeans.

When he'd finished, she noticed he looked a bit glum. 'Hey you. What's up? You don't look like you're having much fun!'

Jack was thinking how useless he was at everything, and was still brooding over those boys at the pool. He pictured them jumping off the highest diving board with ease, whilst he couldn't even go up the smallest one. 'I'm just rubbish at everything,' he said, kicking a pine cone.

'No you're not!' She put her arms around him and kissed him on the lips.

'I am. I can barely ride a bike, I can't go shopping, I can't swim very well – and now I can't even play tennis!'

'Aaah, we are feeling sorry for ourselves, aren't we?' she teased, and kissed him again, but this time lingering.

'It's true, though.'

She looked into his eyes and her voice changed, becoming more husky and seductive. 'I know something you're good at.' Jack's eyes searched hers and then she kissed him properly, using her tongue. It felt amazing and he responded, but before he knew it she was pulling away. 'Why wouldn't you let me near you in the pool earlier?' she said in the same flirtatious voice.

'When?' he asked, blushing.

'Near the end.'

'I don't know. I was just jealous, I suppose.'

'Oh … right. So … why couldn't you get out of the pool then?' She just wanted to hear him say it. But Jack didn't know how to answer: he wasn't used to this sort of talk. Neither was Daisy; she didn't know what had got into her.

She gently nudged her leg between his so that her knee was raised, ever so slightly. Then she took his hand and placed it at the top of her thigh, underneath the hem of her skirt. 'Is this why?' she said. Her thigh was sticky, and it was as hot as hell under there. Jack's heart thumped like a bass drum. He couldn't utter a word – struck dumb in the face of such brazenness – and not even with his cider to rescue him. Again she implored him, 'Tell me what you wanted, Jack.' Her eyes were full of lust and desire, mirroring his; it radiated from both of them. He let his hand do the talking – peeling it off her sticky thigh and tentatively moving it further up, inch by inch. She stopped him by trapping it; not letting him get off that easily. 'Tell me,' she said, firmer now – more insistent. Jack nodded in admission, and from somewhere out there in the world a peacock's strange call rang out as the sun ticked away the swollen seconds. She parted her thighs, letting his hand continue on its journey, until it came up against something that sure as hell wasn't her knickers. Daisy took in a sharp intake of breath, blushed, and said, 'I forgot to pack my underwear.'

There was no turning back for either of them; the urge was too strong. They both wanted – both needed – each other there and then. They slipped further into the shadows and found themselves at the back of the toilet block building. Jack pressed himself against her and her skirt rode up, but she tried to pull it down again; she may have been overcome with lust but she wasn't a flasher. Daisy fumbled at Jack's jeans, but he stopped her from unzipping them. It was no good – they both felt too exposed.

Jack noticed a painted blue door halfway along the wall, and tried the handle. It turned and the door gave inwards. He took her hand and led her in. They were met with a dark and musty cleaning cupboard full of mops, brooms, chemicals and old tennis nets. They didn't care, though – it was perfect. They left the door open just a crack so it wasn't pitch black, and in the dim light they were finally able to be free. Daisy lifted up her vest, and Jack smelt the chlorine from the pool on her breasts as he kissed them. They did it up against a dusty wall, rattling amongst the mop buckets, as she whispered sinful nothings in his ear. Needless to say, it didn't last long.

After they had made themselves decent again, they emerged into the open on shaky legs. They went to collect their bags and tennis kit, which in their haste they'd left under the tree. Then they went to their respective toilets to have a clean-up – being young and in love could be a messy business.

They made their way back through the grounds, holding hands in a stunned silence. Daisy felt a sense of euphoria, as for once she hadn't been drunk; she'd been aware of every little thing. It had felt like a whole new experience, almost like the first time.

'Well, what now?' she said. It was still only just past two o'clock.

'I don't know,' shrugged Jack. There was only one thing on his mind, and that was to go for a drink; but he didn't want to bring it up.

'I know. Why don't we go strawberry picking? We might as well make the most of the good weather, and it's only about fifteen minutes away.'

'Um, yes … we could, I suppose. It's just … I thought perhaps we could go for a little drink somewhere first?' He anticipated a swift rebuke – and got one.

'Trust you!' Daisy scolded him, but half in jest. 'Well, I suppose there *is* a pub on the way, at Rempstone … and you *have* been a good boy.' She squeezed his hand. Although she'd been adamant that today was going to be alcohol-free, that had been more to do with the 'sex sans alcohol' issue than anything else, and they had unexpectedly got that out of the way – she felt a bit like celebrating the achievement. 'Come on then – we should just about get there before last orders!'

CHAPTER 26

A Very English Tea

They drove out of the grounds, more than happy with the day so far, and headed down the main road towards Rempstone. Just over the crossroads, and around the bend on the corner, was the White Lion. It had benches outside by the road – all of them empty, which prompted Jack and Daisy to wonder if they were too late. As it turned out, they were just in time, but the landlord asked if they wouldn't mind taking their pints outside so he could close up. This suited them: frosted pints on a summer's day, watching the world go by – what was there to mind? Much to Jack's bemusement, Daisy made use of their stop-off by drying her bikini bottoms on the hot van roof, saying, 'Well, I can't go strawberry picking without any knickers on, can I?'

Before they set off again, she wriggled back into them, looking both ways up and down the road first and telling Jack not to look. Then they were on their way, with Daisy tapping on the steering wheel to the music – the likes of *Twist and Shout* by The Beatles and *You Really Got Me* by The Kinks. They passed through a village called Wymeswold, and before long came to a big sign with a colourful red strawberry painted on it. Underneath it was a black arrow and the letters P.Y.O. 'What does P.Y.O mean?' asked Jack.

'Pick your own, of course!'

'Oh yeah … course.'

They followed the arrow down a lane and parked near a shed. Jack couldn't believe how many cars there were in the car park. He'd never been strawberry picking before, save for the little patch of wild ones in his garden, so it was a real eye-opener. They got a plastic punnet each from a girl behind a makeshift counter, and she recommended which area they should go to for the richest pickings. They thanked her, and headed in that direction. Daisy led them as far away from other people as they could; so they could be on their own, and so they could secretly eat lots of strawberries.

Daisy loved picking strawberries. It was a family tradition and they did it every summer like most English families – sometimes more than once. It reminded her of being a little girl again, and how magical the fruit used to look to her. It still did now – hanging like precious red jewels, hidden under emerald green canopies. As they were in no hurry, they took their time to search out the biggest and ripest strawberries – eating plenty along the way. They were deliciously sweet and juicy, and Daisy made appreciative noises as she ate, remarking how she loved the shape of them. Jack wondered if it was just his imagination, or was she *deliberately* popping them slowly into her mouth, whilst making those wanton noises?

When their punnets were fit to burst, they headed back to the shed. 'I hope they don't cost too much, we've got quite a lot!' Daisy remarked. The girl popped their punnets onto a scale to weigh them, and they held their breath. They needn't have worried; they were ridiculously cheap compared to the shops.

The seats of the van were red hot, and Daisy yelped as she

settled her bare legs onto them. Jack put the strawberries by his feet on the floor and although he'd eaten lots of them, this had somehow only made him hungrier. 'God, I'm starving!' he said.

'You're always starving! Me too, though.'

Then Jack came out with a rare suggestion of his own. 'Why don't we get some fish and chips on the way back from East Leake?' He hadn't been able to stop thinking of his father's yesterday, and had been craving them ever since.

'Umm … fish and chips, that sounds good!' said Daisy.

They arrived back in East Leake just as the chip shop was opening. It was perfect; they would just have time to eat them at home before Lily got back from work at half five. Daisy felt a certain satisfaction as Jack joined her at the counter; this week had clearly done him good. They got a portion of chips each, and a large fish between them to save money. Jack stared in wonder at all the battered goods on display, as if he was looking at fish in an aquarium. He also marvelled at the speed at which they were wrapped up.

On the way back he sat with the parcels on his legs, enjoying how they scalded him; he tried to see how long he could last with them in one place until he had to move them.

As they rounded the bend heading out of East Leake, Jack suddenly shouted, 'Shit!' (a habit he had picked up from Daisy) and ducked sideways out of view, his head practically resting on Daisy's lap.

'What?!' she cried, swerving in surprise. He popped up again and looked out of the rear window. There behind him was the departing back of a familiar rusty white van.

'*That was my father!*' he gasped.

'You're joking!' said Daisy, searching the rear view mirror and nearly veering off the road again.

'No. I don't think he saw me, though; he was probably too drunk to notice.'

'What – and he actually drives around like that?'

'Yeah, all the time.'

'What if he *did* see you anyway?'

'Well, I should still be at work, remember?'

'Oh yes, of course. I forgot about that.' And she looked in her mirror again, disappointed that she hadn't seen him – this monster, this ogre that she'd heard so much about. 'I wish I'd seen him,' she confessed, and Jack looked across at her, perplexed.

'Why?'

'I don't know. Just to see what he looks like, I suppose.'

'Trust me, you're not missing anything,' said Jack, shaking his head; he still couldn't believe what a close call it had been. He had no idea just *how* close, though; his father was going to the chip shop himself – and any minute now would be standing at the same counter at which Jack and Daisy had been standing at barely five minutes before.

They ate – no, *devoured* – their fish and chips at the table in the kitchen, washing down their meal with a cup of tea. To follow, they had strawberries and homemade vanilla ice cream. The strawberries didn't even need sugar, they were that sweet. Afterwards, with stomachs fit to burst, Daisy washed the pots and Jack dried them. It was as if they were playing house together, and they loved it. Then they retired to the lounge to watch telly for a while before her sister got back. Jack took off his shoes, and they sat side by side on the sofa with their feet up. It was the biggest telly Jack had ever seen. He watched, rapt, as Daisy flicked through the channels with the remote control.

She came across *Blockbusters* and said, 'Ooh I love this!' before immediately proceeding to put Ceefax on anyway. She went straight to the weather forecast, as had become a bit of an obsession of hers of late. It confirmed that the next day, especially later on, the weather took a serious turn for the worse. You wouldn't have thought so looking at it outside, apart from the humidity. This was a problem because they wanted to complete their wish list; they still had their bike ride to do *and* a trip to the seaside. Daisy pondered this for a moment. She looked at Jack. 'How much energy have you got left?' she said, half-joking.

'Erm … enough for a bike ride, I think,' he smiled.

'Really? I thought you'd be worn out!' She raised her eyebrows at him.

'No, not quite yet.'

So it was decided. Daisy gave Jack a lift home, along with his clean washing, which he'd somehow got to sneak into the house. They arranged to meet later at the crossroads to cycle to Wysall and back. If there was a problem, he was to try and ring once.

*****

Back at home everything was exactly as it had been since his sister had left. There was the same mess of pots, bottles and chip papers littering the kitchen, and the sound of his father watching tennis in the lounge. Jack felt oddly detached; as if he was a visiting stranger, a cleaner or home help. He went through the motions of tidying up the kitchen – more to keep his father sweet than anything else.

When they met at the crossroads later, Daisy was sitting astride her own modern-looking mountain bike, making Jack's bike look even more antiquated in comparison. She had showered before coming out to wash away the smell of swimming, and was feeling refreshed and revitalised; she looked it too, wearing her more sensible, but equally delightful, denim shorts.

As they cycled past the Red Lion there were two men standing out front, smoking. Jack recognised them with disdain from the pub garden that very first afternoon they'd visited.

To his surprise one of them said, 'Evening!' to them both, and the other said, 'All right, love!' to Daisy as they passed.

Daisy said, 'Hi' back, but Jack didn't say anything – he just kept his head down. He loathed their familiarity with her, and bet they were both copping a good eyeful of her legs. One of them muttered, 'Nice bike,' and sniggered as they cycled away.

'Just ignore them,' said Daisy, but it was hard for Jack and he silently fumed.

'Are they those regulars you were on about at the bar?' he asked.

'Yes. They're harmless enough, just a bit annoying, I suppose.'

That figured, Jack thought; and they hadn't come across as harmless to him.

They rode down Wysall Lane, retracing their camping trip steps. It was a lot quicker on bikes and everything looked different somehow – even the landscape had altered and turned colour. Neither of them had been down there since that night, and they experienced a shared nostalgia. It felt like a lifetime ago; so much had changed. They had grown so much in such a short space of time – finding themselves through each other.

As they passed the cattle grid and the gate that led up to the wood, they both privately reminisced about that evening. 'Do you know how much I wanted to kiss you that night?' confessed Daisy, making Jack blush as he pedalled along.

'Yes, me too.' She would never know just how much – and how desperately disappointed he had been the next morning.

Jack had never been beyond this point, and as usual got

a kick out of spreading his wings. It took them about twenty minutes to get to Wysall, and by then they were both thirsty. There was only one thing for it, and true to form Daisy didn't disappoint; she knew just the place. They cycled past a church and through the sleepy village, which was charmingly bucolic. A noisy tractor approached from behind, practically taking up the whole road, and they pulled to the side to let it pass. It flung out mud and hay from its giant wheels and left behind a rich, pungent smell of manure.

The Plough was a cosy little inn tucked away up some stone steps; you wouldn't have known it was there. It amazed Jack how Daisy knew about all these places; she seemed to know every pub in every village and town in the East Midlands. They walked across a quirky patio area with old-fashioned lamp posts and big old barrels full of flowers. There was a huge wheel from a cart and, most curiously, a red telephone box.

They entered a welcoming bar that had jugs and tankards hanging from the ceiling and walls that were adorned with old village photographs and farming implements. Considering the pub's tucked-away location, it was bustling with a surprising (and a daunting) number of customers. Daisy ordered their drinks, and they took them outside onto the terrace.

Daisy told Jack that her mum had phoned earlier to see how she and her sister were doing. 'They sound like they're enjoying themselves,' she said. 'Mum says they're doing plenty of walking and getting lots of fresh air, but Dad's struggling with the steep hills a bit, which is a shame – the scenery is stunning, apparently. She also made a point of making me feel guilty about not going with them *and* asked what I'd been up to!'

'And what did you say?'

'Oh, nothing exciting.'

Soon the sky began to darken, and it felt noticeably cooler. They decided to head back and Daisy groaned as she sat on her bike; her legs and bum were already beginning to hurt. 'You ought to try sitting on *my* seat,' said Jack 'It's like sitting on a rock!'

The return journey dragged, with some of the hills becoming positively torturous as they both began to tire; but the road levelled out as they neared the Red Lion. 'One more drink?' Jack said in hope; he really didn't want to go home yet.

'Really?'

'Yes, it's still early – *and* it's my round!' he said, getting into the spirit of this pub thing.

'Considering this was meant to be an alcohol-free day you haven't done badly; this will be the third pub we've been to today!'

Jack grinned and handed her a fiver. 'Can you get some crisps as well please?' Daisy tutted as she handed him her bike. She went in through the front door of the pub whilst Jack walked the bikes into the garden.

When she rejoined him, she said, 'God, they don't let up, those blokes!'

'What now?' said Jack, tensing.

'Oh, "Where's Loverboy?" and "Are you saddle sore from your bike ride?"' She mimicked their voices.

Jack stood up, scowling. 'Do you want me to go and say something, Daisy, 'cause I will!'

'No, no, don't be silly,' she said, putting her hand on his. 'Really, sit back down. Like I say they're harmless enough – not worth getting into an argument over. It just gets boring, that's all.' Jack sat back down. 'Thank you anyway,' she added. It was nice to know that her man was willing to stand up for her. Jack let it go, but still brooded as he sipped his pint. Those men and their snide remarks were starting to become a problem; it was the innuendo that bugged him the most. It made him not want to go the Red Lion anymore – especially after experiencing a pleasant welcome in other pubs that week.

Daisy didn't want to ruin a memorable day, and changed the subject. 'Phew! What a day – I'm knackered!' she exclaimed. Jack smiled in return, trying to lighten up. 'So, Movie Marathon tomorrow night then?'

'What exactly is a Movie Marathon?' he asked; he still wasn't sure.

'Well, basically we stay in – preferably in bed – and spend all night watching movies back to back, eating popcorn and other rubbish. In fact, we could even eat our dinner in bed – I was thinking of maybe a Chinese takeaway!' She'd seen Woody Allen doing this in one of his movies, and had always wanted to do it.

This all sounded pretty appealing to Jack, but one thing troubled him. 'What about your sister?' he asked.

'Oh, don't worry about her; she knows about you anyway … you're gonna have to meet her sooner or later … *and* Mum and Dad, come to think about it. We can't hide you forever… I mean, Lily's already met your underpants!' Jack wasn't amused; he was still mortified at the memory and the whole idea of meeting her family filled him with dread. 'Seriously, though, I was thinking you could come straight to mine on the bus from work so we can make the most of it.'

'But what about … you know, him?' said Jack – meaning his father, and not going home after work.

'I don't know. You don't *have* to go home – it's not like it's a law that you have to be there at dinner time every day. And besides, from what you've said you barely even see each other – never mind eat dinner together – these days.'

*****

That night in bed, Jack contemplated what Daisy had said about the next day. She was right, he supposed; forget ships that pass in the night, he and his father hadn't even been in the same harbour lately. The thing was, this actually suited both of them at this juncture. Jack was being left alone for once, and his father was content that Jack wasn't kicking up a fuss about Anne leaving – not that Jack didn't worry about her; of course he did.

CHAPTER 27

When Jack Met Lily

Jack was dreading going into work. He was half expecting to get called into Peasgood's office on arrival to be told that he didn't have a job anymore. As he entered the factory building he braced himself, but thankfully the day began without incident. He couldn't relax, though, as on more than one occasion he looked up to see Peasgood peering over the balcony at him with his beady eyes. It felt as if they were boring into his skull to see if he'd been lying about his unscheduled day off. This made Jack jittery as he worked. It reminded him of a film he'd watched when he was little: *At the Earth's Core*. It had these huge, prehistoric reptiles with dreadful blinking eyes that sat on high rocks. From time to time they screeched, then swooped down to claim a hapless victim before carrying them off.

The factory clock seemed to go backwards, but finally it was all over and he was back on the bus, heading to Daisy's. As he stared out of the window he had another worry on his mind. Why did there always have to be something for him to fret over? This time it was about meeting her sister. It was the one on one, the scrutiny, the local connection that terrified him; it wasn't like being anonymous in a different place or town.

Meanwhile, Daisy hadn't had anything more pressing to do

than to plan the evening's festivities. This she had done with her usual meticulous precision and down to the finest detail. She'd even got eggs and bacon in – just in case Jack could stay the night; she wanted to cook him breakfast in the morning. The video player had been set up in her room, and she'd agonised long and hard about which films to watch. She was very passionate about her favourites, so this was almost as bad as choosing songs for a compilation tape. They wouldn't have time to watch more than three, and she wanted to avoid renting any from the video shop; it was proving to be an expensive week, and the money her parents had left them was all but gone. Fortunately Daisy preferred old movies, and most of her favourites were already in the house. She didn't even have to consult her list of Top 20 Movies, as she knew what most of them were off by heart.

She wanted each film to be from a different genre to keep it interesting, such as something thought-provoking, something scary and something funny. For her first choice, then, did she go for *A Streetcar Named Desire*?; one of her all-time favourite films and Marlon at his most brooding. Or what about *One Flew Over the Cuckoo's Nest* – another favourite and both tragic *and* funny. They were both pretty long, though, so in the end she opted for *Stand By Me*; not on the grand scale of the other two but in her top five nonetheless. More importantly, she thought Jack would love it; especially the woods and camping element.

For the scary one, no debate; it had to be *An American Werewolf in London*. And for the funny one, it could only be Woody – but which one? There were so many and his humour *was* an acquired taste. Perhaps one of his earlier slapstick ones, she thought, like *Bananas* or *Sleeper*.

The one detail that Daisy *had* neglected was to tell her sister that Jack was actually coming round, and therefore she'd be meeting him. Lily had also neglected to inform Daisy that she'd be late home from work as she had to attend a product meeting about some new lines.

It was an odd feeling for Jack, not getting off at his stop at the top of the hill. Not being at home at dinner time would be breaking a lifetime's habit, and despite everything he still felt answerable to his father. He'd considered telling him this morning as he'd left him his tea, but couldn't be doing with the argument. Instead he'd decided to just leave a note. He'd never written anything to his father before. Who did he address it to? 'Dear Dad'? Even the word made him feel sick. In the end he simply wrote: 'Going out after work, won't be back for dinner.' He didn't sign it – as who else was it going to be from? He left the note on the kitchen table weighed down with a mug, where his father would see it.

Here he was now, getting off the bus in the middle of the village – the village he was forbidden to go into and hadn't even set foot in for sixteen years of his life. Jack drew some stares from people getting off the bus with him, so he waited for them to disperse before heading to Daisy's. This didn't feel right; he didn't feel comfortable doing it at all – and swore he wouldn't do it again.

By the time he reached Daisy's front door (she'd specifically asked him not to climb over the fence into the garden or her sister would think he was weird) he was in a bit of a state – pale, sweating and dying for some cider. Did he knock on the porch door or the inner door? What if her sister answered it? He pictured how awful he must look, and was paranoid about smelling after work. Suddenly the inner door opened, and he thought he was going to faint.

Luckily, Daisy's head peered round the door; she'd been watching out for him. Her face dropped when she saw him up close. 'God, Jack, What's wrong with you? You look dreadful! Here, come inside.'

'Where's your sister?'

'She's not here, so don't worry – I don't know why, though!' Jack looked relieved and stepped into the porch. Daisy went to peck him on the cheek and exclaimed, 'Phew!' as she did so, confirming his worst fears about smelling from work.

She led him into the kitchen. 'Do you want a cup of tea?' she asked, but Jack shook his head. What he needed was a drink ... and then a bath. 'Cider?' she said, moving towards the fridge. Jack nodded and sat down at the table. He cracked open the can she passed him and took a long draught, wishing he'd brought some of his own; he could have done with the stronger hit of it. 'So, what's up? Did something happen at work?'

'No, no it was fine ... well, not fine, you know, just normal.'

'So, what then? You looked a bit ... agitated when you turned up.' It was hard for Jack to say; he felt foolish – he'd been doing so well lately.

'It was just... I don't know, just coming here on the bus from work and ... you know – meeting your sister, I guess.'

'But why?' Daisy replied, pulling up a seat next to him. 'I mean, it's only my sister – and trust me she's nothing to get worked up over!'

Jack shrugged. 'Where is she anyway?'

'I've no idea; she's normally back by now. Probably for the best considering the state you turned up in! Come on, let's go upstairs. I'll show you the films we're going to watch. I've got it all set up – I can't wait!'

Jack picked up his rucksack and they headed upstairs. Her room had that unique, lovely, perfumed smell to it that was so her; unfortunately, this made him want a bath even more. The bed was neat and tidy again, and there were extra pillows for them to sit against. She showed him the video player she'd set up and the snacks and popcorn all laid out. They sat down and she talked about the films she'd chosen, giving her reasons for each choice.

'Right, what do you want to order?' she said, picking up a leaflet from her bedside table and shaking it in his face. Jack looked puzzled. 'Chinese takeaway, remember? You have had Chinese before, haven't you?' Jack shook his head. 'Oh, God! Sorry. Well, are you OK with it? I mean, we don't have to; it was just an idea.'

'No, it's fine. It'll be nice to try something new... I like rice.'

'Well, that's a good start!' she laughed. They thumbed through the leaflet, which had 'The Golden Star' written at the top of it. Jack briefly scanned it – kung po chicken, Peking duck, chow mein, szechuan... It was all nonsense to him and sounded frighteningly exotic. And what was with all the numbers?

'I don't know, Daisy, you choose something,' he said, defeated, handing it back.

'Well, we'll just order something simple – we haven't got much money anyway! So, sweet and sour chicken balls ... everybody likes those. Rice, noodles and chicken with cashew nuts.'

'Sounds OK to me!' said Jack, draining the last of his cider. He was starting to relax into the evening, but was still desperate for a bath.

As if reading his mind, Daisy said, 'Why don't you have a quick shower while I go and order? Then we'll go and get it.'

They went out onto the landing and Daisy grabbed him a large, fluffy towel from the airing cupboard. 'Um, Daisy ... can I have a bath instead?' he asked. He'd never had a shower before but didn't want to say so.

'Well, you could – but it would take longer, and we've got to go and get the Chinese yet … *and* it's sort of getting on.' She looked at her watch. 'We've got three movies to get through as well!'

'Oh, OK, never mind.' Jack shuffled off to the bathroom, clutching his towel.

The bathroom was immaculate, with squeaky clean tiles that smelt of fresh pine. There wasn't a hint of mildew anywhere, nor any daddy longlegs – unlike his. He pulled back the shower curtain and stared at the white shower unit. It gave him the same overwhelming feeling that the washing machine had before Daisy had shown him how to use it. He tried to press a few buttons and turn the dials, but couldn't get it to work. He felt like an idiot again. Downstairs he heard Daisy ordering the food in that grown-up phone voice of hers. This made him smile, and he told himself to calm down.

As Daisy headed back upstairs she noticed there was no sound of running water, and that the bathroom door was still ajar – which wasn't like Jack. 'Are you OK?' she called through the door, then slowly pushed it open. He was still fully dressed, clutching his towel.

'I couldn't get it to work,' he admitted.

Daisy tutted, walked over to a cord that was dangling from the ceiling and gave it a yank. A red light came on, a fan started and the shower hissed to life, making Jack jump and spraying him with water. Daisy laughed. 'Sorry, I should have said!' She leant across him, messed with some of the dials and then tested the water with her hand. 'There you go!'

'Thanks.'

'The Chinese is only going to be about ten minutes or so. I thought it would be at least half an hour … so I'll have to go and get it myself, which isn't ideal. I was really hoping Lily would be back by now.'

Jack looked horrified at this revelation. 'You're leaving me here on my own? What if she comes back?' His voice had gone up an octave.

'Honestly, Jack, it's only my bloody sister: it's not like you're meeting the queen – or even my parents. You'll be fine; anyway, she's probably gone straight out from work or something. Just have a shower, then go and wait in my room. You can get into bed if you want and I'll bring your dinner up on a tray, my lord!' Jack wasn't convinced. 'Well, go on then, get undressed!' And she smacked his bum playfully; sometimes it was like dealing with a child, but she loved it really. 'I'll only be gone for ten minutes. What are the chances of her coming back in that time?' she reassured him.

Jack stripped and jumped in the shower. He felt horribly exposed to the world, not being underwater; he had visions of her sister coming back at any moment and heading straight to the bathroom. It was a shame he couldn't have enjoyed his first shower for longer; the warm jets of water felt good on his body.

He switched the shower off, pulled the cord again and stepped out into the steamy bathroom. After wrapping a towel around his waist, he darted back down the corridor to the sanctuary of Daisy's room, leaving a trail of wet footprints on the landing.

It had barely been five minutes since Daisy had left, and Jack was towelling himself dry when he thought he heard the front door open. That was strange; he hadn't heard her van pull up. And surely she couldn't be back already; unless she'd forgotten something – money perhaps. He tiptoed over to the window and looked out onto the front drive. It was still empty, which could only mean one thing; it had to be her sister!

He strained his ears and heard sounds from downstairs – keys being dropped on a table, footsteps on the stairs. His stomach lurched at the realisation that his worst case scenario was unfolding – and here he was, half-naked in Daisy's room.

In panic, Jack looked for an escape, and briefly considered the window again. But all he had on was a towel; besides, last time had been terrifying. Instead, he shot into bed and pulled the cover up to his chest. His only hope was to keep quiet and pray to God that she didn't come in. He sat upright, his eyes darting from side to side as he listened, not even swallowing or breathing. When he heard footsteps on the landing he clutched the covers tighter around him, as if for protection. The bedroom door slowly opened, and so did Jack's eyes in alarm … then Sookie the cat bounded in, letting out a squeak-like miaow in greeting. He let out a sigh of relief as she hopped onto the bed and began to purr.

Lily waltzed straight into her room in a rush. She'd arranged to meet her on-off boyfriend for a meal and a bit of a 'crisis talk'; things hadn't been going well lately. She was running late as he was picking her up at seven-fifteen, and she'd got to get showered and dressed. She went to pick out some clothes, but couldn't locate the denim skirt she wanted, to show off her legs and let him see what he'd be missing. Jack heard her curse. Just lately, too many of her clothes and make-up bits had been going missing – and they always seemed to end up in her pesky little sister's room. It was ever since she'd met this mystery boy, stopped dressing like a lesbian and gone all girly. Well, she could sodding well go and buy her own clothes!

Lily marched to Daisy's room to retrieve her skirt, along with any other bits of clothing and make-up she'd pilfered. On the way she told herself what a hypocrite Daisy was. It was so rich: she hated anyone going in *her* room, and got all arsey if anyone so much as looked at any of her precious records or tapes. Yet she was quite happy to go around collecting other people's things and hoarding them like some sort of bloody magpie! Then she noticed the trail of wet footprints on the carpet, and reminded herself to give Daisy a ticking off about that too. Without a further thought she swung open the bedroom door.

There, in her younger sister's bed, was a complete stranger – wide-eyed, naked to the waist and petting their family cat. What the hell? And here *she* was, alone in the house with him. She didn't know whether to scream, attack, run or laugh. Instead they both let out a yelp of surprise. There was an uncomfortable silence whilst Lily put two and two together. This was obviously her darling sister's secret boyfriend. On first impressions, the girl had done well; she liked what she saw, and this went a long way towards how she reacted. Fortunately for Jack, this was how her mind worked.

They weighed each other up, studying each other, until Lily spoke. 'So, where's my little sister then?'

It took Jack an aeon to reply as he was still in shock. Daisy's sister cut quite an imposing figure in her white Boots uniform. She looked older than he was expecting and was wearing heels too, making her appear tall as she stood in the doorway – a lot taller than Daisy. She had long, manicured nails and her hair was dyed blonde with darker roots. You could say she was more glamorous than Daisy, but only in a – how could he put it – more artificial way. She wore heavy make-up, and didn't have Daisy's natural beauty. In fact, she barely resembled Daisy at all, he thought.

He cleared his throat and willed his mouth to form words and speak. Come on, Jack, this is it, this is the moment. You can do this. It's time to take part in the real world. 'Erm, she's gone to the Chinese food shop,' he managed to croak.

'Oh right, Chinese, eh?' she replied, smirking at the expression. 'So …you must be the mystery boyfriend then? We meet at last.' Jack didn't say anything; he just smiled sheepishly and blushed. 'Well, have you got a name then?' she asked, looking from him to the cat – whom he was stroking a little over-enthusiastically.

Old feelings came flooding back: this was exactly what he'd been dreading; next she'd be asking him where he lived. There was another awkward pause as Jack considered lying, before deciding against it. 'It's Jack.'

At around this point Daisy walked in through the front door, clutching the takeaway. She was about to shout up to Jack when, to her surprise, she heard voices upstairs. Had he put the telly on? She gently lowered the carrier bag onto the floor and listened. Oh no! That wasn't the telly – that was her sister! Poor Jack. She dashed up the stairs, hearing snatches of muffled conversation. He was actually talking to her and – oh my God! She recognised that tone in her sister's voice; she was flirting with him, the tart!

As Daisy reached the landing she heard her sister say, 'So, Jack … where do you live then?'

'Ahem!' said Daisy loudly. 'What's going on?' Lily turned round with a smug look on her face as Daisy walked past her into the room. She surveyed the scene: she'd only been gone ten minutes, yet Jack had somehow managed to lure every female in the house into her room. Admittedly, he looked a bit shell-shocked – and there *she* was, the trollop, feasting her eyes on him. God, if it's not Sookie, then it's my sister! she thought.

'Oh, me and Jack were just getting to know each other that's all… Fancy leaving him here all alone!' She knew this would wind Daisy up and it did.

She pushed her sister out of the room, saying, 'And you too! Scram!' For a second Jack thought she was referring to him, until she made a move towards the cat, who got the message and scarpered. Then Daisy left too, shutting the door firmly behind her. Jack listened in growing bemusement to the muffled voices that gradually got louder, rapidly descending into an argument. Were they always like this? He heard wet footprints being mentioned and accusations about a skirt and make-up. Names such as 'cow', 'weirdo' and lastly 'tart!' were exchanged before Daisy opened the bedroom door again and slammed it behind her.

She stood against it for a moment, catching her breath. She had colour in her cheeks and looked really angry, until she noticed Jack staring at her. He had a look of amazement on his face, and she suddenly felt embarrassed by her reaction. 'Sorry about that!' she said. Jack didn't know whether she was talking about the argument, or her sister coming back when she wasn't here.

'That's OK,' he said, which it was either way; at least he'd got it over and done with.

Daisy went over to her chest of drawers, pulled out a few bits of clothing and gathered up some make-up. She clutched them to her chest but couldn't find the denim skirt. Jack knew what she was looking for and pointed to a chair.

'Oh, thanks,' she said, embarrassed again. She took everything out, leaving the door open. He heard Daisy say, 'Here!' and then the sound of her sister's bedroom door opening.

As Daisy got back to her room, Lily shouted, 'Well, I can't wear it now! It's all creased and needs washing!' Daisy closed the door on her.

'Right...' she said. 'Shall we have some dinner?'

'Er, yes... Do you want some help?'

'No. You stay there!' She didn't want her sister getting her hooks into him again. Daisy made to leave the room, then turned around with a funny look on her face. 'Please tell me you've got something on under there,' she said, not liking the thought of Jack being stark naked in the same room as her sister.

'No.' And he suddenly whipped back the covers. Daisy gasped and put her hand over her mouth in shock. She burst out laughing when she saw the towel. Jack grinned, pleased at himself with his trick, and was still smiling when she'd left the room. He climbed out of bed to put some clothes on, feeling pretty pleased with himself in general; he thought he'd handled that quite well.

After what seemed an age, Daisy returned with two plates piled high with food. It smelt good and made his stomach rumble. She had to make another trip to get some trays, cutlery, drinks and condiments. Jack offered to help again but she stubbornly declined. The last time she returned, she said, 'At least she's going out now.' She put the first video tape in, closed the curtains and settled down on the bed next to Jack.

As the opening titles came up Jack set about his first ever Chinese takeaway, not knowing what to try first. 'So … what did you think of my sister?' said Daisy as she cracked open a can of cider.

'She seemed nice,' Jack replied, negotiating some slippery noodles.

'Nice?' said Daisy, stopping mid-swig to glare at him.

'Well … a bit bossy perhaps. Erm, could I try some of that sauce please?' he asked, gesturing to the carton on her bedside table.

'No, get it yourself!'

The Movie Marathon began, and each film was memorable in its own way. *Stand By Me* was perilous and goofy in equal measure, and Jack wished he'd had friends like that. They ate and drank throughout the film, and Daisy was over the moon with his reaction, glad that she'd chosen it. After a brief toilet break they slipped back under the covers to watch *An American Werewolf in London*. This absolutely terrified Jack, making him jump out of his skin on several occasions and knock popcorn everywhere. He didn't dare to go to the toilet on his own, which reminded Daisy of when she'd first watched it when she was younger.

To finish off, Woody Allen's *Sleeper* made them both roar with laughter. At first Daisy was worried that Jack wouldn't get it, and would just think, 'Who is this strange little man in glasses and what on earth is he doing?' Which, to be honest, at first he did – and some of the one-liners *did* pass him by. But he was soon sucked in by the sheer ridiculousness of it all, absorbed by the nonsensical slapstick comedy played out to old-fashioned music.

At some point Daisy's sister came back, and during the last film they were laughing so much that she banged on the door, telling them to keep the noise down. Throughout all the films Daisy had made an effort not to keep saying, 'Oh watch this bit!' and speaking the lines as they happened. By the end of the night they were both exhausted, and had square eyes from staring at the television for so long.

Daisy turned off the TV and put her bedside lamp on. They'd totally lost track of time, and when they looked at the clock it had gone twelve o'clock – too late for Jack to go back; he hadn't left his window open. 'Listen,' she said, gesturing to the window, her face half in shadow. It was raining hard against the glass. 'Well, I guess that means you're staying then.' A large rumble of thunder answered for him. It was so snug and cosy here in bed with the rain pelting down outside: how could he refuse?

With some reluctance, they temporarily left the haven of her bed to brush their teeth. Daisy hadn't told her sister that

Jack was staying, but she was past caring; it was none of her business anyhow.

Once back in her room they got undressed in the lamplight. Jack slipped into bed in his boxer shorts, and watched Daisy in the amber glow as she stripped down to her underwear. She turned her back on him to take off her bra and pull a T-shirt on before sliding into bed beside him. As she switched off the lamp there was another rumble of thunder, followed shortly by a crack of lightning which lit up the whole room. 'It must be right overhead,' Daisy said as she snuggled into him. Jack couldn't believe they were going to stay like this all night; it seemed too good to be true. Although they were both tired, it wasn't long before things began to turn amorous, and they were forced to retreat to the floor when the bed made too much noise as they rolled about.

They laid the duvet down by the side of the bed, and to the soundtrack of drumming rain and rolling thunder they began to make love. It was, without doubt, the best time ever for both of them. They'd had enough cider to lose their inhibitions, but not so much that they weren't aware of everything. They were in no rush, and they explored each other in new and different ways. Lightning intermittently painted the room with light, teasing them with flashes of each other's nakedness. They were bolder now and more comfortable with each other – getting accustomed to this love thing. Sometimes there was tenderness between them, with kisses gentle as rain. At other times they banged and crashed against each other like waves upon rocks.

When they sank back into bed afterwards, Daisy was the first to fall asleep. She lay in his arms with her head on his chest, her leg across him and her hair spilling all around him. He drank in her scent, stunned by the happiness he felt. Her heart thumped against him, and if he listened closely he thought he could actually hear it. He wanted it to stay like this forever – and that's what was so overwhelming; it terrified him that it might change or that this could be taken away from him; he didn't know what he would do if it was.

In the morning, Jack was awoken (all too early) by the sound of Daisy's alarm clock. She had set it to go off at six-thirty, so she had plenty of time to make him breakfast. He was dimly aware of her groaning and reaching across him to slap the top of it. He felt her get out of bed, and it was his turn to groan in displeasure. Through bleary eyes, he watched her pad round to his side of the bed in a grey Pixies T-shirt with her black pants showing beneath. She bent over in front of the stereo to put some music on.

Needless to say, he was now fully awake (in more ways than one), and his hand shifted down below. Not for the first time, he swore she did these things on purpose to drive him mad.

'Oh, you're awake,' Daisy said, turning round.

'I wasn't, but I am now!' he replied with a lustful smile, pulling her towards him. She lay on top of him, and could feel him through the covers.

'Jack!' she scolded. 'We haven't got time for this, I've got to make breakfast.' And she pulled herself away. He groaned again in protest and rolled onto his stomach, but was unable to take his eyes off her. She pulled an old blue dressing gown off a hook on the back of her bedroom door. 'Besides,' she said as she wrapped it around her, 'look at my knees, you naughty boy!' They were both scuffed with red carpet burns. He smiled guiltily, and watched her as she went about the room, piling things onto trays. She looked funny in her dressing gown.

As she went to leave, he asked, 'Do you want me to come and help you make breakfast?'

'No, you stay there; I'll bring you a cup of tea in a minute – put the telly on or something.' Jack did as he was told. The news was on, and he tried to be interested in it: at least it took his mind off other things. Daisy soon returned with a mug of tea, kissing him as she handed it to him. She smelt of fried food.

'Does this mean I'm having breakfast in bed as well?'

'Yes, I guess it does.' She didn't like the idea of having breakfast downstairs with her sister on the prowl, flirting and listening in. She disappeared again. Jack sipped his tea, flicking through the channels with the remote control.

After about ten minutes he began to get bored, and was also feeling a little confined in the bedroom. He wouldn't have minded going downstairs and having a bit of a wander about, and was also desperate for a pee. Deciding to chance it, he got out of bed. As he crossed the room he caught his reflection in the wardrobe mirror. He had a few battle scars of his own; there was a bite-mark on his shoulder and scratches on his back. Quietly, he opened the door to poke his head out and look up and down the landing – it was deserted. He smelt frying bacon as he scurried to the bathroom.

He was tiptoeing back down the corridor afterwards when he heard raised voices on the stairs; talk about bad timing. He tried to quicken his pace but it was too late; at that moment Daisy's sister appeared on the landing, followed by Daisy carrying breakfast on a tray. Jack froze and pressed himself up against the wall. Lily was already immaculately made up and coiffed, wearing her work outfit. She was looking behind her and having a go at Daisy: 'Well, it stinks – I can smell it on my hair and clothes already!' Then she turned round to see Jack in nothing but his boxer shorts. 'Ooh, morning, Jack!' she cooed. In her heels she was taller than him in his bare feet. She eyed him up and down. 'We'll have to stop meeting like this.'

Daisy had always felt as if she lived in the shadow of her

older sister, who had always been more glamorous, taller and more vivacious. She felt dull in comparison. Look at her – eyeing up her boyfriend like a bloody praying mantis, while *she* felt like some sort of charlady in her drab dressing gown. She barged between them with the tray and marched Jack back into her room, slamming the door closed. They heard Lily giggling to herself as she walked off. 'God, I hate her!' said Daisy.

Lily soon left for work, and before long it was time for Jack to go too. He did his best to do Daisy's breakfast justice, but wasn't used to eating so much in the morning. Daisy helped him to finish it off, and it was with a full stomach that she saw him off at the door. She kissed him on the cheek and handed him his rucksack as if it was a briefcase, and they were a model husband and wife in a TV advert; she'd even made his pack-up for him. The illusion of convention was somewhat marred by the fact that it was the patio door into the garden. She begged him to come back straight after work, but as much as he'd loved to have done he just couldn't. He'd got to go home … while he still had one.

They arranged to meet, weather permitting, at the pub that evening, so they could discuss what to do about the seaside. It was drizzling heavily as Daisy watched her beau disappear down the long garden. Jack reached the bottom fence and pulled himself up it with ease, vaulted it, and with one last wave was gone She stood there for a moment, watching the rain come down and overcome with how much she felt for him. She noticed that the grass needed mowing; it was ankle deep and her mum wouldn't be pleased.

CHAPTER 28

Locked Out and Barred

It was still raining when Jack trudged down the lane to his house that evening. Mud was sticking to his boots from the fields, and he tried to wash it off in the caramel coloured puddles in the potholes. He hadn't seen his father in almost two days, and not since he'd left that note, so he didn't know what kind of reception he was going to get.

He pushed down on the latch to the back door, glad to be getting out of the rain, but the door wouldn't open. Thinking it was stuck, he tried again, but it wouldn't budge an inch. He rattled the door in its frame, back and forth, but to no avail. There were no two ways about it; it was locked. This was odd for two reasons: his father never locked the door during the day – even when he went out, and his van was there.

Jack cupped his hands over his eyes and tried to peer through the parlour window. It had a net curtain across it, which was hard to see through from the outside. Despite this, he could see there were no signs of life within. 'Bastard!' he hissed, and banged on the door. He cupped his hands to the window again as he waited for a reply, hoping to see some movement. There was nothing, so he knocked again – louder this time – till he was thumping on the door; but still there was silence.

He made his way round the house, peering in at windows and knocking on them. Had he deliberately been locked out? Or had his father just got the telly on too loud and fallen asleep in front of it as usual? What if the old bugger had finally drunk himself to death? Anything could have happened overnight. He despised his father but he didn't want to have to deal with his corpse.

Jack speeded up as he was getting soaked, making a beeline for the bay window of the lounge. When he got there, the curtains were closed, which was also out of the ordinary; they were only closed during the day if the sun was shining on the TV screen. Don't tell me that's not deliberate, he thought, as he banged on the window. '*Let me in!*' he shouted, incensed. Nothing. He pressed his ear against the glass, straining to hear the telly, but it was hard to make anything out over the rain.

He stomped back round to the rear of the house and spotted his father's van on the drive. In desperation, he marched over to it and clambered inside, plonking himself down on the front seat. He felt an unexpected surge of panic at being locked out; it *was* his home after all. OK, it hadn't felt much like that lately, but it was all he had. It was his base; his things were in there, his precious things – his savings, his photograph, Daisy's stereo too.

He sat there for about ten minutes, trying to gather his thoughts as the warmth of his body steamed up the windows. What if his father *was* lying dead in there? Wasn't it his duty to break in? The more likely scenario was that he'd been locked out as punishment for not returning home the previous day; it was too much of a coincidence. The rain had all but stopped, and Jack wiped the fogged-up window with his sleeve. Directly in front of him were the faded green double doors of his father's workshop. An idea came to him.

The last time he'd been in the workshop was when he'd had to ring Daisy to cancel their first camping trip all those weeks before. Today, as he slipped inside, the wood shavings smelt damp from where the rain had got in, giving the place the feel of a giant hamster's cage. It was the phone that Jack headed straight towards, hanging on the wall and covered in sawdust. He didn't know why his father kept it; the line rental could hardly be worth the business it brought in. It wasn't as though he advertised his numerous trades; it was all word of mouth and old acquaintances.

Jack lifted the receiver as gently as possible. The phone made that strange buzzing noise as he pressed it to his ear. There was dust on the dial and he had to blow some of it away to see the numbers properly. Underneath the clear plastic circle, something caught his eye – a combination of small, typed numbers that he'd never noticed before. He frantically wiped away more of the dust so that he could see them properly: 843300. The first three digits were the same as Daisy's phone number – which could only mean one thing. It had to be the elusive number for their phone!

He wasn't quite sure how this could benefit him, but he knew he had to remember it. He dialled Daisy's number, letting the phone ring twice before quickly lowering the receiver. This was the first time he'd used this message (meet me at the phone box as soon as you can) and he hoped it didn't alarm her. After covering the phone with a fresh layer of sawdust, Jack slipped back outside. The evening air felt warm compared with the coolness of the workshop and the sky looked as if it was trying to brighten up a bit. He tried the back door one last time, but it was still locked.

As he picked up speed on his bike, the rain from the road kicked up from his back wheel and sprayed a new line of wet up his back. His thoughts turned to Daisy, and if she had got his call or not; he was counting on her to help him figure out what to do next. If not, there'd be nothing else for it but to go to her house.

Daisy *had* heard the two rings, as she'd been getting ready to meet Jack anyway. They arrived at the phone box at pretty much the same time, both relieved to see each other. 'Is everything OK? I was worried,' she said through the window as she pulled up, then added, 'You look like a drowned rat!' This didn't improve Jack's mood; he was already ashamed at how he looked in front of her.

'Not really. I'm locked out.'

'Locked out? How come? Where's your father?'

'Oh he's there … I think, anyway, but I can't get in.'

'You're joking! God, you poor thing. Well, meet me in the car park and you can tell me all about it.' Her words had an instant calming effect on him.

They sat in Daisy's van for a while without even going in to get drinks. It was spitting with rain again. Jack related his story; and told her he'd shouted and banged on the door and windows to no avail.

Daisy looked at her watch. 'So you've been stuck outside all this time? No wonder you're wet through. You should have called me straightaway. Oh, that reminds me! I was thinking we ought to have another ring for emergencies – so we know whether it's urgent or not…'

Jack interrupted her. 'That reminds me too! I think I've found our phone number.' Daisy immediately wrote the number down on the back of her hand.

'This is great news; we'll actually be able to speak on the phone!'

'How?' he asked, not understanding – the phone was still out of bounds.

'I don't know – you'll have to let it ring three times or something when your father's not about, and I'll ring you straight back to see if it works. Actually, that could be the code – three rings means call me straight back.' They agreed it there and then, and also that they could use four rings for absolute emergencies.

'So if you're convinced he's inside, he must have done it on purpose,' Daisy said.

'Well, yes – probably because I didn't come back home yesterday. That or he's gone and drunk himself to death.'

'God, you don't think so do you?'

'Who knows?' Jack's mind turned it over, and the possibilities that came with it. What if he *was* dead? What would he do with the body? How would he tell the authorities without explaining who he was? What if they thought *he'd* done it and that he was just a stranger passing through? The more he thought about it, the more he hoped it wasn't the case.

'Well, do you want to stay at mine tonight again?' asked Daisy.

'No, I can't,' he said quickly. She looked disappointed and he took her hand. 'You know I'd love to, I really would, but I've got to find out what's going on – even if it means breaking in. The longer I stay away, the worse it'll get.' Daisy nodded, knowing he was right.

The rain had petered out, so Daisy went inside to get some drinks. 'We might as well stay in the van – the benches all look too wet.' When she came back out with two pints, she said, 'Ugh! Guess who's in? Tweedledum and Tweedledee!'

'They'd better not say anything tonight, 'cause I'm not in the mood and I will say something!' Jack snapped. They sat with the van doors open and put some music on whilst they discussed what to do about the weekend. In the end they decided just to see what the weather was like. Their contingency plan, if they couldn't go to the seaside, was to spend the whole day at Daisy's; her sister worked on Saturdays so they'd have the whole house to themselves. Therefore, both outcomes were favourable. They'd have to set off early in the morning if they *were* going, so they agreed that if it was chucking it down Jack was to let the phone ring once by eight. That way they'd both know the trip was definitely off.

After another round of drinks and another bout of rain, they decided to call it a night. Jack couldn't concentrate; he kept going back to the situation at home. Daisy asked if he wanted a lift as it was still raining, telling him in a motherly way that she didn't want him catching a cold. 'Well, I would, but what about my bike?'

'Oh, we can just put it in the back.' The rear of the van had been stripped out over the years, leaving it pretty much bare.

Once the bike was in, Daisy drove out of the car park, then stopped in front of the pub. 'I'll just pop those glasses in,' she said, pointing to them by Jack's feet. She was only in there for a matter of seconds, but when she came back out her face was red, with a stunned look of indignation on it. 'OK, Jack, *now* you can have a word!' she said, clearly upset.

'Why? What's wrong? What happened?'

'He just pinched my bum!'

'Who?!' shouted Jack.

'One of those guys. He went "See you later, love" and pinched my arse!'

'RIGHT, THAT'S IT!' Jack erupted, just like his father in his heyday, making her jump. She'd never seen him like this before and it scared her. 'Which one was it?' he demanded. Daisy was too stunned to answer, and was beginning to wish she'd not said anything. 'WHICH ONE, DAISY?!' he yelled, shaking with pure, white fury.

'The one in the green top,' she said quietly. 'But it doesn't matter, Jack – just leave it. Please! We just won't come here again!' But it was too late; the wheels were set in motion and he was already halfway to the pub. 'Jack, be careful!' she cried through the window, sinking into her seat with her head in her hands.

Jack had never been in a fight in his life, save for some tussles with his father, and he had no idea what he was going to do. He didn't even have time to think about it, which was probably a good thing. All he knew was that nobody, *nobody*, was laying their hands on his girl and making her feel like that. He was already in the mood for a fight, and somebody was going to pay.

He marched straight into the bar, where the two unsuspecting men were standing at the counter, laughing. They soon stopped when they saw Jack heading towards them, a look of thunder on his face and his right hand curled into a fist. The one with the green top froze with his pint halfway towards his mouth. Jack went straight up to him, drew back his fist and exploded it into the man's face with all his strength, putting his entire body weight behind it.

Sixteen years of pent-up rage and shame came out in one blow. Jack felt the man's nose crush under his fist before he went flying backwards onto the floor. His pint glass flew into the air and landed on the other side of the room, exploding into bits. People at nearby tables shot up to get out of the way and then stood there in stunned silence. It was a classic bar room punch out of a Western; once again, Jack's hero, John Wayne, would have been mighty proud of him.

Jack wasn't finished. Still shaking with rage, he went and stood over the man lying on the floor, who was clutching his bloody nose and barely conscious. 'Don't you ever – and I mean *EVER!* touch her again,' he warned, before turning to walk out.

The man's dopey mate, coming to his senses, made a move towards Jack for revenge, but the landlord held him back, saying, 'Leave it, Tony! Leave it! He probably deserved it anyway!' Jack glared at him as he passed, daring him to try. Tony finally relaxed as Jack neared the door, deciding indeed to 'leave it'. 'And you!' the landlord shouted to Jack, pointing a finger at him. 'You're barred! Don't ever set foot in here again!' Jack beat a hasty exit, with the reality of what he'd done sinking in, and his hand beginning to throb.

Daisy was sitting in the van, a petrified look on her face as she heard the commotion unfold. Jack jumped in. 'Drive!' he said, and she sped away. As she did so, she looked down at him clutching his hand.

'Oh my God, Jack, are you OK?'

Jack paused before answering. 'What does barred mean?'

As they climbed the hill to Jack's house, to Daisy's surprise he said, 'Just drop me at the bottom of the lane.'

'But what about your father?'

'I really don't care – for all we know he might be dead anyway.' He felt tired and his hand hurt; too much had happened and he just wanted to get into his house. Daisy pulled in and they both got out. She helped him get the bike out of the side of the van. Jack's face was pale and his teeth were chattering.

'Are you sure about this? Wouldn't it be better if you came back to mine instead?' she said, genuinely concerned.

'No, I can't, really – I've got to get this over and done with.'

'Well, do you want me to wait just in case?"

'No, honestly, I'll be OK. It could take a while – especially if I've got to break in.'

'But what about your hand?'

'It's fine, just a bit sore that's all.' And he opened and closed it to prove it was still working.

She hugged him hard, then put her hands either side of his head. 'Promise me you'll come straight back down to mine if you can't get in,' she said, not wanting to let him go.

'I will, I promise.'

'And be careful, no more fights! Will you let the phone ring just once to let me know you're OK?'

Jack sighed. 'I might not be able to. If you don't hear anything just take it that I'm OK.' Daisy looked dejected, as if she needed more reassurance. 'Don't worry,' he said, kissing her on the forehead. 'And I'll ring once in the morning if it's chucking it down.'

Daisy reluctantly got back into the van and wound down her window. 'Jack!' she called. He turned around, halfway up the lane with his bike. 'I love you!' she said, and blew him a kiss.

'I love you too.'

As she drove away, Daisy felt as if she was going to cry. She couldn't believe what had just happened or that he was leaving her so soon afterwards. She felt alone and didn't want to go back to her house. For the first time that week she really missed her mum and dad – especially her dad, with his easy laugh and reassuring manner. She didn't know how she was going to sleep that night, and there was a guilty part of her that hoped Jack *couldn't* get in. That way he'd *have* to come down to her. Then she could spend the night in the comfort of his arms.

Jack didn't know what to expect as he plodded up the drive. He was pretty much resigned to the fact that he was going to have to break in, and was already thinking about the best method. After parking his bike, he put a trembling hand on the door latch. Pain shot through his thumb as he applied downward force. But to his amazement, the latch gave and the door swung inwards with its familiar scrape. He couldn't believe it. At least it meant one thing; he wasn't going to be dealing with a dead body.

As he stepped inside and turned on the light, his relief turned to anger when he saw the state the kitchen was in; there was two days' worth of mess. Where was the old bugger anyway? Determined to have it out with him, Jack walked straight through the parlour towards the lounge. Sure enough, there he was flopped in his chair in front of the telly. He looked an absolute state: his hair was lank and greasy, and his face was filthy and bearded. Somewhat out of character, he turned and raised his bottle of cider in greeting when Jack walked in. 'Ah, the wand'rer returns!' he slurred, blind drunk.

'Why did you lock me out?' demanded Jack, coming straight out with it. His father ignored him and took a long swig of cider.

'Gez what?' he said in return. Jack was in no mood for games and repeated his question.

'I *said* why did you lock me out?'

His father still didn't reply, but held his bottle aloft and said, 'Beckerz through to the final!'

'Whoopedoo,' said Jack.

'Over four hours it took to see off that Czech basstard Llendl, the longest semi-final in Wimbendon hizt'ry ... course, it was int'rupted by the bloody rain.'

He wouldn't shut up; it was as if he just wanted someone to talk to. But Jack had heard enough; he'd run out of patience. 'WHY DID YOU LOCK ME OUT?' he shouted.

His father turned to him, glassy eyed and swollen nosed, as if hearing him for the first time. 'What d'yer mean, lock you out?'

'You know damn well what I mean, so don't pretend you don't!' hissed Jack, advancing.

His father shrank back a bit. 'I've no idea what you're talking about; I haven't even been out today,' he said, sounding more sober all of a sudden.

Jack digested this new information. Could he actually be telling the truth? If he hadn't been out (which from the state of him he probably hadn't) then it *was* possible the door had still been locked from the previous night. Jack was briefly unsure, but then he remembered his banging and shouting – and knew his father was lying. 'I was banging on the door and shouting. It was pissing it down!' he said.

'Well, I had the tennis on. I didn't hear you.'

'You're a liar. I was banging on the front window too!' He had never spoken to his father like this before.

'Well, perhaps I dozed off or something.'

'Aagh!' Jack cried, turning away in anger; his father was never going to admit it. He suddenly felt drained and wanted to be able to look at his photo of his mother and sister; his 'real' family. And he made to leave.

In doing so, he missed the smug smile which spread across his tormentor's face. Jack had just reached the door when his father spoke, keen as ever to have the last word. 'Aren't you forgetting something?' Jack turned around, without a clue what he was talking about. His father held out a filthy hand and rubbed his thumb and forefinger together. 'Rent. I'm going shopping in the morning.'

Jack's first instinct was to flip; he'd barely been there all week, then he got locked out – and then *he* had the audacity to ask for a week's board! But he couldn't be bothered to argue anymore, and begrudgingly reached into his pocket. He pulled out what was left of his wages and handed over forty quid. It pained him to do so as this left him with only a tenner. His father snapped the folded up notes off him and ferreted them away in his pocket.

An hour later Jack lay in bed, still too wound up to sleep. It irked him that he knew his father had locked him out deliberately, yet he couldn't prove it. He vowed that in the morning, if they weren't going away, he was going to get his own key cut for the back door. Daisy had suggested it earlier, and he hadn't even known you could do such a thing. He had hated the feeling of being locked out, away from his precious few things, and didn't ever want to feel like that again. Now that his father had done it once, what was to stop him doing it again? He clenched his hand. It was bruised and tender, which made him think of his sister; he could have done with some of her nursing skills.

CHAPTER 29
Oh Black Day!

Part One
The Phone Call

The time was nine thirty-five a.m. precisely when Daisy got the phone call. It was one of those life-changing moments, like when JFK got shot. You'd always remember what you were doing, where you were and what time it was … except that this was worse; this was personal. She was in the kitchen at the time, stroking Sookie the cat and staring glumly out into the garden at the incessant rain. There was to be no trip to the seaside, confirmed earlier by a single ring on the telephone just before eight. At least this had meant Jack was OK – she had fretted about him all last night and was missing him dreadfully. Oh, how she'd wanted to pick the phone up when it had rung, just to hear his voice. It had also meant that they'd have the whole house to themselves, she'd supposed. The downside was that she'd had three miserable hours to kill, as Jack had said the previous night that if they weren't going he'd have to catch up on his chores in the morning.

The phone startled her when it rang out again in the silent

kitchen; that was when she looked at the clock and registered the time. Her initial thought was that it must be Jack again – perhaps something had changed and he was able to meet her sooner. She counted the rings in hope, but to her surprise they didn't stop at three; they just kept on going. It must be Mum, she thought and shot up, scaring the cat.

She picked up the phone, trying her best to sound bright and cheery, 'Hello!'

She barely recognised the voice on the other end. 'Daisy … it's Mum.' She sounded awful.

'Hi, Mum, are you OK? You sound strange.'

Carol carried on in a quiet, shaky voice. 'Listen, Daisy … I'm afraid I've got some bad news.' She broke down in tears, unable to go on. Daisy instantly feared the worst. Her eyes began to smart and her scalp seemed to shrink.

'Mum, what is it? Is it Dad? Is he OK?' Carol tried to answer, tried to form the words, but racking sobs caught in her throat again; it was so much harder telling Daisy; she knew how close she was to her dad.

She finally managed to speak. 'No, he's not OK.' Daisy's knuckles grew white as her hand tightened around the receiver. 'Daisy, I'm afraid he's gone.'

'Oh, don't say that, Mum, don't say those words!' Daisy wailed. She felt as if she was standing on the top of a cliff, about to fall off.

'I'm sorry, baby. It's true.'

Daisy let out a guttural howl in the empty kitchen. She let the receiver drop to her shaking chest, forgotten about, as the terrible truth began to sink in. White hot needles of pain stabbed at her and waves of disbelief and despair consumed her; she'd never speak to her dad again, never get to say goodbye. Through her pain, she became aware of her mum's voice coming out of the receiver.

'Daisy! Daisy! Are you there? Listen to me!' Daisy fumbled the phone back to her ear. 'Listen to me. Just stay put, stay strong. Lily will be back soon.'

Daisy hadn't even thought about her sister. 'Does she know?' she said in a quiet voice.

'Yes, I just spoke to her. Someone's giving her a lift home from work, so just stay put, don't go anywhere and certainly don't drive! I don't want you driving, Daisy, do you hear me?!'

'Yes, Mum.'

'Things have got to be sorted here. I'm waiting for the coroner to arrive – it's a mess … it's all a mess, and we'll – I'll be back as soon as I can.' She broke down again.

'When was it, Mum?' asked Daisy through her tears.

'What?' Carol struggled to hear her.

'When did it happen?'

'About quarter past eight this morning. He wasn't even doing anything, just drying his hair. You know how he always had to blow-dry his hair… Look, Daisy, I've got to go, someone's here. I'm so sorry. I'll speak to you soon. I love you. Bye.' And then she was gone, just like that.

'I love you, Mum,' Daisy said, but it was too late; she'd already hung up.

Daisy stood there in shock, the phone still in her hand. She pitied her mum, having to deal with it all so far from home; her dad had always dealt with everything. A fresh wave of tears washed over her as she hung up the phone, stunned. With one phone call her life had changed forever. All she'd been expecting was a quick gossip; instead she'd received the emotional equivalent of a wrecking ball.

She wept uncontrollably as the reality began to sink in. It gripped her as she looked with bleary eyes at the empty kitchen. She needed comforting arms around her; she needed Jack – God, how she needed him. It became the single most important thing – to find him. It was a goal, something to focus on – anything to stop herself from thinking about the dreadful truth that she didn't want to believe. She grabbed the phone in a blind panic, before realising she didn't know his number from memory. He'd only given it to her yesterday – how could she possibly have envisaged she'd need to use it so soon? She wouldn't be ringing twice either; if ever there was an emergency this was it.

She dashed upstairs to her bedroom, where her notebook was kept in her bedside drawer. As she opened it she noticed the little heart she'd drawn next to Jack's number. This made her sob again; she'd only drawn it last night, yet it seemed as if that was a previous life – a carefree one where she'd had a living, breathing father. She ran back downstairs and picked up the phone in the hallway, letting it ring four times before slamming it back down again. 'Please come, Jack, please come!' she said out loud as she grabbed her car keys. Her mum's voice rang out in her head as she did so: 'I don't want you driving, Daisy, do you hear me?' She banished it, pushing it aside.

Her hands were trembling as she tried to lock the front door in the pouring rain. Eventually she managed it, and in direct defiance of her mum's warning she jumped into the van. The tyres squealed on the wet road as she pulled away. She sped through the village and headed over the crossroads towards the phone box. Once she arrived, she waited for Jack with her windscreen wipers on; she wished she had some for her eyes too, as they wouldn't stop raining either.

Daisy sat there numbly, as if she'd been anaesthetised, listening to the thud and squeak of the wipers. Back and forth, back and forth they went, but Jack didn't arrive. This is ridiculous, *where is he?* she thought, and dashed out of the van and into the phone box. She rang his number again, but this time – even though it was strictly against the rules – didn't stop at four but let it carry on ringing. She was past caring, and if his father answered she'd just hang up. She counted the rings – four, five, six, seven – until she screamed, 'Come on, Jack, where are you?!' After about the twelfth ring, she slammed the phone down in a complete state. There's only one thing for it, she thought – I'm going to have to go up there.

As she joined the main road Daisy tried her best to go slowly, hoping to God she might meet Jack cycling the other way. She peered through the window with neither her headlights nor her seatbelt on – more concerned with how soaked Jack would be again, the poor thing. By the time she'd started the climb to his house she still hadn't passed him. 'Damn!' she cried, smacking the steering wheel. It was with a growing feeling of unease – knowing she was doing something so wrong – that she slowed down to put her right indicator on.

Part Two

'Will you Walk into my Parlour?' Said the Spider to the Fly

She turned into the lane, and as she drove up it the bumps and the potholes bounced her about on her seat. Through the rain, she caught a brief glance of the house through the gap in the hedge to the front garden; after that only the roof was visible. When she reached the driveway she slowed down to look. It was empty. Well, at least that's something, she thought – his father's not there. Perhaps Jack didn't hear the phone ring, or perhaps the bell doesn't work anymore. Maybe he's in his room right now, listening to music with his headphones, waiting for it to stop raining.

Despite being in a state of shock, she wasn't stupid enough to park on the driveway; their rules were too deeply ingrained for that. Instead, she found a field entrance on the same side, around a bend, about fifty yards up. This was where Jack cut through the fields behind his house to the bus stop. She jumped out of the van, and without even locking it began to run back down the lane. She'd convinced herself that Jack was at home, so being this close to him her defences weakened, and the tears fell as she ran.

Daisy reached the bottom of the driveway, then stopped; a sudden feeling of dread had come over her. It was seeing the house properly for the first time – or it seeing *her*, which was how it felt. The sky behind it was black and menacing, and up this close the peeling white bungalow looked sinister – as if it had been expecting her. She told herself to stay calm, reminding herself that if his father's van wasn't there it meant he wasn't at home.

Jack had never described the house to her in great detail, so she didn't even know where the front door was. Torrents of water were pouring out of the sagging ends of the gutters as she peered around a corner and spotted a back door. Next to it was a creepy window with a net curtain across it. This exacerbated the sensation that she was being watched, and she shuddered as if something small had crawled down the length of her spine.

Before she lost her nerve, she quickly knocked on the door. Her grief washed over her as she waited for an answer, imploring and beseeching her to succumb to it. No answer came, so she knocked again, saying 'Please, Jack!' as she wiped away a tear. After waiting in vain, against her better judgement, she tried the door; knowing that if it was locked she was doomed to face her grief without him.

To her surprise the door gave and swung inwards with a jarring scrape. The sound went straight through her, and for a second she was terrified that his father would appear. When he didn't, it gave her further hope that Jack would be inside.

'Jack!' she called tentatively through the door. She waited, ear cocked. Then again, louder this time: 'Jack!' But still no answer, no sound of footsteps. Now she was in a dilemma; she didn't know whether to go in or not, as his father could arrive back at any time. And she didn't know where Jack's room was either – she could hardly go round the whole building knocking on every window. After hesitating for a moment, she pushed open the door and stepped inside.

The first thing that hit her was the smell – a mixture of stale air and fried food, with an overtone of gone-off meat or fish. In the background was an eggy, sulphurous stink: the cider, which was at its worse when it was brewing. Jack and his family barely noticed it, but to an outsider it was pretty rank.

The next thing that struck her was the squalor, the mess – an overflowing bin with flies crawling over it, and kitchen counters littered with dirty plates; the sink was full of them. Daisy was shocked and taken aback that Jack could live like this. In his defence, the only reason the kitchen was so bad was because he'd gone on strike in retaliation for being locked out. He *had* got up that morning intending to tidy up but, still fuming at his father, he'd changed his mind.

The kitchen was surprisingly large, with a stone floor of an unidentifiable colour. It was dominated by an old pine table that had fine grains of salt spilt across its surface like sand. The table was stained with rings where tea and coffee cups had been, and sitting in the centre was a huddle of sticky condiment bottles. Directly opposite Daisy was a white door, ajar, which appeared to lead down to a cellar or pantry. She ignored it, and hurried on through the kitchen into a smaller, snug-type parlour that was uncomfortably warm.

Her eyes were drawn to the far right-hand corner, where there was a large display case on the wall. She went over to it, drawn by the colours. To her amazement, inside were neat rows of pristine butterflies. They were all pinned and labelled and went from large to small. There were swallowtails, purple emperors, tortoiseshells and many others. She felt sorry for them. It seemed an unusual collection to have, almost cruel, and made her wonder about the rest of the house. Her overriding emotion was curiosity now – a strange fascination about where Jack lived; she might never get the chance again. Daisy turned to the door that was next to her and pulled it open.

She was met with an L-shaped corridor that was decidedly cooler. There were five or six doors leading off it; any one of them could be Jack's room. She called out his name again, beginning to doubt that he actually was at home. Didn't he say they always left the door unlocked? But she wasn't going to leave until she knew for sure. After seeing all these doors, her feeling of wanting to find out what was behind them was stronger than ever. They were doors onto Jack's life and she had come this far – she wasn't going to turn back now. Besides, it was temporarily keeping her grief at bay.

The first door on the right looked a good starting point. It revealed a darkened bedroom with a single bed. The room was full of clutter – clothes, books, boxes and old furniture. It didn't smell too pleasant either – kind of sour. She couldn't imagine this was Jack's room; those weren't his clothes for a start. She closed the door and moved on to the next one.

This turned out to be a bathroom, which was shabby and smelt of damp. Used toilet roll centres spilled from a bin next to the toilet, and she had to bat away a marauding daddy longlegs. She noticed, repulsed, that a congregation of them was crawling over the dirty net curtain. As she closed the door on the squalid scene, she felt for Jack. He was just a teenage boy after all; he didn't have a mother, and his only sister had left. It made her want to look after him and to clean the place up.

The floorboards groaned and cried out as she crept down the hallway – surely alerting anyone who might be home of her presence. When she reached the last door at this end, she knocked on it and called Jack again, sounding desperate. Getting no response, she pushed open the door to reveal another bedroom. This one was a bit larger, and in direct contrast to the rest of the house was neat and tidy. It was unmistakably Jack's; she could smell his deodorant, which further weakened her resolve. Oh, how she wanted him.

The room was sparse, with only four items of furniture – a single bed, a wardrobe, a small chest of drawers and a bedside table that had a little shelf underneath it. On it was a neat row of what looked like a dozen or so children's storybooks – small and large, hardback and paperback. They were all old and well-worn with damaged spines. Some of them had been Sellotaped several times over. She didn't know why, but it was one of the saddest sights she'd ever seen. It made her think of the lonely, solitary childhood he must have had, trapped there all alone.

She walked over to his bed and laid a hand on it. She had an overwhelming desire to get into it – like Goldilocks – to crawl under the covers and hide away from the world. She could go to sleep, block it all out and pretend that the phone call hadn't happened. Perhaps when she woke up again it would all be a horrible dream and everything would be back to normal. She looked around the room at the bare floorboards and walls. It couldn't have been more different from her own bedroom. It was as if no identity had been stamped on it, making it appear forlorn and drab.

Daisy sat on his bed, and it sank as though the springs in the mattress were worn out. Just like Jack had, she, too, smelt his pillow, and it smelt of him – but fusty at the same time. Unsure what to do next, and becoming aware again that his father could return at any moment, she decided to leave. Giving his bed and books one last lingering look, Daisy headed back down the corridor. She was about to enter the parlour, when she noticed the other doors down the shorter hallway off to the right. Once again, her curiosity got the better of her.

She tried the door on the left, which opened into a lounge. There was an unpleasant odour to the room, similar to that of Jack's father's room: stale sweat, alcohol and unwashed bodies. A strong smell of wet coal emanated from the fireplace, damp from the excessive rain. There was an old-fashioned telly and a dirty, sunken, upholstered chair. It had threadbare arms and empty cider bottles littered about its feet. Clearly this was where his father sat.

Just then, she was disturbed by a stomach-churning noise – the jarring scrape of the front door opening. She quickly exited the lounge, pulling the door closed behind her. She heard sounds from the kitchen, and crept to the open parlour door to listen. Oh God, please let it be Jack, please let it be Jack. She peered through the crack but couldn't see anyone, just some shopping bags on the kitchen floor. A figure then crossed the kitchen doorway to go back outside, and she gasped – but it happened too fast to see who it was.

Cautiously, she stuck her head around the door to look through the netted parlour window. To her absolute horror, out in the rain, she made out a tall, unkempt-looking man rummaging around in the back of his van – her first sighting of Jack's father – this violent monster she'd heard so much about. Daisy had to stifle a scream. What had she been thinking, coming in here? Especially after everything Jack had told her.

She felt trapped, and retreated backwards into the corridor. To her right, she spotted the front porch door at the end of the hallway and dashed towards it. It was locked. 'Shit!' she cried. Looking around the parlour door again, she saw that he'd put more shopping down before heading back to his van. She decided to make a run for it – figuring she could just make it out and down the drive whilst his back was turned.

Well, she got as far as the back door, but that was it; he'd already crouched to pick up the last of the shopping and was turning to head back to the house. Daisy froze. He was a large man with a red face and purplish nose, wild hair and a dirty beard. Worse still, he was coming straight towards her. He walked unsteadily on his feet with his head down against the rain. If he'd looked up at that moment, there's no question he'd have seen her standing at the back door. Daisy turned around in panic, searching for an exit – or at least somewhere to hide. She spied the open cellar door and, with no other choice, ran across the kitchen towards it.

Part Three
Out of the Frying Pan, into the Fire

Quick as a flash, Daisy darted down the stone steps, her head disappearing from view just in the nick of time. She stood out of sight, round a corner, in a wide doorway that led to some sort of cellar. Fighting back the tears, she tried to work out her next move – easier said than done when her heart was hammering like a steam train thundering over the tracks. *Calm down, Daisy, calm down, think!* she willed herself. At least she was as near as possible to the back door. She'd just have to keep watch, and the second he left the kitchen make another run for it.

She peered into the gloom in the vain hope of an alternative escape route, or even a makeshift weapon should she need it. All she could make out was a large windowless basement with three dusty stone walls. These were mainly taken up by as many as four chest freezers that hummed and whined in the dark. A mocking voice in her head said, 'What had you been expecting, Daisy – a magic trapdoor to the outside world?' She noticed that the sulphurous smell was a lot stronger down there, apparently exuding from a huge bucket on the floor with a lid on it. A foot-high stone ledge, which served as a shelf, bordered the left-hand wall. On it were two large upright plastic kegs with taps at the bottom of them and dozens of glass bottles. Daisy recognised these as Jack's cider bottles. On a wooden shelf above was all sorts of paraphernalia – more buckets, funnels, different sachets and the biggest bags of sugar she'd ever seen.

Above her head in the kitchen she heard cupboard doors opening and closing, then the sound of a kettle boiling. She listened in growing dread as this culminated in the screech of a chair being pulled back on the stone floor, making her wince. Silently, she ventured up a step or two, inch by inch, and craned her neck to see what he was doing. Her worst fears were confirmed when she saw him sitting hunched at the kitchen table, tucking into a sandwich. As she looked on, he stopped to take a loud slurp of tea. Then he did something really odd; he sniffed the air and looked around, forcing Daisy to duck out of the way.

When she plucked up the courage to look back again he was well into the second half of his sandwich. He ate like a pig, and she noticed he'd got food stuck in his beard. It didn't take him long to finish, and when he did he stood up again. She willed him to leave the kitchen, desperately hoping for her chance to flee, but instead he went and did that thing again. He stopped and sniffed the air several times – this time with his head cocked to one side, and with a puzzled frown on his face. Daisy's blood ran cold as the sickening realisation hit her: *Oh my God! I think he can smell me!* And as if to confirm this, he began pacing round the kitchen, sniffing, and even stuck his head into the parlour room. It was like some nightmare version of *Jack and the Beanstalk*; any minute she expected him to start growling, 'Fee– Fi– Fo– Fum.'

Just lately, Jack's father had been plagued by a smell – a scent that seemed to be following him around the house, tormenting him. It reminded him of days long gone and of happier times. It was a woman's scent, somehow evocative and familiar. He thought he'd been imagining it, but today it was so strong he could actually put his finger on what it was; it was the perfume of his beloved Carla. But how was that possible? Was it her ghost? Was she coming back to visit him after all these years? Then he actually surprised himself by speaking out loud in the empty kitchen, feeling foolish. 'Carla? Is that you?' And he turned towards the cellar. The hair on Daisy's neck stood on end; it looked as if he was staring straight at her – his head cocked to the side like a mad bird, his dead eyes staring. She held her breath and shrank back into the dark of the basement.

Moments later, she heard the cellar door creak wide open, and the sound of him descending the steps. 'Carla, is that you?' Daisy was overcome with sheer terror as his shadow appeared in the grey light at the bottom of the stairs. There was no way out. She felt like one of those stupid doomed teenagers in a slasher-flick – expendable quarry for a bloodthirsty audience – being stalked to a predictable and grisly death by the local psychopath. Countless times she'd screamed at the screen in frustration at them, 'Why would you go into the house?' or, 'Don't go in the cellar!' Yet here she was, and this wasn't a movie, it was real life – and that was real piss trying to escape into her pants.

Daisy looked around in one last, desperate search for escape, and frantically dashed over to the furthest freezer. She clawed the lid up, and in a split second – without even looking inside – rolled in and shut the lid behind her.

If it had been any other time of the year, there'd have been a good chance that the freezer would have been chock-full of frozen apples. Fortunately for Daisy, it was coming to the start of the new season soon and most of last year's batch had gone. The freezer wasn't even turned on. The most unpleasant thing about it was the stinky brown apple residue at the bottom of it, which normally Anne would have cleaned out – that and the dark confined space…

Daisy lay hunched up in the dark, her neck bent forward, trying to fight the claustrophobia that gripped her. Outside she heard the click and hum of a strip light flick on and footsteps next to her. She closed her eyes and prayed as she heard him sniff and pace the cellar. Just then, she felt the freezer shift, and thought that the end had come. She cowered in fright, trying not to wet herself, anticipating the lid lifting and the light flooding in. Instead, the lid of the freezer bent above her. I don't believe it; he's sitting on my freezer! she thought. Why did he have to pick this one? She came close to passing out. How had it come to this? What crueller hand of fate could be dealt? She'd only found out barely an hour ago that her dad had died: wasn't that enough?

As Jack's father sat there in the empty cellar, he could still faintly smell that perfume – even over the smell of the fermenting cider. Yet there was no one there, and that he didn't understand. For the first time ever, he actually felt uncomfortable alone in his own house. He dismissed it, trying to laugh it off. 'Crazy bastard!' he muttered, and made to get off the freezer. The lid popped back into shape, making Daisy jump. Oh, please don't let him look in here, please God! she prayed. Make him go away. She heard the clink of a bottle and the sound of pouring liquid. Footsteps retreated and the light flicked off again; her prayers seemingly answered. Then there was nothing but the whine of the freezers.

It was pitch black as she clambered out, and the seat of her jeans and the back of her jacket were wet through. She crept across the cellar to peer up the stairs. No wonder it was dark, he'd shut the bloody door! What now? She had no choice but to climb the steps again and listen. She did this as stealthily as possible, then put her ear to the door. There were no sounds at all from the kitchen. What if he was tricking her? What if he was waiting on the other side to leap out and grab her?

After waiting a further five minutes to be sure, and still hearing nothing, Daisy pushed the door open a crack. Through the gap, from what she could see, the kitchen was empty.

She strained her ears for other sounds from the rest of the house. The distant sound of a television could be heard; he must be in the front room. This was it – the opportunity she'd been waiting for. She couldn't hold back a second longer and bolted for the back door. With the last grain of restraint in her spent body, she gently lifted the latch on the door, slipped out, then closed it again behind her. Fresh air (and rain even) had never felt so good. It all came out then – a culmination of the relief she felt and the horror she'd been through. And she ran from the madhouse, sobbing and crying hysterically, all the way up the lane to her van.

When she got in, she immediately locked the door. She fumbled the keys in the ignition as the feeling of being in a horror film remained. She half-expected the van not to start, or for him to come lumbering up the lane after her – wielding an axe or a chainsaw like Leatherface out of *The Texas Chainsaw Massacre*. Thankfully the trusty VW engine gunned to life, and as she shot down the lane she was flung about, her head hitting the roof at one point. She didn't look at the house as she passed it; she never wanted to see it again. The deceptive slope at the bottom of the lane was approaching way too fast, and she suddenly had to slam on her brakes. The van went into a skid on the wet gravel, only just coming to a halt before it slid into the main road.

At that instant, Jack rounded the corner on his bike. He'd chosen an inopportune moment to make it up the hill without stopping – spurred on by his desperate need to find Daisy himself. He tried to brake, but went careering into the passenger door. Daisy gasped in alarm as he was flung against the window with a bump. Still straddling his bike, Jack peered in, a look of shock on his face. 'Daisy!' he cried.

'Jack!' she sobbed. Could this day get any worse?

As it was, he was relatively unharmed. He got off his bike – which had a buckled front wheel – and threw it down. He pulled open the passenger door and cried, 'Daisy, what are you doing here?' When he saw the state she was in, he was taken aback; she looked on the point of hysteria. Her tear-stained face had trauma etched all over it. Her eyes were red and streaming and her hair and clothes were soaked through. Without a word she threw herself against him and broke down, convulsing in violent, uncontrollable sobs. He held her tight and she smelt of damp and perfume. 'Oh my God, Daisy, I've just heard about your dad, I'm so sorry.' Daisy stiffened up, not understanding.

'How? How do you know?'

'I went to your house; I was going to surprise you. Your sister was there – she was in a real state.' Even in her darkest hour, Daisy couldn't help feeling that her sister had again somehow upstaged her – even in grief.

She pushed him away and cried, 'Just get in!' She didn't want to face the truth, and wanted to get as far away from that house as possible.

Jack threw his bike in the ditch – it was useless now anyway

– and quickly jumped in. Before he'd even closed the door properly, she sped away. She had no idea where she was going and was driving far too fast, swerving about on the wet road. It couldn't carry on, and as they neared the lay-by Jack implored her to pull in. She veered off sharply without indicating or slowing down, skidding to an abrupt halt. She killed the engine, then broke down again. It cut through Jack to see her so distraught – he just wanted to help her, to comfort her. He reached across and dragged her like a limp rag doll into his arms. She collapsed against him, and he felt the pain in the sobs ripping her to pieces. He didn't know what to say. What *can* you say? He couldn't imagine how she felt, so he shushed her and rocked her instead, stroking her hair and letting her cry.

After a good ten minutes the tears dried up and she lay still in his arms. He thought she'd cried herself to sleep until she spoke into his chest. 'Where have you been?' It sounded muffled and Jack wasn't sure if he'd heard her right; he didn't know how to answer. She asked again, 'Where have you been, Jack?' raising her head to look at him. Her eyes were bloodshot – almost accusatory – as she remembered the horrors at the house.

'I went to get a key cut for the back door. I cycled down to East Leake. It took longer than I expected; there was a queue and I had to wait.' He'd felt so proud of himself at the time but it seemed so unimportant now. 'Then I thought I'd surprise you on the way back and come round early … that's when I saw your sister…' He trailed off.

'Well, what did she say? How was she?'

'Like I said, she told me what had happened and asked if I'd seen you. She thought you were with me. She was really upset and was worried about you.' Daisy felt a fresh wave of guilt; she should be there with her now. Despite everything she *was* still her sister, and if she was going through anything like she was, she wouldn't want to be alone.

'I should go, Jack,' she said suddenly. 'My sister needs me and my mum might call again. She told me not to go anywhere *or* to drive, but I couldn't help it.' This set her off again and she spoke through her tears. 'I needed to see you and you weren't there.'

'I know, I know, I'm sorry,' he said, cradling her again.

'It was horrible,' she continued as she wept. 'I got trapped in the cellar.' This took Jack by surprise, and it took a few moments to register what she had said.

'Pardon?' And she repeated it. 'You what?' It was his turn to push *her* away. 'You went into the house?' Daisy nodded. He couldn't believe what he was hearing. 'Are you out of your mind?!'

'Don't shout at me Jack!' she wailed. 'Not now!'

'I'm sorry, I'm sorry,' he said, lowering his voice. He took her hands in his. 'What happened? Tell me.'

She relayed her story in a shaky voice: of how she'd been convinced he was at home and had gone in and searched for him. Her voice got shakier still when she said how his father had come back and she'd been trapped in the house.

'He came back when you were in the house?!' Jack interjected, trying his best not to raise his voice again.

She nodded solemnly. 'I ran down to the cellar. I had no choice … and then he came down there. I think he could smell me.' She shuddered at the memory of it, the fear she'd felt still raw. Jack got goose bumps just hearing about it.

'Jesus Christ, he could smell you? But how did you get out? Did he hurt you?' He grabbed hold of her arms. 'Tell me he didn't touch you!'

'No, he didn't touch me. He didn't even see me!'

'But how?' He knew the cellar like the back of his hand.

'I hid in a freezer – he even sat on it. It was horrible!' And she wept again. Jack simply couldn't fathom what she must have been through. All he could think of saying was, 'Have you any idea what he would have done if he would have caught you?' But he didn't; she'd already been through enough. Instead, he lifted her chin up and made her look him in the face.

'Promise me, Daisy, promise me you won't *ever* go up there again.'

'Don't worry. I won't. Not while *he's* alive anyway.'

After holding her in his arms again, Jack said, 'Look, you'd better go, your sister needs you.' It was the last thing he wanted, but he had to do the right thing.

'I know,' she sighed, loath to face it.

'When will I get to see you again?' Jack couldn't help himself from asking. 'I mean, how will I know when? Especially now…'

'I don't know. I don't know anything anymore.' It was strange, but at that point he already felt as if he'd lost a little part of her. It wasn't the kind of thing she would normally have come out with; it sounded too old. 'I guess I'll just have to call, you know … let it ring, I don't know when – hopefully tomorrow. It's the best I can do, I'm sorry.'

'It's OK. You know, just … whenever.' He tried to sound supportive, but at the same time hated the prospect of not knowing when he was going to see her again. He gave her one last hug and made to get out of the van.

'Don't you want me to give you a lift home? It's raining.'

'No, it's fine, honestly. I'll walk, I'm wet already anyway.' He half-smiled but she couldn't muster a smile back. 'I love you,' he said through the window.

'Yes, you too.'

And that was it. She drove off and Jack walked home in

the rain. As he did, a selfish part of him thought: well, I guess it might be a while till I get to see the seaside now.

CHAPTER 30

The Grieving Process

The rain continued to beat down all of that Saturday as if the sky itself was grieving; shedding bucketloads of tears. Even the women's Wimbledon final was called off, to be played on the same day as the men's for only the third time ever. Jack didn't hear from Daisy all day, and Daisy's mum returned home that evening to a tearful reception. Needless to say, her daughters didn't ask her how her trip had been.

Carol looked absolutely shattered. On top of everything else she'd had to pack the car up and drive it back herself. As the years had gone by she'd driven less and less, leaving it more to her husband. Three and a half hours travelling on motorways and main roads, had just about sapped her last ounce of strength. The girls were just grateful to have her back – safe and sound and in one piece. They promptly retired for the night; too exhausted to think, let alone talk.

The next morning, understandably, Daisy couldn't face going into work. Her mum called in for her, and they were more than sympathetic, saying she could come back whenever she was ready. It was a quiet, emotional day interspersed with bouts of weeping. They spent most of it in their pyjamas, not even bothering to get dressed, just sitting, talking, drinking endless cups of tea and looking at photos through teary eyes. None of them could believe what had happened; it didn't seem real. They kept expecting him to walk through the door, laughing and joking. Little things set Daisy off, such as seeing her dad's shoes in the hall or his tablets in the kitchen. As the grey day drew numbly to a close, as much as she wanted to, Daisy didn't feel she could up and leave to see Jack. It seemed disrespectful to think of herself; it was a day of mourning.

Meanwhile, Jack hadn't dared leave the house for the whole weekend lest he should miss Daisy's call. By Sunday evening he was going stir-crazy. He'd tried to keep himself busy by cleaning the place – giving up on his protest as he couldn't stand the mess. Seeing the house through Daisy's eyes, he'd felt disgusted and ashamed. It had made him resent that filthy pig of a father even more. He couldn't help but wonder what rooms she'd been in and what she must have thought. At least *his* room had been tidy and clean, but had she got that far? He was dying to know.

Speaking of his father, all *he* cared about was the bloody tennis. It had been the day of the men's final, so he'd been in a heightened state of animation from the minute he'd got up. He'd then proceeded to get drunk from about ten onwards, as if it was some sort of national holiday. By the time Becker had beaten Edberg in a one-sided match he was steaming.

Jack eventually retreated to his room to mope. He'd planned on putting his personal stereo on to drown his father out, but hadn't even been able to do that in case he didn't hear the phone. As the hours ticked by and it began to grow dark, the harsh reality dawned on him that Daisy wasn't going to call. He'd felt hard done by, hurt and alone; the rejection was overwhelming. How could she not want to see him? He didn't understand.

As he lay there that night, trying to sleep, Jack thought

resentfully of the plans they'd made for the weekend and how they'd all been ruined. He wished he could turn back the clock to the beginning of the week: knowing what he knew now, he'd have slept at her house every night. He'd have spent every moment he could lost in the fragrant felicity of her arms, and buried between her heavenly thighs. When would they get that chance again? If her dad hadn't have died, Daisy would have told her parents about him by now, and he'd probably have met them. He felt ready for it after meeting Lily.

The next morning was the hardest it had ever been to get up for work. What was the point? What was the point in anything? He could barely drag himself out of bed, and certainly couldn't eat any breakfast. It was as if he had some sort of malady. He had; it was called lovesickness. Perversely, and in stark contrast, his father was up and about early for possibly the first time since Anne had gone missing. After the hiatus of the Wimbledon fortnight (where he'd done nothing but sit on his arse for two weeks), he seemed to have gained a new lease of life – like an old clockwork toy that had been wound up again – spurred on by Becker's triumph.

It looked as if he was going to recommence work on the loft conversion; something he'd been threatening to do ever since Jack could remember. He had one of his black and yellow pencil stubs behind his ear, sharpened to a fine point with one of his chisels. Jack groaned inwardly, as this signified he meant business, which, in turn, usually meant extra work for him. His father was at the kitchen table when he left him, looking like Ben Gunn out of *Treasure Island*. He had his plans laid out in front of him, and was licking the point of his pencil from time to time as he scribbled down a list of purchases he would need.

It was a clear, fine day as Jack trudged across the fields to the bus stop. The long grasses and hedgerows glistened with moisture, yet the cracked earth underfoot had absorbed most of the rain like a sponge. The recent storms had disappeared as quickly as they'd come. He wondered what would have happened if it *had* been fine on Saturday and they *had* set off early to the seaside. How would Daisy's mum have possibly got hold of her? It was a strange thought.

It wasn't until about six-thirty that evening that Jack got the precious phone call he'd been so longing for. He and his father were both in the kitchen. Jack was peering aimlessly into cupboards, trying to drum up some kind of appetite when they heard the bell ring out in the yard. It was the first time it had rung in a long time. His father made to get up, but the phone stopped after two rings. Jack tried his hardest not to register any sort of emotion – no mean feat when inside he was dancing for joy. 'Hmmph,' his father muttered; he could have done with some business to lend financial support to his loft plans.

Suddenly feeling hungry again, Jack slapped a sandwich together and sloped off to his room with it. After a swift change and a spray of deodorant, he decided to slip out of his bedroom window; at least that would buy him some time as his father wouldn't know he was gone. He left the window on the latch and took his key with him just in case. Then he ran round the side of the house, off down the lane and continued running all the way to the crossroads. By the time he got there he had a dreadful stitch and rued bolting down the sandwich. The two ring rule had worked fine before, but then again he'd had his bike. Now that he didn't, and his father was back in the land of the living, he realised that he and Daisy had to give each other more time.

Jack briefly considered being a bit off with Daisy at first, just to let her know what she'd put him through – but when he clapped eyes on her these thoughts went straight out of the window. Normally she was immaculately turned out, but today she was plainly dressed. Her hair didn't have its usual gloss and was simply tied back. She had no make-up on and her face was pale and tired. There were dark circles under her eyes as if she hadn't slept in days, which she hadn't – not properly anyway. She'd been haunted by the guilt that she hadn't gone away with her parents, even though her dad had practically begged her. How she wished, just as Jack had, that she could turn back time. She couldn't remember what the last thing was she'd said to her dad.

With the Red Lion now a no-go zone, they drove to the White Lion at Rempstone as it was nearest; Daisy only had an hour. Just an hour, thought Jack, but didn't say anything. They sat outside the pub. Daisy didn't have her normal 'driving drink' – a pint of shandy; instead she had a soft drink. Their conversation was dominated by her dad's death and what she, her mum and her sister were going through. She broke down from time to time, wiping her nose and eyes with a tissue.

Jack listened and comforted her, just happy to be with her. Daisy said that her dad's body was being taken to the local mortuary in East Leake the next day, and she was racked with indecision over whether to go and see him or not. She didn't know if it would upset her too much – and would she be better off remembering him as he was? Or was it a way of saying goodbye? Her mum had said that only she could decide. Before long, their hour was up and Daisy said she had to go. There'd been little physical contact between them and she'd been preoccupied throughout, but who could blame her? It's not every day your dad goes on holiday and comes home in a body bag.

*****

The period between Jim's death and his funeral was, without doubt, the hardest and most trying of Jack and Daisy's entire relationship; even worse than those frustrating early days of shyness and inaction. It was a desolate time of grieving and dark deeds. There were coroners' reports, the endless filling out of forms, phone calls – breaking the news to relatives near and far. Decisions had to be made about the transporting of the body and funeral arrangements. How can you make decisions clearly when your whole world has been ripped apart? Decisions about flowers and venues, burial or cremation; sandwich fillings, for Christ's sake! The only benefit was that this gave Daisy, her mum and her sister something to focus on – anything other than succumbing to the numbing and debilitating grief. It brought them closer together, especially Daisy and her sister. They closed ranks, becoming a tight-knit unit – united by their loss.

Understandably, Jack wasn't involved in any of this, and as a consequence was pushed to the side. Daisy still loved him – that was never in doubt. It's just that he was no longer her number one priority. Let's face it: they'd both enjoyed, and indulged in, a reciprocated monopoly on each other's time and affections, unchallenged, for practically the whole of the summer. That's why it hit Jack so hard. It was as if he'd been given riches beyond his wildest dreams, and just when he was getting used to them they'd been cruelly snatched away. It made him miss his sister, and he found himself thinking about her more often, wondering where she was and what she was doing. Daisy had more than filled the God-shaped hole that Anne had left when she disappeared, but now he felt lonely again and unloved.

All he could do was wait for Daisy's sporadic calls, which was agony. She wasn't neglecting him on purpose, but one grey day blurred into the next. Grief affects people in different ways, and Daisy found herself constantly overcome with tiredness, often falling asleep during the day. As a result, she lay awake at night listening to her dad's old records, such as Bob Dylan and Neil Young. She tortured herself by conjuring up happy memories of days gone by – camping trips and fishing expeditions that they'd shared. When she *did* sleep, her dreams almost invariably involved her dad. She'd decided to go and see his body in the mortuary, but was told she had to wait until Thursday; this was keeping her awake too. And then she was tired again the next day: it was a vicious circle.

That Thursday evening, Jack was staring lifelessly out of the bus window on the way back home from work. Seemingly overnight, and as if by magic, scores of neat cylindrical hay bales had appeared in the sloping field on the approach to Bunny Wood. Jack had always taken great pleasure at the sight of these: they were like pellets deposited by some sort of mythical machine or monster. How did they do that so quickly? You barely noticed the tractors and combines working – or at least didn't pay them any attention – and then there they were.

He was still pondering this when the bus passed Bunny Wood, and he could have sworn he saw Daisy's van parked at the entrance. He hadn't seen her all week and thought perhaps he'd imagined it – wishful thinking. Turning round, he craned his neck to look, but it was too late. As he made to get off, he decided to run straight back down to check, just in case. But then he saw an even better sight: Daisy was sitting on the fence at the side of the road. His heart fluttered, just as it used to, and he suddenly became conscious of his appearance; he hadn't been looking after himself. He was unshaven and his hair needed cutting – he hadn't washed it in days; what was the point if he wasn't going to see her? Now she'd caught him by surprise.

He felt awkward as he sidled up to her, as if they'd become

strangers in a matter of four days. She looked as though she'd
been crying again. He didn't want to hug her because of his
work clothes, but she hugged him anyway. She'd lost some of
her scent, as if her tears had washed it away.

'Hi,' she greeted him.

'Hi.'

'I've missed you.'

A sarcastic voice in his head said, 'Really?' 'Yes, me too,' his
real one said.

They started walking back down the hill towards Bunny
Wood and her van. Neither of them spoke at first. Jack
didn't know what to say; what could he ask her? 'How are
you?' 'How have you been?' He knew the answer to those
questions just by looking at her. Eventually she said, 'I went
to see my dad today.' Her voice was distracted, robotic,
and Jack didn't understand at first: how could she see her
dad? Then he cottoned on. He had to remind himself to
imagine what she was going through, and not to think
of himself.

'How was it?' he asked, taking her hand.

'It was…' But her voice gave way as she was overcome with
emotion.

They'd reached her van now and she leant with her back
against it, her hands covering her face as she wept. Jack felt
helpless. 'Do you want to go for a walk?' he said, and gestured
to the wood. She nodded.

They walked in silence for a bit until Daisy took a deep
breath, trying to compose herself. 'So, as I was saying…' Her
voice was still shaky and she paused again.

'It's OK, take your time,' Jack reassured her. She took
another deep breath.

'It was horrible. He looked so … different. It was a bit
of a shock. I mean, he still looked like Dad but he wasn't

smiling anymore – Dad was always smiling. And his hair was all wrong – not like he'd have had it at all.' She spoke faster now, as if she needed to get it out of her system. 'And his skin was tight and shiny and pale – and when I tried to touch him … oh God, he was so cold, Jack, and that's when … that's when I realised he wasn't there anymore.' She sobbed the last bit and stopped walking, overcome again.

Jack hugged her and shushed her. 'It's OK; you don't have to talk about it.' Quite frankly he didn't want to hear anymore.

'It was Dad but he wasn't there!'

They walked for a little while longer and then turned back. It wasn't helping. Jack didn't feel as if he could change the subject either. 'Do you wish you hadn't been to see him?' he asked.

Daisy considered this for a moment and then shook her head. 'I don't think so. I mean, it would have been nice to remember him exactly how he was, you know, always joking and full of life, but I think I'd always have regretted not saying goodbye.' Jack could understand this; he'd never said goodbye to his sister, and he resented it. 'That reminds me. The funeral's a week tomorrow, on a Friday. Will you be able to book it off work?' She hated talking as if they'd already moved onto the next stage; it made her feel guilty. 'I want you to come,' she said, taking his hand. Their eyes met properly for the first time that day, and a brief pulse went through him. 'I need you there with me; I don't think I can do it alone.'

This was a bolt from the blue for Jack, and he tried to digest what she was asking. He thought of the hordes of people who'd be there and that they'd all know each other. He'd be the stranger on view, a spectacle; something to be stared at. Those old feelings of insecurity came back, making him dizzy. 'But what would your mum say?' he asked.

'Oh she's fine with it, I asked her today,' Daisy replied

casually, but this was a little white lie. She'd already asked her, told her actually, but her mum hadn't said it was fine. It had been something like this…

Once they'd found out the date of the funeral, Daisy had decided straight away that she wanted Jack there with her. She didn't want to ask in front of her sister in case she kicked up a fuss. It was making her sick with worry, so in the end she just blurted it out. 'I want Jack to come to the funeral.' Carol paused from going through the family address book and looked at Daisy over the top of her reading glasses.

'Jack who?' Daisy had clean forgotten that she'd never told her mum Jack's name. Then Carol cottoned on. 'Oh that boy, oh not now, Daisy, I've got enough to think about!' But this didn't dissuade Daisy; she'd got time to work on her mum; she just had to pick the right moment, that was all.

Jack was quiet all the way back to the van; Daisy had put him in a serious quandary. 'Do you want a lift?' she said.

'No, I'd better not. I'll go the back way.' Daisy gave a sardonic half-smile as if to say 'Nothing changes.' He patted his pocket and said more brightly, 'Hey, at least I've got my key with me, so there's no chance of me getting locked out now!'

'No, unless he leaves his keys in the door, that is.'

Jack looked puzzled. 'How do you mean?'

'Well, if your dad leaves his keys or *a* key in the door the other side, you still wouldn't be able to unlock it from the outside.' She said it matter-of-factly, as if everyone knew that. Jack looked crestfallen, then slightly annoyed.

'So what was the point in me getting a key cut?'

'I just meant in general – like if you came back when he was out and he'd locked the door, or if he locked it from the inside and kept his keys with him. It was just an idea; I don't have all the answers, Jack.' And she opened the van door as if she was tired of the conversation. Jack didn't like her tone of voice;

she'd never spoken to him that sharply before. He knew she was under a lot of strain, but she'd changed since her dad had died, and he didn't like it.

*****

As the weekend came around, each day got gradually warmer. On the news there were reports that a mini heatwave was on its way, with temperatures in the mid-eighties predicted. Jack's father had spent the week gathering most of the materials he'd need for the loft conversion. It really looked as if he was going to go through with it. Most of the timber was already on racks in his workshop – stockpiled over the years – and the glass he'd need was already stored in the outbuildings, left over from the demolished greenhouses. He could make the window frames himself and would reuse any tiles that he took off the roof for the dormers. All he needed to buy was plasterboard, plaster, the leading and the insulation. It would, he claimed, cost only a few hundred quid to do, but would add thousands to the value of the house. Jack spent most of the weekend helping his father clear out the loft. At first he was told to stand at the bottom of the ladder, as his father ferreted about in the mysterious space above. This led him to wonder what was hidden up there; maybe some clues from the past, or even better more photos – possibly of his mother. He was handed boxes and various bits of old junk as he dodged the dust that kept falling in his eyes. After a few hours, his eyes were itchy, swollen and red raw.

There wasn't much of any interest, except some old clothes and suitcases; the bulk of it was just files and teaching manuals. As instructed, Jack piled everything on the drive for his father to sort through before he burnt it. Once he was out of his father's view, he eagerly rummaged through all the boxes in the hope of finding something worthwhile. He took as long as he dared until his father bellowed at him from inside: 'Where are you?' As the pile grew, Jack resembled a forlorn, disappointed bird, picking over a junk heap. In contrast to the growing pile, his hope of finding anything important slowly waned. It was most odd – as if their entire family history had been rubbed out.

The most interesting things were the clothes, which could only have belonged to his mother; they were in such a threadbare state it seemed they'd fall apart in his hands. Best of all, in one of the suitcases was a wedding dress, complete with a veil and shoes. With great care, he took the dress out of its plastic cover as he wanted to see how tall she was. It looked and smelt very old, but had been preserved by the plastic and the suitcase. Jack decided he'd like to keep it as a memento – something to remember her by.

Just then a voice barked at him from the kitchen doorway, making him jump. 'What do you think you're doing?' He fumbled the dress back into its wrapper and put it back in the suitcase. His father snatched the suitcase away, then marched back into the house. Jack watched him with hateful, resentful eyes. Selfish bastard, he thought. His father went into his bedroom, and, grunting with the effort, pushed the suitcase under his bed.

Pretty much everything was doused in petrol and burnt. The day was already hot, and the heat from the incinerator was so intense that Jack had to chuck things into it from a distance. He stood there with his shirt off, watching it all burn through a shimmering heat haze, any potential links to his past going up in smoke.

When he was finally allowed into the loft, now that it was empty, Jack was stopped by the ladder. Ladders were his nemesis: he'd hated them ever since the accident when he was little. He didn't mind climbing into the apple trees to dislodge stubborn fruit, but he refused to use a ladder – he simply didn't trust them. The thought of setting foot in the loft was too strong, however, and it was with much trepidation that he stood on the first rung. It gave unnervingly as he put his weight on it, and slowly began his ascent, telling himself not to look down.

It was stiflingly hot up there. Dust particles swirled thickly in the air, lit by two naked light bulbs hanging from the eaves. The eaves themselves hung heavy with decades' worth of cobwebs, mothballs and cocoons. The vast and cavernous loft was T-shaped, following the outline of the bungalow. Jack couldn't believe the size of it. It was funny to think that this had been above their heads all these years, and it was easy to see the potential that his father had seen in it.

*****

By the end of Saturday, when they called it a day, the eaves had been thoroughly cleaned and swept and so had the floor. Jack was hot, drenched in sweat, filthy and irritable. His throat was so sore he could barely speak or swallow, and he itched all over. The worst thing about the loft was that there was no real outlet for the dust. What the place needed was some windows, but they would come later. It also needed some stairs, he thought, as he circled that blasted hole in the floor for the last time; just looking through it to the hallway below made his stomach spin.

His father had relished having Jack under his control again; it was like old times. But he was surprised at the boy's subservience, considering his behaviour of late. He'd noticed that Jack hadn't been disappearing off so much lately, and had seemed subdued and moribund. Perhaps love's young dream had already come to an end, he surmised, with a certain amount of satisfaction: it always did. Afterwards they even sat down at the kitchen table together, for the first time in weeks, to have a late dinner.

After bathing, Jack felt physically refreshed – but the same couldn't be said for his mental state. He had lain in the bath for an age, praying for a phone call that had never arrived. The bathwater was cold and filthy when he'd got out and watched it gurgle away. It left a black stain behind, like the dark thoughts that lingered in his head. He lay on his bed and waited in vain until about eight before accepting he had to let it go. She wasn't going to call this late, and he couldn't stay cooped up in the house indefinitely. He decided to go out for an evening walk – just like he used to. It was a fine evening, so he took some cider with him.

Jack sat on his stile feeling completely forgotten about and tortured by gut-wrenching loneliness. How could he engineer a meeting with Daisy? He hadn't seen her since Thursday evening, and couldn't bear the thought of spending another whole day without her. It felt as if she was slipping away from him. He decided to ring her the next day. He knew she'd said not to call because of her mum, but these were desperate times.

*****

The next morning, Jack and his father set about building a network of timber frames for the walls in the loft. The T-shaped flanks were to be blanked off entirely, making one long room. Cupboards were to be built in on both sides, providing lots of storage space. Sheets of plywood had been measured and sawn so they could be posted diagonally through the loft hatch; his father was adamant they weren't knocking a hole in the exterior of the building again.

They went hard at it all morning, building up momentum as the studding began to take shape. By lunchtime, from a mixture of boredom and having to concentrate so hard, Jack had already had enough for the day. Apart from being terrified of making a mistake, there was only one thing on his mind – phoning Daisy. His father was sweating profusely and looking weary from the physical effort. The heat in the loft didn't help. They broke for lunch at twelve-thirty, and, despite being hungry, Jack announced he was going out for a bit. His father grumbled at him not to be long; he wanted to make a start on the roof batons for the insulation later on. It also suggested to him that perhaps the romance wasn't over after all.

There was no way Jack could phone from the workshop without getting caught, so he had to call from the phone box. Daisy had explained that he wouldn't need money to do this, as you didn't put it in till someone answered. She'd also written the number for the phone box next to Jack's, should she ever need to call him straight back.

After letting the phone ring twice, Jack waited for about twenty minutes in growing disappointment. He cursed the fact that they'd recently decided on at least half an hour's leeway between phone call and meeting – today he was short of time. Then something occurred to him: it was Sunday. Daisy usually worked on Sunday lunchtimes at the pub in the village. He knew it was a long shot, considering how she was feeling at the minute, but he knew how much she relied on her wages. If there was even the slimmest hope … he was desperate enough to take a chance.

Trying to overcome the tremulousness that gripped him, Jack stood at the Generous Briton's door. The small car park was full, and he could hear a bustling Sunday lunch service in full swing. The sounds filled him with dread; it was his idea of hell – entering a small space crammed with people, all looking at him – and so close to home as well. What if she wasn't even there? He summoned up the image of her for courage, and took a deep breath.

He tried to slip in unnoticed, and lingered at the doorway in the hope of seeing her. Luckily there was no one behind the bar to spot him. The pub was crowded and most tables were taken – mainly by elderly people tucking into Sunday lunches. To his dismay, Daisy was nowhere to be seen. He was just about to give up and slip back out, realising what a stupid idea it had been, when the door opened behind him. More people entered the pub, and he was jostled forwards towards the bar. In that moment a man appeared from the cellar door behind the bar, carrying a fresh pack of tonic water, a towel hung over his shoulder. He clapped eyes on Jack. 'Sorry, are you waiting, son?' he said.

Jack froze. Waiting for what? His first instinct was to turn and run – old survival habits kicking in – but he felt trapped, as if he was obliged to order something.

'Erm … pardon?' he croaked, stalling.

'Would you like a *drink?*' the man asked, a puzzled look on his face.

Jack frantically patted his jeans pockets; he didn't know if he had any money on him – he hadn't thought that far ahead. Aware that people were waiting, he began to colour, knowing what an idiot he must look. He could sense the landlord's impatience and heard him clear his throat. Suddenly his fingers found a crumpled-up ten pound note, forgotten about since the night he'd been locked out. He brandished it triumphantly and said, too loudly, 'A pint of cider please.' The landlord paused with his hands on the pumps to give him a long, hard look.

'Are you eighteen, lad?' he said. Everyone was staring at him now. He wanted the ground to swallow him up. But just then there was a familiar voice to his left.

'Jack!'

He turned, and there – dressed in the pub's uniform and holding two plates of food – was his darling Daisy. He could have wept: she was like Florence Nightingale to a dying soldier. There was a look of surprise on her face, but also the hint of a bemused smile that immediately allayed Jack's nerves; at least she seemed pleased to see him. 'Yes, he is, Keith, I know him,' she said, turning to the landlord.

'Well, if you're all right with Daisy, you're all right with me!' he said, giving her a wink and proceeding to pour a pint of cider. Daisy had always been popular at the pub as she was a good, hard worker, and today she'd been getting extra special attention as she'd been brave enough to come in. Immense relief washed over Jack; a disastrous moment had been averted – all thanks to his own guardian angel.

'Sit down,' she whispered to him. 'I'll be over in a minute.' Jack got his pint and thanked the landlord. He found a small, copper-topped table in a corner and plonked himself down, mopping his brow. His eyes searched for Daisy again and there she was, standing at a table of four people with her hands clasped together. It was strange to see her in her work environment – as if she had another life that he didn't know about. Then, as she walked past him, she gave him a half-smile. It was like when they'd first met; he felt privileged – the luckiest boy alive. She looked adorable in her uniform: a plain white blouse, black trousers, a smart black pinny and pumps. But he also noticed how tired she looked. There were bags under her eyes, which he could tell she'd tried to hide with a bit of make-up.

After a few minutes of going about her job – clearing tables and asking people if they'd like to see dessert menus – Daisy had a free moment to talk to him. There was no rush; the cider had gone to Jack's head, and he was content to sit and watch her. His father could wait: *sod him*, he thought. She stood with her back to the bar and asked quietly, but not unkindly, 'What on earth are you doing here?' Jack leant forward before answering, conscious of other people listening in. Out of the corner of his eye, over by the kitchen door, he spotted another two waitresses whispering and giggling. Daisy turned to see what he was looking at and shook her head. This mystery boy turning up to see her had caused quite a stir in the kitchen, and they were all eager to take a peek at him.

'I just had to see you,' he whispered.

'I was going to call tonight.'

'Well, I couldn't wait that long.' Jack searched for some of that old, familiar warmth in her big brown eyes.

'How did you know I was here?' she asked.

'I didn't, I just sort of hoped. I tried calling you from the phone box but you didn't come.'

Daisy looked a little put out. 'I told you I'd call *you*. Mum doesn't need pestering right now.'

The conversation wasn't going well; Daisy felt under pressure as she was supposed to be working. She picked up the ashtray on Jack's table to wipe it down, trying to look busy. 'Look, I'll meet you tonight at about seven at the crossroads – there's things I want to talk about. If I can't make it, I'll just have to call. Now I really need to get back to work – people are waiting. I'll see you later.' And she touched his hand briefly. That was something, Jack supposed, but it was merely parsimonious crumbs of the affection he'd grown accustomed to. After gulping his cider down, he left, and pondered about this all the way home – along with what she wanted to 'talk about'. It sounded a bit ominous. Should he be worried? He already was.

As it turned out, there wasn't anything specific Daisy wanted to talk about – at least not regarding the two of them. She just wanted to know if he'd booked the next Friday off for the funeral. He hadn't. Conversation centred on her dad and the funeral arrangements. She told him they'd received an overwhelming stream of condolence cards, flowers and well-meaning phone calls; this she attributed to her dad being such a popular man. Jack listened and nodded, but grew ever more resentful at hearing what a good man he was, and how much Daisy missed and loved him. He even thought how her dad had gone and ruined everything with his untimely death.

*****

As the week of the funeral arrived, as predicted the weather got hotter and hotter. These were the real dog days of summer – the roasting, sticky marmalade days of July. Jack threw himself into helping his father with the loft to combat the rejection he felt. Now that most of the insulation was in place, the heat up there was absolutely unbearable; it was like working in a sauna; they were both constantly dripping with sweat. Jack couldn't take his shirt off because of the malicious, yellow fibreglass wool – the sole purpose of which seemed to be to scratch and irritate his skin. After a couple of nights he had to make a stand, and refused to carry on unless his father started on the windows to let some air in. The old man, who could be infuriatingly obdurate at times, reluctantly acquiesced. He liked to do things his own way and in his own time, but the weather forecast was more of the same for the foreseeable future; if anything it was due to get hotter, so now was probably as good a time as any.

Jack watched in eager anticipation as his father marked out where the windows were going to go. There were to be three skylights in the roof at the front and two dormers on the back. On the original plans they'd been the other way round. His father declared the change was because of 'better aesthetics'. Jack privately surmised it had more to do with planning permission, something his father had a dubious and somewhat cavalier attitude to.

It was a momentous occasion when the first chinks of daylight flooded into the loft, along with the first breaths of fresh air – like the lid being lifted off a pressure cooker, instantly alleviating the stifling gloom and heat. By the time the second hole was made, there was no need to have the lights on anymore: the loft was actually starting to look more like a room.

The week went on like this for Jack, work by day and work by night, but at least it kept him busy. He was dreading the funeral, and still not a hundred per cent sure he could go through with it. Knowing he couldn't leave it any longer, on Wednesday he summoned up the courage to ask Peasgood for time off. In a situation eerily similar to the previous one, he knocked on his office door. Why had they used a funeral as an excuse last time? It was like some sick, twisted karma – maybe in return for all the evil, resentful thoughts he'd been having lately. But then again, how were they to have known what was around the corner?

Unsurprisingly, Peasgood refused point blank to let Jack have the day off; he thought the boy was having him on. 'Another funeral? Already? You must think I came down in the last shower, laddie!' he barked, craning his neck across the desk. 'If you're not at work by nine o'clock on Friday morning, then consider yourself fired!' Jack left the office with his tail between his legs and an even bigger dilemma on his hands.

Daisy had her own problems. She'd still got to broach the subject of Jack coming to the funeral again, and there never seemed to be a right time. Her mum was always either on the phone, crying or both; or there were annoying well-wishers about that she sat and drank tea with for hours on end. Daisy thought she'd scream if she heard one more person say, 'It's no age is it?' As a result, she ended up retreating to her room to listen to music or just went to sleep to blot it all out. Before she knew it, it was Thursday and she knew it was now or never – it was like important homework that she'd foolishly put off till the last minute.

As before, she tried to pick a moment when her mum was on her own and Lily wasn't about. She tried to sound casual, as if it wasn't a big deal. 'So, is it OK if Jack comes tomorrow?' It took a moment for Carol to register what her daughter was talking about – and then Lily walked in. Daisy groaned. Her mum looked at her, then looked at Lily, who just shrugged.

'Oh I don't think so, Daisy, I've got enough on my plate as it is. You can't just spring something like that on me, not this late; it's not fair.'

Daisy did her best to keep her temper in check. Not fair, she thought – none of this is fair. She replied in her calmest voice, 'But I did ask you, last week.'

'When?' asked Carol, genuinely nonplussed.

'When we found out about the funeral date. Remember?' Her mum still looked confused.

'She did, Mum. You were going through the address book,' Lily said. Daisy was surprised at her sister's contribution, and also wondered how she actually knew – she wasn't even there – but now wasn't the time to ask.

'Well, the answer's still the same I'm afraid. I mean, we've never even met the boy. It just wouldn't be right!'

Before Daisy could say anything in protest, her sister cut in again. 'Oh, I have, a few times!'

Carol looked at Lily in shock. 'When?'

'When you were away on holi– you know, the trip … he seems nice.' Daisy looked down, shamefaced. 'So, you know, it's OK with me,' she finished.

This was a first, Lily fighting Daisy's corner for her, thought Carol: what's got into her? But it made her feel ganged up on, so she refused to budge. 'I'm sorry, Daisy, the answer's still no. I mean it's not like Lily's asked her boyfriend to come or anything.'

'We've broken up, Mum, that's why,' said Lily. This was another revelation for Carol.

'When?' she asked.

Before she could answer, Daisy flipped; this wasn't about Lily or her stupid on-off boyfriend. 'Well, thanks for being so understanding!' she shouted. 'It's the only thing I've bloody well asked for. All I wanted was a man on my arm – and guess what? My dad's not gonna be there!' And she stormed out, slamming the door behind her.

Carol broke down. It cut her to the core to hear Daisy speak such words. Lily tried to go to her. 'Not now, Lily, I just need to be on my own,' she said. She, too, could have done with a man on her arm; *her* man.

Lily left the room and Carol sat there for some time. What would *he* have done in this situation? God, she knew what he'd have done; he was so laid back he'd have said yes to anything – particularly where Daisy was concerned. She'd been so lost in her own grief and loss that she hadn't considered her children enough, especially Daisy. It was no secret that she'd been his favourite, and the feeling was pretty much reciprocated. They'd had their own special bond: it had made her feel a little excluded at times. Lord alone knows what she must be going through.

After about half an hour, she went and knocked on Daisy's bedroom door. Daisy didn't answer, but she went in anyway.

Daisy had her headphones on, as usual, and was sitting on her bed, rocking, with her knees up to her chest. She came across as tough most of the time, but at that moment she looked so young and vulnerable. She glanced up at her mum and took off her headphones. 'I'm sorry for shouting,' she said.

Carol drew her towards her and held her tight. 'No, I'm sorry, baby. I've been selfish. I know how hard this has been for you ... he can come. At least one of us can have a man with us tomorrow. Perhaps we can all share him!' And they both laughed and cried in each other's arms; it was therapeutic to let it all out.

When they calmed down, Carol said, 'But seriously, though, I'm going to have to meet him first. He can't just turn up tomorrow.'

Daisy was thrilled. She couldn't believe it was finally going to happen – no more sneaking around. 'Well, I'm going to meet him in a bit. Shall I bring him back for a while?'

'Oh no! I couldn't. Not so soon.' And her mum made a ridiculous attempt to tidy her hair. 'I look a right state. What would he think?'

'It's not a date, Mum, he's *my* boyfriend!'

Carol thought about it for a moment. 'No, really, I'd rather not tonight. I've got too much to arrange for tomorrow. Besides, we've got Mum and Jean arriving, remember; they're staying here tonight.' This was Daisy's last remaining grandparent and one of her aunts – both on her mum's side.

Daisy looked disappointed; she'd gone from a massive high to an immediate low, and Carol could sense this.

'Look, tomorrow morning will be fine, honestly. Tell him to come early, about nine o'clock, so we can meet him. We could even have breakfast together.' Daisy couldn't imagine Jack sitting down to breakfast with her mum and grandma, and didn't think he'd go for it. 'We might as well get it all over and done with in one go, I suppose,' Carol continued, sighing. 'I'll ring the funeral parlour and tell them there's going to be four in the car instead of three. Yep, it's going to be some day,' she said sadly.

Daisy's stomach sank at the prospect of it. Still, she was buoyed by the fact that Jack had officially been invited *and* that he would be getting to meet her family at last. She couldn't wait to tell him.

*****

There had been clamorous activity in the field directly behind Jack's house since the beginning of the week. The heavy tractors had moved in, filling the air with dust as the giant mowers scythed down the grass and flung it back out again. As a consequence, Jack had been forced to walk straight down the main road from the bus stop to his house. The farmers had been hard at it all week, turning the cut grass over t o dry. Jack had watched them from the roof of his bungalow, determined to find out how those perfect cylindrical hay bales were created.

Despite his best efforts, when he reached the top of the hill that night the bales were already made and the tractors were gone. Typical, he thought. The hay bales stretched in all directions under a strangely coloured sky that had an orange and pink hue to it. Close up, they were a lot bigger than they looked from a distance, nearly coming up to his shoulder. He tried to climb on one but kept rolling off. He vowed to come back later that night to try again.

On arriving home, Jack was just acknowledging the empty drive (his father's van wasn't there) when the phone rang twice. It came as a bit of a surprise, as he almost didn't expect Daisy to call anymore; this would be his fourth straight night in a row without seeing her. For once he didn't feel in a mad rush to go and meet her. He was starting to feel as if he was at her beck and call, and resentment had crept in. Still, the pull was strong; she was like a drug, and he knew he'd never pass up an opportunity to see her.

His father pulled up a moment later. He'd just returned from getting some fish and chips for dinner. For the first time ever, he mumbled to Jack that he'd got him some too. Jack was astounded: his father had never thought of anyone else in his life. Little did Jack know that it was a bit of a sweetener; there was a van-load of plasterboard that needed shifting. That said, it was true that since they'd been working on the loft together they'd reached a sort of uneasy truce. Having a specific goal to work towards had been beneficial for both of them. It had helped keep Jack's mind off Daisy, and his father's off the booze. His father was definitely more stable for it: he'd even shaved off his beard and given his hair a comical trim.

Jack could only pick at his dinner as he still had no appetite. After quickly giving up and excusing himself, he said he was going out. His father, who was still tucking in, was seriously pissed off. Firstly, it confirmed that the romance was still on – but more importantly, it scuppered his well-laid plans for the evening. 'I want you back by eight. We've got work to do!' he snapped, then added, 'Ungrateful bastard.' Jack gave him a look as he left the room; he was pushing it again. The old sod might have bought him fish and chips, but he wasn't his slave anymore; those days were gone.

Taking his time, Jack walked down to the crossroads to meet Daisy, who was eagerly watching out for him. He had his rucksack on his back and was swigging cider. Much to her consternation, he didn't appear to be in any particular hurry either: he seemed more interested in looking up at the sky than at her, which Daisy had also noticed was a particularly striking colour. She'd put a bit of make-up on, and couldn't wait to tell him the news.

As he got into the van, she could tell straightaway there was something up, but she didn't mention it. 'I thought you weren't coming; I was getting worried!'

'Oh, really?'

OK, she thought – trying to ignore his tone. 'So, where do you want to go?'

'Dunno. How much time can you spare – an hour?'

'No … I'm OK for a while. My grandma's coming over later, though, so I'll have to be back in a bit.'

'Oh, "*a while*", that's good then.'

'So, the pub?' she asked, really trying her best.

'What's the point? You probably won't even have a drink,' he said sullenly.

'Jack, what's got into you? What's wrong?'

'Nothing,' he muttered.

'Yes there is, I can tell.' She couldn't believe he was being like this – especially after she'd fought tooth and nail for him to be able to go to the funeral. She was starting to wonder why she'd bothered. For the first time in ages she'd been in a good mood when she'd come out that evening. 'So, what's wrong?' She wasn't going to ask again.

'Is it always going to be like this from now on?' There: he'd finally come out and said it.

'Like *what*?' she replied after a pause.

'Like this. Where I don't see you for days on end and I'm just hanging around waiting for you to call. And then I'm expected to just drop everything and come running – and then when we do see each other, it's only for an hour and we don't even go near each other anymore!'

Daisy was gobsmacked; she couldn't believe how selfish he was being and felt stung by it. She turned on him, her voice shaking. 'Jack, I've just lost my dad! He's not even been dead two weeks. You couldn't possibly know what I'm going through *or* how that feels!'

'No. How would *I* know how it feels? It's not like *I've* ever lost anyone, is it?'

'Well, it's not quite the same, is it? You never even knew your mum, and as for your sister – well she's not dead, is she? You're still going to see her again one day!'

'Am I? Am I really? She might as well be dead. I can't see her or speak to her, can I? And at least you got to know your dad and spend time with him. I never got to know my mum – can you imagine how *that* feels?'

'What is this, a competition?' she cried, and glared at him. Jack didn't reply. He'd had enough.

There was silence then, save for Daisy crying. After a few moments she noticed that he too was crying silently; tears spilling down his cheeks. For the first time she realised how hard everything must have been on him as well. She softened, and put the back of her hand on his cheek. 'I'm sorry, Jack. It's just been so hard, and Mum's needed me too. I haven't meant to shut you out, I promise, and what with the funeral coming up and everything it's been horrible. I just feel numb and in limbo, and want it all over and done with.' She took his hand. 'Please, Jack, hold me. I don't want to argue anymore – life's too short to argue.' And they reached across and hugged each other.

'I've just been so lonely, Daisy – with Anne going and that… I couldn't bear to lose you too.'

By the time they'd made up properly, they'd been sitting in the van for a good quarter of an hour. 'So, the pub then?' she asked again.

'No, I've got something I want to show you.'

Jack told her to drive up past his house to the top of the

hill. They parked down Ash Lane, opposite his bus stop. Jack led her by the hand, back over the road, and into the fields where the hay bales were. They headed towards his stile. Daisy hadn't seen it before, and Jack offered her the familiar seat. He stood next to her, swigging from a bottle of cider, as they both surveyed the stunning view. 'Wow!' she said; but it wasn't just the sight of the hay bales that took her breath away; it was the sky – a canvas of apricot, mandarin, salmon-pink and lilac, cut through with ribbons of white jet streams.

'It looks like God's spray-painted it with his own hand and signed it off,' said Jack, offering the bottle to Daisy. To his surprise she took it from him, and had a swig herself before replying.

'I don't think there is a God anymore, Jack.' She said it in the world-weary voice that had become so familiar of late – a shadow of her former self; as if she'd lost something. And as she stared sadly out at the sky, she seemed to Jack to be like an angel with clipped wings.

CHAPTER 31

The Funeral

It was hot on the morning of the funeral – too hot. Funerals should be played out against a backdrop of grey, under a respectful leaden sky, with perhaps a smattering of sympathetic drizzle; not under a spotless, blue firmament and unforgiving molten yellow sun – callous in its brazenness and indifference. Jack had never been so nervous in his life – and that was saying something; the only thing that could compare was when he was thrust out into the world on his first day of work. At least on that day there had been a modicum of expectation and excitement after being cooped up for so long. This, however, was pure dread.

The prospect of the funeral itself – of being on show and spending the day in such close proximity to hordes of other people – would have been horrific under any circumstances. Add into the mix the small matter of meeting Daisy's family for the first time, and you'd got a neurotic's jackpot on your hands. What made it worse was that he'd gone back into his shell of late, almost reverting to his old self – the pre-Daisy Jack. He'd done nothing for the last two weeks, save for the brief moments he'd had with Daisy, but go to work (where he didn't speak to anybody) and then go home. Old habits had returned – the rucksack, the cider, the insecurities, the fear of people. His old adversary the black spot was back; it menaced him in the corner of his eye as he set off to the crossroads.

Jack was already on his second bottle of cider. Not a good idea on an empty stomach; he wasn't used to it now, and instead of calming him down it was making him feel nauseous. He hadn't known what to wear, and this was at the forefront of his mind. Daisy hadn't given him any instructions the previous night as she'd been too preoccupied; something she'd realised later on. Before she'd gone to bed, she'd dug out a tie and a jacket that had belonged to her dad, just in case. Even Jack knew that you were meant to wear black for funerals, but he didn't have anything except for his black drainpipes and Converse boots. These he'd donned, along with his white T-shirt that he'd ironed himself. He'd tried his best to comb his unruly hair into place with shaking hands, but still felt uncomfortable and hopelessly underdressed.

He was a bit early when he reached the crossroads, so he stood by the phone box and waited. This didn't help his nerves; he was jigging about like a marionette by the time Daisy pulled up. They both looked each other up and down when he got in. What immediately struck him was the colour of her hair; it had changed. It was wet and scraped back, making it look darker, but it was definitely a different colour as well – a deeper, blacker red, the colour of black cherries. It looked unnatural to him, mainly because it was a bit of a shock, and he didn't think he liked it. He didn't like change at the best of times – and certainly not this morning. It saddened him as he'd loved the colour of her hair.

As the summer had gone on it had lightened Daisy's naturally auburn hair: it happened every summer, but more so this year with all the sunshine. It had become too light for her – too rust coloured; as though autumn had come early. So, on a whim, she'd dyed it a darker shade. This wasn't something she'd done before but it suited her mood perfectly.

'Your hair,' was all Jack could say.

'I know. I dyed it. I felt like a change.' She appeared a little nervous and agitated herself.

She leant to peck him on the cheek (which was a nice surprise) and she was fragrant from the shower, but her hair smelt funny. She could smell something on Jack too. 'Have you been drinking already?' she asked.

'Well, yes – just a couple.'

'A couple? Jack, it's only nine o'clock in the morning and you're about to meet my mum and grandma for the first time – you can smell it!'

'Well, I was nervous,' he said, hoping she'd understand – the old Daisy would have done. When had it been such a problem?

She started the engine and made to pull off. As she did so, she looked across at him again and at what he was wearing. He was pale-faced and clutching his rucksack, which looked full and clinked on his lap as his leg tapped up and down. 'And you won't need that today either,' she said, gesturing with her head. He knew she was stressed out – it was understandable – but it was as if she was picking at him. He felt himself shrinking further into his shell, and he slumped down into his seat as they headed into the village. 'I've got a jacket and tie of Dad's you can wear. You can't go dressed like that… We'll see if there's a shirt that fits too – I'm sure Mum won't mind.'

A vision of spending the day in some ridiculous, oversized suit, like some sort of freak on display, flashed through Jack's head, and he totally lost it. She was making him feel as if she was ashamed of him. 'I don't want to wear any more of your dad's clothes!' he shouted. Daisy looked at him in shock. Where had that come from? 'Stop the van. I can't do this!'

'I'm sorry, Jack. I didn't mean anything by it!'

'Stop the van, Daisy!' he yelled again, and this time she did as he said, screeching to a halt.

Before the van had even come to a standstill, Jack had opened the door, grabbed his rucksack and was off sprinting down Church Lane. Daisy was distraught. How could this be happening? She was counting on his support. Had she been that harsh? Or should she be mad at *him*? How could he do this to her, today of all days, leaving her in the lurch? Worse, what on earth was she going to say to her mum? She needed to find him, that was for sure. 'Oh, Jack,' she sobbed; and crunched the gears into reverse.

She drove down Church Lane, keeping her eyes peeled. Rounding the bend, she expected to see him at any moment – running with his rucksack bobbing on his back – but there was no sign of him. She passed the church, where in less than three hours they would all be assembling for the funeral. It made her feel sick just to look at it. Bearing left, she negotiated the narrow lane past the cemetery where her dad was to be buried. The same feeling of dread came over her. It was like a bad dream. She went as far as she could, but when she reached the kissing gate at the end Jack was still nowhere to be seen; it was as if he had vanished into thin air, like Lord Lucan.

Daisy screamed in frustration before reversing down the narrow lane. Twice she had to stop as, in her panic, she kept misjudging and backing the van into the hedge. Finally she reached Main Street. On the corner was the Generous Briton pub where they'd all be going for the wake. It was as if she was doing some hideous run-through. She didn't know whether to turn left and head back up the main road to Jack's house or not. Knowing Jack, he'd have gone cross country, and in any case her mum would be wondering where she'd got to.

Defeated and deflated, she headed back to her house. What

was she going to say? She cursed herself for being so hard on him, but she'd been on edge all morning. It wouldn't have really mattered what he wore; him being there was all that mattered – she realised that now. The hardest part was going back into the house and breaking the news to her family. She felt so foolish after all the song and dance she'd made to get him there. They all looked up expectantly when she entered the kitchen. But their faces dropped when they saw Daisy's tear-stained face. 'He's not coming. We had an argument,' she confessed, and broke down again. She looked so helpless and forlorn that they all felt for her; even Lily's heart went out to her.

Carol took the news stoically, and came over to hold Daisy tight. 'It's just us now, love, just us family. That's all that matters.'

Over her mum's shoulder, Daisy could see her grandma shaking her head in disgust. 'What kind of boy treats a girl like that on a day like this? It wouldn't have happened in my day!' she said.

After calling the funeral directors to inform them there would only be three in the car, Carol made a decision. She pulled a suitcase down from the top of her wardrobe, laid it on the bed and unzipped the inner pocket. Inside was an envelope that had been hidden there since the ill-fated trip to the Lake District. On the front it said simply 'Daisy' in her husband's handwriting. Her lip quivered at the sight of it. She took in a deep, jerky breath, trying to compose herself, before heading to Daisy's bedroom. She knocked softly on the door. 'Daisy? Can I come in?'

Daisy was sitting in front of her bedroom mirror, wearing her funeral outfit and trying to put make-up on. Carol still hadn't got used to her daughter's recent transformation. She looked so beautiful and grown up. What had happened to that tomboy she used to know? 'How are you doing?' she asked, putting her hand on Daisy's shoulder. Daisy smiled sadly at her in the mirror by way of an answer, and continued to try and apply her make-up; her hand was trembling and her eyes wouldn't stay dry for long enough. 'Here, I wanted to give you this,' her mum said, and held out the envelope. Daisy gave her a quizzical look, and then she noticed her dad's handwriting. Her face furrowed into a frown, which nearly set Carol off again. 'Don't worry,' she said, squeezing her shoulder. 'It's nothing bad – it's meant to cheer you up. Go on, open it.'

Daisy looked down at the envelope. She couldn't begin to imagine what it contained, especially with her dad's writing on it. And that was the surreal thing: that he'd held this in his still warm hands – touched it, breathed on it, written her name on it – and now he was gone. She turned the envelope over and pulled the flap open. Inside were two tickets, which she gently pulled out. They had swirls of pastel colours on them and big, bold lettering that said:

SJM CONCERTS PRESENTS
'THE STONE ROSES'
BLACKPOOL EMPRESS BALLROOM
SATURDAY 12th AUGUST 1989

Daisy gasped in disbelief. And just for a second, just for a brief moment, her sorrow lifted due to an injection of pure joy; but then the reality came crashing back in. She was more confused than ever and tears spilled down her cheeks – one of them smudging the uppermost ticket. It felt like being handed a winning Pools coupon but not being able to celebrate.

'Hey, don't cry!' her mum said, not heeding her own advice as she pulled Daisy round to face her. 'It was meant to cheer you up!' They hugged each other.

'But, how come? Why now?' Daisy said.

'They were meant to be for your eighteenth birthday next month, but I thought you needed some cheering up. Your dad bought them while we were away – I think he secretly wanted to go too. You know what he was like!'

This struck Daisy as so tragic, but it was typical of her dad. He liked to keep up with the new bands, thinking he was cool. She went silent, wondering whom she'd go with, and how she'd get there. She'd never been to a concert before and had certainly never driven that far.

As if reading her mind, Carol said, 'You could always go with Claire from college, or what about Loverboy? If you make up with him that is. Does he drive?' For some reason Daisy found this hysterical, and she snorted with laughter. It must have been the stress she was under, she felt almost giddy with it, but the vision of Jack driving was absolutely ridiculous. He would be the worst driver in the world – a total bag of nerves; just like Woody Allen.

When her mum had gone, Daisy tucked the precious tickets into her diary-cum-notebook, where they would sit forgotten until after the funeral.

*****

Jack was prowling the fields on the outskirts of the village, indulging in a severe bout of mental flagellation. When he'd left Daisy he'd run as far as the brook before stopping – racked with hurt, shame and self-hatred. He wanted to hurt himself so badly – like that day he'd burnt his hand at work; something to make the other pain go away. He wanted to throw himself in the brook and drown himself, or bash his head with a rock till it bled. Why couldn't he be normal like everybody else? Daisy had made him feel like that for a while, until all this had happened – and he cursed her dad again; but then felt guilty. What a terrible thing to think. It wasn't her dad's fault *or* Daisy's. He'd forgotten to make allowances for her again – to consider what she was going through. As he didn't care if his own father lived or died this empathy didn't come naturally, and now he'd gone and deserted her on the day of her dad's funeral. She'd never forgive him; and he wailed at the sky.

He wandered along the bank of the brook, as lost and lonely as a party balloon wrenched from a child's hand and blown away in the wind. Soon he came to a familiar spot where the water was still – the place where he and Daisy had first kissed. The bittersweet memory of it tugged at his heartstrings. Things had seemed so simple then, and he sat down to reminisce, taking off his T-shirt and cracking open another bottle of cider. He stared at the water, lost in reverie. He could remember exactly what she'd been wearing that day – the white blouse tied at her waist and her denim shorts. How she'd laughed as they nearly fell in, and how the sun had shone down like honey as they'd kissed. He conjured up their images – like shimmering apparitions beamed up on *Star Trek*. Jack smiled sadly as he pictured it. He picked up a stone and threw it into the water, breaking the surface into rings and banishing the images.

He continued throwing stones into the brook, lost in thought, for hours, deliberating over what to do as the hot sun beat down. He'd finished another bottle of cider and it hadn't helped his thought processes at all. But it *had* given him some 'Dutch courage'. He decided he was going to face his fears, make amends and go to the funeral. It was the right thing to do – to pay his respects for Daisy's sake and to try and salvage the rest of the day. Using the sun as his gauge he figured it had got to be getting on for midday, and for better or worse he slowly made his way back through the fields to the village.

Jack was staggered by the number of cars lining the lanes up to the church, and his courage quickly vanished. When he saw all the mourners congregated around the gate, he stopped dead in his tracks. There were hordes of them – it looked like hundreds to him – all dressed head to toe in black; they flocked, flapped and fidgeted like a murder of crows. He'd intended to sneak in and sit quietly at the back, but this plan went straight out of the window. Nobody saw him as he melted back into the shimmering heat haze on the lane, around the corner and back the way he'd come.

The worst bit for Daisy, and for all of them, was seeing the coffin properly for the first time – and the subsequent noise that escaped her mother's throat. That was when reality hit hardest: her dad was actually in there. The finality of it was impossible to comprehend or bear. She felt as though her dad should be standing next to her, giving her a reassuring look. It made her miss Jack. And it was awful to hear the vicar say 'James Alexander Jones' as if he was a stranger. That wasn't her dad's name – it was Jim; everyone called him Jim, except his late mother, who'd always called him J.J.

Jack loitered behind the churchyard throughout the service, listening to the sombre singing and prayers within. Finally, organ music played loudly, seeming to signify something, and he peeked over the church wall. After a moment the coffin appeared, carried by men in long coats. People were pouring out of the churchyard, following the coffin down the road. Where were they going with it? And where was Daisy? He sat down again, breathing heavily and listening to the exodus. They must be heading to the cemetery, he thought.

He set off through a gaggle of young silver birches – their thin striped trunks like a herd of zebra's legs. After a brief trespass through someone's garden, he burst through a hedge at the back, then cut across a field to the rear of the cemetery.

Desperately, he searched for a vantage point where he would be hidden but could still watch. He felt a need to be part of it, to see what went on – but most of all he wanted to see Daisy.

About ten to fifteen yards away he spotted a small, broad field maple tree that was bushy and in full bloom. It was ideal as it had low boughs, and he ran over to hoist himself up it. Soon he was immersed in its welcoming canopy. Subterfuge was his thing; he'd been doing it his whole life; and right now he felt as if he was little again – lurking in the shadows, behind a curtain of five-pointed leaves that hung down like a thousand green hands.

Jack lay full length on a branch, out of sight, as the funeral procession entered the small, sun-drenched cemetery. At first he didn't recognise Daisy, but when he did her beauty took his breath away, and he nearly fell out of the tree. He'd forgotten she'd dyed her hair. It was now done up movie queen style – like Bridget Bardot – parted in the middle then back-combed into a beehive. Long, plum-coloured tresses hung down either side of her face. She looked stunning, almost regal, in a black fitted jacket nipped in at the waist and a matching pencil skirt; a combination that accentuated her hips. She was wearing heels – another reason why he hadn't recognised her; he'd not seen her in heels before and she looked a lot taller. Daisy and her sister glamorously flanked a smaller woman in a hat and veil – obviously their mother. They walked arm in arm, following the coffin. Even from where Jack was he could see the identical expressions of pain on their faces, and how their mascara was running.

There were only a dozen or so mourners – led by a vicar dressed in a white smock – who stood in a horseshoe shape around the coffin as it was lowered into the ground. Jack couldn't hear what was being said, but he could see their shoulders shaking as they threw flowers and earth into the grave. It was the most harrowing sight he'd ever seen and he wanted to go to Daisy. He wanted so much to hold her and comfort her and to say how sorry he was. He reached out at one point, and nearly fell out of the tree again. When it was over, there was much hugging and crying. Daisy, her mum and her sister seemed reluctant to leave, and they were the last to go.

Jack didn't know what to do; he was at a complete loss, so he lay there for a while feeling sad. Where had everyone gone? He couldn't see where they were heading – presumably back to Daisy's house. Although he badly needed to see Daisy and to speak to her, would she even want to speak to him? How could she forgive him? He couldn't just turn up at her house if there were people there. There seemed no other option than to bide his time, wait till everyone had gone and then ring her. Yes, that's what he'd do – he'd call her later and beg her to see him. But what could he do in the meantime?

An overwhelming desire to get blind drunk seized Jack. He jumped down from the tree, pulling his rucksack behind him. It was reassuringly heavy, and he was glad that he'd brought a good supply of cider. Whilst Daisy and the rest of the mourners were drowning their sorrows at the Generous Briton, that's exactly what he did as well.

*****

Some considerable time later, Jack woke up feeling like crap. His stomach was in agony, his mouth was bone dry and he had a pounding headache. He was stiff and sore and could feel something digging into his back. Worst of all was a burning sensation down one side; he felt as if he was being grilled alive. Where the hell was he? And what time was it? He gingerly opened his eyes and winced at the brightness.

He was in a vaguely familiar field, full of hay bales. The unrelenting sun was high in the sky, so it couldn't be that late. He rolled away from it and tried to piece together what had happened. His argument with Daisy came back to him and he groaned. Then he remembered trying to go to the funeral but chickening out, and he groaned again. He then recalled seeing Daisy at the cemetery, and how beautiful she'd looked. After that it was all a bit of a blur, and he was left with an overwhelming feeling of disappointment – as though he'd badly let her down.

Jack looked around, trying to get his bearings. He was surrounded by empty cider bottles. He remembered trying to get some respite from the sun, seeking refuge in the shade of a large hay bale, which he now had his back against. He must have fallen asleep. But during the afternoon, the sun had moved round, leaving him half-exposed. His ravenous thirst returned, and he heard distant running water, confirming he was still in the vicinity of the brook. This was enough to pull him to his feet. He collected up all his bottles then pulled on his T-shirt, which chafed his tender, red skin.

Jack made for the part where the water ran fastest, its rushing and gurgling teasing and tormenting him. He pulled out one of his bottles, filled it, then drank long and hard. He'd never needed a drink quite like this, and he filled his bottle several times over. Then he poured another couple of bottles over his head, face and neck. It felt amazing, except for the side where his neck was burnt; that stung even worse. The water sobered him up, and he began to think more clearly. What should he do now? His overriding urge was to see Daisy. He'd got to speak to her – to apologise – and just hope that she'd forgive him. This had been his original plan, he recalled, before he'd gone and got blotto. His biggest problem was that he still didn't know what time it was, so he didn't know if the funeral party would be finished or if he could go home yet. There was only one way to find out – and that was to call Daisy.

As he climbed the bank to the bridge a bus went past on the main road, which was a stroke of luck; this meant that it was, more or less, on the hour. He didn't see anyone he recognised on the bus, so it couldn't have been his usual one. This meant it had to be five o'clock – it definitely wasn't seven yet. Again, this was a bonus: perhaps he could still get home at the right time too. He crossed the main road and headed down the lay-by to the phone box.

Jack pulled open the creaking red door and squeezed inside. He picked up the clunky receiver and, before he lost his nerve, dialled Daisy's number. He let it ring three times, praying that no one answered it, before putting it back down.

Three phones in Daisy's house rang out in unison, yet were still barely audible over the music. A hard core of close family and friends – those who liked to drink – had come back to the house after the wake. They were now having a bit of a knees-up around the bar in the dining room. Spurred on by alcohol, and in true Jones family style, the day had turned from a sorrowful occasion into a celebration of Jim's life. 'It's what he would have wanted,' they told themselves; the tears would return later.

Lily was the first one to hear the phone: she was in the hall, on the way to the kitchen for more ice. Daisy, who'd just emerged from the bathroom upstairs, heard the last ring too, and then her sister saying 'Hello. *Hello?*' in a drunken voice. Daisy's senses became sharper; she was also a little tipsy, but not drunk enough to join in the inappropriate frivolities that had sprung up. Had they forgotten what today was? Now that the funeral was over she wanted everyone to go home; she was missing Jack, and that was all she could think about. She listened intently as she descended the stairs, stuffing her blouse back into her skirt. By the time she reached the bottom step, her sister had already put the phone down. 'That's funny. That's 'bout the third time that's happened jus' lately,' Lily said, slurring her words.

'Who was it?'

'Dunno. It rang off before I got to it; there was no one there.'

Daisy was fully alert now; it had to be Jack. What if he was in trouble? What if he needed her? 'How many times did it ring?'

'I don't know,' said Lily, looking at her sister oddly, before tottering back towards the kitchen.

'How many times?' shouted Daisy, grabbing her arm.

'I don't know! What's got into you?' Lily yelled back, removing her arm from Daisy's grip. 'Three, I think. What does it matter? I wasn't counting – sorry!'

Daisy ran back upstairs, chanting to herself like a mantra: 'Three rings, call me straight back, three rings, call me straight back.' Lily stared after her as if her little sister had gone completely cuckoo. Daisy ran into her mum's bedroom, picked up the phone, and punched in Jack's number.

To her surprise, instead of Jack picking up straightaway, the phone rang and rang. That was odd, she thought. Why wasn't he answering? But then, on the sixth ring, the phone *was* picked up. She was about to say 'Jack?' when a gruff voice that sent a chill through her said: '843300.' She slammed down the phone: Jack's father – she wasn't expecting that. Why hadn't Jack answered? Perhaps he'd been caught out. But why would he have taken the risk of ringing three times if his father was about? Maybe Lily had got it wrong: it wouldn't be surprising; she was plastered. It was then that Daisy remembered the phone box – perhaps he was calling from there? Surely he must have gone home by now. She raced into her bedroom to retrieve her diary, thinking, it had to be worth a shot.

Jack had vacated the phone box and was heading dejectedly for home when he heard a muffled ring behind him. He dashed back inside and picked up the phone. 'Daisy?' he cried.

'Yes.'

'It's me, Jack!' She felt a mixture of emotions at hearing his voice. At first she was relieved to hear that he sounded OK, and inside it made her want to melt, but it was also a reminder of what had happened between them that day. Deep down she was still mad at him for leaving her in the lurch: it was like being stood up at the altar.

'I know it's you, you just rang me,' she replied noncommittally. There was an awkward pause. Now that Jack had got hold of her he didn't know what to say; and it was strange hearing Daisy's voice on a telephone line at last.

'So, how are you?' he said, and immediately felt foolish – what a stupid question.

'Well, I buried my dad today, so – you know…'

'I'm sorry, Daisy, about everything…'

'I needed you today, Jack.'

'I know, and I'm sorry. I tried to come, I really did, but there were just too many people.'

'When?'

'To the church today, but you couldn't get near it.'

Daisy considered this for a while. 'Well, it's probably best you didn't. My grandma might have hit you with her handbag.' Her joke was an attempt to lighten the mood, but it had an element of truth in it. Unfortunately it only served to bruise Jack's already fragile opinion of himself. Great, now even her grandma hates me and I've never even met the woman, he thought.

'Can I see you, Daisy? I want to make it up to you. Can you meet me?'

'I can't, not now. There are still people here.' She spoke quietly as if to emphasise the fact. 'Besides, I've had too much to drink to drive.'

'Well, later then. You could walk to the crossroads.'

It would be nice to get some fresh air, thought Daisy – to sober up and get away from all these hangers on: she wished they'd just piss off. 'I want to, I really do … but I don't feel I can just up and leave. It seems rude, and I don't know what time it'll go on till.'

His disappointment was palpable, and she remembered their argument from the other night – and how it had been between them lately. She didn't want him to feel neglected anymore. She didn't *want* to neglect him anymore – she needed him too. He was her solace, her emotional tourniquet. 'I know. Why don't you come here as soon as it's dark?' she said.

Dark, he thought – he couldn't wait that long; he'd go insane! 'But that's ages away, and I mean, how? What about all the people?'

'I know it's a while, but at least then we can spend some proper time together instead of me worrying that I've got to rush back. They should all have gone by then; if not I'll kick them out myself! Meet me at the bottom of the garden. I'll slip out.'

'Whereabouts?' he asked. But just then Daisy heard her mum calling her from downstairs.

'Under the willow,' she whispered. It made Jack go funny inside.

'OK, as soon as it's dark… Daisy?' But she cut in.

'I've got to go Jack, she's coming! I'll see you later. Wait for me under the willow.' And she was gone. He'd wanted to say how sorry he was again, and how much he loved her, but it would have to wait till later.

Jack trudged home. It was the last thing he wanted to do as it meant getting involved with his father and work. He wasn't in the mood. At least it would pass the time, he supposed; dark couldn't come soon enough. After a pauper's dinner of soup and stale bread, which seemed to leave him even hungrier, he reluctantly headed up to the loft.

This was really taking shape now. His father had been busy, and Jack could sense him looking for some sort of approval or acknowledgement. Jack refused to give it; old habits die hard. But he *was* impressed: all three skylights had been cut out, making it light and airy – and this was without the dormer windows. The walls had been finished and, along with the peaked ceiling, were neatly stuffed with that hated yellow insulation. It was all ready for the plasterboard to go up.

Jack tried to keep his sunburn away from his father as they worked: he either didn't notice or didn't care enough to ask about it. They made good progress, grafting for a few solid hours. When the light started to go, Jack said he was calling it a night: he wanted to freshen up and head out just before it got dark. His father was displeased as usual. 'Rent's due,' he muttered in retaliation.

Having a bath was a painful experience. Jack could only have the water lukewarm. Afterwards he searched for some cream or ointment, but there was none to be found; since his sister had left, nothing like that had been replaced. As he looked in the mirror, he cursed himself. He looked like a striped stick of rock. What would Daisy think? At least it would be dark.

Jack left the house as dusk was descending. It was amazing how quickly the days began to get shorter again, not even a month since Midsummer Night. It felt like old times being out this late. There was a sprinkling of stars in the sky and a waxen, yellowy half-moon. He was desperate to see Daisy – to hold her in his arms and to make amends. He broke into a jog, wishing that he had his bike; he had *got* to get that fixed.

Peeping over Daisy's fence, Jack could just make out the willow tree in the twilight, but couldn't see Daisy. Lights were on all over the house, flooding the patio and top of the garden. Apart from that, there were no signs of life from within, and certainly no one in the kitchen. He vaulted the fence and scurried towards the safety of the tree. The smell of honeysuckle was in the air, not as strong as before, yet still powerfully evocative.

Jack crouched down and waited, watching the house through the hanging beads of the weeping willow. Some lights went off upstairs, then another light went on and he heard a toilet flush. Then this light went off, leaving the whole first floor in darkness. Still he waited, for maybe another five minutes. An owl hooted in the dusk. Despondent thoughts crept in. God, I hope she hasn't forgotten; she couldn't have, could she? Finally there was movement in the kitchen. Even from this distance there was no mistaking that hair; it was Daisy. His stomach spun as he watched her make her way towards the patio door.

There she was now, looking behind her before sliding the door open. He could see she was still wearing her clothes from the funeral, minus the jacket. She looked grown up, like a secretary, and again it struck him how he barely recognised her. She pulled the patio door closed behind her and bent to unbuckle her shoes. Her pencil skirt clung tightly to her, leaving nothing to the imagination. Then she removed her shoes and took a pin out of her hair, shaking it loose, before tiptoeing out of the light and into the gloaming.

He watched her shape float down the lawn towards him. 'Jack!' she whispered.

'Psst. Over here!' he replied, and emerged from under the skirts of the tree. Suddenly they were standing face to face for the first time since that morning, Daisy still clutching her shoes. It wasn't quite dark, and they searched each other's faces, looking for signs to indicate where they stood with each other. Jack wanted to touch her but didn't know if he was allowed – not yet; there were things that needed to be said first. 'I'm so sorry … about today, about your dad,' – she flinched when he said the word –'about the way I've been acting lately, about everything.'

She stopped him then. 'No, Jack, it's not just you. I'm sorry too. I know I've been a bitch lately.'

'No, it's not your fault. I've been selfish. I should have been more understanding – especially this morning – and I just want to make it up to you.'

Daisy looked up at the house, as if they could be seen or heard, then took him by the hand and led him behind the tree.

'Are there people still here?' Jack said.

'No, they've all gone – except for Grandma and Aunt Jean. They're in the spare room, but they've gone to bed now. Everyone has, even Mum.'

'How is your mum – and Lily?' he asked, trying to say the right things.

'Mum will probably have one hell of a hangover in the morning, put it that way! There were quite a few tears at the end as well, but I dare say there are more to come.' She looked sad. Jack touched her face for the first time, tentatively, putting her hair behind her ear. 'I missed you today. I needed you so much,' she said, and her voice trembled as if she was going to cry – which she didn't want to, not now. There had been enough tears today already, and enough these last few weeks to last a lifetime.

Jack figured he wasn't quite forgiven, not entirely, and he

put his arms around her neck. When he spoke his voice was thick with emotion. 'I'll never let you down again, Daisy, not ever, I swear, as long as I live – do you hear me?' He lifted her chin up to look at him, to show that he meant it.

'Do you promise?' she said.

'Yes, I promise.' They hugged each other then, tightly, their bodies almost as one – until Jack recoiled and let out a yelp.

'God, what's wrong?' she asked.

'I fell asleep today and got a bit sunburnt.' And he showed her his face and neck.

Daisy gasped. 'Jesus, Jack, that looks so sore, you poor thing!' She ran her fingers over his tender skin and kissed him softly there, her lips brushing his cheek, her hair tickling his face. The feel and smell of each other up close stirred familiar feelings. From the very start, theirs had been a physical attraction; from the moment they'd set eyes on each other, to the first time they'd touched and been zapped by static. How apt that it should have begun that way, because that's how they felt now – electrically charged. Their lips sought out each other's, unable to help themselves. They hadn't kissed like this since before the fateful day when Daisy had heard the news about her dad – and it had been too long. They were like addicts who had gone cold turkey; each was the other's drug. And once they were tempted again by their weakness, their vice, they were powerless to resist.

She led him by the hand, across the bottom of the garden and into Honeysuckle Cottage, just as she had on Midsummer Eve. Once inside, the faint smell of the honeysuckle added further spice to the mix; a little bit of alchemy – an aphrodisiac. Her blouse felt silky under his fingers, slightly open at the front with hints of lace underneath, exuding that sweet musk at her throat. Her bum felt somehow fuller in the skirt than he remembered; it had been so long since he had touched her that she was a stranger to him, yet wonderfully familiar at the same time…

*****

It was a cathartic experience for both of them, especially Daisy, and she shed tears afterwards. It was a release, after weeks of numbness, to feel something real. Jack wanted to tell her about losing his job but decided to wait – it would only raise questions about his plans and their future … America. Now wasn't the time. Instead, he professed that he was starving hungry as he'd barely eaten all day. Daisy said she'd slip back to the house to get something left over from the wake; there was loads of it. She also said she'd get some cream for his sunburn.

When Daisy returned she lit a candle, as everyone in the house was fast asleep. Soon the inside of Honeysuckle Cottage was bathed in a soft orange glow, and their flickering shadows danced on the walls like puppets. It was good to be able to see each other properly. She'd brought a plate back with her, piled high with food. Jack accepted it gratefully. It was only sandwiches, sausage rolls and quiche, but to Jack it was food from the gods. By candlelight she watched him eat. His over-long hair hung in his face as he tucked in with abandon. She smiled at the almost feral quality he still had about him – one of the things that had so endeared him to her in the first place. She reminded herself that she should never look down on him for it; something she'd been guilty of recently.

When he'd finished, Daisy told him to take his shirt off so she could put some cream on. He was looking thin, more so than usual, and she chided him for this whilst feeling sorry for him at the same time; it was hardly his fault, what with no one to look after him. This was what Jack had missed so badly –

being taken care of and some motherly attention. And perhaps he exaggerated those little winces of pain, just a tiny bit, as she rubbed in the soothing after-sun ointment and cooed at him not to be such a big baby.

Whilst she was doing his back, Daisy said, 'I take it you don't like the colour of my hair then?'

'Erm, I didn't say that,' he replied, glad he was facing the other way.

'You didn't have to. I could tell by your reaction this morning! Don't worry, it comes out after a few washes.' Jack smiled at his shadow on the wall.

CHAPTER 32

A Walk in the Cemetery

Things began to settle down a bit after the funeral. Relatives disappeared back whence they came and visiting well-wishers stopped turning up on the doorstep, leaving the Joneses to grieve in peace. Despite this, you certainly couldn't say that everything returned back to normal; far from it. Daisy had lost her dad, so she wasn't that happy-go-lucky girl that she'd been. It had taken that bit of magic out of the world and had made her grow up a little too quickly, a little too soon. Each day was an obstacle course – hurdles to overcome, reminders to avoid – and she still felt guilty doing her own thing or thinking of herself.

As for Jack, he no longer had a job – which was another big change in their lives. It was something he was going to have to come clean about, to both Daisy and his father – sooner rather than later. He seriously wasn't looking forward to telling his father, and he tried to keep him sweet all weekend by continuing to help with the loft. By Sunday, all the plasterboard was up and two holes had been made in the roof for the dormer windows, opposite the skylights, overlooking the back garden and orchard. It was strange to be able to see the orchard from this new viewpoint, and it was a damn sight easier to check up on the apples from there. Jack could see them in their green abundance as he looked out: they looked like frozen peas.

Most of the work for the dormers had to be done from the outside. But much to his father's annoyance, Jack refused point blank to climb up the precariously extended ladder propped against the wheel of the van. Instead, he passed bits of wood and tools to him from the bottom rung. His father descended the ladder and called out, as a surgeon would to his assistant, opening and closing his hand impatiently. Jack was somehow expected to know what things were, despite the fact that he'd never heard of some of them. He now knew what 'two be two' was, and a spirit level, fair enough; but what the hell was a bevel?

*****

Jack met Daisy on Sunday at the end of her shift. They'd arranged to visit the cemetery to look at the temporary marker that should have been placed on her father's grave. He snuck into the pub early so he could have a crafty pint and, more importantly, just sit and watch her work – something that gave him an exquisite and infinite pleasure. She looked a lot healthier than the last time he'd seen her working, with a healthy glow back in her cheeks from rushing about.

Afterwards, they took the short walk down Chapel Lane to the cemetery, Daisy clutching a bunch of flowers. It was a perfect summer's afternoon, and Jack was proud to be walking hand in hand with his girl, glad that things were getting back to normal. He took the opportunity to tell her about losing his job. Daisy was incensed. 'What a bastard!' she cried. He decided not to tell her about the wages he'd missed out on (for good) by not going in on Friday. He'd only realised this when he'd gone to get his board money for his father the previous day.

'Well, what are you going to do? Are you going to try and go back in on Monday?' Daisy felt a terrible twinge of guilt at the sacrifice Jack had made for her; which in the end had proved pointless anyway.

'No, I don't see the point. Peasgood made it perfectly clear that if I wasn't there on Friday I was sacked.'

'But he can't just sack you for going to a funeral! Workers have rights and things these days – my dad was always harping on about it!' She'd got her hackles up now, more like her old self.

'I don't have any rights. It was just an arrangement between him and my father; he could say I never worked there if he wanted – I don't exist, remember.' Daisy had kind of forgotten about this aspect of Jack's life. Being around him, he just seemed like any normal person – and it was a stark reminder of the life he'd led.

'Well, it's just not right. I mean, where are you going to find another job – especially without a reference or anything? And what's your dad going to say?'

'I wish you wouldn't call him that. He's not my dad – not like yours.'

'Sorry, your *father* then.'

'I don't know; that's what I'm worried about. I might not even tell him.'

They'd reached the cemetery gates. Daisy passed Jack the flowers whilst she prised open the stubborn rusty handle. The cemetery looked contrarily pretty in the afternoon light. Shadows danced and flowers nodded in the light breeze amongst the headstones. Jack passed Daisy her bunch of flowers and he sensed her tensing up; he could see it in her face. It had seemed like a good idea – to come back sooner rather than later – to get it over with. But now she was here, the reality hit that all she'd got left of her father was a grave – a mound of dirt; not even a proper headstone yet. The thought of it made her wobble, and Jack put a steadying arm around her as they made their way down the path.

Daisy knew exactly where the grave was but didn't look up; she didn't want to see it, not yet. Instead, she walked slowly, preparing herself. Jack knew exactly where it was too, but let her lead the way. He didn't want to let on that he'd watched that day – she might think it was weird.

The grave stuck out like a sore thumb. It was covered in wreaths and flowers, and the dug-over earth was still fresh. They stood there solemnly and read the writing on the marker, whilst Daisy tried her best to hold back a sob. The marker wasn't much more than a plaque on a stick; almost like something you'd put on a pet's grave. It read: 'In loving memory of JAMES ALEXANDER JONES. APRIL 1940 – JULY 1989. Devoted husband and father'. 'The headstone will say more, but that was all they could fit on this,' Daisy said in a tearful voice.

Jack put his arm around her again. It all seemed so cold and matter-of-fact to him – an entire life condemned to history; nothing more than a few words on a plaque and some expensive flowers that would be dead themselves soon. He wondered what would be written on *his* father's headstone – or if he'd even have one. 'Devoted father…?' He didn't think so. To his surprise, Daisy said: 'Do you mind if I have a moment?'

'No, course not,' he replied, and kissed her on the side of her head. He was glad to have a wander; all this was making him feel a bit depressed.

As he turned away, Jack couldn't help but watch out of the corner of his eye as Daisy knelt down and placed the flowers at the base of the marker. They looked slightly limp, as if she'd strangled them half to death in her hands. When he heard her speak, 'Hi, Dad,' he quickened his pace and shuffled away; it felt too much like eavesdropping.

He meandered through the tombstones and crosses with Daisy's voice still in the background. She was talking to a man who was no longer alive – and it struck him what a strange thing this 'death' business was. Who was it worse for? The ones who'd died or the ones who were left behind? He knew he'd rather be dead himself if Daisy died, but the thought of lying there, under the ground for all eternity, was equally unappealing. It made him feel panicky and claustrophobic, and he shivered despite the sun's warmth.

Some of the graves were overgrown, with headstones that were slanting, ancient and weather worn, covered in tangles of creeping ivy and vines. He read the inscriptions on some of the newer ones, trying to find the most recent date before Daisy's dad's. But there were so many of them that he soon began to lose interest, barely registering what he was reading.

Just then, something on one of the headstones caught his eye, and he stopped to retrace his steps. It was the surname Hemsley – *his* surname. Nothing too unusual in that, he supposed; there were probably hundreds of Hemsleys in the world. But on closer inspection, the first name made the hair on the back of his neck stand up: it was Carla. As if on cue, the black dot floated into focus. Had he just stumbled upon his own mother's grave? And just a few miles from his house? The headstone was in pretty good nick and didn't look that old – comparatively speaking anyway. Stranger still was that there were flowers on the grave; dead flowers admittedly – but they had been placed there in the last few weeks or so.

He frantically brushed some ivy away from the stone to read the rest of the writing. 'Here lies CARLA HEMSLEY. 1932–1967. Loving mother and wife, taken away too soon.

R.I.P.' There was something about the year 1967 that didn't make sense. He tried to track backwards from sixteen to the year he was born – something that he rarely thought about. He'd never been good with figures, but by his reckoning he was born in or around 1973. That was at least six years later! This woman – his mother, Carla, whom he'd held so dear – had died years before he was born. How could that possibly be? And then there were the flowers: who had put them there?

Jack kept going back to the dates, thinking perhaps he'd made a mistake and added it up wrong, but nothing made sense. He tried to think again but his brain kept slipping. He had a dreadful feeling, both physically and mentally, as if he was going to sink into the grave itself. Something precious that he'd had to hold on to – a sense of belonging, an identity – had been wrenched from him. He felt cast adrift, in the dark, and motherless. 'Daisy!' he cried, 'Daisy, come here!' His voice was shrill with panic – a cry for help from a drowning man – and it startled her. She looked up from her dad's grave where she'd been lost in contemplation. Across the cemetery she saw Jack on his knees, clutching a gravestone, his face ashen.

It took Daisy a while to understand what he was gibbering about – he wasn't making much sense. He kept pointing at the headstone and muttering about dates, photographs and his mother. She read the inscription, and as soon as she saw the name the penny dropped; the lady from the photograph – the woman Jack had assumed was his mother. Quite clearly, judging from the date she'd died, this wasn't the case. She knelt down, put her arm around him and rested her head on his shoulder. 'I'm so sorry,' she said. She knew how much this had meant to him – how much the photograph had meant to him.

'I just don't understand,' he said, not taking his eyes from the gravestone. 'It doesn't add up.'

'I know,' Daisy replied. She'd done the figures herself.

'The photograph. I mean, why would Anne leave it me if it wasn't of my mother?'

'I don't know; it doesn't make sense. Unless she was just leaving you a photograph of herself to remember her by – perhaps it was the only one she had.'

Jack felt foolish, as though he'd pinned all his hopes on something that wasn't real. 'I need a drink,' he said, getting unsteadily to his feet.

'Well, you're out of luck: the pub's closed. Besides, what you really need are answers.'

As they got up, Daisy noticed the flowers. 'Look,' she said, pointing. 'Someone's left those fairly recently.'

'Yes, but who?'

'It must be your father or sister, obviously.'

'Him? No way!' Jack snorted. He couldn't imagine his father picking or buying flowers; he didn't have a tender bone in his body.

'Well, it's got to be your sister then. This means she's still in the area!' Daisy grabbed Jack's arm and his heart leapt in hope. The feeling was fleeting, though. Daisy had voiced something that he didn't want to consider. The possibility that Anne had known about this all along, yet never told him – especially after all the times he'd pestered her – really hurt. Why would she keep it from him? If only she was still around to ask. And that was the other thing: if she *was* still around, why hadn't she been in touch? This stung even more. 'God, I wish she was still here. She'd have to tell me the truth now.'

'Well she's not, and there's only one person who *could* tell you the truth.' She didn't need to speak his name.

'That bastard won't tell me anything!' Jack replied bitterly. 'He doesn't know what the truth is; he's probably not even my father either!' Daisy pitied him: he really was a sorry and confused mess. It must be awful – not knowing who your parents are or where you came from.

'I don't see you've got any other choice but to ask him,' she said, leading him by the hand away from the grave. It was Daisy who had her arm around Jack for support as they walked out of the cemetery, as though their roles had been reversed.

They closed the cemetery gates behind them, the proper reason for their visit side-tracked. But Daisy didn't mind – unfortunately there were going to be many more days ahead when she'd be able to visit her dad's grave. Right now, she was more concerned about Jack. She gave him a big hug and said: 'Give it a go: you've got to.' He nodded, still unsure at the prospect of confronting his father; he'd given up on that years ago. 'Good luck. And ring me twice later if you can. I'll pick you up from the crossroads – we'll go for that drink.'

Jack psyched himself up on the way back home, preparing what he was going to say. This *had* gone on long enough. He'd got no choice but to have it out with his father. No wonder he hadn't wanted him going into the village all these years. The scary thing was, seeing the grave had been pure chance. What if he hadn't gone with Daisy? He'd have lived the rest of his life thinking Carla was his mother. Perhaps that would have been better: he'd have been content with that. They say ignorance is bliss, but it was the *not* knowing that gnawed away at him.

He walked through the kitchen door and headed straight down to the cellar. God, he needed a drink: for the shock, and to drum up some courage. He filled up a cider bottle and drained nearly half of it in one go. Back in the kitchen, he heard his father banging away in the loft above. Before he lost his nerve, he made his way down the hallway to the ladder. He took a deep breath and slowly ascended it.

His father was leaning out of one of the dormer windows. When Jack spoke, it disturbed him in more ways than one.

'I want a word with you.'

'Do you have to go creeping around like that?!' he snapped.

'I want to know who my mother is and what happened to her.' His voice was shaky.

His father carried on hammering. It was nothing he hadn't heard before – just not for a long, long time. Jack felt that old familiar frustration and rage bubble up inside, like when he was a child; there was nothing worse than being ignored. 'I asked you a question!' he said. His father kept on hammering – figuring that if he just ignored him he'd go away; that's how it normally worked. Jack moved closer to him, and in his mind briefly pictured pushing him out of the window and being done with it. 'OK... Who's Carla then?' he demanded, changing his tack. At the mention of the name, his father struck his thumb with the hammer and cried out in pain.

'Now look what you've gone and done!' he shouted, clearly ruffled. He made a big deal out of shaking his hand and putting his thumb in his mouth, playing for time. Meanwhile his thoughts were racing. Where had he heard that name? *He'd* never told him it ... or had he? Perhaps when he'd been drunk. He cursed his weakness. Then again, it could have been that no-good, conniving sister of his. Now he'd got to say something to shut the boy up.

He was aware that Jack was standing only a foot away from him, watching and waiting. 'Your mother, God rest her soul, died when you were young and that's all you need to know.'

'So who's Carla then?' Jack fired back, feeling he could trap him now. There was a momentary flicker again at the mention of her name, and then, just like that, his father erupted. It was like flipping a switch. He swung down from the window with the claw hammer in his hand, bending low beneath the sloping ceiling. Jack took a step back.

'She's your mother, and I don't want to hear you mentioning her name again! Now that's the end of it! No more questions!' And he barged past Jack, towards the loft hatch.

This was how he responded when he felt cornered and the noose was tightening – with silence, violence or both. Jack could sense the menace and physical threat, but he still refused to back down, spurred on by his search for the truth. Before he could stop himself, he said, 'No she's not, she died before I was born!' His father, who had his back to Jack, was not expecting this; it was like a blow to his solar plexus. How could he possibly know?

'You don't know what you're talking about. You're spouting rubbish!' he growled, without turning round. 'And I wouldn't pay attention to anything that loopy sister of yours has told you either!' And he began to climb down the ladder, still clutching his hammer.

The more distance between them, the braver Jack felt. '*She* didn't tell me! She's not loopy and it's not rubbish either! I've seen the grave myself. I know she's not my mother!'

His father couldn't believe what he was hearing. He stopped on the ladder, half in, half out of the loft. 'I warned you to stay away from the village. It's that bloody girl, isn't it, I bet, stirring up trouble, putting ideas in your head.'

Jack hated hearing him talk about Daisy; it stoked his anger further. 'It's got nothing to do with her, so don't bring her into it! It's about finding out the truth!'

'I'm warning you for the last time,' his father said, shaking with fury. Jack tensed. He was backed into a corner, and his eyes flickered to the hole of the nearest dormer window. 'I don't want to hear another word about it. Do you hear me? Don't make me come up there again, so help me God! Stay away from the village and keep your filthy little mouth shut. And keep out of my way as well if you know what's good for you. You don't have to live here, you know; you can piss off anytime you like. I don't need your help anymore.' He waved his hammer about to emphasise this, then stormed down the ladder, leaving the insults ringing in Jack's ears.

It was the reality, though; he wasn't wanted there. He was just an unpaid labourer. Once again, his father had avoided the truth and left him raging with the unfairness of it all. 'Bastard!' he shouted to the empty loft, their brief truce well and truly over.

When Jack returned to his room, angry and defeated, he went straight under his bed and got out his tin. He lifted out the photograph; the photograph that had meant so much to him, but now meant nothing, save for something to remember his sister by. He'd wanted so much for her to be his mother; she'd looked so kind. Perhaps he'd wanted it so much that he'd believed it was true regardless. He counted his money twice, slowly and carefully, to make sure he'd got it right. There was just over one thousand one hundred pounds – perhaps not quite as much as he'd hoped, but still a considerable amount of cash; more than enough.

The longer he stayed, the more this money would get eaten into; he certainly wasn't going to go grovelling back to Peasgood, that was for sure. He unfolded his map of America and ran his fingers over it. Right now, he wanted to get as far away from his father as possible, but he had to be patient; it was still too soon to talk about it with Daisy. Even *he* realised that. His father's voice rang out in his head: 'You can piss off anytime you like. I don't need your help anymore.' Well, soon he'd get his wish. Then let's see how he copes – trying to pick all those apples for his precious cider on his own.

*****

After returning from the cemetery, Daisy bathed to wash away the smells from work. The heat from the bath made her feel dizzy and light-headed, so she lay down on her bed for a while. She pulled out that week's *NME* (which had sat there untouched since Wednesday) to catch up on the latest news from the music world. With flushed cheeks and a towel round her head, she thumbed through it; it was nice to relax for a change.

The paper alerted her to the fact that The Stone Roses' latest single *She Bangs the Drums* had been released that week – something she'd totally forgotten about. She quickly turned on the radio, hoping she hadn't missed the start of the charts. She hadn't – and to her absolute joy the single *had* made it into the Top Forty. It was only at number 36, but this lowly position didn't matter to her; it was a massive breakthrough for her favourite indie band.

She recorded the event in her diary. In blue biro she wrote down the date, 'Sunday 23rd July', and the words: 'Today will go down in musical history. The Stone Roses entered the UK singles charts for the first time at No. 36 and they are going to be massive!' This made her even more excited at the prospect of seeing them live, and she flicked to the back of the notebook where the tickets were tucked. She'd decided to ask Jack if he'd go with her; it would do him good, she thought. It would do both of them good.

At this point the phone rang twice, then stopped. Daisy hadn't expected Jack to call so soon. Her mum, who'd begun to cotton on to these coded phone calls, pre-empted Daisy when it rang off. 'You haven't had any dinner yet!' Daisy smiled to herself; something she hadn't done in a long while.

They drove to The Plough at Wysall for a change, and on the way Daisy told Jack about The Stone Roses breaking into the charts. 'Wow! That's amazing,' he said, but couldn't really see what the big deal was: he had a lot more on his mind. She also said she'd got something to ask him, which *did* sound promising.

Once at the pub, Jack was pleased when Daisy ordered a pint of shandy. She seemed in an upbeat mood. He told her how his father had reacted to his questions. 'You need to get away from there, for your own good – and before something serious happens,' she said in response. Jack glanced up at her in hope, probably reading more into her words than was intended. Daisy didn't notice. 'You know that photo your sister left for you?' she said, and Jack nodded. 'Well, surely there's got to be more of them somewhere, maybe in her room – or hidden somewhere else.'

'No, it's empty; it was all cleared out when she left. My father took care of that, just like everything from the loft – burnt and gone.'

'What about your father's room? There are boxes in there.'

Jack looked puzzled for a moment; his father's room was the biggest no-go zone in the house. 'How do *you* know what's in his room?'

'Well, I sort of peeked in there when I was in your house; I was trying to find you.'

'Really?' He couldn't believe it; they'd never had chance to talk about that day.

'Yes, I went in *your* room too!' She smiled mischievously, and Jack grinned back. It was so good to see her smile again. It was a joy to be talking like this – about normal things for a change, and nothing morbid or miserable.

'So, what else did you see?' he asked, intrigued.

'I don't know … your books … oh, they're so sweet, Jack. I wish I'd kept things like that from when I was young – they looked so old.'

'They are; they were my sister's...' He trailed off, growing solemn again at the mention of her.

Daisy put her hand on his as he took a long gulp of cider. 'Anyway, you've got to look in your father's room. God knows what he might have hidden in there.'

'I know, that's what worries me.' Jack's face screwed up at the thought of it. 'And I don't see how it's possible; he's always there – he never goes anywhere.'

'You've just got to bide your time. There'll be an opportunity, and when it comes up you've just got to take it – you'll see!' Daisy was right, as usual. One did come up – and much sooner than Jack expected.

CHAPTER 33

Mr Spence

'Are you OK doing this, Daisy?' Jack asked. 'You know, going into town and that. We don't have to.' Her face was pale and puffy, as if she'd had a bad night. It was Monday morning and they were on the way to Loughborough in her van.

'Yes, I'm just feeling a bit peaky that's all. I didn't get much sleep last night, I kept feeling like I was going to be sick; it just sort of came on in the night.'

They'd decided to have a day out in town, partly so Jack could get away from home for the day, still pretending he was at work, and partly so he could get his bike fixed up. Daisy felt so sorry for him having to walk everywhere again. She knew of a second-hand bike shop that also did repairs. The owner, Mr Spence, was an old friend of her dad's and would probably do it at a reduced price. Today would also be a good opportunity for Jack to get his hair cut at a proper barber's; something that Daisy had suggested and Jack was dreading. He was looking forward to it about as much as most people look forward to root canal surgery.

As for Daisy, she felt she could do with a bit of 'retail therapy'. Some benevolent relatives had expressed their condolences to their poor bereaved nieces and granddaughters with cards that had contained more than words of sympathy; most with an accompanying PS along the lines of 'A little something to cheer you up'.

'Well, only if you're sure,' Jack said.

'Yes, it's fine, honestly. It's good to be busy. It's nice just to be getting out and trying to get back to normal a bit. I'm looking forward to going back to college, believe it or not … and I never thought I'd say that! It'll be good to catch up with Claire again… I might give her a ring this week actually – it's been ages.'

Jack was slightly put out by this and shifted in his seat. It wasn't just the reminder that she had another life without him, but more the fact that going back to college didn't exactly fit in with his plans. What about America? It was like when she'd asked him about that concert the previous night. He'd agreed, after a fashion, because she'd been so excited about it. And what with her father getting the tickets for her as well … he didn't want to let her down again; he'd promised not to. He hadn't envisaged sticking around that long, though – it was weeks away yet – and this was a problem that had kept him awake most of the night too.

They parked on the outskirts of town, near the bingo hall and as close to the bike shop as possible. Jack pulled the remaining two-thirds of his broken bike out of the van. It had lain in a ditch, hidden in the undergrowth, since the day of the accident and was in a sorry state. He'd removed the buckled front wheel that morning and buried it, deep in the long grasses behind the top orchard.

Jack pushed the bike on its back wheel as they made the short walk down the street. The bike shop was the last in the row, with many bikes lined up outside, both new and old. The sign above the shop read 'E. Spence and Sons' – and proudly declared it had been established for twenty-five years. The shop was run by a kindly chap, in his sixties, called Eric Spence. Daisy's family had always used the shop for repairs and purchases, so had visited it most birthdays and Christmases – or when the girls had grown out of their bikes. Despite the 'and Sons', Daisy couldn't ever recall seeing anyone except Eric, leading her to the conclusion that he was one of the sons himself.

A bell dinged when they entered. Mr Spence recognised Daisy straightaway – even though it must have been two years since she'd been in. 'Aah, Lily, isn't it?' he greeted her. He hadn't changed a bit; still wearing the same old, oil-stained, blue boiler suit and flat cap, and still getting their names wrong.

'No, Daisy,' she said, blushing.

'Oh, that's right. I always get you two muddled up, yer looking so grown up now.' Daisy blushed further. She could remember going in as a freckly little girl and demanding Grifters and Tomahawks, rather than conventional girly bikes. It had always made Mr Spence chuckle. 'And you are?' he said, leaning across.

'Er, Jack.' He was surprised at this stranger taking such an interest.

'The boyfriend, eh?' he said, giving him a cheeky wink and Daisy a twinkly-eyed smile. This was how he worked: he could make anyone feel at ease. 'And what 'ave we got here then, Jack? 'Alf a bike by the looks of it! Ooh, she's a beauty, though, an old Raleigh. Local. I like that. You don't see many of these anymore. Looks like she's 'ad a bit of a prang, though. An accident?' He always referred to bikes as females – as you would a boat.

'Erm, you could say that,' said Daisy, and looked at Jack.

'Still, I should be able to sort 'er out. These forks just

need a tweak – you're gonna need a new wheel and maybe a mudguard. You 'aven't still got the old wheel, 'ave yer?'

'No,' said Jack. 'It's erm…'

'Tatered?' Mr Spence finished for him. This was an East Midlands term, short for potatoed, meaning 'done in' or 'knackered'. 'Well, that's OK; you'd be surprised at what I've got out back. Yep, leave it wi' me; should be done in a few hours or so. I've got nowt else on. Could do with some oil as well, we'll 'ave 'er right as rain in no time. 'Ow is the old man anyway, Lil– sorry, Daisy. Still making them amps?' There was a sudden and unexpected silence. Jack looked at Daisy, then down at his feet.

This is going to happen, thought Daisy – I'm going to have to get used to this. She took a deep breath. 'I'm afraid he … he passed away recently.'

There was another awkward silence as Mr Spence put his hand on Daisy's shoulder, leaning heavily on the counter with his other arm. He looked as if he'd been slapped. She could smell a combination of oil and some kind of cleaning alcohol on his hands. 'Oh, my darlin'. I 'ad no idea; I'm so sorry – me and me big mouth running away wi' me as usual. I don't believe it… When?'

'Just over two weeks ago.'

'Just over two weeks ago, you say … well I'll be … and 'ere you are out and about, getting a bike fixed for yer laddie here. Yer made of sterner stuff then I am, ducky, that's for sure, 'ats off to yer.' He paused again. 'Yep, 'e were one of the good uns, your old man… I remember when my Mikey was into 'is music thing; thought 'e was gonna be a big rock star on *Top of The Pops* 'e did. Well your dad sorted 'im out proper; cost price, free leads, the lot, even set it all up for 'im. Nothing was too much trouble. Yep, 'e was one of the good uns…' He trailed off. 'Anyway, yep, give us a couple of hours, we'll get 'er sorted.'

And he shuffled off with the bike, still muttering 'Well, I'll be,' as if he couldn't quite believe it.

Jack smiled supportively at Daisy and shrugged. He took her hand and led her out of the shop. The bell dinged again as they left and they were back on the pavement outside. 'So, what now?' he asked, studying her face; he didn't know how she was going to react after that. She was still looking a bit pale, but otherwise OK – as Mr Spence had said, she was made of stern stuff.

'Well, we've only got a couple of hours, so maybe get the haircut out of the way first in case there's a queue.' Jack pulled a face at this; he'd been hoping that she'd forgotten. 'And then the shops, I think. Grandma gave me and Lily fifty quid each, bless her. So, The Left Legged Pineapple next; it's been too long and my wanted list is piling up! Then maybe some clothes shops as well – do you need anything?'

'Er no, I'm trying to watch my money actually; I've got to be careful now – what with losing my job. Plus, I've got my bike to pay for … *and* a haircut,' he added, thinking who pays for a haircut?

'Yes of course, poor you. Well, we'll see – I might be able to treat you to that.'

As Jack had expected, it was, without doubt, one of the most humiliating experiences of his life – not *the* worst, but certainly in the top five. Daisy dragged him in like a sulky child, even instructing the barber what he wanted done as Jack refused to speak to him. He sat and wriggled, twitched and squirmed throughout as if he actually *was* in a dentist's chair.

He found the whole thing totally invasive – the touch of a stranger's fingers, the smell of his cheap cologne, the whistle of him breathing through his nose and the stink of his coffee breath. The barber, who was of Mediterranean descent, even lost his rag a couple of times – tutting at Jack to keep still and roughly tilting his head this way and that. Daisy didn't know whether to laugh or to be genuinely concerned.

The ordeal was over, and the only thing to be thankful for was that there weren't more people there to witness the sorry spectacle. Daisy paid the barber, whilst Jack fled to the sanctuary of the street. She found him rubbing at his neck and staring at his reflection in a shop window, a vengeful look on his face. The sadistic bastard had totally ignored what Daisy had said and cut it far too short, making his ears appear to stick out – nothing like how Anne would have cut it; she knew how he liked it. Daisy felt a bit sorry for him. She'd had no idea he was going to react like that, and didn't know if she should apologise. At least he managed to mutter thanks to her for paying.

After an hour or so of being dragged round the shops (with Jack spending most of his time staring into shop mirrors at his hated new haircut), Daisy coerced him into a quick visit to the Job Centre. He refused to sit at one of the desks with everyone else, but stood next to her and peered noncommittally at all the cards in the windows. Daisy pointed out a few that looked suitable and were also either local or on a bus route. Jack didn't appear to show any interest. He'd no intention of getting another job whatsoever. Privately, the thought of working somewhere else – in a totally new environment – absolutely terrified him. In the end Daisy gave up and they headed back to the bike shop.

Mr. Spence was on his lunch break when they went in, sitting at his counter with his feet up, clutching a cheese sandwich in one of his swarf-stained hands and reading the newspaper. He looked up and smiled as if he'd been expecting them. "Ello, you two, been doing some shopping, 'ave we?' he asked, indicating Daisy's bags. Daisy looked down guiltily. Why did she feel so guilty all the time? 'Well, don't blame yer, don't blame yer at all. Cheer you up a bit. Short back and sides, eh, Jack?' He never shut up, but in a nice way. Jack grimaced, still smarting from his drastic chop. 'Well, I'll just go and get 'er, won't be a minute!' And he hobbled off, spryly enough, but clutching the base of his back.

He returned some moments later with a satisfied smile and pushing what appeared to be a brand new bike. Daisy and Jack looked at each other in puzzlement. 'There she is!' he announced. 'Good as new!'

'Mr Spence, sorry, but this isn't Jack's bike!' said Daisy.

'Oh that's 'er all right; it's amazing what yer can do with a bit o' polish, an old rag and some chrome cleaner!'

˙ They inspected the bike more closely and, sure enough, it *was* Jack's. They were both speechless. The frame was black and polished and the chrome of the wheels shone and gleamed. The cogs too, formerly a dull, rusty brown, glistened blackly with oil. The front forks were back in position and it had a new front mudguard and wheel. Mr Spence had well and truly weaved his magic. It made Jack gulp in apprehension at how much it was going to cost; he'd only brought thirty quid.

'Yep, you need to look after a bike like this. Yer don't see many of 'em about anymore!' Mr Spence said, whipping out an old rag from his back pocket and giving the bike one last rub.

'Mr Spence…' began Daisy.

'Call me Eric, darlin', please,' he interrupted.

'Eric, it's amazing – but how much do we owe you?' she said, also concerned.

'Not a bean.'

'But Mr Spence … Eric, we can't possibly accept that. You've got to let us pay you!'

'No! Yer money's no good to me, so you can just put it

back in yer pocket – you don't say a lot, do yer, sonny!' he said, giving Jack another wink.

'But…' Daisy tried again, but he cut her off.

'No, look at it as returning a favour. It's only a wheel that's been 'anging round out back for years – I'm pleased to find an 'ome for it! An' a bit o' spit 'n' polish too, like. And as I said before, your old man were one of the good uns. 'e looked after *my* son and I'm just sorry for your loss is all … an' glad to be of some 'elp, so be on your way both of yer and I won't 'ear another word about it – and send my condolences to yer mother as well, God bless 'er, *and* that sister of yours!'

And that was that. They muttered their thanks, then wheeled the bike out of the shop in dumbfounded silence. Out on the street, the refurbished bike sparkled in the midday sun. They were both shocked at Mr Spence's generosity. Jack was also starting to realise that Daisy was a pretty useful person to know – and her old man; it made him feel even worse about all those resentful thoughts he'd had about him.

They walked the bike to the van and stuck it (more carefully) in the back. Jack couldn't wait to try it out. They covered it with a mat so it wasn't on show, then slid the side door closed. 'I don't know about you, but I feel like a drink!' exclaimed Jack, suddenly cheering up.

'You always feel like a drink.'

'Well, you know – I feel like celebrating.' Daisy shot him a look. Jack immediately cottoned on and downgraded his enthusiasm. 'Not celebrating. I mean – you know, getting the bike fixed and that … for free.'

'I know. He's one in a million, isn't he?' she said, aware that she was being a party pooper. But she really didn't fancy a drink: she was feeling a bit groggy again. Perhaps she needed something to eat as she hadn't had any breakfast. 'I *am* hungry – so we could have a bite to eat at the Three Nuns, I suppose.'

Jack's face lit up. 'OK, my shout. I'd have spent it on the bike anyway!' he said; and they locked the van.

'Does that mean I'm forgiven then?' Daisy asked on the way to the pub, tousling his newly cropped hair.

Daisy tried her best to eat her lunch, she really did, but only managed to get halfway through it before she had to dash to the toilet. Once there, she brought up what she'd just eaten, which was a shame because she'd been genuinely hungry. When she came back to the table she looked dreadful – clammy and washed out, her eyes watery. She wiped them with a tissue and picked up her glass of lemonade to get rid of the foul taste in her mouth. 'God, I feel dreadful. I'm starting to think I've got food poisoning or something from that buffet stuff that's been hanging around. I've been picking at it all weekend. Have *you* been OK? You had some of it the other night.'

'Yes, fine,' he replied, emphasising the fact by helping himself to her leftover lunch.

'Well, they do say it can take up to forty-eight hours. Do you mind if we just go?' She pushed her plate away: it was making her feel ill looking at it. Jack looked disappointed; he'd been looking forward to another pint. 'I'm really sorry, Jack – I didn't mean to ruin our day out.'

'Don't worry – it's not your fault. Perhaps you just need some fresh air.'

'Yes, maybe,' Daisy replied, gathering up her bags, glad to be leaving the thick, smoky atmosphere. Jack picked up her lemonade and drained that too. She watched him, perturbed. 'You shouldn't do that; you might catch it!'

'Not me, I'm invincible!' he announced with a swagger. The cider had gone to his head. God, this beats being at work, he thought.

It was a relief for Daisy to be outside again and it instantly made her feel a little better – but not better enough that she didn't want to crawl back into bed. 'Thanks for lunch. I just wish I could have eaten more of it.'

'That's OK. What do you want to do now?'

'Can we just go home? I think I need my bed. I won't be much fun like this.'

Jack was crestfallen. He'd been expecting to spend the whole day with her, but now the familiar, aching hours of waiting until he could go home stretched out before him. He reminded himself to consider her feelings. 'Well, at least we got the bike fixed I suppose.'

They were both quiet in the van on the way back. Daisy was trying not to give in to the queasiness that was building again, whilst Jack was preoccupied with what he was going to do with the rest of the afternoon. It was the same old depressing dilemma; he was sick of living like this. Why couldn't he go back to Daisy's like a normal boyfriend? Why did everything have to be so difficult? It made him think of America again, and going away together to a place where they didn't have to sneak around and stay out of people's way.

He was actually on the verge of bringing it up, but chickened out at the last minute. 'Daisy?'

'Yes?'

'Er, do you think I'll be able to come back to your house again…? You know, not today – I mean, soon.'

'God, yes. 'I wish you *could* come back today: you could look after me and make me hot drinks and things.'

'I'd like that,' he said sadly, picturing her room.

'Same here, although I'd probably only throw up over you!' As she said this, a fresh wave of nausea washed over her, and she had to wind down the window and stick her head out for a bit. When her stomach had stopped churning, she sat back again but kept the window open. 'Sorry about that …

where was I…? Oh yes, soon. We'll have to arrange it again. I'll speak to Mum – but give it a week or so, when things have died down a bit. It's only a few days since Dad's funeral after all.'

By now, they were driving down Rempstone hill and approaching the crossroads. 'Do you want me to drop you at the top of the hill near home?' Daisy asked.

'No, I can't. He thinks I'm at work, remember.'

'Oh no, I'd forgotten all about that. God, you poor thing. What are you going to do? Are you going to go home and tell him? You can't just keep wandering the countryside every day for the rest of your life!'

'Yes, I will… It's just that we're not really speaking at the minute – after yesterday and everything.'

'Well, I don't blame you – but you really need to get that sorted as well, you know, get to the bottom of it one way or another.'

Easier said than done, he thought; it wasn't as if he hadn't tried. On the spur of the moment, he said, 'Here, drop me at the crossroads. I think I'll go for a ride – try out the new bike.' Daisy indicated, turned right and pulled over near the phone box. Jack got the bike out of the side of the van and slid the door closed again. 'Will I see you later?' he said, more in hope than anything else.

'I'll have to see how I feel. I'm just going to go to bed for a bit. If I'm feeling better later, I'll give you a ring.' Jack lingered by the van, sitting astride his shiny bike and scuffing his boot on the ground. Her heart went out to him. 'I'm really sorry again about today.' He gave her his best smile. 'I won't kiss you; I don't want you to get it.' And she blew him a kiss, adding, 'I love you.'

'Yes, you too.'

'Hey, I might even start work on another tape for you this

afternoon if I feel up to it. You must be getting bored of the old one by now!' she said as she drove off.

'So, which way then, Jack?' he said aloud to himself. He decided to head towards Wysall again, but this time keep on going and explore some new places. Lord knows he'd got plenty of time on his hands. He set off, and the bike felt amazing. The tyres were fully pumped up, and because the chain was oiled and greased, once Jack had built up speed it went into third gear for the first time. It was kind of therapeutic – cycling along in no particular rush, the wind in his hair and nothing but his thoughts for company. Soon his mind began to wander and race: about America, about Daisy and about his mother.

If Anne was around, he was sure she'd put him out of his misery. Actually, looking back to the time before she left, it had felt as if she was on the verge of it; as if she had wanted to tell him something. And what about those flowers on the grave? Could she really still be in the area? It itched at him like a wound that wouldn't heal – the fact that she'd never said goodbye. Why hadn't she contacted him to give him an address? Probably because she didn't want to risk *him* finding out where she was. He'd only try and hunt her down, to keep her prisoner again, waiting on him hand and foot – no, she was better off keeping quiet. But there was another dilemma: if he went away himself, how would they ever contact each other again?

And then there was Daisy – dear, darling Daisy; his Maid Marian, his funfair – all candy floss, helter-skelter and ghost train. Before he'd met her, he'd felt as though he was just waiting for something to happen. Now he couldn't imagine life without her. And he certainly couldn't contemplate going to America without her.

Jack was still desperately hanging on to that post-coital pledge as gospel – the one she'd made in sleepy haste that crazy afternoon in bed, all those weeks ago. But even he wasn't entirely convinced by its sincerity now. So much had happened. That's why it was so hard to ask her: he wanted affirmation but was scared he wouldn't like the answer. It was driving him crazy, but so was staying at home with all the loose ends that it seemed would never be tied up. He felt as if he was ready to move on, but he couldn't do it without Daisy.

Jack rode and rode with all these thoughts going through his head, smoothly using the bicycle gears without even thinking about it. It wasn't long before he reached Wysall, and he cycled straight through to uncharted territory. He followed the road for miles, past the east entrance to Bunny Wood, until he came to a crossroads. It appeared like an augury in the middle of nowhere, and he quickly came to a halt. He was faced with three choices: turn left to go back home, go straight on towards Bradmore or turn right towards Keyworth. The latter two would definitely kill a lot more time *and* take him to unknown places – which, after all, was his original plan. 'Which way, Jack?' he said to himself again.

Then he made a surprising decision that would prove to be significant. He was sick of living a lie and keeping out of his father's way; all the wasted days and hours whilst he pretended he was at work. Well, no more. He was going to go straight home and tell his father about his job. Sod it: he was still getting his board money, wasn't he?

Jack took the left turn and headed down a small lane. After about a mile or so, the lane came to an end when it joined the main road. There was the smell of bonfires in the air. He turned left again to commence the gradually more gruesome climb of Bunny Hill. Never before had he tackled it from this side on a bike: it was pure torture, and before long he had to get off and walk.

He soon came across the source of the smoke: the air

was thick with it, making him cough and his eyes smart. The large, sloping field on his left that bordered Bunny Wood, and not so long ago had been littered with hay bales, was now devoid of them. They'd been replaced with small clumps of hazy smouldering fires – as if the bales had spontaneously combusted. Through the thick fog he saw dark shapes of men in hats with cloths over their faces, circling the field with sticks like sinister shepherds.

Jack scurried past with his head down, pushing his bike for what seemed like hours; the arduous, unforgiving slope went on forever. By the time he reached the main entrance to Bunny Wood, his throat was parched and his back was killing him. Fortunately the smoke had cleared, which he saw as a good reason to get back on his bike. He finally reached the plateau, the road levelling out before sloping rapidly downhill again. He freewheeled the rest of the way home, resting his aching legs. It felt like heaven.

Jack's attention turned to his father. He listened out for sounds of him on the roof, but there weren't any. Must be having a late lunch, he thought, which made him wonder what time it was. This is it then, he said to himself as he cycled up the lane. Imagine what he's going to think – me turning up at this time of the day with a new haircut and on Anne's bike.

He braced himself for the challenge, but when he turned into the drive, his father's van wasn't there. This was unexpected. Or perhaps his father often went out during the day? He barely ever went out in the evenings or if Jack was at home – almost as if he didn't want to leave him on his own in the house. Jack could probably count on one hand the times that this had happened. He parked his bike in full view under the kitchen window anyhow, as if he was setting out his stall of things to come.

Chapter 34

Can't see the Wood for the Trees

As Jack rounded the corner to the back door, it was dawning on him that this could be just the opportunity he'd been waiting for – an empty house. He didn't know how long his father had been gone or how soon he'd be back, but right now he'd been given some precious minutes alone to investigate – and that could be all he needed. He speeded up, not wanting to waste a single second.

An overwhelming sense of déjà vu washed over him when he tried the door; but although it was locked, this time he had the means to change the outcome. It was a satisfying feeling as he used his secret key for the first time. The fact that his father had locked the door further enhanced the creeping suspicion that he'd got something to hide – something probably hidden in his bedroom; the forbidden place.

He'd never actually *wanted* to go in there – not since he was little anyway: it reminded him of his father too much, even emitting his smell into the corridor from time to time. Jack took a deep breath and turned the handle, pushing the door open slowly. The air that hit him was stale, musty and rank, and did indeed reek of his father; as if the room was one giant lung breathing him in and then exhaling him again. God only knew when the bedclothes had last been washed or the windows had been opened; probably not since Anne had left. It made Jack feel queasy and loath to touch anything, lest some of his father should rub off on him.

There were boxes in stacks everywhere, clothes and old furniture too; it was a hoarder's room. Everything was covered in dust as if it hadn't been moved in years. Jack didn't know where to start. He didn't want to go disturbing anything or leaving fingerprints and tell-tale marks everywhere. Where would I hide something I didn't want anyone to see? he thought. He got on his hands and knees, grimacing at the tackiness of the carpet, and lifted the bedcover with his thumb and forefinger. This unleashed a fresh wave of dust, making him sneeze and his eyes itch as he peered underneath.

There must have been at least half a dozen more boxes and bags crammed under there. Jesus, what had he got in them all? Nearest, he noticed the suitcase from the loft that had contained his mother's wedding dress. Damn! His sister's mother's wedding dress; he still hadn't got used to that yet. Next to the suitcase, a bit further in, was a wooden drawer that caught his eye. It was covered, inside and out, with flowery print wallpaper. But more noticeable still it wasn't just covered in thick dust like the rest, but also camouflaged in a network of cobwebs… Cobwebs? The loft! This must have been brought down and hidden along with the suitcase.

Jack's pulse quickened as he pulled it out, wincing at the dust it kicked up. The drawer was neatly stuffed with all manner of documents – folders, envelopes, paper wallets and what looked like cards. His mind boggled at the secrets they could contain and also at the urgency of the situation; part of him wanted to pick the drawer up and run with it to his room. He frantically brushed the cobwebs aside and, kneeling on the filthy bedroom floor, began to pull out various envelopes and bits of paper.

His initial search didn't yield anything of major significance – none of it made much sense – just deeds to the house, solicitor's letters and bills. He kept on going, and things got a bit more interesting. There were various medical documents with Carla's name on, mainly concerning hospital appointments. Then he found a battered, brown envelope containing a bunch of yellowing certificates. They had old-fashioned writing and signatures on them. The first was a certificate of death, confirming that Carla Hemsley did indeed die in 1967. Cause of death: cervical cancer. There were two signatures, one of which was his father's. So it was true – that part anyway.

He looked at the next document. This was a birth certificate. Surely he must be on the threshold of something now. Again it belonged to Carla. He kept thumbing through the papers. The next, again, was old and fragile but was also (somewhat predictably) his father's birth certificate. Where the hell were his and Anne's? Agonisingly, the last one turned out to be a marriage certificate for his father and Carla. There was nothing more, and he felt bitterly disappointed – cheated and let down.

After shoving the envelope back, Jack continued his search with renewed haste. There were wedding cards, engagement cards, baby congratulations cards … dozens and dozens of them. He picked some out at random, in the vain hope that they might give up some answers, but they all related to either his father and Carla or to Anne. On further perusal there were even a handful of birthday cards: a rare sight indeed. So … they must have celebrated birthdays once upon a time, he thought, or at least Carla must have done. They were all for Anne, though, and petered out after the age of four. Needless to say, none of them were for Jack. Where were *his* baby cards? Where were *his* birthday cards?

He carried on rifling through the drawer until, unexpectedly, he came across two shiny black and yellow wallets. They were tucked away, hidden right at the back. Jack yanked them out and opened them. Inside, to his amazement, were dozens of photographs. He had *never* seen any photos in the house before, save for the one that his sister had left him. Daisy was right; the bastard *had* been hiding something.

Beginning to look through them, he was spellbound. The first wallet contained pictures of his father and Carla, all black and white, both of them looking impossibly young and fresh faced. It was shocking seeing his father like that, and smiling too. It was also disturbing to note how much of a resemblance he'd had to Jack when he'd been younger. He was a caricature now, practically a gargoyle, of his former self. As for Carla, she looked so healthy – vivacious, full of face; so different from the photo he had of her.

They always seemed to be outside pubs, laughing and joking, or sitting in old-fashioned sports cars. Their clothes were also old-fashioned, she in high-necked dresses and scarves or short-sleeved sweaters, and he with slicked back hair, wearing suits. It was like looking through a magical window into the past. They looked so happy together; and there was no doubt that the man was his father. This dusty box from the loft had answered two questions, but what about the big one? The one he really needed the answer to.

Jack started flipping the photos over to see if there was any writing on the back. There was the odd bit, in the same handwriting as *his* photo, but more humorous comments or place names than anything else. There was one actual date, but it related to the house; on the back of a photo of his father holding a spade, it said 'Digging for Victory –'62'. Bizarrely, he was surrounded by chickens.

Jack reluctantly put the photographs back and moved onto the next wallet. These were even more astounding as there were some of Anne, mainly as a toddler, and some were in colour. Looking at them made him feel happy and sad at the same time. She always seemed to be on her own, except for a few with her mother when she was very little. There was one particularly touching image that showed her in the snow, giggling and clutching a basket full of shiny chocolate eggs. There were footprints all about her, and the caption on the back read 'Frozen Eggs!'

As he went through the rest of the pictures, Jack realised there didn't appear to be any of her over the age of about four again. There was something about this that nagged at him: it was as if her childhood had just stopped. Perhaps that was when Carla first fell ill. This also made the photo Anne had left him more of a curiosity. Where had she got it from? Had she got more like it – all the in-between ones? Had she seen these photos too? Not being able to ask her drove him mad. Even more frustrating was that there were none of him whatsoever – not a single one.

After rummaging through the rest of the drawer in increasing desperation, Jack was still no closer to his or his mother's true identity. He'd been through every wallet and envelope, shaking them to make sure there was nothing trapped inside. In the end he'd searched the entire drawer twice, but to no avail. He even turned it upside down, giving it a good shake too, as if in a last ditch attempt he could bully it into relinquishing something – anything at all. As he did so, a single colour photograph fluttered to the floor. It had been trapped between the wallpaper lining and the inside of the drawer. Jack picked it up with trembling fingers.

It was of Anne, an older Anne. She was wearing a red dressing gown and standing next to a Christmas tree with blurry, coloured fairy lights. At her feet, to Jack's utter joy, was a little baby, propped up and surrounded by presents and wrapping paper. He melted inside at finally finding a photograph of himself as a child; maybe even taken by his mother – proof that someone had actually cared that he existed. It was worth all the previous disappointment. He turned it over, his heart thudding, and his mouth dry. In the same handwriting as before, Carla's handwriting, it said simply 'Anne's first Christmas'.

He had that same, familiar, pit of the stomach sinking feeling that he'd had at the cemetery. Surely this had to be a mistake! Surely it was meant to say 'Jack's first Christmas'. It didn't make sense. If this was Anne's first Christmas and *she* was the baby, then who the hell was that older girl – lurking by the Christmas tree like the ghost of Christmas past? He turned the photo back over and inspected the girl more closely. Wait a minute, what was he thinking? If that was him as a baby, that couldn't be Anne – she'd have been at least twice that age. This girl was maybe six or seven. It was definitely the same girl as in the Carla photograph, which meant – what? That she wasn't Anne either! As he stared at her, the hair on the back of his neck stood up and her face jumped towards him in stages – closer and closer – accompanied by those piercing, orchestral stabbing sounds from the shower scene in *Psycho*.

Just then, he heard the dreaded crunch of gravel on the drive. 'Oh shit!' he cried out loud. It was his father! Why now? Why did he have to come back now? Jack began shoving everything into the drawer in terror – but made a split-second decision to stuff the photo wallets into his back pockets instead of replacing them. He wasn't relinquishing *them* – not yet – not after what he'd discovered; he needed more time. It was a risk he was willing to take. He shoved the drawer back under the bed before darting for the door.

After hiding the photo wallets under his bed covers, Jack sat with his chest heaving and his forehead clammy with sweat. He cocked an ear to listen. In the corridor he heard his father march straight down the hallway, then stop outside his own bedroom door. There was a pause before he opened it, then it closed a few seconds later. To Jack's growing alarm, his father came and stood outside *his* room; he could see the dark shape of his feet under the gap in the door. Jack stared at the door handle, expecting it to turn, his face riddled with guilt.

He held his breath, but true to form his father didn't come in – he just banged on the door instead. Jack didn't answer, hoping he'd go away. And so he banged again, harder. 'What?' called Jack, trying his best to sound normal.

'How did you get in?' his father said through the door. It was the first time they'd spoken since the loft incident. *Shit*, thought Jack – he'd left the door unlocked. If he'd locked it again he could have said 'through a window', but it was too late for that now.

'What do you mean?' he replied, stalling for time.

'You know damn well what I mean! How did you get in the house? The door was locked!'

'No it wasn't!' said Jack. It was *his* turn now to play dumb – just like that day when he'd been locked out. He'd deny everything and let the old bugger think he was going mad – give him a dose of his own medicine.

It appeared to be working, as there was a pause whilst his father considered this. *Had* he locked it? He wasn't so sure, and he shook his head, trying to remember. He was positive he had: he'd done it deliberately. 'Why aren't you at work?' he demanded. It was the dreaded question, and now was the time for Jack to tell the truth. When it came to it, though, he just couldn't do it.

'I was ill, so I got sent home. You can't work with food when you're sick, you see – food poisoning and all that.' An idea borrowed from Daisy. His father's silence suggested that he'd bought the excuse.

'And what are you doing with that bike?' he said, determined to find Jack guilty of something.

This was starting to feel like Twenty Questions. Now that the initial fear of being caught out was abating, he wanted to look at the photographs again. 'It was Anne's. I got it fixed up.'

'I know whose it is! Where did you get it from?'

'It was in the shed!' Jack shouted back.

'Well, you had no right. You can just put it back where it came from.' And with that, he stomped off. No right? thought Jack; it was just sitting there gathering rust. His father was probably just jealous at how it had been fixed up. He had no intention of putting it back.

When Jack was sure that his father had gone, he fished the photos back out. He studied them, absorbed, for half an hour or so and tried to sort them into some kind of order. He kept returning to the one that he'd found separate, as if it had been forgotten about – or more likely deliberately hidden. It stood out from the rest as it was the only one showing two children. That girl by the tree haunted him. He pulled out his tin to compare the photo with the one Anne had left him; it looked like the same girl, but a couple of years earlier. Who the hell was she? Some cousin of Anne's on Carla's side that he didn't know about? A step-sister, maybe? The idea seemed preposterous: why weren't there any more photos of her? Why hadn't she been mentioned? He needed to get them to Daisy – and fast. *She'd* be able to figure it out; perhaps she could see something that he couldn't. It was like that old expression: 'can't see the wood for the trees'.

Before he left, Jack took a couple of photos of his father (one with Carla) out of the first wallet and stuck them in with the pictures of Anne; they might come in handy. The rest he didn't need at the moment, so he stuck the wallet back in his tin and replaced it under the floor. He slipped out of his bedroom window, ducked under the kitchen window to retrieve his bike, and pushed it stealthily down the drive.

As Jack whizzed down the hill, there was smoke drifting across the road from the field that surrounded the spinney; they'd been burning the stubble here as well. It seemed as if the whole countryside was on fire today, he thought, closing his eyes and mouth as he cycled through the smoke. He realised that he liked the smell of it, though; there was something evocative and autumnal about it.

*****

Daisy wasn't totally enamoured with being dragged away from her bed, but she figured it had to be for something important; Jack wasn't in the habit of calling for the sake of it. She'd been unable to sleep anyway. When she pulled up to the phone box he was looking agitated, and clutching a photograph wallet in his hand. Maybe he'd found what he was looking for. He got in the van and she kissed him on the cheek and asked if he was OK.

'I'm not sure,' Jack replied, and passed her the wallet.

Daisy flicked through the photographs in silence, not seeing anything out of the ordinary at first. There were about a dozen photos of what was presumably his sister when she was little. She looked really sweet. There were also a couple of his father when he was much younger – you could see the resemblance to Jack straightaway. He didn't look anything like that bearded ogre she'd encountered on the hill. Well, at least that answered one thing, she thought. Jack let her carry on looking without saying anything, not wanting to influence her in any way, leaving her to draw her own conclusions.

When she got to the photo of the two children and the Christmas tree she stopped. After studying it for a few seconds, she looked at Jack with raised eyebrows. It gave him that creepy feeling again and the hairs on his arm stood on end. 'Look at the writing on the back,' he said, prompting her for the first time.

She flipped over the photo and read what it said: 'Anne's first Christmas'. She repeated it out loud, and this time a frown came over her face. Something didn't add up, but she couldn't quite put her finger on it. 'Wait a minute,' she said. 'Where's that photograph of Anne and your mother?'

'You mean *Carla*?' he replied sarcastically; the pressure taking its toll, making him fractious.

'Yes, sorry, Carla.'

'It's in there somewhere, further down.' She quickly thumbed through them until she found it. It stood out as it was one of the few colour ones. Holding it next to the Christmas photo, she studied them both hard. Then she flicked through some of the photos again, stopping at some and flipping others over to see if there was any more writing on them. He was dying to know what she was thinking, and after a while he couldn't take it anymore. 'What?' he cried 'What are you thinking?' She was thinking something all right; something terrible – possibly too terrible to comprehend – but she wasn't willing to voice it yet, not until she'd figured it out properly herself.

'I'm thinking I need to get these laid out,' she said; and Jack sighed in frustration. 'It's a shame the pub's not open.'

'Yes, you're right there, I'm dying for a drink!'

'No, not 'cause I want a drink! Just so we can lay them out on a table properly… Wait, I've got an idea.' She tucked the photos between her legs and started the engine. 'Get on your bike and follow me!'

Jack pedalled along behind the van, trying to keep up whilst wondering where the hell she was going. She drove about halfway down the lay-by, then pulled up behind some tall hedges and got out. As Jack caught up, she was opening the side door. She waited until he'd dismounted before saying, 'Come on, we're going in the back.' He propped his bike against the van and followed her inside.

Jack had never been in the back of the van before, not properly, and it was surprisingly spacious. Once he was in, she gestured for him to close the door. 'So they don't blow away,' she said, holding up the photo wallet. He came and sat next to her – finally cottoning on to what she was thinking as she began to place the photos on the floor in front of her. With a clearer head than he, she was able to sort them into a rough chronological order a lot more efficiently than he had done. Jack was too attached to them; he lived each photograph as if it was a whole newly discovered world.

Daisy carefully laid them out using the growing Anne as a guide. The Christmas photo and the photo that Jack's sister had given him were the last two to be put down. Jack noticed that her hands were shaking slightly. She braced herself, taking a deep breath before speaking. 'Have you noticed that there aren't really any photos of Anne over the age of about four?'

'Yes, I had sort of – except for the original one she left me. That's why I thought she was the girl next to the tree at first in the one that was hidden. She looks just like her, only a bit younger.'

'When you say "hidden", how do you mean?'

'Well, the Christmas one,' he said, pointing to it. 'It only fell out when I shook the drawer.'

'That would make even more sense then,' said Daisy, as if her worst fears were being realised.

'What would make even more sense? Tell me, Daisy! I need to know!'

'How old do you think your sister is? I mean, really – if you had to be specific.'

'I don't know. Like I said before, maybe late twenties?'

'That's not specific.'

'Well, I don't know. I've explained to you about the birthdays and that, so it's hard for me!' he protested.

'I know, and I'm sorry – but it's important. Let's say she's twenty-eight, that's what you said before. Does that sound reasonable?'

'Yes, I guess so.'

'Right, let's work it out. If she was twenty-eight now, she'd be born when?'

'Don't look at me,' said Jack. He couldn't work things out at the best of times, never mind under duress.

'I'm not, I'm just trying to work it out myself,' she said.

'That means she'd have been born in or around 1961. Is that right? Yes,' she confirmed to herself. Jack shrugged. 'Well, how do you explain this then?' she said, holding up the original Carla and Anne photo. Jack looked at the photo, then back at her, not quite seeing what she was getting at. 'Carla died in 1967! We've seen her grave. And she may look ill in this photo, but she's not at death's door, so I reckon this was taken a little while before she died. Which means Anne would have only been about five or six then, and the girl in this photo is about nine by my guessing.'

Thinking about it, Daisy was surprised she hadn't figured this out before. But she'd had other things on her mind, and as far as *she* was concerned, Anne *could* have been about thirty; it wasn't as if she'd ever met the woman. She'd only seen this photo once before, and thought the girl had been younger.

'But how do you know Anne's not older than twenty-eight?' asked Jack, as if he couldn't accept it.

'Oh, I reckon it's the other way. I reckon she's younger than you think. Look, the photographs prove it. There's no doubting that those two older girls are one and the same, and

Anne's only a baby in the Christmas one when *she's* about six. Therefore it follows that she would have been no more than three or four when the later one was taken. And then there's that age again – four. There are no photos of Anne over the age of four ... and why do you think that is?'

'Because that's when Carla died,' Jack replied, visibly shaken. 'So what you're saying is...'

But she finished for him. 'That you had another sister, an older sister, older than Anne – maybe even six years older.'

Jack was shattered by this revelation. How could he have had an older sister whose very existence had been wiped from the face of the earth? Someone who even Anne had never mentioned or spoken about? It seemed too absurd to be true, even by the crazy, screwed-up standards of his sorry excuse for a life. He didn't want to believe it. 'Well, what makes you think it's a sister? It could be a cousin or something,' he said, clutching at straws.

'I'm sorry, Jack, I know this is hard to believe. I mean it could be – but look at this too.' And she picked up the Easter photograph. 'Look at the footprints in the snow. Look at them closely; there are four different sized footprints!' She was right; she was good. There were huge ones – only a couple (obviously his father's before he'd lost interest in the exercise), some medium-sized ones, which would have been Carla's, some tiny ones that led directly to little Anne and her basket of eggs, and then some small to medium ones. These darted about everywhere when you looked closely – made by an unseen and energetic child of probably eight or nine.

Jack sat back against the side of the van and closed his eyes. Daisy watched him with a worried look on her face, but also as if she was holding something back. When he spoke again, his voice was distracted. 'Do you know what the worst part of it is? That after all this ... after all these revelations –

like finding out the woman I *thought* was my mother died before I was even born… I mean, can you imagine how that feels, Daisy?' He opened his eyes and looked at her. She shook her head and turned away; the pain in his eyes made her want to cry. 'And now I find out I've got some older sister that I didn't even know existed … it's like… It's like the more I look, and the harder I try, the further I actually get away from the truth … and do you know what the worst part is? I'm still no nearer to finding out who my mother is! That's all I want, Daisy, that's all I've ever wanted!'

He broke down in tears then, and Daisy took him in her arms. 'My poor baby,' she said as she rocked him. The pity she felt ripped through her. But the *actual* worst was yet to come. Daisy could see now why his sister had lied to him all these years, and taken the easier way out – not that it could have been easy in any way. But when it came down to it – when the truth was just too horrific to deal with, sometimes not knowing was the better option. That wasn't her style, though; that wasn't how her dad had brought her up. 'I reckon you're closer than you think,' she whispered in his ear.

'How do you mean? How's that possible?' he mumbled.

She pulled away from him to place her hands on his shoulders and look into his bloodshot eyes. 'Will you be brave, Jack? For me?' He searched her face, not understanding. ''Cause I need you to be brave, and I need you to calm down and listen with a clear head to what I'm going to tell you, because … otherwise, I don't think I'm going to be able to do it – and if *I* don't tell you this, then I guess no one else is going to.'

Once Jack had pulled himself together, Daisy began. 'Right, let's start from the beginning and go over some facts; what we know to be true.' She spoke authoritatively, and despite the gravity of the situation Jack couldn't help but feel that his girlfriend was turning into Velma from *Scooby Doo*. 'One, you've never met your mother – which means she either died when you were a baby or were certainly less than one or two. This Carla woman died in 1967 and you were born in 1973, so that rules her out; she wasn't your mother. Two, your sister is how old? Twenty-eight? I think she's about twenty-six – the photos tell us that; there are none of her over the age of four – which is when Carla died in 1967. That means that she was born in or around 1963 – so she would be about twenty-six now; ten years older than you. Therefore that isn't her in the photo taken just before Carla died that she left you – and needless to say, *she* isn't your mother either! Which leads us on to this mystery girl…' She paused: this was the hard bit. 'This mystery girl, this sister of Anne's – which means she's *also* probably a sister of yours, was six-ish in the Christmas photo.' She held it up. 'And it follows that in the Carla photo of around 1966 or '67 she'd have been around nine. That's her; it all makes sense.'

Jack interrupted. 'But we still seem to be going over what we already know. What about my mother?'

Daisy guessed she was going to have to spell it out for him. 'Well, I hate to say this, but you were born in, what, 1973?' Jack nodded. 'This mystery girl, your unknown sister, would have been fifteen or sixteen then, and yet you never saw her! Why do you think that was? And why do you think Anne left you that photo before she left, baby?' She still couldn't bring herself to come out and say it outright.

'I *thought* because she was showing me my mother.'

She looked at him to see if it had registered yet, but she didn't think it had – not quite. 'She *was*, Jack; you were just looking at the wrong person, that's all.'

'You mean?' He couldn't say it, but Daisy knew the penny had finally dropped when he scrambled open the van door to retch.

He leant against the side of the van and emptied the contents of his stomach onto the ground. It happened quickly and violently. Jack was rarely sick: it was another phobia of his – something that he was fearful of. It seemed so unnatural to him; that stuff should be on the inside, not outside on the ground. He didn't want to know what was sloshing around in his stomach; it was gross. Daisy came to him and tried to stroke his hair, but he retched again. This time nothing came out. He pushed her hand away – disgusted at himself and how he must look.

When he'd finished, he clambered back in and closed the door in a hurry – not wanting her to see it or indeed to smell it. 'Don't look out there,' he said. He had tiny red dots around his eyes.

'It's OK, don't worry about it.' Daisy passed him a tissue. He took it from her, thanked her and wiped his mouth. The enormity of what had just been revealed struck him again and he rocked on his knees. 'Are you OK?' she asked, steadying him. She was really worried about him now – surely there was only so much one boy could take.

He didn't answer. His mind was elsewhere – churning over and over. Could this girl really be his mother? And if so, what had happened to her? Where was she? Why hadn't Anne ever told him about her? He thought of the lengths that had been gone to keep it hidden, maybe by her *and* his father, and that really hurt. He could see now, through the photographs that were left, how a whole life had been cleverly edited and erased from existence; two lives if you included his. And could she really have been, what, fifteen, sixteen years old when she'd had him? That was younger than he was now – younger than Daisy. 'Jack?' she said. But he couldn't bring himself to look at her, couldn't speak. He felt ashamed – dirty and ashamed. He'd felt like it his whole life; his father had made him feel that way. But it was worse than ever now that he knew where he'd come from.

His shame turned, via indignation, into seething anger and hatred at his bastard of a so-called father. He was going to get the truth out of him if it meant killing him – or them both; he just wanted to hear him say it. He swept the photos off the van floor – as if he didn't want to see them anymore – and stuffed them back into their wallet. 'I've got to go, Daisy!' he cried.

She could see how badly affected he was, and feared for what he was going to do. She'd seen that look on his face before, outside the Red Lion before he'd gone in and punched that guy's lights out. 'Why don't you wait a bit? Let's talk this through; there could be another explanation. We could see if there's a pub open somewhere.'

'No, I've waited long enough – I want answers now!' And he climbed out of the van.

'Do you want me to come with you? He's less likely to lie or get violent if there's someone else there!'

Jack gave a bitter laugh as if to say, 'You don't know my father.' Besides, he was more worried about what he was going to do to *him* than the other way round. 'No, this is something I've got to do alone – I don't want you around.'

She looked hurt, like a wounded child, and he realised how it must have sounded. She was the one who'd figured all this out, after all. It tempered his anger to see her like that, and he came and stood next to her, straddling his bike. He bent forward to kiss her on the forehead, but drew back again when he smelt sick on himself. It disgusted him – there was no way he was going near her. 'I mean, I just don't know how this is all going to end, that's all,' he said.

'I know. That's what I'm worried about.'

'Look, I've got to go.' He was keen to get off while he was still angry. Anger was good; it was a weapon.

'Please be careful – and promise you'll call me as soon as you can. I won't be able to sleep tonight till I know you're OK.'

'I will,' he said, but she held onto his shirt sleeve – loath to let him go. It slipped through her fingers and he was away. She sat there for a moment and watched him from the side of the van. Suddenly, she came over queasy again. And it wasn't the smell of Jack's vomit drifting up from the ground; it was what she'd just discovered in the photographs.

CHAPTER 35

'Of Smoke and Mirrors'

J ack made it home in no time, drawing boundless energy from his anger. He turned into the drive and skidded on the gravel, throwing his bike down. His father was up on the roof, hammering felt onto the side of one of the dormer windows. He ignored Jack's dramatic entrance – pissed off at him for going out without telling him.

Jack stood at the foot of the ladder, smouldering with renewed anger at the sight of him. Why did he have to be up on the roof? Despite his ire, he was unwilling to go charging up there; extended as it was, the ladder seemed to go on forever. There was something about the angle it was propped at as well: it reminded him of the angle it had been propped at on that fateful day. He pulled the photo wallet from his back pocket and brandished it in the air. 'How do you explain these?' he yelled. Out of the corner of his eye, he could see the black spot dancing in the blue sky next to his father's head on the roof.

His father, unwilling to get drawn into Jack's tiresome questions, paused, hammer in hand, and turned to look down. From up there, he couldn't quite make out what the stupid boy was holding. He hadn't seen Jack since he'd had his hair cut and was somewhat distracted by this at first; it made him look slightly unhinged. It took him a good deal of scrutiny to register what the photo wallets were – he hadn't seen them in years. When he did, he stumbled in shock – and then reacted with genuine outrage. He couldn't believe that Jack had actually been in his room, snooping around. Was there no end to it?

He spat out some flat-headed tacks he'd been holding in his mouth and they pattered down the roof into the gutter. 'Where the hell did you get those from, you little thief?' And he began to descend the ladder with the intention of putting a stop to this once and for all. Seeing the look of murder on Jack's face, however, and the way he stepped on the ladder to meet him, he thought better of it. They were like a pair of sparring stags, facing off at each other.

'Never mind where I got them from! I want to know what happened to my mother. I know who she is now; I've found out for myself, I've seen her photo!' bellowed Jack as he climbed up another rung.

His father sprung off the ladder and back onto the roof. 'Don't you come up here. I'm warning you! You're gone in the head; you don't know anything!'

Despite the threat Jack posed, in his crafty old mind, his father still felt he'd got the upper hand and that the boy was bluffing: first, there was no way he could have seen a photo of *her*; they'd all been destroyed – he'd made sure of that. And second, he knew how scared Jack was of ladders: he'd never climb all the way up to the roof.

Well, the old man was right in one respect. There was no way of getting to his father from inside either, as the loft hatch was too high. He just wanted to get near enough to see his face up close when he showed him the pictures of the girl – his poor mother; the ones he'd tried so hard to hide. And also close enough to strangle him if necessary.

Jack rummaged through the photos until he'd found the ones he was after. A couple of them fluttered to the floor in the process. 'Who's *she* then?' he demanded, holding up the pictures. His father stared wearily down, but when he saw the hidden girl, staring back at him, the colour drained from his face and his knuckle gripped the hammer tighter. It was as if a ghost had come back to haunt him. He swayed on the sloping roof and had to steady himself against the window frame.

Jack cautiously advanced up another rung, clutching the ladder with one hand and holding the photos out in front of him with the other. It was as if he was taunting his father with them, as you would with a crucifix to a vampire. 'Who is she and what have you done with her, you sick bastard?' he hissed. He couldn't believe he'd just spoken to his father like that, but he was too far gone now; too outraged. He wasn't getting away with it, not this time.

His father grabbed hold of the ladder, lifted it off the tiles and began shaking it violently. 'Don't you dare speak to me like that! And I told you not to come up here!'

Jack had no choice but to jump back off. There was a brief tussle over the ladder, but his father refused to relinquish his grip on it; he had one arm linked inside it, the other one holding onto the ledge of the dormer window. The photos weren't helping Jack's cause, and he stuffed them back into his jeans, yelling in rage, 'Come down here, or I swear I'll burn this bastard house down with you on top of it!' He kicked the ladder in frustration, then stomped off up the drive in the direction of the log pile and the caustic tank.

He had no intention of burning the house down, not just yet anyway, but he would if he had to. What he wanted right now was a weapon. If he was going to get up onto that roof (even if that meant climbing onto a window ledge or up a

drainpipe), he was going to need something to fight with –
preferably something bigger than his father's hammer.

It took him a while to locate what he'd been looking for, and
he had to cover his nose whilst he searched for it: he'd never
known the tank to smell so bad. He spied the handle of the
axe, sticking out, right at the back of the log pile – not where
it normally was, stuck into the chopping block. As he went to
retrieve it, he heard an unexpected clattering noise from the
roof. His father, who'd been watching, was still banking on the
fact that Jack wouldn't come up there. But when he saw his
very angry (and possibly demented) son pick up the axe, he
decided he wasn't going to take any chances.

Jack turned at the noise and watched as his father hurriedly
began to pull the ladder up onto the roof – feeding it through
the dormer window and into the loft. By the time he'd realised
what was happening, it was too late; the bottom of the ladder
had already passed the gutter and out of his reach. This
thwarted part of his plan – he'd intended whipping the ladder
away himself so that his father would have no means of escape.

In sheer frustration, Jack swung the axe as hard as he could
into the side of the caustic tank. It clanged loudly on impact,
sending the flies that had been hovering above the surface to
scatter for cover, rocking the tank as the axe became wedged in
the side of it. This seemed to wake some dormant monster in
there, as the impenetrable liquid belched and bubbled to life in
response – worsening the already rank stench.

He turned up his nose at the smell and put his foot on the
side of the tank to remove the axe head. On hearing the initial
clang, his father had looked down in disbelief. Disbelief was
replaced by fury as the caustic solution began to seep out of
the hole in the tank. His voice boomed out across the yard.
'DON'T YOU DARE FUCKING DO THAT AGAIN!'

Jack looked up in complete amazement; he had never, ever,

heard his father use the 'f-word' before. This was a man capable (and guilty) of many despicable acts – happy to beat a woman or child black and blue – but he never resorted to using that word. He prided himself on it; it was possibly his only admirable quality. At worst, he said 'bastard', 'bloody' or 'sodding', but *never* the 'f-word'. Jack was shocked, but kind of satisfied that he'd drawn it out of him.

He stared up at his father with a smug look on his face, then swung the axe back in a big arc before burying it again in the side of the tank. Once more, the tank wobbled and its lethal contents slopped about. He removed the head straight away this time, and had to jump back as jets of evil-smelling ebony liquid spurted out. His father was literally hopping mad on the roof – doing a tap dance of rage on the tiles. 'GET AWAY FROM THAT FUCKING TANK!' he roared. Ah, there was that word again, thought Jack – delighted at the effect he was having; for once he'd managed to capture his father's attention.

He swung again, puncturing another slit in the tank. In his anger and frustration, he knew he'd found a way to get his father down from the roof. Out of the corner of his eye he saw him frantically trying to pull the ladder back out of the loft. 'Yes, that's right!' Jack shouted, renewing his efforts 'You come down here and tell me the truth!' And he made his way round to another side of the tank to avoid the vicious spray. He swung again and again, aiming lower now as the liquid level began to drop. 'Come and tell me the truth, you bastard! Tell me the truth about my mother, you sick bastard!' It was as if he'd gone berserk himself.

There were so many holes now that the tank resembled a giant square colander, with jets of fetid black soup pouring from its holes. Jack was just standing back to admire his handiwork when something thin and pale appeared, protruding from the tank. At first glance it looked like a large bent nail or screw, sticking out of the end of some long-forgotten furniture. On closer inspection, the thing it was sticking out of seemed to be curved – like the end of an armrest of a half-stripped pine chair.

So what was sticking out of it? As the black solution dripped from it, it got paler still, until it was creamy and off-white; even worse, what it was attached to wasn't just peeling, but ribbed too. In growing horror, as Jack covered his face from the smell, he realised he wasn't looking at stripped furniture at all … but the grisly, curled claw of a human hand with a pointing, accusatory finger.

He looked up, following its instruction. It pointed directly at his father's ashen face as he peered over his shoulder – as if it was singling him out. He too had watched its unwelcome appearance in mounting dread, whilst trying to yank the ladder out of the loft at the same time; one of its rungs had got caught on a window latch.

With one last act of violence, he managed to yank the ladder free, but he pulled too hard – losing his balance on the sloping roof and his grip on the ladder. The momentum sent him hurtling backwards, head over heels. The ladder joined him in a clattering race down the tiles as he let out a scream of surprise. This was cut short by an almighty thud as his head smashed into the cast-iron guttering, and he bounced off the roof and into the air.

On any other day he might have landed differently, like toast landing butter side up, but that's fate for you; today wasn't his day. When he hit the gravel of the drive, he landed butter side down – on his neck, at an awkward angle. His head snapped forward with a sickening crack, accompanied by one final utterance – a yelp of surprise. His body went limp and he finally lay still. The ladder did a brief, spinning waltz on one leg before it, too, came crashing down on top of him. And then there was silence.

Silence, that is, save for the drip-drip of the caustic tank. Jack stared across at his father, lying there between the house and the van, not moving, his boots sticking out from under the ladder. He didn't need to go and check if he was dead: he already knew it by the sound he'd heard when his father landed. The unnatural angle of his head was a giveaway too; he looked like a chicken that had had its neck wrung.

Jack didn't feel a great deal at his passing – his tormentor of sixteen years. Not right away anyhow. Perhaps a little queasiness at the manner in which it had happened – and maybe some relief too; but mainly indifference. Right now he was only concerned about whose hand was slowly appearing out of the injured tank as it bled its secrets. He feared the worst.

It was agonising waiting for the level to drop. Jack went and sat on the log pile – as far away as he could and with a better viewpoint. Whilst he waited, he fashioned himself a makeshift mask by tying his shirt around his face. His heart thumped, his legs shook and the black spot marauded his vision like one of those damn flies, making him want to bat it away. More and more of them had returned now, drawn by the smell. They voyeuristically buzzed about, hovering and congregating above the tank in renewed interest.

To make matters worse, as the solution retreated it seemed to be getting thicker – as if it was coagulating. As a result, it began clogging up the holes and they started sputtering, stemming the flow of the liquid. But the tank had emptied enough to confirm sickeningly to Jack that what he was looking at was a semi-stripped arm. It was jutting vertically up, and he braced himself for a body to be revealed – or even worse – a face appearing in the murk.

What *was* revealed next was not what he was expecting at all. Substantial lumps of rock and breeze blocks began to appear; like a miniature Atlantis – an underwater city, dripping blackly. The gunk had all but stopped receding – it was either too thick, or the holes were too high for it. Jack reluctantly jumped off the log pile, picked up the axe and walked round to the far side of the tank. He had the intention of making some lower holes, but just then he spied something in the bottom corner – a tap with a short, wide spout – clearly to drain the tank.

At first the tap wouldn't budge, which was hardly surprising as he'd never known the caustic tank to be drained. And now he knew why. In grim determination, he began to bash it with the square, blunt end of the axe head until it gave way with a rusty groan. He turned the tap fully open, but to his dismay, nothing came out.

Jack picked up a long stick, stuck it in the spout and wiggled it about. Slowly but surely it started to cough and splutter, spitting out the foul black mess like coffee grounds spewing from an old percolator. It glooped steadily onto the yard floor and over the edge, dripping onto the grass bank where the daffodils sprouted in spring.

He peered into the tank, and saw the ooze was on the move again. The stench was now so bad that it made him gag. He whipped his shirt off his face and bent over to retch. His stomach cramped and spasmed, but there was nothing left to throw up. Squatting on his haunches, he spat bile, not wanting to look in there again, not wanting to see – but he *had* to know if what he feared was true.

When he looked back again, a huge, door-shaped sheet of corrugated iron – the type they had on their outbuilding roofs – had been revealed. The large stones and bricks were sitting on it, weighing down and trapping what lay beneath. The flayed arm was sticking out from the side of the sheet; it must have come free – and that's why it had floated up to the surface. It lay resting on the sludge by the side of the corrugated iron – as if it had done its job in drawing attention to its poor owner.

Jack didn't know what to do next; it was hard to think. He knew what he *should* do but was dreading finding out what seemed to be inevitable. He wanted to put it off as long as possible. An idea came to him, and he walked across the yard to turn on the hosepipe. First, he aimed it at the bothersome swarms of flies, trying to disperse them, then he directed it into the tank. He began spraying down the corrugated iron and rocks, washing them off and hoping to dilute the foul-smelling gunk. The arm he tried to avoid, as he didn't want to damage it any further; heaven forbid it should come loose and float away.

He let the hosepipe run into the tank whilst he donned his protective gloves. After batting away some stubborn flies, he took a deep breath before bending over the tank. The breeze blocks were easy to shift, but the rocks were heavy and slimy. Fighting the urge to retch again, he began to chuck them out of the tank. As he did so, the corrugated sheet began to shift and move upwards of its own accord, startling him. He jumped back as the ghastly arm began to bob about as if whatever lay beneath it was trying to get out. Because the liquid level was getting higher again the sheet was trying to float. Jack rushed over to turn the hosepipe down to a steady trickle.

On returning, he let the tank drain for a while before attempting to remove the last few large stones. They were impossible to get hold of, so he pushed them off the edge of the sheet and into the hidden recesses of the tank. They clanged dully on the bottom. This was it then ... the moment of truth he'd been so dreading. He could barely breathe through his shirt. It felt as if someone was squeezing his windpipe, cutting off his air supply, as he lifted up the sheet of metal to reveal what lay beneath…

*****

It was that beautiful Midsummer Night. Anne was in Jack's bedroom, trying to escape her father and dashing towards the window in her nightdress. She bounded onto Jack's bed, using it like a gymnast's springboard to reach the window sill. She ducked down and flicked the latch up with one bare foot whilst kicking open the window at the same time. It flew back and a gentle breeze kissed her body as she crouched to jump, preparing herself for the sting of gravel on the soles of her feet as she landed. She imagined it as if it had already happened, and she was free, away in the night, the wind in her face as she ran and ran.

If she'd cropped her hair short, as she'd wanted to so many times when she'd felt down, she'd probably have made it. Her head was even out of the window when her ponytail was grabbed in a vice-like grip. She yelped in pain as she was dragged backwards onto the bed, smacking her head on the window frame. 'Where do you think you're going, you little whore?' her father hissed in her face.

Anne fought and kicked like a sack of cats about to be drowned – a mass of flailing limbs in a billowing nightdress. By pure chance, she caught him a corker with her elbow under his chin, making him bite his tongue. In surprise, he let go of her hair, and she made a dash for the door.

He grabbed at her gown as she fled, ripping it down the back. It flapped about her as she went screaming down the corridor. She shot through the parlour to the back door, where one hand scrabbled at the latch and one hand reached for the key that was always left in the lock. *Oh no! The key! He's got the bloody key*! It was if he'd planned it all along. She was trapped; helpless. What chance did she have? As she heard his footsteps enter the parlour, her legs buckled beneath her and she sank against the door.

She felt like collapsing entirely; giving in. She was never going to get away from this place; he wouldn't let her – and certainly not with a man. She thought of her new beau, and how kind and gentle he'd been to her – how he'd treated her with an affection, a respect and politeness the like of which she'd never known. With his simple, old-fashioned manner and parted hair, he'd be waiting for her in the butcher's shop, looking out of the window for her; wondering why she hadn't been in. Perhaps he'd think she didn't care for him anymore – and she couldn't abide that; he didn't deserve that. The thought was enough to draw her back from the dark tunnel of despair and into the light.

She rushed over to the sink in search of a weapon just as her father appeared in the doorway. Frantically, she scanned the draining board for her kitchen knife. Where the hell was it? She flung open the top drawer, clattering through the cutlery tray; maybe she'd put it away. She was aware of her father's sinister presence behind her, negotiating the kitchen table. Why wasn't he drunk? Why hadn't that bloody sleeping pill taken effect? She was also aware she'd run out of time. Grabbing the first thing she could lay her hand on, she whipped round with it.

She held it out in front of her, keeping the table between them for added protection. Her weapon was a potato peeler, and it looked pathetic in her hand. The blade was barely three inches long – but at least it was pointed. He laughed as they faced each other. There was blood on his lips and teeth from where he'd bitten his tongue. Go on, laugh, she thought, despising him. I can still put out one of your eyes with it if

I have to. She noticed his gaze shift downwards and linger, causing her to look down. Her ripped gown had come off one of her shoulders, exposing the top of her chest and bra. She pulled it to her, clutching it to her neck, whilst warding him off with the peeler.

All of a sudden, he shoved the table across the floor to trap her against the sink. She managed to move out of the way, but only just in time, and the corner of the table crashed into her hip. She yelled in agony as she freed herself and limped, wounded, to the other side of the kitchen. The pain was excruciating and she wanted to cry, but she bit her lip and sucked in air instead, refusing to give him the satisfaction. 'Stay back! Don't you come near me!' she shrieked as he slowly advanced, backing her into a corner and blocking her entry to the parlour.

'I know what you've been up to. I know where you were sneaking off to. You're no better than that whore of a sister of yours. Except even *she* never tried to drug me!' Anne let out a whimper at this revelation; the fact that he knew she'd been slipping him pills confirmed she was in grave trouble.

'Stay back! I'm warning you. I'll tell Jack!' She jabbed the pointed end of the peeler towards his face.

'He can't help you now; he doesn't care about you. He's off gallivanting with his own bit of strumpet. It's just me … and you.' He edged closer with his hands up.

'Get back!' she shouted, jabbing towards his eyes again with the peeler, but this time he was too quick. He grabbed her wrist with the weapon in it, and with his right hand dealt her a cracking blow to the head. The peeler flew out of her hand as she fell to the floor in a heap. Her night gown rode up. She lay there with her legs splayed, momentarily stunned. There was that sickening leer on his face again, and something clicked in her head. She kicked out as he approached. 'Get away from me! I'll tell the police everything! I know what you did, you murderer! You rapist pig!'

He lunged at her in outrage, grabbing both her arms, their faces only a foot apart as they struggled. Suddenly, and without warning, Anne spat in his face. She couldn't believe she'd done it … and neither could he; it was the ultimate insult and they both froze. The spittle hung off his swollen nose and dripped down his chin. He let go of one of her arms and slowly wiped the mess away with the back of his sleeve. The tactic had worked. She saw her opportunity and slammed both her feet into him. He lost his grip on her and fell back. She jumped up to a crouch and sprang away like a sprinter out of the blocks, hoping to reach the bedroom window before he could stop her.

As she fled, he made one last desperate swipe with a large paw, catching her ankle. It was enough to knock her off balance, headlong into the ironing board. This clattered to the floor along with the iron, whilst Anne sprawled onto her front on the stone tiles. Winded and battered, she dragged herself up, but she was losing the fight now and started to sob. Her hair hung down as she tried to crawl away, and with no weapons left but words, she taunted her father through swollen lips and a chipped tooth. 'Jack will find out the truth, he'll know what you did, you sick bastard.'

Her father had heard enough and just wanted to shut her up – once and for all. He picked the heavy old iron off the floor, and brought it careering down on the back of her head. Just by chance, she moved at the last minute and it glanced off. 'Go on, kill me!' she cried, wanting it all to be over too. 'I want you to! I'm clean, I'm going to heaven! You're going to hell!' He hit her again with the iron, making proper contact this time with a dull thud. 'Go on! Kill me! Jack will find out the truth anyway!' She was gurgling blood now, muttering, barely conscious. Why wouldn't she shut up? Crack! He dealt the fatal blow. Something gave way and she slumped to the floor – her wish granted at last.

*****

When Jack flipped the corrugated sheet over, despite his worst fears, nothing could have prepared him for what was underneath. His dear sister, Anne, rose up to meet him in greeting, as if she'd missed him. He jumped back in terror, screaming at the grisly sight. Pulling the shirt off his face, he bent over to retch for the third time that day.

Once he'd recovered from the initial shock, he covered his face again to peer into the tank. The body had settled back down, floating on the silt, and there was no mistake: it was definitely his sister. Instead of starting a new life somewhere, with a dog and her new man, she'd got no further than the caustic tank yards from their home.

Jack felt cheated, robbed, overcome by the sickening pain of loss. 'BAASTAARD!' he yelled, sinking to his knees in despair. He threw off his gloves, held his head in his hands and wept. This hurt more than anything he'd ever known. Forget the revelation in the churchyard, forget the photographs; they didn't compare to this. He felt so much pity for her and so much sorrow for himself: it was a bitter pill stuck in his throat. Now he really knew what Daisy had been going through these last few weeks. And that's when it struck him what Anne had really been – his mother – and she had been all along; maybe not biologically, but in every other sense. She was the one who'd brought him up, changed his nappies, fed and clothed him, dressed his wounds and taught him to read and write; he'd have died without her – literally. She'd sacrificed her entire life for him. He could see that now she was gone, and he wanted more than anything to be able to tell her, to thank her – and now he'd never have the chance. It was too late.

His hatred for his father burned brighter in death than it ever had before. It was as though, even now, he'd had the last laugh and left one last thing to torment him with. All this time he'd been carrying on as if she'd snuck off and run away. It made Jack sick to the stomach to think how he'd been helping with the loft those past weeks. And now there was nothing he could do to hurt him or to get him back. He looked down the drive at him again. 'You bastard,' was all he could mutter through his sobs.

Jack slipped into a daze. It was as if all the stress and trauma caused his body to shut down to protect itself. Some minutes later, when he came back round, the first thing he noticed was the sound of the tank emptying over the bank; the hosepipe had been running all the time. He pulled himself together and peered into the tank, queasy at the thought of seeing his sister's body again. The constant flow of water had cleared the sludge considerably and the smell wasn't quite as bad. His eyes searched the bottom of the tank, deliberately avoiding the body. It was full of all manner of junk – rusty springs, rocks, old bits of wood and metal, even mini-skeletons of poor creatures.

His gaze returned to his sister. Her skin was flayed and eaten away and what was left was bloated and swollen. It killed him to see her like that. Most of her hair was still intact, though, and he could still make out her profile. Some tattered remnants of her night gown were stuck to her, but melted into her sunken flesh. It seemed that being trapped under the sheet had somehow preserved her; her arm in comparison was practically stripped to the bone. The question was, what did he do with her now? He couldn't possibly leave her like this – at the mercy of every scavenging animal and insect in the vicinity. It was undignified. She needed a proper burial, but how could he possibly move her? The thought conjured up the most dreadful imagery.

He peered closer at the body, trying to establish the extent of the decomposition and whether she was too fragile to move. She seemed to be raised off the bottom of the tank, as if lying on some sort of nest. He picked up the hosepipe and began to spray around her, clearing any remaining gunk. He concentrated on a spot near her leg where something was sticking to it, almost curled around it. The more it was revealed, and the lighter it got, the more it looked hauntingly familiar – as if he'd seen something similar not so long ago. It was off-white in colour and pure bone ... the unmistakable remains of another human hand. And it wasn't Anne's. He felt wobbly again, dizzy; he put his fist in his mouth and gasped. Surely there couldn't be one last twist of the knife, could there?

He sprayed up and down the length of his sister – more urgently now, more frantic – the sight of her body not bothering him, for the moment at least. He directed the spray around and underneath her head, again trying his best not to damage her any further. Her hair floated around as he sprayed and the sludge it was containing ran clear. It was as if he was washing her hair for her, rinsing the black suds away like a hairdresser. Slowly but surely, through her hair, what he'd been grimly expecting began to appear – the stained, ivory dome of another human skull. Like the hand, it was cracked and entirely stripped of any flesh or hair – as though it had been there for years and years.

He turned off the hosepipe to let the tank drain properly. Now he could see more clearly what Anne was lying on: a skeleton – almost identical in length to her. And he had no doubts whatsoever as to whose it was; it was her sister, the girl – his mother ... he'd finally found her. How fitting that they lay there together in a final, loving embrace. How ironic too that after all these years, all that soul-searching and all those questions, that she should be in his own backyard all along. It wasn't quite the earth-shattering revelation he'd expected it to be. He'd had so many shocks of late that nothing surprised him anymore. It only reinforced what he'd realised when he discovered Anne; he'd already found his mother. This other one wasn't real. She was an ideal or a fantasy – and always would be.

Jack gazed into the tank for some time, looking but not seeing, as he decided what to do. The thing was, even with gloves on he didn't think he could bear to touch Anne's body, let alone move it. He was terrified she'd fall apart – and what then? Shovel her up in pieces? At least in the tank she was intact and at peace; it seemed a shame to move her. And then there were the other bones to consider – the bones of the girl. They'd need moving as well. What if he missed some of them and they got left behind? And he'd have to dig a hole to act as a grave, which would take time.

Just then, another option came to him: cremation, a funeral pyre. Isn't that what the Vikings used to do? This seemed much more practical, the perfect solution; it would be a proper send off. Flies were starting to congregate and alight on Anne again. It wasn't decent. He didn't want to see her anymore, not like that; it was too upsetting. This made up his mind.

Once decided, Jack worked quickly, and he made his way to the house to get some bedding and matches. As he negotiated his father, he resisted the urge to kick him. He was about to take his filthy boots off before entering the house when he realised there was no point. He couldn't stay there any longer anyway – not now – not with all those dead bodies around. And certainly not after what his father had done. Jack remembered what he'd said to him earlier about burning the house down. The image of fire filled his head and a plan hatched in his mind. If he left that night – if he was *really* going to go through with it – he'd have to get rid of every shred of evidence that he ever existed. He was going to raze this place to the ground; *his* house, *his* fortress. He wouldn't stop until there was nothing left – nothing but ashes and dust.

After laying bed sheets and duvets in the bottom of the tank, he sloshed them liberally with petrol. The petrol can felt disconcertingly light, which was a worry given what he'd got planned. He only gave his sister a light sprinkling; it seemed disrespectful to douse her in petrol. He said 'forgive me' in his head as he did it, glancing at her briefly one last time as he laid a blanket over her. This was a mistake: as soon as he saw her face he buckled. The pain and sorrow returned, followed by anger and bitterness. It was hard not to cry again as he went about his work, tucking the blanket in at the sides before drenching it in petrol.

Next, he went into the workshop and shovelled up two bin liners full of wood shavings; another of his chores that had been neglected lately. These he emptied into the tank, spreading them in an even layer like down, but piling a good mound over Anne's body. He grabbed a load of the wood chippings that they used as kindling and added them to the pile too.

Now it was ready – his family's funeral pyre. Before setting it alight he sloshed one last load of petrol over the wood chippings, knowing he was using too much, but not wanting to take any chances. After washing his hands under the hosepipe he took a deep breath, and, standing a good distance back, lit a match with shaking hands; there was still something about fire that terrified him. He chucked the match into the tank. For a millisecond, nothing ... then 'BANG!' There was a sudden blast that singed his face and sent him stumbling backwards. It reminded him of that time with the lawnmower when he was little, only a hundred times worse.

The whole of the tank was a huge, orange square of fire. Panic set in as it licked at the high bushes surrounding it, scorching them black and threatening to set them on fire. What had he done? Overdone it with the petrol, that's what! You idiot, Jack! he cursed himself; the last thing he wanted to do was to draw attention to the property. The only good thing was that every fly in the vicinity had been toasted; they were peppering the yard around the tank with a biblical rain. The smell was disgusting.

Jack was forced to retreat to the log pile. After a few minutes, thankfully, the initial blast began to die down. He started tossing in logs from the pile, aiming for the middle and feeding the fire while it was still hungry. There was a large, but manageable, blaze now in a centralised mound, like a flaming pyramid for someone noble. This struck Jack as appropriate, and a tear rolled down his reddened and grime-streaked face. He felt he'd given them a proper send-off; that he'd done them proud.

'Goodbye, sister, goodbye, Mother,' he said aloud, which confused him as each of them was both of these things. He realised he'd never even know her name – his actual mother: only Anne could have told him. He choked back a sob, feeling suddenly lonely, and thought of Daisy. He needed her then so badly, as he watched, transfixed by the flames, until a new smell filled the air; the smell of scorched bones. It soon became unbearable, and he knew that his job was done. There was the sense of some kind of closure at least – the end of a chapter in his life; nothing was keeping him there now. He jumped down from the log pile, picked up the petrol can and walked away, leaving his family to burn.

CHAPTER 36

A Fire

Returning to the house, Jack couldn't wait to wash the stench off him; he'd got plenty of time before it got dark anyway. So, bath first – no, *cider* first, then bath, then food.

It gave him a strange feeling, filling a bottle of the last brew ever to be made there. He looked around the cellar at the freezers, the funnels and the mash bins as he drank. The cider had been such a big part of his life, of their lives, ever since he could remember. It was a relief in a way to know that he'd never have to prepare another brew, but it also made him sad.

After stripping down to his boxers, Jack chucked his stinking clothes out through the back door ready to toss on the fire later. Still clutching his bottle, he padded through the house in his underwear to run a bath. He felt surprisingly calm, almost contemplative; perhaps it was just the cider.

As he soaked in the bath, he went through his plan. His thoughts became distracted as they returned to Daisy. This was the one detail that kept niggling at him. He still hadn't had a chance to speak to her. The last few days had been a whirlwind – all this had happened too soon. He thought about phoning her, and that was when another revelation hit him. If he wanted to call her, he could; who was there to stop him? He could do anything he wanted. He could stroll out there to the workshop, pick up the phone and ring her. But what if her mum answered? What would he say? How could he possibly word it? 'Oh, hi, Daisy, my father's dead now, and my sister was in the caustic tank in the yard all the time – along with my mother – so I've just set fire to them both. Oh, and by the way, pack your suitcase; we're leaving for America tonight.' It sounded ghoulish and preposterous. No, better to leave it to the last minute; then he couldn't back out of it – and neither could she.

After bathing, Jack wrapped a towel around his waist and walked back to the kitchen – something he'd never normally have done. The calm and relaxed feeling came over him again. It dawned on him that this was probably because, for the first time in his life, he'd got the house to himself. He'd never known what it was like; to enjoy his own home without his father presiding over it, ruling him. And that was the difference now that he was gone: his presence had disappeared, his threat had been removed. *He* was the king of the castle now – and he liked it.

Jack continued to entertain these thoughts, letting himself daydream, whilst he prepared a simple dinner of fried eggs and beans on toast. As he sat down to eat his ceremonial 'Last Supper' he was still thinking. Right now he could be sitting there with Daisy, eating dinner together at the kitchen table in his own home. They could watch telly together afterwards, spend the night together – they'd have the run of the house. His mind was racing now. Maybe he could keep the house on and they could live there together – him and Daisy, like husband and wife. It seemed like the most wonderful idea he'd ever had!

But for how long would it last? How would they pay the bills? He didn't have a job and Daisy was at college. How would he get another job? How would he get a bank account to write cheques with? Hell, he couldn't even drive. There'd be letters, demands for money – why hadn't his father paid the bills? The electricity and water would be cut off. It wouldn't be long before 'the authorities' came calling. Then there'd be questions: Where had his father gone? What had happened to him? Where had Jack, this imposter, come from? They'd think *he'd* killed him! They'd search the premises and find three sets of bones – human bones. They'd take him away and put him in prison for murder, triple murder; he'd never see Daisy again!

Jack sat at the table in the empty kitchen, his eyes wide in fright, his knife and fork clenched upright in his hands. The bubble had burst. Back to reality. Whilst he stayed there, he'd always be an outsider, an outlaw – a criminal with no identity. That's why he needed to get away and start afresh; a new life in a new country – far, far away. Best stick to the plan: don't get distracted.

His dinner had grown cold, half-finished; he'd lost his appetite anyway. As the reality of the situation set in, Jack had his first real jangle of nerves. He pushed his plate away and went to tap another bottle of cider. This really *would* be the last one, he told himself. The time had come for action.

He went about his work methodically. His whole life had been leading up to this moment, and now it was really happening. First, he got dressed in the clothes he was travelling in, then set about packing the things he'd need to take with him; everything else could be burnt. He checked his tin had his savings, his map of America and Daisy's stereo in it, before adding the other photos – the important ones. The tin went into his rucksack along with a spare set of clothes, deodorant, a compass, a toothbrush, soap and a flannel. There was more than he'd expected and his rucksack was nearly full. There wasn't even going to be any room for cider – he'd got to pack some food for the journey yet.

The hardest decision was what to do with his books. They were the only material thing that he cared about in the whole house. He couldn't bear the thought of leaving them behind but, equally, knew he had to be practical; he could hardly go lugging them around the countryside with him. Deep down, he knew it was time to say goodbye to the past and leave these relics from his childhood behind. He allowed himself one book to take with him and agonised over the choice, wasting valuable time. In the end he opted for *Lamont the Lonely Monster* – a character he'd more than empathised with over the years. It was a sad tale but had a happy ending. Perhaps it would bring him good luck – perhaps *his* life would turn out the same.

The remaining books he piled up with the rest of his meagre belongings and clothes. It was shocking how little he had; it only took him two trips outside with his arms full. He scooped up the stinking clothes from outside the back door on the way. Carrying them at arm's length, he headed up the drive to the property's new incinerator. I'm sure Anne won't mind, he thought, as he began throwing his clothes into the tank; it's only my things after all. I certainly wouldn't put anything of *his* in here.

Lastly, he fed his beloved books into the pyre – his books that were once hers. It felt right in a way – as if he'd borrowed them from her as you would from a library. Now he was returning them; better this way than them going up in smoke in the house. They quickly caught light, and he chucked another half dozen logs on them to make sure they all disappeared.

He went back to his room, taking the petrol can with him. There, he dragged the furniture into the middle of the floor, leaving behind pale shapes on the walls. The walls themselves were thick with dust and inhabited by an array of creepy-crawlies – families of woodlice and the odd, indignant spider – annoyed at being disturbed after so long.

Lastly, he yanked the faded brown curtains that he'd always hated down from the window. He draped them on top of the furniture. This was where the fire was going to be lit. Picking up the petrol can, he tipped it upside down and sloshed the remaining contents all over the curtains until there wasn't a drop left. He was no longer alarmed by this: he'd already thought of a couple of new sources of fuel.

Taking the empty can with him, Jack went outside again. As he left the house he noticed his bike on the driveway. It couldn't stay there. He picked it up and wheeled it to the junk shed; he was going there anyway. After cramming the bike in, he reached up to the wall for the clear, plastic siphon tube that hung in a loop on two rusty nails. He'd watched his father siphon petrol on numerous occasions over the years, but for Jack this was going to be a first.

Under a darkening sky, he knelt next to his father's van and unscrewed its petrol cap, relishing the smell that hit him. If there wasn't enough in here, he'd have to do the lawnmower too. He fed one end of the tube into the tank until it hit the bottom, then blew into it to make sure it was fully submerged. There seemed to be plenty of petrol. Here goes then, he thought. He took a deep breath and started sucking.

It was harder than he'd expected. He'd been bracing himself for a sudden rush of petrol, but it was a gradual process. He watched, cross-eyed, as the liquid rose up the tube, creeping closer and closer towards his mouth. He let it get as near as he dared before pinching the end of the tube shut tight and letting out a big lungful of air. Keeping his thumb over the end, he carefully pointed the tube into the petrol can. Then he took his thumb off and prayed. The petrol began to pour out, rattling on the bottom of the can; it was working!

It took him half a dozen goes until he was satisfied he'd got enough. And all the while, he had an unnerving feeling that he was being watched by his dead father. Jack still hadn't decided what to do with him yet. By the time he'd finished his face was bright red, he felt dizzy and there was a foul taste in his mouth. Glad it was over; he carried the half full can back into the house.

Once inside, he worked his way from room to room, following the same procedure each time. First he checked for anything belonging to him – any evidence that he'd ever existed – and then he sprinkled the room in petrol, singling out choice items. Then he left the door open before moving on to the next room. There was barely anything at all of his left in the house, save for a few old coats and shoes in the hallway. These all went into the tank outside.

In his father's room, he symbolically placed the drawer of their edited family history onto his bed before covering it in fuel; this would go up in seconds. In the lounge, he took great pleasure in dousing his father's chair with the stuff; it was the embodiment of him, and would provide perfect fodder for the fire.

Before leaving some rooms, he lingered briefly, surveying the scene and allowing himself a few moments of sentimentality. Childhood memories came flooding back. He gazed fondly at the warm rug by the stove where he'd spent hours being schooled by Anne when he was little. In the kitchen there was the stained pine table where, again, he seemed to have spent a lot of his childhood, watching his sister cook. She would throw him titbits when his father wasn't around, or give him bowls and spoons to lick. That and the countless hours they'd spent there chopping apples together or stirring the cider mash. He picked up the matches from the table before sloshing it with petrol.

He was nearly done now. Outside, the night had crept in with the stealth of a silent assassin. The sky was a dark and enticing indigo colour, dusted with a smattering of stars. And the moon was smoky and smudged, as if it had been coloured with white chalk and a finger had been rubbed across it. It was the perfect night for travelling and adventure. His stomach lurched at the thought of it – that this was really it; the time had come.

The whole house reeked of petrol, making him feel high as he headed down the creaking corridor for the last time. After placing the can outside his bedroom door next to his rucksack, Jack walked a few feet into his room. He nudged open the cardboard drawer of the matches, studying the box with glazed eyes. Swan Vestas: yellow, red and green with a white swan – his father had always insisted on them: so innocent, yet so deadly. It was frightening to think of the power he wielded with them.

With twitching fingers, he pulled two matches out for extra effect, their two red heads nuzzled together like conjoined twins. He paused for a moment before striking them. His childhood home was about to go up in smoke … and there'd be no turning back. The matches flared brightly in the darkness. Before he could chicken out, he tossed them towards the pile of furniture. They appeared to float through the air in slow motion, lighting up the room, before landing. And then 'PUFF!' … they went up – quieter and more understated than the caustic tank.

The blaze quickly took hold and soon reached the ceiling. Jack panicked, turned to shoulder his rucksack and grab the petrol can. From the doorway, he trickled the last of the petrol onto the bedroom floor so that it led out into the corridor. Walking backwards, he left a trail down the hallway, through the parlour and kitchen to the back door, until it was all gone. Without looking behind him (he'd already said his goodbyes), he dashed out of the door and up the drive to the workshop. He had one final job to do – and that was to call Daisy.

On his way, he bounded over his father, who was still lying exactly where he'd fallen. Jack pulled up abruptly. 'Shit!' he said aloud; he'd forgotten all about him, and now it was too late. The thought of moving him, even if he could, made him feel ill. He nudged his father's leg with the toe of his shoe. It felt leaden and solid. Jack shuddered; that decided it for him – he could stay where he lay. Let fate decide what happened to him. With any luck the house would collapse on him and cremate *him* too.

On the spur of the moment, he placed the petrol can and the siphon tube next to his father's outstretched hand, rubbing them both with his shirt sleeve first; he'd seen them do it on telly. This way, if his father *was* found, maybe they would figure he'd gone crazy and set fire to the place himself before falling off the roof. It would have to do.

Jack ran into the workshop and up to the phone. It was almost pitch black and his eyes weren't accustomed to it. Banging his hip on the bandsaw in the dark, he cried out in pain. He hobbled to where he thought the phone was, fumbling his hands over the chisels that were hanging next to it. Finally he located it, then knocked the receiver off so that it dangled by its coil. He cursed before yanking it back up again, pressing it to his ear.

In his panic, he couldn't remember Daisy's phone number. It was as if his brain had frozen on him. He had to repeat the number out loud, over and over, until he'd got it. He'd intended to let the phone ring four times – the emergency ring – but, to his utter shock, someone answered it right away. His heart nearly went into cardiac arrest.

It was Daisy. She'd been sitting by the phone, increasingly anxious as it grew darker. 'Hello!' she said breathlessly.

'Daisy!' Jack croaked in surprise, his voice hoarse from the petrol fumes and smoke.

'Are you OK? You sound dreadful. I've been worried sick!'

'Daisy, meet me at the phone box in ten minutes.'

'Why? What's happened? Are you OK?' she asked again.

'I haven't got time to explain. Just meet me at the phone box … and bring a rucksack of clothes.'

'But…'

'And walk. Don't bring the van!'

'But why, Jack? It's dark out,' she pleaded.

'Daisy, I've got to go!' Through the grimy workshop window, he could see yellow and orange flames had already spread throughout the house. 'Just meet me in ten minutes. I love you.' And he put the phone down.

The phone clicked dead in Daisy's ear and she returned it to its cradle. She sat there for some moments on her mum's bed and started to cry. She'd badly needed to tell Jack something. Hearing his voice had set her off – and now he was gone again.

Jack rubbed the receiver clean of fingerprints and ran for the door. He could see better now, and as he skipped around the bulky machines lurking in the gloom, it occurred to him that he'd forgotten to torch the workshop; and he'd got no petrol left. But who needs petrol? he thought. This whole place was one giant tinderbox; the wood shavings were waist deep in places. He patted his shirt pocket for the matches, pulled them out and struck two of them; this was getting addictive. He shoved them back into the box and threw it into a large pile of shavings. There was a bang and a pink glow – like a firework going off as the box exploded. The shavings smoked before bursting into flame. Jack beat a hasty exit.

The fire had now reached the parlour; Jack's petrol trail had done its trick a little too well. As he sprinted down the drive he shielded his face from the heat. His bedroom window blew out behind him, missing him by inches. He ran for his life, dashing across the lane and through the long, wild grass of the meadow. He hurdled the ditch that bordered it, then stopped for a moment, crouching down to allow himself one last look at the house.

The whole bungalow was ablaze. It had gone up so much quicker than he had expected; he thought he'd be miles away before the fire got going properly. Jack set off again, desperate to put some distance between himself and the house. He ran through the dark of the spinney, negotiating the familiar territory with ease.

Once out the other side, he noticed he could still smell smoke. He was running through thick clumps of it. Stranger still was the sensation underfoot; the ground felt hot beneath his feet. The whole field surrounding the spinney was still smouldering from the stubble burning earlier that day. This worked in Jack's favour as it diverted attention from the house. Pretty much the whole area surrounding his home had been on fire for the last few days: what was another bit of smoke and a few flames on the horizon?

Jack made it to the brook and climbed up the bank by the bridge, breathing heavily from running with his backpack on. He checked for cars, then headed down the lay-by, sticking to the shadows, towards the phone box. The Red Lion was open (something he hadn't thought about) and he regretted arranging to meet near it. As he reached the bottom he peered expectantly round the corner. He couldn't wait to see Daisy; it seemed as if it had been days … and there she was, illuminated by the light from the phone box. He breathed a wondrous sigh of relief. God, it was good to see her.

He was glad she'd followed his advice and not brought the van, but as he jogged over he couldn't help but notice she didn't have her rucksack with her. 'Jack!' she cried as they met, and she embraced him, holding onto him for some time. He returned the compliment, hugging her tight. She smelt and felt wonderful – the total antithesis of him, who reeked of smoke and petrol. 'Phew, you stink!' she said as she finally let go.

She examined his face and was shocked; he looked wired, manic, his pupils dilated. He pulled her away from the phone box and spoke urgently. 'Where's your rucksack? Where's your clothes?' She looked down, ashamed.

'Why do I need clothes?'

Jack didn't understand; he'd had only one thing on his mind, one mission. 'Because it's time to go!' he cried.

'What do you mean, time to go? Go where?'

'To America! Where else? We need to go now!'

'Why now? What's the sudden rush? And why do you smell of petrol?'

'Anne's dead.' He said it so matter-of-factly, she didn't know whether she'd heard him right.

'Dead! How do you know? Did she come back? Or did *he* tell you that?'

'No, she never *went* anywhere! He killed her, Daisy! My mother too!' He garbled something about a tank that she didn't quite catch, and then his eyes glazed over – as if he was remembering the atrocities of some far-flung war that he'd just returned from.

'Jack, you're not making any sense! What tank?'

He snapped out of his trance and grabbed her shoulders in renewed urgency. 'He killed them both, Daisy – and now *he's* dead too. The house is on fire and that's why we've got to go – right now!'

'Oh my God, Jack! What did you do?'

'I didn't *do* anything! He fell off the roof earlier on and broke his neck. He deserved it. I've been waiting all evening till it got dark so I could torch the house; that's all *I've* done. And that's why we've got to get away, now – before the authorities come. There's nothing left, nothing to go back to.'

Daisy couldn't comprehend the horror of what she was hearing, or what he was asking of her. She crumpled under the pressure. 'I'm sorry, Jack, I can't go with you. Not right now.' And she began to sob. Jack's hands dropped to his sides in stunned disbelief. It briefly crossed his mind to slap her. The urge flared up, just like that, just like his father – and then it was gone again.

'But you promised! You said you'd come with me!'

'I didn't promise. I said I would … one day, maybe when I've finished college, maybe in a gap year perhaps – but not now, especially after … you know. Mum needs me, she's still in a state.'

'*I* need you, Daisy! I've got nothing left, nothing without you.'

'I'm sorry,' she wept. 'Please don't make me make this decision. You know I love you! There's something I need to tell you as well.' She put her hand on his arm, but he snatched it away – he couldn't even bring himself to look at her. Her words meant nothing right now and he turned as if to go; he couldn't bear to – not without her – but in his manic state, the rejection and betrayal he felt were all consuming. What else could he do?

Daisy held onto his arm, pleading with him. 'Please don't go, not like this. Look at me! I'm begging you! Where are you going to go at this time of night? How are you going to get there? I mean, you haven't even got a passport, have you? Have you actually *thought* of that?'

'I don't need one!' he said defiantly, turning to her. 'I'm going on a boat!'

'You still need a passport!' she cried. He looked confused then, unsure; it wasn't as though he'd ever discussed the specifics with anyone. He'd always figured that you just wandered on, mingling with the other passengers like in the old movies, and just got a ticket on board or something. 'I mean, what did you think you were going to do? Stow away?' Jack didn't answer; he had fallen silent. 'Honestly, you can be so naïve sometimes, Jack!'

As soon as it was out of her mouth, she wished she hadn't said it. It came out wrong; she hadn't meant it in a cruel way at all – it's just that his lack of worldly experience could be so frustrating. Jack looked at her as if she'd stuck a dagger through his heart. This was all going wrong – he hadn't pictured it like this. In his dreams he'd imagined them waltzing off hand in hand into the sunset, sailing off on a ship with the ocean spray in their faces. 'I'm so sorry, baby, I didn't mean it to sound like that. It's just … well, I don't think you've thought this through properly… Come back to my house and meet my mum. It'll be OK. She won't mind, and then we can figure out what to do. She could help us – *you* haven't done anything wrong, remember! You look tired. Come home with me. Let me take care of you.'

Jack remained stubbornly silent, but she could sense his resolve beginning to weaken, so she carried on, encouraged. 'We've got my birthday to look forward to *and* Blackpool – the Stone Roses gig…' She knew she was clutching at straws now, and possibly being selfish, but she was running out of ideas. Jack's face changed. He glared at her as if she was stark raving mad. Had she been listening to a single word he'd said? He'd found his dead mother *and* sister today, both murdered in his own backyard – and she's talking about pop concerts?!

Daisy opened her mouth to speak again, but just then – at precisely the wrong moment – the piercing wail of a siren startled them both. Ice ran through Jack's veins. To him it represented the dreaded threat of 'the authorities'. The sound was coming from the direction of the village. It got louder and louder until it was almost deafening. Suddenly a fire engine appeared at the crossroads before turning left, its blue lights flashing. The sight of it sent Jack into a renewed panic; he'd stalled far too long and had *got* to get away fast. His gaze returned to Daisy's desperate, tear-stained face, taking it all in for the last time. She shook her head, as if to say 'please don't do it'. He lowered his eyes, his mind made up, and walked quickly away.

She moved into the light of the phone box and screamed after him, distraught, 'Jack, please don't go! You can't keep hiding forever!' But it was no use; he was gone. The last she saw of him was when he was lit up by the yellow light of the pub window as it spilled across the lane, before he melted into the shadows. He was heading east – the nearest way to the coast as the crow flies – sticking to the back lanes and fields. Just then, there was the sound of another fire engine, but this time coming down the hill from the direction of Loughborough. It too got steadily louder, until it screamed past in the direction of Jack's house. The landlord of the pub came out to stand in the porch, to see what all the fuss was about. It was a quiet night, a Monday. He sniffed the hazy air before lighting a fag, silhouetted in the doorway.

He noticed the girl standing half in, half out of the light of the phone box. She looked vaguely familiar, but from this distance he couldn't be sure. She appeared to be upset and lost in thought; she was. Daisy was thinking about all the happy times she and Jack had shared in the short time they'd known each other. They ran through her head like a montage of flashbacks from a film.

She remembered how they'd first met, and how he'd zapped her with static on the bus. She thought of their first date in Bunny Wood – the bluebells and sitting on top of the mine together, and his fainting on their ill-fated trip to town. She remembered their camping trip and how much she'd wanted to kiss him by the fireside. And then when she finally had – that beautiful day at the brook. The long, glorious, sun-drenched summer days and evenings they had spent: Midsummer Night, Honeysuckle Cottage – their lovemaking and drunken afternoons dressing up.

There was the swimming at Stanford Hall, the strawberry picking, the movie watching, and his defending of her honour by punching that creep's lights out. She recalled the songs they'd shared … how they'd laughed, and how they'd loved. And despite the situation, she found herself smiling at the memories whilst a tear spilled down her cheek – bittersweet – like a rainbow of sun and rain. The movie finished as she pictured them sitting high up together in a place they'd never been before, on a ledge at the edge of the world. They looked at each other and smiled, before she took his hand in hers and they both jumped off.

The landlord had stubbed his fag out, crushing it underfoot half-finished, and had gone back inside, deciding not to get involved. He didn't see or hear the girl as she moved her hands down to stroke her stomach underneath her jacket and cry, 'Jack, wait!!' But he looked up briefly from drying some glasses as a shadow flitted past the window, somewhere out there in the smoky, summer night.

ABOUT THE AUTHOR

Inspired by reading Nick Cave's *And the Ass Saw the Angel* in 1990, lifelong book and music addict, Adam Longden, began to write the novel that would later become *The Caterpillar Girl* the following year.

A career in the catering industry got in the way. But the story always remained.

Fast forward to 2012. After finishing a long stint at running a pub restaurant, Adam found he had Mondays to himself. Utilising decades' worth of scribbled notes, work on *The Caterpillar Girl* began in earnest. Little did he know how long it would take...

Adam resides in Rutland with his wife, three children, Frodo the cat and Chilli the tarantula.

Printed in Poland
by Amazon Fulfillment
Poland Sp. z o.o., Wrocław